150
D1711284

Prologue

A TWIG CRACKLED in the stillness of the October night. A gossamer mist hung over the grass of the orchard and made a shimmering incandescence beneath the low-spread apple tree boughs. An owl shrieked somewhere far off in the woods which lay sharp-etched under the autumn moon, and even farther away, perhaps six or seven miles, so still was the frosty air, came the sharp, insistent piston-beat of a city-bound train.

A shadow moved across the icy grass, seemed to hesitate, and then blended with the darkness under the trees. The moon shone clear and cold, its silver light making a steel engraving of the low sagging profile of the house, where the bloom of interior lamps broke up the great mass of the façade. Two thin coils of smoke ascended directly upward from the ancient chimneys toward the moon, looking as though they had been drawn mathematically straight by the hand of some master craftsman.

The owl sounded once again, mournful and forlorn above the muffled progress of the train, and then that too died. A few moments later, when the last echo of the engine's beat had faded across the valley, an uninterrupted, almost oppressive silence prevailed.

Inside the house a smartly dressed man had paused in his packing. He frowned at the grandfather clock which stood in a shadowy corner of the spacious study. Its sonorous tick fell heavily upon the heart and made a melancholy background to his hurried movements. Once he paused and went to the window, staring out over the frosty grass of the lawn to where the brilliant globe of the moon rode high in the clear sky above the fretted edge of the far woods.

Nearer, the shadow glided slowly across the lawn, moving ever closer to the large room whose French windows threw deep yellow rectangles of light onto the paving of the ice-rimed terrace. A boot gritted on the edge, and all sounds seemed to stop in the depth of the night. Footprints were crushed into the grass now as the owner of the shadow skirted the terrace.

Back in the study the watcher at the window had quitted his post. He was over at the desk, hurriedly going through his papers. There were travel documents, railway and steamship tickets to be examined and noted. The traveller was meticulous about such matters; he checked and counterchecked before he set out on a journey.

He glanced again at the big clock in the corner. He would have liked some refreshment before his departure, but it was late. The housekeeper had long been in bed, and she slept in a remote corner of the mansion. He would not disturb her again. He went on with his packing, oblivious of everything else.

The man on the terrace was very close. He pulled the astrakhan collar of his heavy coat about his face, a thick plume of breath making a smokelike cloud in the freezing air.

He could see into the room now. He watched intently, very still and silent so that his hunched figure might have been taken as part of the shadow of a great vine thrown onto the house wall by the brilliance of the moon. Then he moved slowly along, taking his time, searching for a part of the house whose windows were dark, looking then for a sash whose catch was rusty or insecure.

A knife-blade glinted in the moonlight, and he gave a slight

The House of the Wolf

Contents

Basil Copper

The House of the Wolf

DRAWINGS BY STEPHEN E. FABIAN

ARKHAM HOUSE PUBLISHERS, INC.

For Ann Suster,
With My Love

Library of Congress Cataloging in Publication Data

Copper, Basil.
The house of the wolf.

I. Title.
PR6053.0658H6 1983 823'.914 83-3747
ISBN 0-87054-095-5

Printed in the United States of America
First Edition

grunt as he started to work the hasp of the lock to and fro in the crack between the two window-frames. The owl screamed again and he paused for a moment or two, waiting until all was quiet before resuming his furtive task.

Inside the study the man had finished putting things into his valise, and he rested it on a settee, the lid still open, while he looked around him in case he had forgotten anything. His thick plaid overcoat was lying across a chair in the far corner, and he went to fetch it, placing it and his heavy walking cane with his luggage.

He paused and lit a cigarette, taking it from the slim gold case he produced from an inside pocket of his elegantly cut suit. The house was quiet apart from the faint creaking noise the timbers made as they settled down for the night, the heat from the coal and log fires kept burning during the day dying out. A fainter creak which ran like a thread through the others escaped his notice.

He went over to sit at the desk, writing a last-minute note to be added to the instructions for his housekeeper. The scratching of his pen seemed an intrusion in the silence, and he became uneasily aware of the lateness of the hour and the loneliness of his situation.

After a little he got up and drew the thick curtains at the French windows, hiding the bleached silver of the moonlit grounds from his sight. As he did so a long shadow glided across the parquet of the corridor outside. The man in the study coughed faintly as he crossed the room back to his desk.

He reseated himself and reached for an envelope in which to enclose his message. At almost the same moment the echo of another train's progress came faintly down the valley. The man at the desk again looked anxiously toward the clock in the corner; he knew the time almost to a minute, but it was obvious that he was concerned.

He still had half an hour to get to the station to meet his train. There was no hurry, as it would take him only some five minutes to get there. It was apparent now that the train was not the one he intended to catch. He was still facing toward the clock when there came a low clicking noise as of claws on the parquet of the room. Before he could turn, a great shadow passed across the lamp.

He had no time to call out before long, incredibly sharp teeth had fastened in his throat. With a low snarling noise the thing was pinning him with its heavy body. The man at the desk fell to the floor and died almost before his glazing eyes had time to take in the monstrous creature which had torn his throat out.

A faint bar of moonlight fell across the trembling fingers of his outstretched hand as the thing continued to savage his mangled throat with a low worrying sound. Presently all was quiet and still again.

The moon, riding high in the sky, shone blandly down on the great bulk of the house in its well-kept grounds. The lights in the study were out, and one French door gaped blackly in the silver sheen. The tall man with the fur-collared coat came out cautiously, bowed under the burden he carried over his shoulder. He had cleaned the floor, replaced the overturned chair, and tidied the desk.

When he had carried the body far into the grounds, deep among the rhododendron clumps at the deserted edge of an estate wall, he returned for the luggage, stick, and coat. A silent grave, dug some hours previously, yawned beneath the evergreen leaves, brightly gleaming in the light of the moon.

The body was quickly tipped in, followed by the other articles. The coat was spread over the remains last of all. Within ten minutes, working with ferocious strength, the man in the heavy overcoat had filled in the gaping hole and tamped down the half-frozen earth with his boots. When he was satisfied that the ground in this remote spot appeared undisturbed, he wrapped the newly purchased spade in sacking and carried it back toward the house with him.

It was unlikely that the body would be found until the following spring, if then. He would be out of the country within hours and did not intend to return. He was safe enough. He reentered the study, still carrying the wrapped spade, and went minutely over the room by the light of the moon spilling through.

Everything seemed normal. There was no evidence of anything untoward, let alone traces of a crime.

He carefully locked and rebolted the windows, drawing the heavy curtains. All was quiet in the house except for the ticking of the clock. He went over to the desk last of all, looking at the travel documents, tickets, and other material he had placed there. Everything he needed.

He paused, carefully adjusted the angle of the chair in front of the desk, and straightened the dead man's envelope in the middle of the blotter where the housekeeper would be sure to find it the following morning. A church clock was chiming from a long way off when he finally quitted the house, easing the heavy hall door back until it had clicked quietly to behind him.

Still carrying the spade, he made his way down the drive and then branched off through the undergrowth. The documents made a faint crackling noise in his pocket as he hurried down the side-lane which led to a little-used entrance.

Here, by the iron gate, was tethered the big bay, warm beneath its blanket, harnessed to the shafts of the smart dog-cart. It whinnied softly with pleasure as he came up. He reached in his pocket for a cube of sugar, listening for unusual sounds as he took off the blanket. The horse munched contentedly as he got up into the cart, putting the spade down at his feet.

The horse's hooves were muffled on the short grass of the overgrown private lane as he turned its head. A few hundred yards farther on the cart rumbled over the wide wooden bridge spanning the lake. Its black depths gleamed in the moonlight as he brought the bay to a halt with his steellike gloved hands.

He looked round in the pale light. There was woodland all about him and no-one near to see. The sacking-enveloped spade dropped into the turgid depths with hardly a splash, and he was already urging the horse on. The train-whistle sounded as he came into the outskirts of the little town. It was almost midnight now. The last train of the day. He would take the boat tomorrow. He would catch it with plenty of time to spare.

Lugos

THE RUNNERS of the sledge grated over the ice as the two horses in their elaborate harness, nostrils steaming in the bitter air, breasted a rise in the track leading to the village of Lugos, whose jumbled roofs and glittering spires looked as though they had been carelessly thrown down by the hand of God on the frowning heights above them.

To Coleridge, muffled in furs behind the driver, nursing his portable luggage at his numbed feet, the journey appeared endless. It seemed years since he had left the civilised comforts of Pest for this forsaken corner of Hungary, yet in reality it had been only yesterday.

Since then he had rattled endlessly along in fussy local trains, in largely unheated rolling stock, eventually to be decanted at the nearest station, a mere three miles from Lugos, where his driver and his droshkylike vehicle had awaited him.

He wondered, uncomfortably, whether he was expected at all today. Coleridge had missed the train from the capital he had originally intended because he had stayed on for the final sessions of the Congress. He had not realised conditions were so primitive at the other end, or he would have made more careful arrangements.

But as one of the organisers and principal speakers at the Congress, he had felt it politic to stay on, though to tell the truth there had been only some twenty-five or so delegates for the final lectures and discussions. But it had been a success, a great success, and Coleridge had been left with the pleasant afterglow of a task well accomplished as he sat hour after hour in trains which got progressively more uncomfortable as he rattled on his interminable journey.

It had been a disappointment that he had no colleagues to travel with; no less than six, at least, were due at the Castle for a ten-day gathering which was to act as a corollary to the main Congress. But all of them had cried off staying in the city until the Congress sittings had concluded and had departed to catch their trains a day or two before the proceedings terminated.

Now Coleridge ruefully knew the reasons why; his driver, who mercifully understood a good deal of English, had explained that the Tuesday express from the capital had excellent connections, with buffet car facilities on most of them, and that the primitive conditions existed only for the last three hours on the local train, which stopped at every station.

But the ordeal was over now, and the professor was looking forward to the magnificent hospitality at the Castle and the facilities of its superb library, where learned discourse and earnest discussion on their favourite subjects would continue late into the night.

He fell against the freezing handrail at the side of the sledge as it lurched over the ruts, the driver swearing at the two great black horses which pulled the contraption. He pointed with his whip into the far distance, where the jagged turrets glinted in the moonlight on a height which looked impossibly precipitous.

"The Castle, sir. You will be most welcome."

Coleridge glanced dubiously at the big silver-cased watch he brought from one of the capacious pockets of his fur coat. He did not hold it long, for the metal was already extremely cold. It was late, and it might be expeditious for him to present himself at his host's door tomorrow morning rather than at this time of night.

"Is there an inn in the village? I wish to go there first."

The driver turned his pitted face toward his passenger. With his weathered features and drooping black moustache he looked like one of those old Magyar prints Coleridge was so familiar with.

"The Golden Crown, sir. You are expected. It is the best. We stop there for drink?"

There was such an enthusiastic gleam in his eye that Coleridge was inwardly amused. And such hospitality as he might extend to his driver was expected, he knew. The Hungarians, with their admixture of Eastern European nationalities, were a hospitable race, and whatever refreshment as he might afford this man would be more acceptable to him; whereas a tip, the normal procedure in a capital like London or in his native America, could well give offence.

"Yes, indeed," Coleridge said laconically, inwardly resolving to have some message sent up to the Castle to see whether he might be received this evening. It was already half-past nine, and he was extremely hungry. Judging by their present progress, the professor realised that at least another half hour would be required to reach Lugos, and the Castle gates and inner doors might well have been locked for the night.

His musings were interrupted by a low mournful howling that rose and fell on the wind that was beginning to blow, stirring the tops of the dark pine trees and whipping small whirls and eddies of snow from the dancing boughs.

"What is that?" he said sharply.

The driver gave him an amused glance from beneath his thick fur hat.

"Why, wolves, sir. What did you think?"

Coleridge looked at him in surprise.

"I did not know that there were wolves here."

The driver spat expertly into a frozen snowdrift at the side of the road. He had slowed the horses to a walk now, to spare them on the upward incline. Coleridge could see the faint fret-mark of the road, like a scratch in the gigantic landscape, as it zigzagged down toward the moonlit village before again ascending the cliff that he understood led to the higher town and the Castle itself.

"There are wolves everywhere in these mountains," the driver said. "But they have never come so far down toward Lugos for many years."

He spat again.

"It will be a hard winter if you are here, sir. By January you will see something."

Coleridge huddled deeper into his thick clothing.

"God forbid," he said. "I could not imagine anything worse than this, and it is only the second week in November. I shall be gone before the month is out."

The driver shrugged, his expression regretful.

"That is a pity, sir. We have many sports and diversions in the winter. Some of them at least you would enjoy."

Coleridge wondered what they might be, but he kept his own counsel.

Now they were descending the steep track, which led to a large timbered bridge over a frozen stream. For some while there had been a brittle clatter in the distance, and Coleridge saw, in the clear sharp light, a group of horsemen who were now crossing the bridge, the breath of men and horses reeking up like steam in the frosty air.

They passed the sledge at a walking pace, the men's faces red and frozen over the collars of their heavy overcoats, sabres and accoutrements jingling and creaking. Their leader, a slim, dark-moustached officer who rode a white horse, courteously saluted the savant as they passed, the horses walking in single file at the edge of the road.

Coleridge returned the gesture with a low bow, watching over his shoulder until the long procession had begun to fade round the bend in the road.

The driver had noted his interest.

"The Forty-first Cavalry Regiment," he grunted, urging on the horses with the reins. "They have their barracks at the edge of the town."

"And who was the officer?"

"Captain Rakosi. He is a well-known character hereabouts. You will no doubt be meeting him up at the Castle."

They were coming off the end of the bridge, the houses of the village creeping up the skyline, and Coleridge roused himself and looked about with more interest as the buildings began to close about them.

It was obvious that Lugos was larger than he had expected.

Many of the houses were seventeenth century and older, solidly built with stone and much timber, now fringed and festooned with fantastic patterns made by the icicles sparkling like diamonds in the moonlight. A few primitive oil lamps burned at street corners and on the façades of the more imposing buildings.

The place was really a cross between a village and a town but was possibly rated in smaller terms on population grounds, Coleridge supposed. He looked around eagerly as they traversed a large square, but there were few people about: one or two passersby who hurried quickly into the sheltering warmth of a tavern and, once, a creaking cart containing firewood covered by a tarpaulin and drawn by a team of two patient black oxen.

The sledge skirted the edges of the square, following the icy ruts which were frozen as hard as tramlines, and the professor realised the centre of the square was now impassable, as the heaped snow had solidified into a mountainous mass whose texture and rigidity denoted a surface as hard as steel.

The runners of the sledge made an ugly grating sound which echoed and reechoed back from the façades of the buildings, and they turned up the third avenue where there was a sort of side-street; in fact, the square merely continued for a hundred yards or so into a cul-de-sac where they were evidently bound, the large buildings at the edge of the square composing the two sides. Light showed from a massive timbered structure set at the end of the cul-de-sac and which made up its third face.

The sound of a violin and piano sliced through the keen wind that set the elaborate golden signboard swaying and creaking, and Coleridge thought the mellow glow of lamps that glimmered through the leaded bay windows had never seemed so welcoming.

Even the horses seemed glad to be home because Coleridge knew that they were bound for the shadowy stable yard that loomed beyond a timbered archway to the right.

The driver passed his gloved hand across his frozen lips, his eyes bright with anticipation.

"As you command me, sir. The Golden Crown."

The Track of the Wolf

COLERIDGE WAS OVERWHELMED with the noise and warmth in the great hall after the frozen silence of the endless wastes he had traversed to get there. He was bewildered by the luxury of The Golden Crown. Instead of the simple inn he had expected, here was a hostelry in the grand style: a parquet floor that was polished to an eye-aching dazzle, skin rugs scattered about, a huge log fire burning in the vast stone fireplace, boars' heads and other game trophies on the tapestried walls, a great balcony that ran around three sides of the entrance hall and presumably led to the bedrooms above.

The noise was coming from doorways leading off to the right, and when a girl dressed in peasant costume opened one the professor caught sight of a crowded barroom, discordant with the sound of clinking glasses and jumbled conversation. Above, two great crystal chandeliers shone down a mellow light from their electric candles, and through a glass screen up ahead Coleridge could see a restaurant where people dined discreetly among evergreen foliage. That door opened too, and a man in evening dress came out so that the half-frozen visitor could hear the noise of an orchestra playing; his ear caught the sharp, brittle notes of a zither and cimbalon.

His driver was standing near the entrance doors, Coleridge's luggage piled around his feet, as though too awed to come any farther. He smiled faintly as he caught the professor's expression.

"Good, yes?" he ventured, moving a little closer.

"More than good," said Coleridge drily.

He went over toward the big pine reception counter in the far corner near the restaurant, where a bearlike man with a shock of black hair and a dark beard that made his white teeth look even more brilliant was advancing toward him. Coleridge guessed, correctly, that he was the proprietor. He did not speak any English, unfortunately, but he listened with deep attention as the driver explained Coleridge's presence and his business.

He waved the professor over to a great carved chair near the fireplace, where he thawed out gratefully. A waiter had appeared from somewhere, bearing a tray on which stood a wine bottle and glasses. The manager had bustled out again now, giving Coleridge a reassuring smile, while the driver came and stood deferentially behind his chair.

"You are expected, sir," he explained. "Mr. Eles has a message for you from the Castle. Dinner will be ready for you in a quarter of an hour."

He came round the other side of the table, warming his hands at the fire also, his eyes looking approvingly as the waiter finished pouring the sparkling wine into the glasses.

Coleridge picked up his goblet and tasted tentatively. He felt the warmth permeating his body.

"Excellent."

The driver, at Coleridge's invitation, raised his own glass.

"You may well say so, sir. Tokay! The wine of the country."

He looked at Coleridge reflectively.

"I will be available to drive you directly to the Castle after supper, sir."

Coleridge understood that it was not really socially proper for his driver to drink such an excellent wine with him in such an establishment, and he felt a momentary discomfiture. The man could not sit down, so he stood up also to put him at his ease. He was grateful for his help, and his excellent English had certainly smoothed the path this evening. What he had originally taken for taciturnity was obviously the driver's natural reserve.

"Please order whatever wine and food pleases you and have the management put it on my bill," he told the other, brushing aside his stammering thanks. He glanced up anxiously at the ornamental gilt clock that stood on the mantelpiece. His feet were warming nicely now. The driver had intercepted his glance, stooping to unobtrusively refill his own glass.

"They keep late hours at the Castle, sir. We have at least until midnight before it would cause embarrassment."

"That is good," Coleridge told him. "Shall we say an hour?"

"Very well, sir."

The driver bowed with great dignity, drained his glass regretfully, putting it down on the table, and went out of the hall into the bar where all the noise and conversation was coming from.

Coleridge settled himself gratefully, his feet out to the logs, and refilled his own glass. He was still sitting there contentedly some ten minutes later when Eles, the bearded proprietor, came silently back across the parquet bearing an envelope for him.

Coleridge read the letter for the second time. It was a most warm and cordial welcome from the Count. He had left instructions that all the entertainment and refreshments at The Golden Crown should be at his expense. He felt, as a courtesy to his guest, that it might be more convenient for his honoured visitor that he should pause and refresh himself awhile before the final stage of his journey to the Castle. But the writer assured Coleridge that he and his family would be awaiting his arrival in person, however late the hour.

Coleridge was overwhelmed at the generosity of his hosts, but all his expostulations through the driver had carried no weight with Eles, who had simply smiled, wagged his bearded head, and refused all offers of payment. Instead, Coleridge had made an arrangement with the proprietor that his driver should be rewarded with further refreshment at his fare's expense, just as soon as he had returned from the Castle. With that the professor had to be content.

Now he had resumed his outdoor clothing and stood at one side of the hall, warm and replete, while the driver finished his conversation with the proprietor. The dinner had been startlingly lavish, and the wines choice and well selected; in fact, Coleridge mused, he could not have dined more rewardingly at any of the great restaurants of London or Paris, which was surprising indeed for such a small place as Lugos.

He guessed, rightly as it happened, that the inn was under the direct patronage of the noble family in the Castle above, who liked to have such facilities available for their guests and who no doubt also patronised the establishment from time to time.

Eles now came forward affably and pumped Coleridge warmly by the hand, conveying through the latter's guide his wishes for a pleasant and comfortable stay at the Castle. With his smooth manners and assured, self-confident air the savant guessed that he was an educated man who had devoted his life to The Golden Crown and its standards of excellence. There were many such people, he mused as he followed his guide down the steps, who chose such obscure places in which to practise whatever profession they had chosen and who were content with a somewhat narrow world which they had entirely mastered. And who was to say they were not right in eschewing the clamour and rough competition of the wider world?

Certainly in 1895, Coleridge reflected, things were becoming intolerable in the great cities with their obsessive noise and stifling proximity of man to man, which was why his scholar's soul luxuriated in such an atmosphere as that expressed by Lugos. And his deep studies in the folklore of bygone ages impelled him backward into even more remote periods of time.

Not that he despised the swiftness of travel in the present age or the comforts personified by such establishments as those of Herr Eles. Coleridge supposed that he was an elitist; like so many people he wanted all the advantages of a modern society without being obliged to share them with millions of others.

He smiled faintly before once more returning to the biting cold and icy streets of the village. His driver had already disappeared within the shadows of the yard at the side of the hotel, and a few moments later, as Coleridge loitered on the pavement, conscious of the keen wind and the breath which smoked painfully from his nostrils, he could already hear the impatient hoofbeats of the horses and the grating of the sledge-runners across the frozen ground.

He walked down a way, pausing beneath a lamp, and as soon as the vehicle appeared, wormed his way quickly beneath the thick blankets and heavy fur coverings of the passenger's portion of the sled. The heavily moustached driver had already stowed his baggage carefully to one side, and now Coleridge checked, making sure everything was there.

He already had his heavy leather briefcase, which he kept with him at all times. It contained the notes of the major lectures he had delivered to the delegates of the Congress and other important material which he hoped to research and discuss with his colleagues at the Castle.

Now, at a nod from his passenger, the driver gently urged the horses on, the heavy sledge-runners making a crisp, brittle noise which seemed an intrusion in the silence of the streets. The moon was obscured by cloud and it was dark, though the brilliance of the snow and the lamplight of the town made it appear a good deal lighter.

They again skirted the square and took a broad side-road which led slightly upward; they crossed another bridge shortly after, this time a rather grandiose stone affair whose buttresses and elaborate balustrades, thickly capped with frozen snow, bespoke some antiquity.

There were few people about in the streets, though lights shone dimly from behind blinds and shutters, and once they passed some sort of tavern where shouting and drunken revelry, interspersed with wild violin music and the noise of breaking glass, made a vivid contrast to the silent, dignified streets through which the horses threaded their unerring way.

Once they were across the bridge, the moon came from behind the clouds and illuminated the wild and rugged landscape beyond. To the left-hand side of the road the terrain dropped swiftly to a savage valley where another frozen stream glittered like a photograph in the pallid light.

Dark pines and firs made a sullen fringe of forest in the glacial whiteness of the snow, and far above rose jagged ice-capped peaks. A chill wind blew here, and Coleridge huddled deeper into his thick clothing, conscious that Lugos represented a thin veneer of civilisation. Once out of the streets or a few yards off a known road, and a man could be lost and die here in a few hours. A man like himself, at any rate, Coleridge mused wryly.

To his right the houses of the village continued, and now the road began to rise and turn, doubling back on itself, to where the frowning towers and spires of the Castle started to reveal themselves on the battlements above.

But before that there had come a curious interruption; Coleridge was aware of a faint, faraway noise above the harsh grating of the sledge-runners and the panting breath of the horses as they thrust themselves into their collars and settled to the work. The driver had caught it before him, and now he reined in the horses, enjoining silence on his passenger with a peremptory motion of his hand.

Coleridge sat stock-still, his breath smoking from his mouth, while his eyes searched the frozen slopes below them. They had halted almost at the edge of the track where it started to ascend in a spiral toward the Castle. Up ahead there were more houses clustered about the foot of the rock on which the Castle was built and another street which formed a sort of suburb of Lugos.

At the point where the sledge had paused was a dog-leg of road, protected from the precipitous drop into the valley below only by a rough wooden fence. The driver's gaze was fixed on the near distance where the lower slopes debouched from the fringes of thick forest that Coleridge had earlier noted.

Two rifle shots echoed out sharp and clear in the frosty air, slapping echoes from the cliff-face beyond. At almost the same moment the savant noted a small, melancholy procession which was emerging from the tree-line opposite. Now the moonlight was clear upon the slope, and Coleridge could see that it was made up of a long file of men, thickly clad in furs, like black insects against the whiteness of the snow.

In the centre of the file they were clustered about a smaller group which moved slowly and painfully as though they carried a heavy burden. The horses shifted uneasily in the sledge-harness, snorting heavily through their nostrils, and Coleridge cast an interrogatory glance toward the driver, whose immobile back showed no inclination to move.

Something of the man's rapt attention transferred itself to the passenger, for he again felt his eyes fastened on the group in the valley below, limned in the faint and eerie light given both by the moon and by the reflected radiance of the snow. They were closer now, and he could make out that the men in the centre were carrying a sort of rough wooden stretcher on which reposed a shapeless mass that was covered with furs.

The two men sat in a tense silence as the sombre party seemed to glide almost imperceptibly toward them, making for a small bridge and a path which would eventually bring them out upon the road on which the halted sledge stood.

Coleridge felt a vague, indefinable sense of doom as the ghostly tableau came on, slipping and stumbling occasionally, its progress now audible as the crunch of footsteps in the snow. A chill wind blew, and on it, as though from vast distances, came the low, menacing howl of wolves from the forest beyond.

The Priest's Tale

AS THE MELANCHOLY PROCESSION came nearer, its members slipping and stumbling on the hard-packed ice of the rutted road, the professor could see that it was formed exclusively of grim-looking, mostly bearded men who wore stout boots and clothing composed largely of fur. Some of them carried rifles in their gloved hands, and pale lantern beams shone across the snow. As they neared the main road the lamps were extinguished, being now quite eclipsed by the light of the moon.

Coleridge guessed that the lanterns had been necessary to dispel the darkness and gloom within the woods. He wondered idly what they could have been shooting at this time of night; perhaps there had been an accident and the man on the rough wooden stretcher, made up of thick wooden poles hacked from the living tree and lashed together with leather belts and thongs, had been wounded.

Then the men with their burden came fully into the light, and Coleridge perceived that the occupant of the stretcher was dead because the face was covered. It was just a heaped mass of fur which lay there, its only human indication a bare arm which dangled below the edge of the covering, the fingers and forearm covered with rivulets of black blood which had frozen in the bitter air.

Their progress was slower now that they were coming upward on the steeper path to the spot where the sledge stood, and Coleridge could see that the tall, distinguished-looking man who headed the procession, walking alone and mumbling something from a small leather-bound book he carried, was either a priest or some sort of civic dignitary.

Coleridge's guide briefly removed his heavy fur hat as the cortège came up to the level of the sledge and then quickly replaced it. The savant guessed that there would be danger of frostbite under these conditions, and he quickly checked the earflaps on his own headgear. He was much impressed with the respect and natural dignity the driver exhibited, and he admired the way he was now calming the restive horses with smooth, experienced movements of the reins.

The guide inclined his head as the tall man leading the procession stopped and gave the passenger a courtly bow. The professor saw that he was indeed a priest, for an elaborate silver pectoral cross glistened at his breast as it caught the rays of the moon.

"Father Balaz," the guide mumbled to Coleridge in his heavily accented English.

The professor inclined his own head to show courtesy to the priest and wondered whether he should get down from the vehicle, but the tall man indicated with a gloved hand that he should remain where he was.

Then followed a muttered conversation that Coleridge was unable to grasp, but he had forgotten the cold in his absorption in his guide's discourse with this strange and arresting figure. Father Balaz had a long, ravaged face like that of a mediaeval saint, with great grooves that ran down from beneath his eyes, passing the corners of his mouth and ending just short of his chin.

In the silvery light of the moon they looked like the streaked tears Coleridge had seen depicted on the faces of religious statuary in some Latin American churches. Balaz almost resembled a living statue as the mumbled colloquy continued.

In the meantime the procession had passed, the feet of the men making crisp crunching noises in the crusted snow, each and every one giving a slight bow to the man in the sledge as he went by. Coleridge saw, to his horror, as the rough stretcher passed, that there was a good deal of blood on the tumbled furs which covered the immobile figure and that the hand which protruded from beneath the covering was much torn and mangled.

There had been an accident, then. He controlled his patience as best he might and waited while the long file of men and their burden moved on toward the streets of Lugos. The priest concluded his business with the sledge-driver at the end, drew himself up, looked at Coleridge with deep-set melancholy eyes above the greying stubble of beard, and made the sign of the cross in the air.

Coleridge received the benediction with another courteous half-bow and shifted awkwardly beneath his thick coverings as he watched the priest hurry off to rejoin the others. The driver was silent too as he stared after him in turn. There was an odd interval, broken only by the impatient snorting of the horses. The guide turned in the seat of the sleigh and answered his passenger's unspoken question.

"There has been another death. Father Balaz is extremely perturbed."

He shrugged.

"The people hereabouts are very superstitious, you see."

Coleridge found impatience welling up within him, cutting through the numbing cold.

"I don't understand," he said, more irritably than he had intended.

The driver crossed himself, still staring after the dark figure of the priest, now a black speck on the icy road before he too turned an angle of a building and was lost to sight.

"Another killing, sir," he said, lowering his voice as though they might be overheard in that remote place. "The third this year."

Coleridge looked at him sharply.

"What do you mean, killing?"

The guide put his lips together in a straight line.

"A local villager. A woodman. Torn to pieces by a wolf."

The driver could not stop the trembling which visibly agitated his frame now.

"A great black wolf which leads a pack hereabouts."

He fixed the professor with mournful eyes.

"The villagers say there is something supernatural about it. The beast has been sighted and shot at on a number of occasions, but it seems to have a miraculous ability to avoid bullets."

As an expert on the folklore of Europe the professor was intensely interested in what the man was saying, but his commonsense side was momentarily in conflict with the academic in his nature. A grain of sense told him that there could be nothing miraculous about a wolf and its ability to avoid bullets; nothing, that is, but animal cunning.

But his special interests were aroused. This was really the raw stuff of folklore, and it was ironic that the two sides of his nature should be tested in this way; he had not come across it before.

But his manner was noncommittal as he replied.

"I am sorry you have such troubles in Lugos. Perhaps I could help. I am an expert shot."

The driver shook himself as though he were emerging from a bad dream.

"The authorities would be grateful for your assistance, sir. I believe the Count has also offered the family's help to the local Chief of Police."

His eyes were grim as he turned back to the reins.

"The soldiers have been out already. They saw no sign of the beast. It is cunning, you see. But it had returned to the body when our people came across our poor friend, the woodman. They were unable to hit it, according to Father Balaz, though it was less than a hundred yards away, in clear snow."

He whipped up the horses, and the sledge creaked on toward the Castle. Coleridge felt a bleakness in his soul that was far more searing than the cold.

The Castle

THE CASTLE ROSE above them, gilded silver by the moonlight and looking as unlikely as some eccentric iced cake, Coleridge thought. As they drew nearer, the splintering passage of the sledge was echoing back from the street of small houses which led up to the main entrance, and mingled with it was something else. At first it sounded like the magnification of their own passage, but he then became aware that there were other horses and vehicles approaching from the opposite direction.

The first visible indication was two great staring eyes which jerked about the dusky road, now in shadow from the ancient tumbled façade of the buildings opposite and the deeper mass of the Castle walls at their left as they went on down the frozen street. The eyes presently resolved themselves into a pair of lanterns suspended from short poles and set out at angles from a solid wooden cart built of massive timbers and drawn by four coal-black horses.

Other carts followed, each painted in gaudy colours, some decorated with elaborate carving that now threw back the rays of the lamps as they swayed and flickered at the end of their poles. A low animal rumbling sounded deep from within a wooden slatted cage that stood on one of the open vehicles, and through the opening in the tarpaulin that surrounded the cage on three sides to keep off the wind, the professor glimpsed the dark snout and burning red eyes of what appeared to be a large bear.

The men who drove the carts, with swarthy women beside them, had dark, sullen faces and wild eyes above their fierce moustaches; they looked neither right nor left but tugged moodily at the reins, one or two smoking elaborately engraved silver pipes. Coleridge could hardly take his eyes off them until the creaking cavalcade was again swallowed by the dusk.

He realised it was the third procession he had seen since his arrival in Lugos a few short hours ago, each one more extraordinary than the last. His guide, who had sat hunched on the seat of the sled while the bizarre caravan passed, now straightened himself, cleared his throat, and spat reflectively.

"Difficult and dangerous people, Professor."

Coleridge turned back in his seat and huddled deeper into his protective furs.

"But who are they?"

The driver stroked his chin with his free hand, his left skilfully controlling the horses so that the vehicle avoided the worst of the ruts which fell to a sort of ditch or moat which hugged the edge of the road. Above them the great sheer walls of the Castle, not a light showing this side, looked as though they were made entirely of frost.

"Hortobagy!"

The driver struggled for the English equivalent.

"How do you call them in your country?"

Then he turned with quiet triumph.

"Gypsies. They are a wild folk, sir. They are here for the first of our Winter Fairs, which starts in a few days' time."

"That sounds interesting."

The driver shrugged.

"It is interesting enough. But there is much quarrelling and drunkenness, too. Though it brings good trade to the village and business for the likes of me, so perhaps I should not grumble overmuch."

He turned back to the reins, pulling the powerful team round.

The road curved now, easing away from the village street, which continued onward past the main wall. There likewise was curving of the great mass, which angled inward as though anxious to be quit of the village.

Coleridge glimpsed lights at ground level which shone and glinted on the thick ice of the moat and on vast iron-studded doors with a courtyard beyond. Above that hung the immense bulk of the Castle, hereditary home of the Homolky family. Those windows in the façade which were still lighted exhibited delicate tracery of stone and lozenges of different coloured glass which glinted ruby and green and gold, almost like church windows, but with a secular splendour foreign to churches. To Coleridge, in the biting cold of the street, they seemed to beckon with all the warmth and comfort of civilised values.

"We have arrived, sir!" said the professor's guide, pointing with a flourished whip. "The House of the Wolf!"

The horses' hooves rang steel-hard on the drawbridge as they clattered across to where the great mass of the Castle awaited to ingest them.

Coleridge paid off the guide, cutting short the man's mumbled thanks, and followed the bearded servant, who tucked his luggage beneath his gigantic arms as though they had been nothing more than feather bolsters. The professor kept his briefcase and removed his heavy fur hat as he followed the man across the stone floor of what looked like a gatehouse within the inner arch of the Castle courtyard.

The clatter of the horses' hooves across the cobbles in the icy air was already receding and was then cut off altogether by the slam of the massive gatehouse door. They reemerged into the open air again, crossing a smaller courtyard where the snow and ice had been meticulously cleared from the massive setts.

Facing them was a graceful arched portico whose glass doors, set back in the shadow, showed forth slanting beams of yellow light. The servant held the door courteously aside for Coleridge to enter, and he was at once aware of the rush of warm air. He blinked as another servant, more elegant than the first and in smartly cut livery of a military pattern, ushered them across a black-and-white tiled hall.

A large log fire burned in a vast fireplace at the right, and sporting trophies were ranged about the uneven stone walls. A marble balustraded staircase made right-angled turns in the far corner as it ascended to the upper floors, and Coleridge made out the carved blazons on the heraldic shields which bore the coat of arms of his noble host and which were set at intervals in the staircase balustrade.

Three enormous brass lanterns suspended from the darkened beams of the far-off ceiling held quivering banks of large red candles, which cast a shifting, mysterious light downward onto the tiling of the floor as Coleridge followed the two men across to one of a number of doors set into the fireplace wall. Already his painfully tingling ears were attesting the return of circulation.

The second servant patiently waited while Coleridge divested himself of his heavy outer clothing. He sat down by the fireplace and changed into indoor shoes while the bearded man removed his boots and other garments to some inner chamber.

When he had thawed out and felt himself to be sufficiently presentable, he picked up his briefcase and followed the uniformed man, who was patently some sort of household major-domo, toward the far door which the white-haired man held ajar for him.

It was a smaller room into which he showed the guest, panelled with some rare wood and furnished with great taste and elegance. The lighting here came from electric bulbs set into wrought-iron wall lanterns and from overhead chandeliers, and Coleridge guessed that this was a more modern part of the Castle, though still of great antiquity.

There was no sound except for the faint sputtering of the logs on the fire and the sonorous clicking of a large-pendulum clock which meticulously measured out the minutes against the far wall. So far as Coleridge could gather in his first glimpses, there was no-one in the room, and he looked about curiously as the servant courteously indicated a great carved chair at the right-hand side of the fireplace.

It was almost a repetition of the scene at the inn earlier, and Coleridge felt a certain inward satisfaction that he was at last at his journey's end and would not have to venture out into the bitter air and on his seemingly endless travelling again tonight. He put down his briefcase on the huge polished refectory table which stood near the chair and thawed out.

The majordomo had reappeared from behind him with an embossed silver tray on which stood several tall crystal goblets of amber glass and a flagon of some reddish wine. Despite the professor's protestations he filled a goblet and put it down on the tray within the guest's reach.

It was obvious the man did not speak English, as he merely smiled without answering Coleridge's thanks, and the American then saw with a slight sense of shock that he had no tongue; only the remains of a pink root which showed like a gaping sore in his mouth before he closed it again.

It was a barbarous glimpse of something of which Coleridge had been dimly aware on his journeyings in Hungary, and it merely emphasised the civilised veneer of this great house, a veneer which covered the cracks in the façade of this huge and largely backward country.

The majordomo smiled again, this time without exposing his deformity, and pointed with a gentle gesture toward a door in the far corner of the gracious room. Then he went out the same way he had come in, leaving the professor to his sombre thoughts. He wondered whether the man had been involved in some bizarre accident; it did not seem likely that he had been the subject of a surgical operation. It was improbable that things were so advanced in this remote corner of Europe.

There remained two other possibilities—that the man was the victim of some congenital deformity that had been with him since birth. Or was there something even more sinister, a practice that might have persisted since the days of the Wallachian tyrants who had ruled this blood-soaked land? That the man's tongue had been literally torn from his mouth to render him mute and prevent him from speaking about his betters' affairs? Coleridge's expression was grim as he raised the goblet of wine to his lips. As he had expected, it was excellent.

He was still sitting there in the mellow firelight sipping the dry and subtle vintage when he became aware that the far door was open. A tall, thin man with a shock of white hair stood there regarding him with a sardonic expression.

The Host

PROFESSOR COLERIDGE, I presume?"

There was warmth and humour on the face now as Count Homolky turned, closing the door behind him and coming across the room with extended hand.

"I expected a very much older man."

Coleridge had corresponded with his host for years on the specialised subjects which so absorbed them, but the two men had never met until now and the professor's initial reaction was one of disappointment as he rose hastily from his chair and went to meet the tall man who spoke such impeccable English with the very faintest trace of an accent.

"I hope you are not disappointed, sir?"

Homolky shook his head, clasping the younger man's hand in a warm, dry grip. He wore evening clothes as though he had just risen from table, and now that they were closer Coleridge could see that his face, though one of great distinction, was much ravaged. There was, it was true, a certain hard-bitten quality about it as though he spent much of his time out of doors in icy weather, but there was also something beyond that; some secret sorrow which lurked in the corners of his eyes and eroded him from within so that Coleridge almost felt he could see the living bone beneath the tightly stretched flesh.

"I fear my tardy arrival has kept you from your bed."

Homolky shook his head.

"Not at all. My family and I keep late hours here."

He smiled thinly, revealing perfectly kept, even teeth, which came to sharp points.

"My house is yours, but I gather you would not require any further refreshment tonight. I trust The Golden Crown lived up to its reputation?"

Coleridge smiled also.

"I could not eat another thing, sir. I hope I may repay your generosity there at some future time."

Homolky shifted uneasily, his head on one side as though listening for something in the far corridors of the vast Castle.

"Perhaps, Professor, perhaps."

He rubbed his hands together and became brisk, as if remembering his duties as host.

"You will be reunited with your six colleagues in the morning. They ask to be excused and have already retired."

Coleridge glanced over at the big clock in the corner which, as though prompted by his look, commenced to chime the hour of midnight.

"You had a good journey, I trust?"

The professor shrugged, dropping back into his chair at the Count's insistence. His host went to stand in front of the fire, twisting his thin hands behind his back as he spread them to the blaze.

"A trifle uncomfortable at this time of the year."

Coleridge hesitated, then plunged on. After all, the Count would hear of it in the morning if news of the incident had not already percolated within the walls of the Castle.

"There was some trouble in the woods near the village. I understood from my driver that marauding wolves have been seen. A villager was killed. A woodman, I believe."

Homolky's face became white, and he controlled himself with

an effort. Slowly he turned from the fire to confront his guest directly.

"The devil, you say, Professor!"

Coleridge got up from his chair.

"I am sorry to bring bad news. It is not the first death, I believe."

The Count put his lips together in a grim expression.

"No, it is not the first time, Professor Coleridge. And curiously, it constitutes the material of the purest folklore. Ironic, is it not, when it is the very subject which has brought us all together here."

Coleridge nodded, setting his empty goblet down on the table. He felt a sudden weariness permeating his limbs. The Count, who had brilliantly penetrating eyes, evidently noticed this, for he laid a sympathetic hand on the other's arm.

"Not a word of this tonight to my family, Professor. We have had trouble enough, and one is able to face things more resolutely in the daylight."

He led the way across to the door through which he had come in.

"They have been eagerly awaiting your arrival, and there is just time to greet them before retiring."

"We have waited long for this moment, Professor!"

The tall, dignified woman who rose from a carved chair at the end of the vast library gave Coleridge a smile of great nobility.

The visitor felt a faint flush of embarrassment as he came down the room with its serried ranks of books lining the shadowy walls. It was something he was learning to control; a feeling which had come back to him again at the Congress just past. One would have thought that he would have become used to such recognition at the age of forty-six.

But it was always the same at the opening of a function, or, as now, when meeting new people who knew his standing in the field in which he had gained his reputation. It would disappear within a short while, but in the meantime it was vaguely disconcerting.

His host, at his side, gave a faint smile as though he had glimpsed something of the guest's thoughts.

"My mother, the Countess Irina," he said, sotto voce. "Though almost eighty she is a remarkable old lady. I fancy you will find her well-versed in your works."

He put his hand on the other's arm and steered him round a huge circular walnut table whose surface was littered with books.

"You are among friends, Professor."

Coleridge felt reassured.

"That is good to know," he said.

As they moved closer to the carved wooden fireplace where a heaped fire of logs blazed, throwing dancing shadows across the spines of the books and the sheen of the furniture, he made out the figures of two much younger women who stood either side of the mantelpiece; like two carved nymphs supporting the structure, they appeared stately and still in their evening dress until they stepped forward to add their greetings to those of the elderly lady.

The Count made the formal introductions in English, and it was obvious all three women were fluent not only in that language but in others, because they occasionally dropped into French and German among themselves as the conversation proceeded. Coleridge bowed low over the hand the Countess extended to him, conscious of a remarkable countenance and a pair of grey eyes of piercing sharpness which were turned upon him.

The other two women were both elegant and beautiful, and the Count introduced them as his wife and daughter. Coleridge did not properly catch the names during the sudden buzz of conversation. If the ladies were tired, they did not show it; Coleridge had rarely seen such animation and comeliness in the opposite sex, and it was equally clear that the Count's mother had herself been a notable beauty in her youth.

They led the professor to a place of honour in another carved chair near the fire and sat about him on cushions and stools as though he were the head of some regal court. It was obvious that the Count's wife was a great deal younger than he; she could not have been more than thirty-eight or forty, and her dark, clear-moulded beauty would have stood out in any company.

Her daughter was about eighteen, slim and tall like her parents, but with hair of a subtle blonde texture that shimmered and gleamed in the firelight as it fell in long, careless waves across her shoulders. Coleridge had only a few moments to take in the general aspects of these remarkable-looking women before they were plying him with questions, as though he were some university lecturer and they the students.

"I am *au fait* with your latest work, *The Essence of Lycanthropy*, Professor," said the Countess Irina in a low, well-modulated voice which, like her son's, had little trace of an accent. "I should place it within the canon of your most important works; among the top three of your most significant books to date."

Coleridge was astonished. The book had been published in America only the month before, and he would not have thought the English language version could have penetrated into this far outpost of Europe.

"You are too kind," Coleridge murmured, aware of the eyes of the other two ladies upon him. The granddaughter had caught his expression, for she said with good-natured irony, "We have excellent bookshops in Pest, Professor. The city is noted for its culture and learning."

Coleridge smiled easily. He felt more relaxed now.

"I am well aware of that," he conceded.

His host was smiling too.

"We hope you will enlarge upon your theories at our gatherings here," he said. "There will be a free day tomorrow, as you must be tired after your journey. But we have a full programme from Saturday onward. The library and all the facilities of the Castle are open to you. And your colleagues' own papers promise some verbal fireworks!"

His eyes sparkled with a mischief which was very far removed from malice, and Coleridge smiled round the circle. He did not make friends very easily, but he was beginning to feel at home here already.

The Countess Irina, now that he had more time to study her, seemed even more striking close up than she had from a distance. Despite her great age her hair was only slightly powdered with grey, leaving raven strands at the sides of her head and at the temple. The hair was drawn back and secured with a silver comb, no doubt in order to fully reveal the fine bone structure of her face.

She wore a light coating of powder over features which were surprisingly free from wrinkles, and her grey eyes were now so dark that they appeared almost jet-black. Her teeth were finely kept when she smiled and appeared to be entirely natural; her lips were still full and rosy, though Coleridge imagined their texture was maintained with the skilful use of makeup.

She wore a heavy dress of some thick material, with a high-fitting collar to hide her wrinkled throat and sleeves descending to her wrists. From the right hand a handkerchief of fine lace showed as she moved her long, slender hands restlessly in her lap.

Apart from the silver comb she wore little jewellery, merely a single row of pearls which hung loosely over the bosom and two antique silver rings set with diamonds on her left hand. Altogether she made a remarkable impression on the visitor with her general vivacity and the vitality reflected in her voice and gestures.

Countess Sylva, her daughter-in-law, was of an entirely different mould, the professor judged. She was dark, like the older Countess, but there the resemblance ended. With her rosy cheeks that owed little to makeup, smooth broad brow, and deep, almost cobalt eyes, she would have passed muster in any salon of Paris or Vienna. She too had very little accent in her English, but from the way she spoke French he guessed she might well be a native of that country.

She was dressed simply but with great elegance, and her body moved with slow, voluptuous undulations beneath the heavy evening gown. The ladies' clothing was obviously adapted to the rigours of the climate here; bare necks and shoulders would have invited pneumonia in some of the draughtier stone corridors Coleridge had traversed with his host on the way to the library.

The daughter, Nadia, was equally as attractive as the mother but, again, in an entirely different way. She wore a dress that was cut in a younger style, and beneath the long blonde hair that streamed across her shoulders her brown eyes were clear and candid. Her mouth was broad and generously made, and like the other two female members of her family she had extremely fine teeth, though they looked a little sharp and predatory whenever she opened her mouth wide.

Now she got up from her stool, as though conscious of her guest's meditations.

"You must be tired, Professor. And we are thoughtless in keeping you up so late after such a long and exhausting journey."

Coleridge got up too, again aware that he was very tired, now that the girl had spoken of it.

"The end of the journey was worth the rigours of its attainment," he said gallantly.

The mother raised her eyebrows.

"An old Hungarian proverb?" she queried.

Coleridge smiled, conscious of his host's approval.

"An old American one," he said, "but equally applicable here."

The Count joined in the laughter, rising quickly and guiding the group over toward the door.

"You are perfectly correct, my dear, nevertheless," he told his daughter. "Say goodnight, and I will show our guest to his room."

Coleridge stood by the door to the corridor, shaking each of the ladies' hands in turn as they took their leave. He was left with an impression of beauty, animal warmth, and a faint, elusive perfume hanging in the air after they had gone. The Count had obviously noted his guest's favourable impression, but with consummate tact he ignored it and led the way along a broad corridor hung with tapestries and lined at intervals with heavily carved, somewhat primitive, occasional furniture.

There was no electric lighting here, and the silver lamp Homolky carried cast great fleeting shadows over the huge hammer beams above their heads. He smiled as he caught Coleridge's expression.

"We have our own electricity-generating installation here, Mr. Coleridge. The first in Lugos. It does not run to the entire Castle, it is so vast, you see. So I illuminate only the principal apartments."

He smiled again.

"Those that I wish to impress my guests."

Coleridge felt a rapport with this man already; he had a gift of putting the visitor at his ease.

"And you run the surplus to The Golden Crown," he said.

The Count looked at him shrewdly from beneath the shock of white hair.

"You are most perceptive, Mr. Coleridge. I have a commercial arrangement with Herr Eles. And I and my family use the hotel a great deal. It seemed mutually advantageous."

He glanced around him as the two men came out upon an elaborate stairhead where intricately carved balustrades curved both up and downward in the flickering gloom.

"And as you can imagine, Mr. Coleridge, I have many expenses here. The world is changing. Too quickly, perhaps. And so one must move with the times."

"You seem to have the best of both worlds," Coleridge ventured.

The tall man shrugged, the golden lamplight dancing over his saturnine face.

"I am a survivor, Mr. Coleridge. One has to be in a place like Eastern Europe. But you would not know that, coming from such a prosperous and enlightened place as the United States."

Coleridge gave him a wry smile.

"We also have our problems," he told his host politely.

Count Homolky had paused now, and he flung open the thick oak door in front of them to reveal a distinctive but comfortable chamber in which nothing had been spared for the guest's needs. A blazing fire burned in the stone hearth; the panelled walls shone with wax polish; there were thick rugs on the parquet floor; and the yellow light from silver-based lamps set about on tables and the mantel shone on the carved bed, the thick tapestry curtains, and the decanter and glasses set out at the bedside table.

The Count made a subtle gesture with his shoulder, indicating another pool of yellow light farther down the corridor.

"The bathroom is just along the passage, Professor. Lights burn there all night."

He gave the guest his hand to shake in a grave, formal manner. Coleridge saw that his luggage was arranged neatly at the foot of the bed. He had carried his briefcase up with him, and now he transferred it to his left hand as he said goodnight to the Count.

"I will leave you to unpack. Breakfast is at half-past eight, and if you ring the bell one of my staff will escort you down."

Coleridge went on into the room, closing the door behind him, listening to his host's footsteps dying out along the corridor. He went to the window and drew back the thick drapery. The light of the moon and the reflections from the snow created a fairy-tale illustration of Lugos; and the tangled turrets, walls, and cupolas spread out below Coleridge to the courtyards made his iced-cake simile more valid than ever.

He stared over toward the dark fir forests on the horizon, clear-cut in the brilliant light of the moon. Was it his imagination or had there come a faint, insistent howling that hung briefly in the icy air before being dissipated by the wind?

A vivid impression of the mangled thing on the stretcher came unbidden and unwanted into Coleridge's mind. He shivered suddenly, drew the thick curtain against the night, and stepped back into the warmth of the room.

COLERIDGE WAS WOKEN from a dreamless sleep the following morning by a soft-footed manservant who brought hot water and towels. After he had washed and dressed he pressed the bell, which brought the dumb majordomo to his room. It was just half-past eight and still pitch-dark when he descended to breakfast.

The meal was served in a vast chamber warmed by a roaring fire and whose pine-panelled walls were burdened with barbaric relics of the chase: boars' heads with glaring eyes, deer with vast spreads of antler, and even the heads of wolves, whose tarnished plaques proclaimed that they had been slain in the eighteenth century.

Coleridge was the first at table, and so he had time to study his surroundings while girls in traditional peasant costume bustled about, first bringing scalding hot coffee in a silver pot before the main breakfast which would presumably be served when the host and the rest of the guests arrived.

Coleridge inferred that the room had once been the Castle armoury in ancient times. Apart from its huge size, it had a flagged floor made up of gigantic slabs of stone which were now wax-polished and covered with occasional rugs of what looked like bear-skin, and there were racks of weapons at ground-level with shields and other lethal-looking implements, including axes and pikes, spread out in artistic patterns on the walls.

They were high up here, and though there would have been a magnificent view down to the rest of the Castle and the village in broad daylight, the enormous windows that broke the massive stone walls at the professor's back were still covered by thick tapestry curtains, no doubt in order to keep out the draught.

Despite all the evidence of the rude arts of the mediaeval huntsman spread about him, the room was not without comfort, and Coleridge revelled in the rich taste of the coffee, agreeably aromatic on the tongue; the snow-white linen of the tablecloth; the glinting silver at each placing; and the gratifying warmth that the stone fireplace threw out from the opposite wall.

He had been there only a few minutes, tasting the coffee, his eyes occasionally catching those of the deferential servants who passed and repassed, or staring into the roseate flames of the fire with his mind agreeably blank of any specific thought, when there came the muffled sound of footsteps from the flagged corridor outside the room door.

It was still only ten minutes to nine, and familiar faces were advancing down the length of the room toward him. His host was in the forefront, leading a party of Coleridge's fellow delegates from the Congress, but there was no sign of the women for the moment. Coleridge made as though to rise from the table, but Homolky pressed him back.

"You are early abroad, Professor, particularly after your late night and journeyings of yesterday. I trust my people have made you comfortable?"

"Everything is admirable, Count."

Coleridge acknowledged the smiling greetings of the six other men as they ranged themselves round one end of the huge refectory table, their host dropping into a rudely carved wooden chair which had a boar's-head motif engraved on its back.

"The ladies are not joining us, then?"

It was the black-bearded man nearest to Coleridge, reaching out for the silver-plated coffeepot. The servants were coming back en masse now, bearing the main breakfast.

The Count shrugged. He wore a hunting jacket with deep-flapped pockets this morning, and a red silk handkerchief made a splash of scarlet as it peeped from his breast pocket.

"Alas, no. They are taking breakfast in their rooms and begged to be excused."

Coleridge himself was wearing a thick tweed country suit, and as he leaned back in his chair and waited for the meal to be served he felt a good deal more comfortable and at his ease than yesterday.

A young man with a clipped black moustache, who was sitting almost opposite Coleridge, caught the other's eye and made a wry face. Coleridge, with one of his moments of deep penetration, could not resist a slightly waspish comment.

"Delightful ladies, are they not?"

The Count quietly watched the two men as he reached forward to raise the cover on one of the big dishes a servant-girl had placed in front of him. A familiar and agreeable aroma permeated the room.

"Indeed," the dark-haired man mumbled.

"Particularly Miss Homolky," put in George Parker, the black-bearded man sitting to Coleridge's right.

The Count dabbed fastidiously at his lips with a silk handkerchief as he put his coffee cup down.

"You have made a conquest, Dr. Raglan," he told the young man smilingly.

"My daughter was speaking of you only last evening, just before the professor's arrival."

Raglan flushed and bent over his plate to hide his slight confusion. An awkward pause had ensued, and Coleridge, conscious that he had started the conversation on this tack, hastened to make amends.

"What is the programme for today, gentlemen? I realise we have no official business, but I would be glad of a tour of the Castle and perhaps a walk in these agreeable surroundings. Unless the weather is too severe."

The Count pushed one of the dishes over toward his companions, the servants hovering in the background and looking slightly anxious to Coleridge's eye.

"Eggs and bacon, gentlemen," Homolky exclaimed with a short laugh. "A favourite with the English and the Americans also, is it not?"

"You are too kind," Coleridge said.

Truth to tell, he was exceedingly hungry this morning and he felt he could do justice to the breakfast before them. He took a slice of the coarse-looking brown bread and spread it with butter. It was warm—fresh-baked, in fact—and tasted delicious.

The Count had taken up the thread of their earlier conversation.

"No, I do not think the weather will be too severe if walking be your pleasure, Professor. Providing you are accompanied by one of the members of my family or my staff. It will not snow, if that is what you meant."

A sombre image had again floated back into Coleridge's mind. He shook his head.

"No, I did not mean that, Count. I was referring to the wolf."

There was a sudden silence round the table. Dr. Menlow, a tall, gaunt Englishman with sandy hair and a drooping moustache of the same colour, paused with the butter-knife halfway to his toast. The others stared at Coleridge uncomprehendingly. The latter was quick to sense the atmosphere, and he looked apologetically at his host.

"I trust I have not inadvertently . . ."

Homolky shook his head, his face serious beneath the shock of white hair.

"No, no, Professor, it is quite in order. The affair is all over the village by now."

A dark shadow passed across his mobile features.

"That is why the ladies have not joined us this morning. They are rather upset about the business. The man did a good deal of work for my estate. And, as you know, this is not the first time."

Coleridge nodded, aware of the puzzled expressions of his colleagues.

"A man was killed by a wolf last night," he said. "I saw the body brought in as I was on my way here."

A visible shiver passed through the servants bustling about in the background, despite the warmth of the room. The effect Coleridge's words had had on them was not lost on the Count.

"Leaving aside superstitious nonsense," he said sharply, "I should be glad of your help, Professor. It is time a proper hunt is organised for the beast. I understand you are a superlative shot."

Coleridge shrugged, again feeling exposed and inadequate as the eyes of the other six men, who had fallen silent at his news, were turned upon him.

"I would not say that, Count. But adequate, yes. I have hunted in my native mountains and in those of Europe. But not for what you call sport. Only from necessity."

The Count raised his eyebrows, but before he could reply, Professor Shaw put in sharply, "But superstition is surely why we are here, Count?"

Coleridge was certain their host would have been annoyed at this, but he smiled thinly at the savant's interruption.

"An admirable observation, Professor. You are right, of course. But there is a difference between properly conducted scientific research into primitive superstition and the mindless acceptance of old wives' tales, as I believe you call them."

He waved a heavily built man in steward's uniform away from the table. He looked round the vast room, stilling the murmur. Keeping his penetrating eyes fixed upon the middle distance he continued, lowering his voice almost to a whisper so that the breakfasting company had to strain their ears.

"These are very simple people, gentlemen. They are admirable in many ways. But they are like frightened children when something like this happens."

"But what has happened?" put in George Parker with mild exasperation.

Coleridge waited for his host to go on, but he remained silent, so the professor took up the story.

"There is apparently a large black wolf which leads a marauding pack hereabouts. The wolf—or the members of the pack—has been responsible for the deaths of three people from the village. And the local inhabitants say there is something supernatural about the animal that leads the pack. They have continually fired at the creature but have been unable to hit it."

"Perhaps it's because they're such beastly bad shots," put in Dr. Raglan sotto voce, causing fleeting smiles to run round the table.

To Coleridge's surprise the Count shook his head.

"I think there is a little more to it than that, Doctor."

He glanced about him again, making sure the nearest servants were out of earshot.

"There is something strange. Not supernatural, in my opinion. But the beast which leads the pack is certainly cunning and quite out of the ordinary."

He fixed the company with his piercing eyes.

"I have never come across anything like it. And I am an experienced hunter, both here and in other parts of Europe."

"You have taken part in the hunts yourself, then," said Coleridge.

The tall figure of their host was erect now, as though he were listening for something above the crackling of the fire.

"Indeed. And there were some surprising incidents."

He held up his hand suddenly.

"Though I would not wish this information to reach the ladies. They have been much troubled by this business already."

"I do hope all this will not interfere with the business for which we have gathered here," put in Dr. Abercrombie, a burly, bearded Scotsman who had not yet spoken.

"You need have no fears on that account, Doctor," Homolky replied smoothly, his eyes sweeping round the company.

The eighth man at table, who had been silent hitherto, was sitting diagonally across from Coleridge. He wore a suit of dark brown plus-fours, which made him look as though he had strolled off a Scottish grouse-moor, Coleridge thought.

Middle-aged, and with a greying beard, he was a noted expert on vampirism and witchcraft. He had arrived late for the Congress, having been detained on medical consultations in Paris, but had promised to read some important papers containing original research during the ten-day programme the Count and his household staff had organised.

Now he drummed with thick spatulate fingers on the immaculate white cloth before him, the steam from his coffee cup making little blurred images of his features as it rose past his face toward the ceiling. He stared thoughtfully across at Coleridge.

"It has already been touched on, of course, but if there does turn out to be something odd about this creature, would it not be extremely interesting?"

The Count had a momentary expression of annoyance on his face but disguised it as he again turned down to address himself to the heaped plate before him. Coleridge's own bacon was getting cold, and he also resumed his interrupted meal, the others following suit.

"I mean," Dr. Sullivan went on, almost dreamily. "This is the very stuff of our own studies. The observation of primitive superstition at close hand and under such circumstances would be absorbing, to say the least."

The words seemed to hang in the air far longer than one would have thought, Coleridge felt.

Sullivan had just the faintest touch of malice in his smile as he glanced around the table.

"Or is it the difference between comfortable scholarship in agreeable surroundings and the rigours of fieldwork which might turn out to be extremely dangerous?"

The Count dabbed at his mouth with his napkin, his manner formal and correct.

"We shall see, Dr. Sullivan," he said. "In the meantime the food is getting cold."

An uneasy silence fell over the table, which persisted until the end of the meal.

Confidences

A LOW DISPIRITING MIST lay over the landscape, cloaking the salient features, and through the darkness of the fir trees which made up much of the surrounding forest, individual trunks stood out blackly like the bars of a cage. That was the impression given to Coleridge as he stood, warm and well-fed, by the windows of a great reception room on an upper floor of the Castle, enjoying the afterbreakfast solitude.

His colleagues had dispersed to their rooms, and his host had gone to see his family regarding their plans for the day. The professor was momentarily alone, apart from the dumb majordomo who stood with his arms crossed at the far end of the room, ready to cater to the guest's whim, but in reality looking as though he were on guard, Coleridge thought.

He watched his own reflection in the pane, occasionally obliterated by the dancing gleams of the fire at the opposite side of the tapestry-hung chamber. The end of his cigar glowed an even red, and he relished its fragrant aroma.

He was glad of the break. There was no noise here, though he could see massive wooden carts negotiating sharp bends that took the road past the Castle. He followed them idly with his eyes for a moment or two; they looked like more gypsy arrivals for the Fair his sledge-driver had spoken of. He hoped he would have an opportunity to visit the Fair during their stay. Coleridge enjoyed such gatherings with their crude vitality and gusto, and the gypsies, particularly the Eastern European variety with their vivid dances and wild stories, were the very essence of folklore.

In his library at home Coleridge had upward of forty thick notebooks stuffed with the data he had amassed during his travels the length and breadth of Europe in recent years. But then his thoughts reverted to his host and his attractive family. Apart from the cloud cast by the death of the woodman yesterday, the visit promised to be a delightful break from the rigours of the Congress.

The Count's guests were hand-picked, though not all had been Coleridge's first choices for this private gathering; all were English-speaking and generally congenial spirits. It was true that Coleridge did not know every one of them in person. Some he had met for the first time in the capital, others he had corresponded with.

But they had impressed him favourably with their outward-looking ideas and the depth of their scholarship. Really, this visit to Castle Homolky should have been the highlight of the Hungarian trip. And yet . . .

Coleridge broke off frowningly and turned away from the window, seeking the deep carved chair by the fire. The incident yesterday he had referred to, in his own mind, as a cloud. Yet it was more than that. The Count and his family were obviously troubled. And the guide and the priest, if he remembered correctly, had both spoken of a projected wolf-hunt. He had even agreed to take part himself.

He bit his lip, knocking out the ash from his burning cigar on a massive wrought-iron firedog in the shape of a fiercely snarling wolf. He had not noticed it before and was somewhat startled for a moment; the unknown mediaeval craftsman had fashioned the likeness so skilfully as to give the image an expression of unbridled ferocity.

Coleridge shifted his gaze over to the left-hand side of the fire, ignoring the impassive figure of the white-haired man in the military-style uniform who stood so patiently near the door. The image here was even more interesting: the wolf had something down between his forepaws and, with head lowered, was tearing at it. The effect was so unpleasant that Coleridge felt an involuntary shudder pass through him. Then he was himself again.

He remembered that his guide had referred to the Castle as The House of the Wolf; that was curious in itself, and now here was the wolf-motif on the firedogs. If there were historical precedent, then the wolf-motif should logically appear in the Count's coat of arms. He got up again and walked over closer to the fireplace. The heat was intense, but he forgot that as he looked up at the carved heraldic shield that occupied the central panel high in the gloom.

It was difficult to make out at that distance, and the professor went back and resumed his chair and his disconnected musings. He had brought some notes for one of his principal papers down from his room, and now he took them out and spread them on his knee, running down the subheadings frowningly as he looked for errors and turned over half-formulated ideas.

He stopped at last, glancing back to the first page with a sharp crackle of paper. He had passed an agreeable few minutes, the only sound being the musical chime of an ancient clock with metal and gilt figures which wheeled about with a faint noise of clockwork before beating out the quarter hours with tiny hammers.

The thing was a quaint conceit but all of a piece with Castle Homolky and the antiquity of their host's family, Coleridge thought. He frowned again at the paper's heading, his cigar burning out unheeded in the fingers of his right hand. He stared at the title.

"On Lycanthropy." It seemed a little austere even for such a function as that on which they were engaged. If he knew George Parker, he would have chosen something much more colourful for his opening paper. Coleridge grunted.

He leaned forward, searching in his breast pocket for his pen. He crossed out the heading, conscious of its dry inadequacy. He thought for a moment, his eyes half-closed. Then he rapidly scribbled in a substitution. "Some Aspects of the Werewolf Myth."

He smiled faintly at the conceit, as though he were proposing something greatly daring in such a title. The smile was still curving his lips when there came the click of a door in the silence and someone came out onto the carved wooden balcony which overhung the end of the room and stared down at him.

After a moment or two Coleridge made out that it was the Count's daughter, Nadia. She gave him a hesitant smile as she caught his eye and then moved over to the head of a small spiral staircase which led down to floor level. Coleridge got up and walked over to meet her. He heard another noise then and, turning, was just in time to see the majordomo disappearing through the far door. The girl had evidently given him some discreet signal, indicating that she wished to talk alone with her guest.

Coleridge awaited the girl at the foot of the stairs with faint trepidation. Firstly, he often felt ill at ease with such young women; he had had some embarrassing experiences with his own students when lecturing in America. The modern young girl was inclined to be intense and romantic and often read subtle implications into Coleridge's lectures which he had certainly never intended.

He was no prig, and he smiled briefly as the thought swiftly chased itself across his mind. And he was certainly not too old for young women, though he preferred those of more mature years; the early thirties was a sensible age, he believed. Now as he waited, one hand on the carved wooden balustrade, listening to the clattering of the girl's heavy boots on the treads above, he hoped she would not make him the recipient of some unwanted and unlooked-for confidence.

Coleridge was aware that subtle influences were gathering around him; from attending a highly enjoyable and relaxing private gathering of like-minded savants he might well find himself enmeshed in something far more complicated.

The thought was ridiculous on the surface, but the old adage about coming events and their shadows was much in Coleridge's mind, though it did not show on his face as he gave Nadia Homolky a welcoming smile as she reached the foot of the spiral.

This morning she wore some sort of masculine hunting costume which showed her full figure to advantage. The effect was delightful, Coleridge thought, and was certainly practical in such a country and in such weather conditions as prevailed outside. She caught the approval in his eyes and smiled again, the mellow light of the overhead lamps making a shimmering mass of her shoulder-length hair.

"I am glad to find you alone this morning, Professor," she said in her clear-minted English, every syllable precise and correct in a way in which native-born English-speakers never enunciate. There was nothing mechanical about it, but it proved to Coleridge that she had had the finest teachers who had not been satisfied until the slightest trace of an Eastern European accent had been eliminated. He guessed that her father had had a good deal to do with her schooling.

The two walked back toward the fireplace, a faint, elusive perfume Coleridge had noted the previous night emanating from the girl's hair. He supposed it might have been the pomade or whatever it was that young ladies washed or dressed their hair with.

Coleridge had not ventured an answer to her first remark, and now the girl turned her head sideways to give him a penetrating look. He was beginning to find her close proximity a little overpowering, and he moved quickly away to the other side of the fireplace. Nadia Homolky appeared not to have noticed, but the savant was aware that this member of a remarkable family was just as percipient and quick-witted as the rest of them.

"There was something I wished to discuss with you, Professor," she went on, hesitating and resting one slim hand on the back of the big carved chair near the fire. Coleridge waited politely for her to sit before he took the chair opposite, a small occasional table between them.

"I am at your disposal, Miss Homolky," he said, turning his eyes from her face to the details of her costume.

She wore green velveteen breeches tucked into tan riding boots, and they gave her a masculine look that was offset by the decidedly feminine curves of the legs beneath the thick material. A belted corduroy jacket of the same colour circled her trim waist, and a dark brown shirt, open-necked at the fine pillars of her throat, was topped by a red silk scarf which was knotted carelessly, with the art that conceals art, and thrust into the bosom of the shirt where firm breasts swelled beneath the jacket.

Coleridge knew he had been wise to put the table between them; he was not normally an impressionable man, but he knew this girl could have a powerful effect on members of the opposite sex. He had already noted the attraction that she had for the good-looking and enthusiastic young Dr. Raglan.

She moistened her full lips and went on rapidly, keeping her eyes turned down to the polished parquet which dully reflected the dancing flames of the fire.

"I believe you witnessed an ugly incident which had taken place a short while before you arrived at the Castle?"

Coleridge inclined his head.

"That is so. Your father seemed rather upset and asked me not to mention it in front of the family."

The girl made a little dismissive gesture with her right hand, raising her eyes to fix his own.

"Father has already told us the broad details, Professor. You may speak quite freely with me."

Coleridge felt faint surprise rising within him, but his manner was noncommittal.

"I know very little about it, Miss Homolky. I merely saw the remains of this poor fellow being brought back, and I gathered the details from my guide, who spoke to the priest about it."

The girl nodded, her eyes still on Coleridge's face.

"Father Balaz. Yes. He is a good friend and often dines here. I have a particular reason for asking you about the matter. The man who died worked for my father and had been a loyal companion to me during my childhood."

Her voice trembled a little, but her gaze was steady as she continued to regard her guest.

"We are very close-knit in these communities, Professor Coleridge, even though we may appear to be separated in station and style of life from the village people. My mother and grandmother were also very upset."

She broke off and looked almost fiercely into the fire before resuming.

"There have been many wild stories in circulation. I would be grateful if you could tell me what you saw and heard last night."

Coleridge shrugged.

"There is little enough to tell, Miss Homolky."

He related the events of the previous evening, his eyes turned down toward the parquet where the flames of the fire were reflected. The girl sat with one hand on the arm of the carved chair, her small knuckles showing white where she clutched it. Coleridge told her everything he could remember, leaving out the bloodier detail to spare the girl's feelings.

There was no sound in the vast apartment except for the faint noise of the fire, and when he at last finished the girl gave a low, vibrant sigh that startled Coleridge by the depth of sorrow in it. His surprise must have shown on his face, for the blonde girl flushed slightly and put up her hand to brush the hair from her eyes.

"You are a stranger here, Professor," she said gently, "and can know little of childhood ties forged under the dark and tragic circumstances of such an unfortunate country as mine."

Coleridge looked her full in the eyes.

"I can assure you I do understand, my dear young lady," he answered softly. "I am sorry to be the one to bear such news which can only cause distress to those who knew the man."

The girl was staring into the fire, as though she had not heard Coleridge's last remark. She turned back to him again, her jaw set.

"What do you think about this wolf, Professor? You are an expert on folklore, like Dr. Raglan and your colleagues here."

"I?"

The surprise in Coleridge's voice was unconcealed.

"What can I say, Miss Homolky? There are many wild superstitions abounding in such lonely and mountainous communities as you have here. I have written much about them, as you know."

The girl shook her head impatiently.

"I did not mean that, Professor. Even the soldiers say there is something weird about this wolf—that he is impossible to shoot, possessed of almost supernatural cunning, and so forth."

Coleridge shook his head.

"The wolf is a very courageous, enterprising, and cunning animal. It is hardly surprising that a pack-leader such as I have heard described should have gained such a reputation. But I would be extremely doubtful whether the same animal had killed three times. Normally they kill other animals only for food or when cornered."

The girl's face now was white.

"Exactly, Professor. That is what is so strange about it. Dr. Raglan too was sceptical when he came here. But now he agrees with me."

Coleridge smiled at the girl, conscious of the warm flush spreading across her cheeks.

"Dr. Raglan is a very clever and highly-thought-of young man in his profession, Miss Homolky. If you will forgive me for saying so, you make a handsome pair. And it is hardly surprising that he would agree with someone so delightful as yourself . . ."

He broke off, conscious that the girl was smiling too. She shook her head violently as though in disagreement, but the smile grew.

"I take your point, Professor, but I did not mean that, I can assure you."

She became more serious after a moment or two, glancing around as though uneasy that they might be overheard.

"There was something else you wished to tell me, wasn't there?" Coleridge went on, trying to put his companion at ease. He sensed all sorts of questions in her eyes.

She bit her lip and turned away from him, her gaze again seeking the flames, as though she could see things there that were hidden from him. The dancing reflections of the firelight glanced on the iron eye-sockets of the two heraldic wolves on the firedogs, making them momentarily alive.

"There was something, Professor," she continued after a moment. "But it is almost too fantastic for belief."

Coleridge felt a quick stirring of interest.

"Is it something to do with this house? Or the subject of our Congress?"

The girl sat stiffly now, her face turned away, all her concentration seemingly on the molten mass at the heart of the fire.

"The locals call this The House of the Wolf," Coleridge went on. "It seemed a strange conceit to me until I saw the heraldic devices in this room."

The girl was facing him again. Her eyes were troubled, and her breasts rose and fell with her agitated breathing beneath the open-necked shirt.

"Yes, it is to do with this house, Professor. And with the Congress, if you like."

She got up and came forward impulsively to put her hand on the savant's arm.

"What would you say, Professor, if I told you something that seems utterly, wildly impossible?"

Coleridge's smile died on his lips as he looked into Nadia Homolky's agitated features.

"I should probably say there was some logical explanation and that you should not distress yourself."

The grip of the girl's hand tightened on Coleridge's sleeve.

"Late last night, Professor, I was reading in my room. Someone tried the door-handle. I saw it move as clearly as I see you now. It turned several times, and then the door itself was violently shaken."

She bit her lip again, her eyes haunted by the recollection of something her listener was unable to fathom.

"I am rather nervous, and this Castle has a strange atmosphere at night. I called out, and the noise stopped. I got out of bed and went over to the door and was actually going to open it . . ."

She broke off, pulling her hand violently away from Coleridge's restraining grip. Her eyes were wild and her face ashen now.

"Professor, I am as certain in my mind as I am that we are here that as I put my hand on the key I heard the snarling of a wolf not a foot from where I was standing, and the click of a wild animal's paws on the floor of the corridor!"

The Thing in the Corridor

"YOU ASTONISH ME!"

Coleridge's bewilderment and momentary inadequacy were all too palpable on his face. The girl's features had a little more colour, but her expression was still grim as she stared at her companion.

"I intended to, Professor. Can you imagine my situation late at night and to all purposes alone and undefended. I cried out, and then I heard the thing running down the corridor outside. After that I must have fainted because I awoke on the floor of my room deathly cold and found by my bedside clock that almost an hour had passed."

The girl came closer again, looking at her companion with a mixture of terror and apprehension.

"You do believe me, Professor? I can assure you of my sanity."

Coleridge took the small, chill hand she held out and rose from his seat.

"I believe you, Miss Homolky. But there must be some logical explanation. Could a wild beast have gained access to the Castle?

I noticed earlier today that there is a break in the ancient perimeter wall where it gives on to the open countryside. You can see it from the window here."

He led her toward it, more with the hope of distracting her from her distressing memories than of providing a rational explanation of what she had told him. She followed his pointing finger downward through the misty air.

"It is possible," she said slowly. "But not likely. How would such an animal have got through all the locked and closed doors between the inner courtyard and my room? Besides, you are forgetting that the thing tried the door-handle."

There was a trace of hysteria in her tones, and Coleridge ushered her swiftly to a great side-buffet where bottles and glasses glittered. He poured her a small glass of the local spirit, her teeth catching on the rim of the crystal. When she was calmer, the colour fully restored to her cheeks, Coleridge led her back to the fire.

"You have not told your family of this?"

Nadia Homolky shook her head vigorously.

"It did not seem appropriate. They have many worries, you see. I do not wish them to know."

Coleridge ventured another approach.

"Is it not possible that a servant first tried your door and, being unable to gain entrance, went on down the corridor? And then this beast passed along a few moments later."

The girl's burning eyes were holding Coleridge's own.

"Possible, but not likely, Professor. I know what I heard."

She gulped at the raw spirit again.

"And no-one else saw or heard this creature? It was not mentioned at breakfast."

The girl put her small hands together round the rim of her glass. Again she looked very vulnerable and frail at that moment.

"That was one of the reasons I decided to say nothing."

Coleridge read her glance correctly.

"And you would like me to investigate this incident for you? As discreetly and quietly as possible."

The girl was smiling again now. For a moment Coleridge almost wished he were Dr. Raglan.

"If only you would, Professor. I would be tremendously grateful. You are such an authority. And if anyone can assign a mundane explanation for this weird happening, it would be you."

Coleridge put his hands together in his lap and frowningly examined his nails.

"You flatter me," he said.

And after a moment of sombre silence between them: "Why do you keep your bedroom door locked?"

Nadia Homolky shrugged, her fingers still firm round the glass.

"I am happy here. This is my home. But the Castle is a strange and gloomy place at night, as I have said. Since I have been an adult my parents have encouraged us to lock our doors at night."

Coleridge raised his eyebrows.

"Us?"

"I am referring to the family and the household staff, Professor. Those that sleep within the Castle itself, in the residential wing here. It seems a reasonable thing to do. If you have lived in this country . . . It is remote and savage, as you have seen. And we have wild animals that are unknown in places like France and England."

"You have made your point," Coleridge conceded. "But it could be awkward if someone were taken ill and unable to summon help."

The girl raised her glass to her lips.

"Father holds master keys in case of emergencies," she said.

She again smiled briefly.

"You are not suggesting that one of these superintelligent wolves is clever enough to use one of the master keys to gain access to the Castle?"

Coleridge was constrained to smile too.

"I hardly think so, Miss Homolky. But let us just take a look at this room of yours, and perhaps I may be able to set your mind at rest."

The girl led the way back up the curved staircase so swiftly that Coleridge was hard put to it to keep pace with her. Their footsteps echoed from the beamed ceiling and seemed to stir reverberations that hung in the air long after they should have dispersed, or so the guest felt as he hurried in the girl's wake.

He paused as she turned to a small octagonal table in a dark corner and picked up a silver-banded oil lamp which had already been lit.

"It is so dark in some of the corridors we are reduced to this," she said. "I have been pestering Father for a long while to extend the electric lighting to our bedrooms, but he prefers to augment his income by diverting it all to the guests and staff of The Golden Crown."

Coleridge thought it politic to say nothing and wrenched his features into a blank expression. Nadia Homolky saw through him immediately and seemed amused. She turned up the wick of the lamp, throwing a golden glow onto the ancient panelling and the sombre-visaged oil portraits that hung in gilt frames on the balcony on which they found themselves, and opened a small, low door set into a stone buttress.

Coleridge was amazed at the proportions of the wall, which made a short corridor to a connecting door. It must have been almost eight feet thick and aroused his antiquarian interest, as this sort of thickness was usually reserved for outside defence.

He glanced at his silver-cased watch as the girl opened the far door. It was still short of eleven o'clock in the morning, but it might have been midnight for all the light that penetrated here.

The girl led him down another very short stair with beautifully carved balusters. Coleridge perceived that this was modern work and guessed it might be one of his host's own improvements, for private use by the family. So it proved a few moments later, for Coleridge realised with faint surprise that he was again back in the corridor leading to his bedroom and down which he had walked to the main staircase on his way to breakfast.

The girl put the lamp upon a table they passed and left it burning. They were at the main stairhead now, and she ushered the professor up another staircase to the right which evidently led to the private apartments of the family, for here were more intimate touches: flowers carefully arranged in pale blue porcelain vases on occasional tables and the bright light of the snow shining through great vaulted windows at their left, which had gaily coloured scenes of some ancient battle with knights in armour, all carried out in stained glass of particularly rich shades of green, gold, and red.

They cast a bizarre patina on the faces of Coleridge and the girl, and she gave a delighted laugh as she glanced at him sideways as they hurried on down the corridor. They were passing a section where gold-coloured glass depicted the sky, and as Coleridge caught the girl's eye he saw for one indescribable moment all the beauty of her face transformed into bronze, as though she were herself some Arcadian nymph cast by a master sculptor.

Coleridge was amazed at the ramifications and elaboration of the Count's life-style. To produce the flowers he must have hothouses somewhere within the Castle, and he had probably provided the incongruous blooms he had already noted at the inn in Lugos. Incongruous, only in the sense that they were wildly unlikely not only in this savage corner of Hungary but in the existing weather conditions.

Coleridge realised the whole atmosphere of the Castle led one into a world of fantasy; it was an ideal setting for the scholarly purposes on which they were gathered here, but he did not at all care for it as a background to the somewhat more sinister incidents which appeared to be unfolding at the moment.

The girl again glanced at Coleridge from beneath her long-lashed eyes.

"A strange place, is it not, Professor? You must suppose we are all tainted with this bizarre atmosphere."

"Not at all," Coleridge said in disavowal but felt constrained to add: "That is, I would find it a wonderful atmosphere for a family like yours. But it makes a sombre setting for such an incident as you have described."

The girl nodded.

"Precisely," she said crisply.

They were almost at their destination now, for the corridor turned at right-angles and the guest saw that they were in a cul-de-sac; the passage, which had doors leading off both sides, being lit by one large window at the end through which the harsh glare of the light off the snow struck dull reflections from the polished parquet underfoot.

The girl paused and stood for a moment or two as though in thought.

"Tell me, Professor, why was it Father, with his intense interest in folklore, did not attend your Congress in the city?"

Coleridge glanced down toward the glare from the far window.

"A fair question, Miss Homolky. The Congress was reserved for professional scholars, historians, and folklorists only. Your father is a gifted amateur, and I mean that in no pejorative sense."

The girl made a little shrugging motion of her shoulders.

"So you arranged your own Congress here in which Father could take part and hear the distinguished professionals pontificate on their own pet fields."

Coleridge smiled faintly.

"Something of that sort," he admitted. "It might be expressed in that manner, though whether my colleagues would find your description pleasing is another matter."

The girl put her head on one side and looked at him with such a grave expression that it seemed for one moment as though she were a person of advanced years. Coleridge had seen such a look many times on the faces of elderly scholars who were scandalised by or opposed to his views, and it inwardly amused him, though nothing of this showed on his face.

The girl had moved on now, and she threw open an elaborately carved door to the left. It was obviously her bedroom, as Coleridge could see a large bed with a pink counterpane beyond and a glass case in which were beautifully carved dolls dressed in colourful folk costumes. But he had little time for them; he had bent to his knees, his professional instincts reasserting themselves, and was minutely examining the bottom panel of the half-open door.

The detail was readily visible by the light spilling in from the windows of the bedroom, and he gave a low exhalation of breath which the girl immediately seized on.

"You have found something?"

"Look at this."

Coleridge moved over, and the girl knelt at his side; again he was uneasily aware of the faint, elusive perfume she used, and he drew back slightly, disturbed by her closeness. Miss Homolky was oblivious of this, being completely absorbed by the panelling in front of them. Her hair hung down in a cloud of gold about her face, and she moved closer to take in the deep scratches indicated by the professor's pointing finger.

"Were these here before?"

She shook her head.

"I don't think so."

"I thought not."

Coleridge could not keep a slight trembling resonance from his speech. He had produced a small pair of metal tweezers from somewhere, and he delicately picked out a large splinter of wood from the detailed carving, leaving a clearly incised groove. There was something adhering to the splinter; the girl made it out to be wool or fur and perhaps a fragment of skin.

"What is that?"

Her own voice was somewhat unsteady to her ears.

"We shall know a little better when I have analysed it," said Coleridge crisply.

He got up and carefully dusted the knees of his trousers.

"In the meantime, not a word about this to anyone."

He had already moved back along the corridor and was examining the parquet with the eye of a trained observer, according it the same minute scrutiny he had already given the door. A moment later the girl, who had quickly joined him, noticed the mark which had drawn his own attention. It was another clearly incised groove in the smooth waxen surface of one of the blocks; a cut that could have been made by a sharp metal tool or perhaps by the claw of a large animal.

Nadia Homolky gave an audible shudder, her eyes very bright as she stared at Coleridge.

"Well, Professor?"

The pair were still in a crouching posture when the lean form of Dr. Raglan came noiselessly round the angle in the corridor and discovered them motionless on all fours.

The Break in the Wall

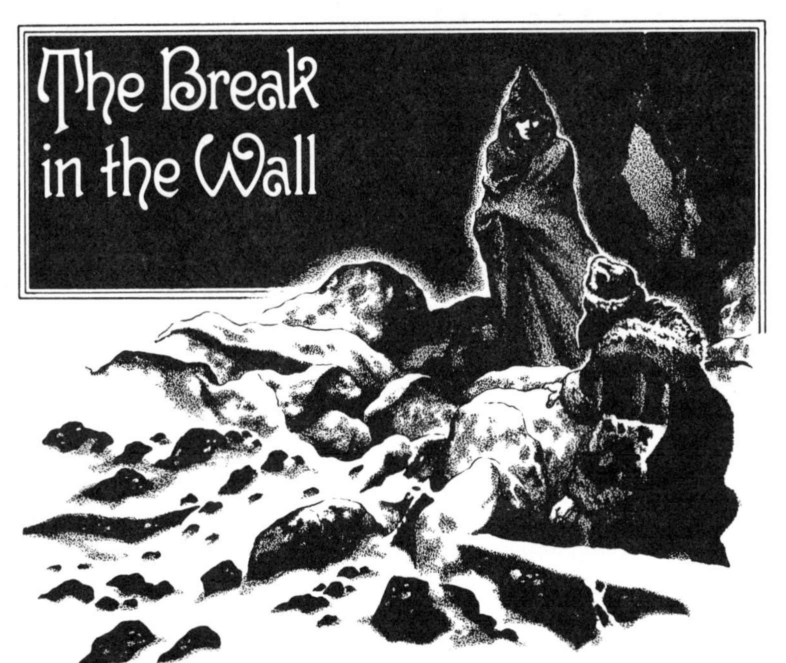

COLERIDGE IGNORED the injured expression in the other's eyes. He got up carefully, still holding the tweezers, and put the fragment of wood and fur into a small brown paper envelope he took from an inner pocket.

He sealed the envelope and wrote something on it with a silver pen, aware all the time of the looks the two young people were exchanging. If the situation amused him, he was too skilled a diplomatist to let anything of this show on his face.

"I think I may have some news for you a little later," he told the girl tactfully, giving his colleague a friendly glance.

The latter cleared his throat, a baffled look in his eyes as he stared first at Coleridge and then at the young woman. The former thought it might be a good time to take his leave, but Nadia Homolky had not yet finished.

She ignored Raglan and fell into step with the professor as he started back down the corridor.

Coleridge half-turned. Raglan had taken a step after them as though he meant to follow but was halted in his tracks by the peremptory, almost savage, gesture the girl made with her right hand, which she kept behind her back. Coleridge was left with the image of Raglan's face, half-angry, half-baffled. He felt uneasy; he did not wish to get between this charming but apparently fiery-tempered girl and a young colleague who was obviously interested in her.

"I did ask you a question, Professor," the girl said to him gently.

The brown eyes, so clear and candid, had an appealing expression in them now. The professor, who could be inflexible when the occasion warranted, knew when to bend with the wind.

"I am sorry," he said by way of being placatory. "My mind was much occupied with what you have just shown me."

"Then you do think an animal was outside my room," the girl persisted.

"I did not say so," said Coleridge cautiously.

He went on, forestalling any interruption.

"It is possible. But we are far from knowing it was a wolf."

"When will you know?" the girl asked.

Coleridge admired her tenacity while at the same time deploring the way in which she was continually pressing him for an answer.

"In a little while, perhaps," he said. "When I have had this material analysed. One of my colleagues is an expert in these matters. If he has his microscope with him . . ."

"Oh, there is no problem about that," Nadia Homolky broke in. "Father has a well-equipped laboratory at the top of the Castle. You will find everything you need there."

Coleridge was about to smile at the girl's earnestness, but another look at her face convinced him of her deadly seriousness. He put his hand on her arm in a consolatory gesture.

"Do not distress yourself further, Miss Homolky. I know how gravely you regard this matter."

They were back at the stairhead now, and they paused again. Coleridge fixed his gaze absently on the glaring, glassy eyes of a wild boar's head which hung on the panelling of the staircase. The Castle, he now understood, was full of such barbaric mementoes of the chase.

He heard, too, the faint footfalls on the parquet along the angle of the corridor. Raglan had followed them, then. He realised the doctor would have to, of course, because the corridor was a cul-de-sac. Nevertheless, the young man's proximity gave him an uneasy feeling; he felt there might be a scene between him and the girl, and he had no wish to be party to it. He took his hand off her arm. He was relieved, therefore, when she led the way down the staircase at a fast pace.

"Natural or unnatural," he added, "we ought to examine the place in the Castle walls where the beast could have gained ingress."

"I am just going to show you," she said over her shoulder.

"I shall need my boots if we are going outside," Coleridge rejoined with his native practicality.

The girl laughed musically.

"Nonsense!" she said. "We can see well enough from the inner courtyard. And there is plenty of thick clothing in the entrance hall, which Father keeps there for the use of guests."

Coleridge shrugged. He was content to leave things to this rather extraordinary girl who, although obviously well educated and gently brought up, had a swift decisiveness about her that cut through the veneer of conventionalised ideas.

They passed down the staircase to the great black-and-white tiled hall the visitor recognised from the previous night. The majordomo appeared from one of the side-doors as though he had been summoned by some inaudible bell.

The guest realised then that the girl had, in fact, pressed a button set beneath an enormous oil painting at the bottom of the stairs. She spoke to the majordomo in her own language, and the grey-haired military-looking man immediately withdrew.

"Perhaps you would like some coffee before we go out," the girl said. "I understand that is your custom in your own country."

The humour was back in her eyes now, but Coleridge ignored it. He was completely absorbed in the problems which were currently presenting themselves to his mind.

"When we return," he said. "Then I really must rejoin my colleagues. I believe your father has some sort of itinerary planned for us today. Everyone will wonder where we are."

Nadia Homolky raised her elegant eyebrows, the humour still in her expression.

"I think not, Professor," she said softly.

Coleridge raised his glance to the gloom at the stairhead. He could now see the vaguely questioning form of Raglan hovering there. He felt uneasy and was glad when the unhurried footsteps of the majordomo were again heard on the parquet.

He shrugged on the heavy fur coat the man presented, followed by the enormous flapped cap, and accompanied the girl across to the main entrance of the Castle.

Their breath came reeking from their mouths as they crossed the courtyard, their feet gritting on the frozen granules of snow in the interstices of the cobbles. The going was tricky indeed, and more than once Coleridge felt his footing slip from beneath him, saving himself by clutching his golden-haired companion's arm.

On each occasion she smiled at him mischievously before the savant realised that her heavy boots were evidently fitted with special cleats, because they made a sharp grating noise from time to time.

He wished he had worn boots also, but it was too late now. They were off the courtyard and under an arched colonnade which followed the ancient walls round. It was warmer and dry in here, and Coleridge stamped his feet, getting rid of crusted fragments of snow. The girl kept hold of his arm as though she were either concerned with his balance or anxious about something.

Coleridge came to the latter conclusion after glancing at her because she stared from side to side as they went on down the gloomy cloisterlike arcade. There was no-one about, and it was almost as dark as night beneath the shelter of the wall. They walked on for a few moments in silence before the girl stopped before a massive iron-bound door set into the heavy masonry.

It was unlocked and opened easily to her touch. There was a glare of snow after the darkness of the inner court, and Coleridge blinked, closing his eyes against the suddenness of the light. As they stepped forward into the crispness of the humped and frozen whiteness, he realised they had left the main Castle buildings behind. This was some sort of outer courtyard whose walls were in a sorry state of repair, which he had already glimpsed from his bedroom window.

Looking back, the professor could see that the bulk of Castle Homolky and the entrance area which faced the moat and the road was behind them and to their right. The vast demesne also continued to their left until it was masked by a curtain wall which ran out to join the sprawling curve of a ruined battlement which lay in front of them.

Beyond it, Coleridge could see sloping ground which debouched from the far edge of Lugos. There was a frozen stream which lay in a fold of ground and, beyond, the sinister stillness of dark pine forest, looking like a crayon sketch by some mediaeval artist. The smoke from a few chimneys hung in the sky like the vague scribblings on a child's slate.

There was a confusion of footprints in the trampled snow leading to and from the jagged gap in the tumbled walls. They were much closer now, and Coleridge bent to examine the muddled impression of many feet. He turned to the girl, who was watching him with grave anxiety.

"A great many people pass in and out this way."

Nadia Homolky nodded.

"The Castle staff mostly. They come and go to collect wood and on various errands. It saves them a long journey round by the Castle entrance and the main road. Father frowns on the practice, but there is great practicality in it for the people concerned, so he does not insist."

Coleridge stroked his chin with a hand which was rapidly becoming numb. He thrust it deep in the capacious pocket of the fur coat he had borrowed.

"Your wolf could have come this way. And if that side-door had been unlocked. . ."

The girl said nothing, but her downward-cast eyes showed her companion brief glimpses of her disbelief. He did not labour the point. It would be best to find out more before coming to any definite conclusions. He walked over to where the great jumbled blocks of masonry lay about the breach in the wall.

"How long ago was this done?"

The girl shrugged.

"Centuries, perhaps. In some ancient siege, I believe. Father has the details if you are interested."

The visitor noted that there was a well-defined pathway between the blocks which led to a sort of plateau, probably of heaped earth, where it would be easy to get through. From the other side of the wall another readily apparent path led down to the meadows beyond.

Even with the thick coating of snow Coleridge could make out the heavy indentation where thousands of feet must have trod over the years. And there were deep ruts made by carts passing and repassing, probably with firewood and the implements of forestry. He was silent for a few moments, the weight of centuries suddenly pressing on his mind, mingled with a sense of the impermanence of human beings and their transient affairs.

Then his practical side reasserted itself. He bent down toward the heaped ice and snow, trying to make sense of the blurred impressions produced by many passing feet. He soon saw that there was something apart from footprints and the ruts of a wheeled cart: a series of slotlike indentations in the frozen upper crust of the muddied snow made by some large animal. He followed them back, lips pursed grimly. The traces died out on a large sheet of ice. They went in the general direction of the door in the wall leading to the pillared arcade.

The girl had seen the tracks too, and she came to join him, her breasts rising and falling beneath her thick fur coat with the quick breathing engendered by her emotion.

"An animal, Professor," she said ironically.

"A large dog, perhaps," Coleridge answered. "From your father's household."

The girl shook her head, strands of golden hair escaped from her fur hat falling across her eyes.

"I think not, Professor," she said slowly. "I know a wolf-track well enough when I see one."

Before he could answer, Coleridge became aware that someone was watching them.

Frozen Falls

THE COUNT CAME out from behind the buttress which had concealed his approach. He looked searchingly at his daughter and her companion, but his voice was bland and unconcerned.

"Ah, there you are, Nadia. And you, Professor. We had wondered at your absence. I saw you from the window and took the liberty of coming to fetch you."

"I am sorry, Father," the girl said quickly, shooting Coleridge a warning glance. "I was showing the professor some of the more interesting parts of the Castle."

"So I see," Homolky muttered drily.

He turned to Coleridge, his manner suddenly brisker, and the three started to walk toward the door in the wall which led back to the colonnade flanking the inner courtyard.

"Hot coffee and brandy await us, Professor."

He gave his guest a somewhat wolfish smile, the latter thought.

"It will fortify us for the excursion before us."

He looked at Coleridge anxiously.

"Unless you find the conditions too severe this morning. . ."

Coleridge experienced faint confusion again, though there was no reason he should not have been walking the boundary walls with his host's daughter. He wondered if the Count had noticed the tracks in the snow. Coleridge knew Homolky wanted to keep all worries about the wolf-pack and the deaths in the village from his family. He felt he might have inadvertently breached the host's conception of good manners in a guest and was anxious to make amends.

But he need not have worried, for it was shortly obvious that the Count was in good spirits when he smilingly commenced a dissertation on the history of his ancestral home. Emboldened by this, Coleridge felt encouraged to ask him something which had been on his mind for the past hour or so.

"It is a remarkable place," he said in answer to a proffered remark by the tall man with the white hair, making a startling contrast to his black fur hat.

"I was interested to learn that the village people called it The House of the Wolf. And I noticed the wolf-motif in the firedogs. I presume it is also in your family coat of arms."

The Count smiled politely, and once again Coleridge noticed the sharpness of his teeth.

"That really relates to an ancestor of mine," he said. "The armorial bearings originated from his exploits."

He shot an amused glance at his daughter as they regained the door in the wall. Coleridge waited for his host to precede him but was ushered firmly in to the darkness of the colonnade.

"It is a longish story, and I will reserve it for this evening, with your permission."

Coleridge felt a quickening of interest, and he mentally decided that he would return to the subject if Homolky showed no inclination to do so. In the meantime he had the girl's problem and the fragments of fur and flesh in the envelope in his pocket. He must have a discreet word with Menlow; perhaps there would be an opportunity on their walk.

They were halfway along the shadowy arcade now, and it was somewhat warmer in here, sheltered from the wind. Coleridge had lagged behind, and he hurried to catch up with his companions, his footsteps echoing sepulchrally on the flagstones.

"Have you made arrangements about the wolf-hunt, Father," the girl was saying.

"There has been no time," said Homolky somewhat curtly. "But I hope to have a word with Colonel Anton later in the day."

He turned back to Coleridge.

"Our local Chief of Police," he explained over his shoulder. "It is not strictly a police matter, but he likes to be kept informed of all that goes on in the area."

"I can imagine," said Coleridge blandly, his mind elsewhere for the moment.

They had regained the house now, and Homolky led the way with quick, nervous steps to the hall where the same mute major-domo took their outdoor clothing. Coleridge moved over to the fire, aware that his fingers were frozen to the bone. He held them out to the healing warmth, conscious of the Count's somewhat mocking expression.

Too late, he realised he had left the gloves in the pockets of the coat. He should have worn them, of course; it was dangerous in this climate. There was always a distinct possibility of frostbite if one did not take extreme care.

The girl moved over near Coleridge; her eyes spelt out a mute warning to him. Coleridge found the message difficult to read. He was not sure whether she was asking his discretion regarding their conversation over the supposed wolf outside her room, or whether she was trying to alert him about something else.

A few moments later the tall form of Dr. Raglan moved into view. There was a puzzled, resentful look on his face, and Coleridge edged toward him, offering a reassuring smile.

"I am sorry about that just now," he said in a low voice that the Count could not possibly have heard. "Miss Homolky was rather concerned about something. I am sure she will tell you all about it in due course."

Raglan's face assumed its normal frank, open expression, and he smiled too, all the tension and restraint dropping away from him.

"I did not mean to intrude, Professor, but I was anxious to discuss something with Miss Homolky. I was rather surprised to find you there."

"It was a surprise to myself," Coleridge assured him. "However, you will no doubt have ample time to discuss these matters at coffee."

The Count was standing rather impatiently, and as the two men and his daughter joined him he led the way back at a fast pace to the Armoury, where his wife presided at a silver coffee urn and a black-bearded servant dispensed glasses of spirits.

The room was full of brightness and conversation from the people gathered there, and Coleridge's spirits lightened as he and the other members of the small group hurried forward to join them.

The air burned like fire as Coleridge took it deeply into his lungs, and his boots crunched with brittle punctuations in the icy snow as he followed the black crocodile of figures down the forest trail between the pine trees. They had come through the village in a procession of horse-drawn vehicles which were now returning to the Castle, the hoofbeats sending back reverberating echoes from the house-fronts.

He looked idly at the slim figure of the girl, in her stout boots and fur garments, who walked lithely ahead in the middle of the procession. She was now deep in conversation with Raglan, and her light laughter, metallic in the rising wind, was flung back fragmentarily toward him. Engrossed as she seemed in the young man's banter, he knew she was absorbed in the problems they had earlier been discussing, and he thought again of the samples of flesh and fur reposing in the envelope in his inner pocket.

He hoped to find a moment to confer with his colleague, but the man he wanted was far ahead at the moment, walking with their host. The Count's wife was also present, her tall, graceful figure the absolute mould of her daughter's as she strode at the side of her husband. Coleridge was content to remain in the background for the time being, absorbing the strange atmosphere of this extraordinary land and quietly observing his companions.

He was conscious too that the gathering should have been truly an international one, but two French savants whom he had invited had to decline for personal reasons and a distinguished Hungarian folklorist, whose name was a household word in his native land, had had to return to his remote province because of a family illness.

Therefore, as he had already noted, the English-speaking community which had gathered at Castle Homolky was not strictly the party he had wished for, and one or two of its members were unknown quantities so far as their personalities and the depth of their scholarship were concerned.

It did not really matter, though, because the colleagues Coleridge could personally vouch for and whose work was known to him represented a quality that would make the private Congress due to start in the morning well worthwhile.

His thoughts were proceeding in this mundane fashion when they were interrupted by a harsh roaring noise, and his eye was drawn to the ridge above them on which the village stood and from which drifted great clouds of smoke billowing above the rooftops. He glanced inquiringly at a black-bearded man, almost abreast of him, who appeared to be one of the senior house-servants from the Castle. He broke into a flood of harsh, guttural sentences, which Coleridge could not make out. The tall, emaciated Englishman called Shaw, who was walking just ahead on the path, had dropped back, and now he listened attentively.

"He says that the gypsies are encamped in the village, Professor," he explained in a soft voice. "They are preparing for their Winter Fair."

Coleridge was surprised, though he tried to keep it out of his voice.

"You speak Hungarian, Shaw? I did not know you were so gifted."

The silver-haired man shrugged, his teeth gleaming beneath the drooping moustache.

"It is nothing, Professor. I am able to pick out phrases here and there."

He laughed shortly.

"But friends who know such things tell me my accent is abominable when I try to speak."

They were proceeding lower now, and even the rooftops of the village had sunk beneath the darkness of the trees, as though the last of civilisation was being submerged in their savage and barbaric surroundings.

The image of the great bear he had seen in the wooden slatted cage as they passed the gypsies on their way to the Castle the previous night floated unsummoned into the professor's mind and somehow filled him with sadness. He had said nothing to his host of his feelings on the matter, but he abhorred the shooting of animals and birds except on matters exclusively concerned with food-gathering or survival.

But he had lived in remote parts of the world from time to time where expertise at firearms as a protection against humans as well as animals would appear to be prudent, and so he had taken pains to ensure that he was expert at their use.

Most of his shooting had been, in fact, at nothing more vulnerable than targets, but he was certainly an expert shot and he knew he could give a good account of himself against a man-eating wolf on open snowy ground, conditions under which both trained huntsmen and the troops of Rakosi's detachment had failed.

Shaw had gone ahead again now, slipping and slithering on the icy path, and Coleridge turned aside, walking on the ridges of frozen snow where the footing was more secure. The village had abruptly disappeared from sight as though it had never been, and it was again borne in on the American that a few yards off the path in this country could mean long hours of fruitless wandering and an agonising death for a so-called civilised European.

Even the peasants were better equipped for life here, and he resolved to remember that and take his host's advice in all things related to this rugged country into which they had hardly begun to penetrate. He turned to look back for an instant: only the farthest pinnacle of the Castle was now visible, and a second later it too had disappeared beneath the green-and-white ice-covered foliage of the topmost tree-branches.

The savage roaring again came loud and clear from the direction of Lugos; Coleridge was not startled now. He knew it was probably the bear he had seen on the gypsy cart; possibly the poor brute was signalling for its midday meal or perhaps being prepared unwillingly for some rustic circus turn.

Walking at the side of the path at a faster pace, he had already overtaken some of the party and was now somewhere toward the middle of the column. The Count was up at the head, but almost at once Coleridge found himself behind the gaunt figure of Dr. Menlow. He was deep in conversation with the Count's wife, and once again Coleridge admired the heavy voluptuousness of her figure moving beneath her thick fur garments. He kept a yard or two behind, and after a little while longer she excused herself and went off at a faster pace down the path, moving with quick, lithe movements to rejoin her husband.

Menlow had glanced around and, noticing Coleridge, waited for him to come up, stepping aside to join his colleague on the rough snow at the side of the track. This was the man Coleridge wanted to see without arousing any attention from the others, and he could not have planned it better. Menlow stared at him with red eyes from pinched features. He glanced around with a shiver.

"This is a wild place, Coleridge. I shall be glad to get back indoors again."

The professor shrugged.

"I don't know. It gives one an appetite for lunch."

Menlow grinned wryly, falling into step with his colleague as they crunched slowly along.

"You are better covered than I," he murmured. "And I fancy my blood is thinner than yours."

They had come down into a steep valley, and the trees were falling away; a stream debouched at their right in long, curving sweeps that bisected the whiteness of the snow. It was completely frozen and gleamed like gun-metal in the clear light. Below them, almost in the centre of the valley, was a spectacular waterfall where the stream fell about eighty feet to a pool; it too was frozen and descended in a series of stalagmites that sparkled like some bizarre confectionery in a patisserie window.

The Count had obviously brought his guests to admire this extraordinary place, and already there were polite murmurs of astonishment from guests and household staff as they went in single file down toward a heavy wooden bridge which spanned the pool at the foot of the petrified fall.

Coleridge was alone with Menlow now beneath the shadows of the trees.

"I have something I would like you to analyse, Doctor," he said softly, looking sharply about him. "I would prefer no-one to know about it but we two."

Menlow raised his eyebrows but said nothing. Coleridge thought he could rely on his discretion if his reputation was anything to go by.

"I have only simple apparatus. . ." the other began, but the professor stopped him.

He took out the envelope from his inner pocket and passed it over.

"It is a very mundane matter. Merely a sample of hair and skin. I would be grateful if you could let me have your valued opinion by this evening."

Menlow nodded slowly, his sandy moustache looking as though it were carved from ice, so cold did he appear. He took the small brown envelope in his gloved hand and put it into his pocket.

"Would it be indiscreet to ask why you want this done and what you expect me to find?"

"It would," Coleridge said with a smile. "But we shall discuss it again this evening when you have your findings."

"As you wish," said Menlow affably. "I will respect your confidence."

"I understand the Count has a well-equipped laboratory which can be made available if you need to do any elaborate tests," Coleridge said.

Menlow opened his mouth to reply, but the sentence was never uttered.

A dark shadow passed at the edge of the trees, and at the same moment a loud explosion startled the ears and reverberated with hideous suddenness across the icy landscape.

Enter the Colonel

COLERIDGE BECAME AWARE of flame and a puff of smoke as another crash awoke the echoes. The great grey-black wolf went by very fast about a hundred feet away, a blurred impression between the dark tree boles, splinters of ice thrown up in long plumes from its claws.

The party on the bridge spanning the pool beneath the waterfall were as still and solid as the frozen water suspended in a composition of hoary spray. The wolf was in the far distance now. It moved with incredible speed, and Coleridge realised, as a big man in a fur coat came out in a clearing below them, that it was putting the tree-boles between itself and the menace of the rifle. The man swore in a heavy guttural accent and flung up his unoccupied hand in a gesture of disgust.

The scattered groups were breaking up as though they had thawed and liquefied, and the murmur of startled conversation came up to the two men by the spiralling path. Coleridge stood stock-still, his heart pounding slightly, watching the faint grey image which imperceptibly merged with the darkness of the tree-line.

The paw-marks clawed in the snow were clear-printed on the slope and widely spaced. The brute had been immense and of high intelligence because it had taken the only angle in its upward flight at which the man below had been unable to use his weapon. Somehow it knew this, and Coleridge was impressed more than he cared to admit with its reasoning power.

He had a sudden, absurd idea that the scrap of fur in the envelope in Menlow's pocket had come from the same great beast. It was ridiculous, of course. His host had said, and the sledge-driver's earlier conversation confirmed, that there were many wolves in these parts.

The girl's story had affected him more than he realised, and he thrust the thought impatiently back in his mind as he and Menlow hurried down the path to where the man with the rifle stood as though in solemn thought.

Coleridge felt in his bones that the beast they had just seen was the one the whole village had been talking about, but he kept silent, putting his gloved hands deep into his capacious pockets, listening to the bewildered voices as the other members of the party converged on the big man as though he were some magnetic source of attraction. He stood with easy confidence, his legs in the heavy leather riding boots thrust widely apart.

He wore a military-looking cap on his head, which bore some tarnished badge which glinted dully in the low winter light, and there were scarlet epaulettes on the shoulders of his heavy fur coat where pieces of leather had been specially let into them.

There was a black belt buckled round his waist, and the butt of a revolver protruded from a leather matching holster, the white lanyard from the metal ring in the butt leading to one of the heavy metal buttons of his coat. He turned as the two men came up.

They were the first on the scene, and he rested the rifle barrel against a nearby tree and straightened himself. Coleridge had the impression of a great, watchful face with hooded eyes and a heavy black moustache. The lips were thick beneath the moustache but not unhumorous. He gave a stiff half-bow and briefly touched the peak of his cap in a military salute.

"Ezredes Anton!" he said in a clear, clipped voice that was used to command.

"Colonel Anton," Menlow translated. "The gentleman the Count was telling us about. He is the Chief of Police hereabouts."

Coleridge went forward to take the colonel's extended hand. He felt his fingers held in a bone-crushing grip. The big man laughed slightly at his expression, revealing strong yellow teeth. By now the Count had hurried to the colonel's side. The officer gave Homolky a very smart salute indeed and bowed more deferentially than he had to Coleridge and Menlow.

The former guessed that their host wielded a good deal of power in the locality. The two men conversed together earnestly for a few moments while the rest of the party came up. Coleridge could understand nothing of the interchange, but it was obvious from the police officer's gestures and the occasional glances of the two men up toward the far trees on the horizon that they were discussing the wolf.

"The colonel believes the beast to be the one which killed the woodman yesterday," explained Menlow, who had been listening closely. "It has just badly injured an old man in the village."

There was a cry of horror from the servants and those Hungarian-speaking people in the group, and some of the former, after asking the Count's permission, detached themselves from the main party and started off at a clumsy run for Lugos, stumbling and sliding on the icy path in their eagerness to get there.

Coleridge was vaguely aware that the Count's wife and daughter had joined the edge of the group. Raglan was there too, and he held the girl's hand tightly as she stood with a white face listening to her father's questioning of the police chief.

Menlow went on translating at Coleridge's elbow.

"Anton cannot understand how he missed the beast," he went on in a low voice. "He caught up with it at the edge of Lugos, just after it had attacked the old man. His rifle is very accurate. It should have despatched the wolf. But it seemed to know his aiming points and avoided his shots every time."

Coleridge felt a strange sensation enveloping him. Despite the intense cold he had become oddly warm and had difficulty in focusing his eyes. More of his colleagues were jostling their way through the group now, their questions chopped into disparate segments by the wind. Some of them were panting heavily, and he guessed they had run a good distance from the bridge, mostly uphill all the way.

Coleridge blinked rapidly and had control of himself again. He felt the girl's eyes on him and recalled once more her strange story of the previous night. He wondered if she were given to hysteria; that and the brooding atmosphere of certain parts of the Castle, which had been growing on him over the past hours, might have been responsible.

But on brief reflection he dismissed the possibility. She had impressed him as being very tough and cool, and from the little contact he had had with her he would not have put her down as being overfanciful. That also left out of account the scratches on the door and the parquet and the beast-hairs that reposed in Menlow's pocket.

The Count suddenly seemed aware that Coleridge was close beside him.

"Forgive me, Professor," he said curtly. "This is a very upsetting matter, as you can imagine."

"Do you wish to return to the village?" Coleridge asked. "We can visit the falls some other day."

Homolky caught the police officer's eye and shook his head.

"There is no point. The man is injured; the village doctor is doing the best he can for him, and the beast will be miles away by now."

He stared grimly up toward the tree-line where the tracks of the wolf could be faintly discerned in the frozen snow.

"There will be another time," he said softly. "We will organise a proper hunt if the animal is not shot soon."

"Is it the same one, then?" Menlow ventured.

The Count shrugged.

"Perhaps, Dr. Menlow."

He glanced quickly at his wife and then seemed to recollect his duties as a host.

"You have met Colonel Anton. Colonel, this is my distinguished guest, Professor Coleridge from America."

The Chief of Police gave another of his half-bows. As he turned toward the savant and moved his arm, a brilliant golden medal irradiated light, making a splash of molten liquidity on the breast of his uniform.

He smiled thinly as Coleridge's eyes rested on it.

"The Star of Krasnia, Professor. For services to the Emperor," he said in passable English.

"It seems as though half of Lugos speaks English and half of the visiting delegation Hungarian," said Coleridge mildly, his eyes held by the strange spectacle of the frozen icefall. Menlow smiled faintly.

"Hardly, Professor," he admonished his companion. "They have excellent universities in Hungary, and English and French are favourite languages among the aristocracy and upper classes. I speak passable Hungarian, and I believe we have two others among our party. You are not usually given to exaggeration, Professor."

Coleridge relaxed, his eyes lowered from the falls to the girl, her mother, the Count, and Colonel Anton, who stood in a tight group at the far end of the wooden bridge with Raglan like an isolated fragment some yards from them. The main party were spread out on the far slope, beyond the bridge and the pool, where there were said to be some locally celebrated caves.

"That is true," he said in answer to his companion. "Nevertheless, it is a little disconcerting at times. One hardly dares speak one's thoughts aloud in English."

Menlow smiled again.

"That depends on one's thoughts," he said softly.

Coleridge decided to leave it at that. Problems appeared to be gathering on his horizon instead of dispersing as they usually did when one relaxed after a Congress. Nadia Homolky's wild tale seemed to be bulking inordinately large in his thoughts ever since she had first told it to him in that strange galleried room back at the Castle. But wild as it sounded, there was undoubtedly a germ of truth in it.

And the terrible spectacle of the mangled corpse on the bier was ever before Coleridge's eyes. He was the only one of the Castle party who had actually seen it. He would wager that his colleagues would not be so flippant had they been present as the funereal cavalcade approached last evening.

He realised he was anxiously awaiting Menlow's report on the specimen in the envelope. He hoped he would take it seriously enough to carry out the microscopic examination he had promised. A few moments later, as though he had read the professor's mind, Menlow excused himself and detached himself from the main group.

Coleridge saw his lean figure striding back up the slope that led to the village. The Count had seen him also, because he despatched one of the bearded servants. The man went after Menlow at fantastic speed and in a few moments, it seemed, caught him up on the path. The professor noticed that he carried a rifle suspended in a sling over his shoulder. The Count was coming across the bridge toward Coleridge, his face dark beneath the heavy fur hat.

"That was a very foolish thing to do, Professor," he said curtly. "This is not your Central Park. It can be extremely dangerous here, as you may have gathered just now. I must ask you to impress upon your colleagues the foolishness of wandering off alone, especially when there are wolves about."

Coleridge bit his lip. He had no wish to upset his host, and it was obvious that the Count was considerably annoyed. As he had every right to be under the circumstances.

"You must forgive me, Count," he said quickly. "It is entirely my fault. I asked Menlow to carry out some tests for me."

He looked at the host's blank face, forcing a smile.

"For one of my lectures," he explained. "With so many experts present it is necessary to check and countercheck one's facts."

He had said the right thing. The Count's features relaxed, and the cloud lifted from his brows.

"Ah, I see. Well, in that case, the matter is closed. But I think perhaps it would be well if I emphasised the point myself."

He hesitated, looking round the dazzling white landscape broken only by the darkness of the pine forests and the sky, which was becoming cloudy again as though more snow threatened.

"But over the lunch-table would be more appropriate."

He became brisk, straightening his tall figure.

"I think it is time we returned to Lugos. I am inviting everyone to take wine with me at The Golden Crown before we lunch at the Castle. It is one of your New World customs, is it not."

Coleridge smiled.

"And a very agreeable one."

The tall man nodded, seemingly wrapped in thought.

"Perhaps you would be kind enough to escort my wife back to the village while I collect the rest of our guests."

He gave Coleridge a bantering look.

"I fancy Nadia is quite satisfied with her own escort for the moment."

And he strode off back across the bridge, barking instructions to his servants and rounding up the party as though they were a wayward flock of sheep.

A Toast to the Emperor

I AM SORRY that these tragic incidents should have cast a shadow over your visit," the Countess Sylva said.

They were in the square in front of The Golden Crown now and had drawn some hundred yards ahead of the party, which was straggling back into the main street of Lugos behind them. The Countess's fine teeth glinted appealingly in her smile, and she linked her arm intimately through Coleridge's as they negotiated a jagged pile of frozen snow which blocked the pavement at this point. Again Coleridge was aware of the yielding voluptuousness of her body as she leaned heavily against him while he helped her over.

"It cannot be helped," said Coleridge mechanically, hoping that the Count was not watching them.

The ladies of his family were dangerously attractive, and he would not wish his host to think for one moment that he was taking liberties. The thought was absurd, of course, but Coleridge was not familiar with the social customs of this corner of Europe. What he had seen among the peasantry on his trip so far must give a civilised man pause, and he felt again the shock he had experienced the previous night when he had glimpsed the pink stump of the dumb man's mutilated tongue.

They were through the great heap of frozen snow and walked on slowly, waiting for the others to catch up. The Countess's cheeks were pleasantly flushed with the exertion of the walk, and she appeared impervious to the cold, the breath ascending in smokelike clouds from her mouth to merge with Coleridge's own in the air above them.

But nevertheless Coleridge sensed some deep-down lurking uneasiness within his companion, and it seemed that more than once on their walk she had been on the point of imparting some confidence to him, except that the trivia of everyday polite conversation had kept intruding and driving away the gathering intimacy between them.

Perhaps it was just as well, the professor reflected. Already he had a commission from the daughter; unlooked-for problems connected with the mother might be too much. And yet the sense of horror which the wolf-deaths seemed to have brought with them was gathering like a visible aura above the fairy-tale icing of the Castle on the heights, and the sombre surroundings only reinforced and emphasised the brooding thoughts that seemed about to be given verbal expression between the visitor and his hostess.

The tall woman was looking at him sideways from under long eyelashes now, ostensibly watching the approaching party over his shoulder but in reality searching his face. For what, Coleridge wondered. Signs of knowledge he perhaps did not possess? Or was there a perfectly innocuous reason for her seemingly artless questions? There was definitely something troubling her. Perhaps beyond the worries engendered by the admittedly horrible events which had affected many people in Lugos.

"You find my daughter attractive?" was her next question.

Coleridge nodded, turning his head briefly, his eyes seeking the commanding figure of the Count, who was heading the long stream of stragglers coming into the square. They were at the foot of the steps of The Golden Crown now, and Herr Eles was coming out of the main doors to greet his guests. Coleridge followed the Countess up toward the main façade.

"Who would not, madame," he said, answering her question. The Countess gave him a wry look over her shoulder.

"She is a very imaginative child. I should not let her wilder flights of fancy distract you from your main purposes here."

"I shall not do that," Coleridge returned blandly.

Despite the numbness of his hands and feet from the biting cold he kept his wits about him. The Countess's last remarks were obviously pertinent to the affair on which the daughter had asked his help. After what Nadia had said and the secrecy to which she had pledged him, it was unthinkable that she would have confided in her mother.

Nevertheless a doubt persisted in Coleridge's mind as the two slowly picked their way up the icy steps. An inspired guess, perhaps. Or was there something darker and more pointed beneath the seemingly innocent questions with which she had gently plied him on their return from the falls?

It was obvious that both she and the Count were extremely shrewd and worldly people; their daughter took after them in those respects. And it was equally clear that the Count had observed him and Nadia in deep conversation by the Castle's ruined wall. Another thought struck Coleridge then. Had the Count suspected the subject of their conversation?

Was it possible that he himself had heard something the previous evening; that the beast had prowled the corridor and had come to his own room door during the course of the night? It was a possibility which Coleridge could not discount. And yet if that had happened, why had the Count himself not made some investigation or, at the very least, roused the Castle?

Coleridge's head was beginning to ache with the thoughts that were whirling around inside it, and he caught again at the thread of the Countess's remarks. She was waiting at the entrance to The Golden Crown, the professor some half-dozen treads below. Eles, after shaking her hand and exchanging some pleasantries, stood discreetly to one side, his eyes averted from Coleridge and fixed on the main party which had arrived at the foot of the steps. He seemed oblivious to the cold.

Coleridge was glad when they were inside and in the warmth of the hotel lounge. He was drowned in a sudden buzz of conversation and, after divesting himself of his outdoor clothes, was grateful simply to move with the slow tide of humanity in the general direction of the hotel lounge.

* * *

The light from the ornate chandeliers blazed down on the dazzling white linen of the lunch-table and struck crystalline sparks from the silver cutlery and the engraved goblets set at each elaborate placing. The noise that rose from the assembled guests was deafening, and mingled with it was the pattering as the servants brushed past, fetching and removing the various courses.

It had been a memorable meal not even spoiled by discussion of the latest wolf-attack, and now that the dessert was reached Coleridge felt the rigours of the Congress and of his bleak journey to Lugos completely erased by the luxury of his surroundings.

He sat next to the Countess in a place of honour; they were in an extraordinary dining room, with richly panelled walls on which hung a few family portraits in oils and two huge fireplaces, one at each end. There was an intricately carved gallery which ran around all four sides of the room, about eighteen feet from the parquet floor, and above it the great hammer beams of the roof looked almost misty and insubstantial, as the bulbs from the electric chandeliers could not penetrate that far.

The Count presided at one end of the long table with his mother, the Countess Irina, at his right; on his left sat Colonel Anton, mellowed and beaming now in the glow of his host's hospitality. Coleridge and Countess Sylva were halfway down the length of the table, and almost opposite was Nadia Homolky, with Menlow on one side of her and the long, ravaged mediaeval priest's face of Father Balaz on the other.

Coleridge was glad he had not been placed next to this austere prelate who spoke no English, but the good Father had relaxed considerably since their last meeting and he was even smiling affably in the greying stubble of his beard at something the girl had just said. On this occasion he had abandoned the black soutane and wore a dark suit with an ecclesiastical collar, the silver pectoral cross glinting in the lamplight every time he moved.

On the balcony at the far end of the room, above the second of the great fireplaces, sat a small rustic orchestra in peasant costume, presumably recruited from Lugos, whose surprisingly tuneful efforts sent vibrant, harsh, and exciting polka and czardas melodies down the room, cutting vividly through the heavy surge of conversation.

Coleridge felt inwardly amused. The whole affair reminded

him of the *Très Riches Heures de duc de Berry*, and he realised he was fortunate indeed to see some of this luxurious, privileged, almost feudal life before it was finally engulfed by the encroaching flood of industrialised civilisation, so-called.

His palate felt cleansed and refreshed. The courses had been excellent and most delicately cooked and marinated, and the exotic fruits they had just enjoyed were refreshing and astringent to the taste. Another product, he imagined, of the host's hothouses. With the dessert they were drinking something special, Coleridge had gathered.

"Aszú-Eszencia," Countess Sylva had announced. "Tokay, of course. Our finest dessert wine."

It was indeed, and the vintage was important enough for the Count to rise from his seat and propose the health of his guests and the success of their gathering in his house. Then it was the turn of the guests to stand and drink the health of their host, his family and friends, and the people of Lugos.

Coleridge had made a simple little speech which he thought effective and appropriate to the occasion. It was well received by the Count and his family; he caught the approval in the eyes of the Countess and her daughter and felt a flush starting to his cheek.

When he sat down he found his glass had already been refilled. His eyes sought Countess Sylva's over the rim of the goblet.

"This could become a habit."

She smiled, revealing the fine, strong teeth with the slightly pronounced sharpness which seemed to be a characteristic of the whole family. The orchestra had recommenced its labours, giving the company a waltz this time, and Coleridge savoured the wine on his tongue. It was an orange amber in colour, and he found it fresh, elegant, and sweet.

His eyes swept round the company. Something of the dark oppression which had been stealing over him seemed to have lifted, but it was only momentary, he knew. It was something more subtle than the natural gloom cast over Lugos by the wolf-attacks and the deaths of several of the villagers. Something which seemed to have soaked into the stones of this old Castle and to have permeated the very fabric.

The discussion had ranged far and wide over the matter, of

course; the attacked villager was recovering well, the doctor had said. But these dark subjects had been dispelled temporarily by the present pleasant gathering, and they had nothing to do with the Homolky family as such or the luxurious quarters of the Castle they occupied. They were more concerned with the gloomier, older, and more austere parts of the Castle which Coleridge had already glimpsed: damp, echoing corridors where, presumably, the servants hurried about their errands; cheerless flights of stairs; and dusty, secluded corners such as the closetlike passage where Nadia had guided him with the oil lamp.

It was there, in neglected, forgotten crevices of such a vast edifice that remote, atavistic forces held sway and an imaginative man such as himself could imagine gibbering fear in the night.

For the first time he realised something of the strain a sensitive girl like Nadia Homolky could undergo in such an atmosphere—an atmosphere slowly darkening under the subtle pressure of the fear that obviously overhung Lugos, of the menace of the wolves, and now of something even more sinister and disturbing. The vivid image of the firelight flickering on the eye-sockets of the wolf-heads on the firedogs came unbidden to his mind.

He snapped his attention away from these sombre imaginings, thinking forward to the time when his colleague would come to him to say that his microscope had discovered something quite harmless in the sample Coleridge had submitted. A burst of laughter finally cut through his musings and restored him to normality. The Count was discussing with some of his guests the possibilities of their afternoon's entertainment.

The Fair proper did not begin for two days, but the consensus of opinion seemed to be that it would be a pleasant and relatively short outing for the party to walk down to Lugos and visit the gypsies in their encampments. There would be stalls and sideshows, and, said Homolky, braziers and bonfires would make a comparatively warm enclave for the entertainment of his guests. He had, in fact, already despatched a messenger to make sure the gypsies knew they were coming.

"Supposing they do not wish to entertain us," said Abercrombie, the bearded Scot, his teeth gleaming in the depths of his hairy smile.

The Count looked at him mockingly. He had changed into a

dark grey formal suit, and he appeared both elegant and distinguished as he raised his glass in a silent salute to the company.

"They are gypsies, Doctor," he said slowly. "They are there to wheedle money from the inhabitants of Lugos. They will entertain us all right, have no fear."

Menlow shot Coleridge a fleeting glance. He was seated almost opposite at the long table. He tapped his breast pocket significantly. Coleridge felt relief. He knew his colleague would ascend to his room after lunch to begin the tests he had asked for. He was placing an absurd importance on something so relatively simple, but it would be good to know the girl's fears were ill-based.

The Count was on his feet, glass in hand. His eyes raked the room, resting on each person at table in turn.

"I would like to propose another toast now," he said. "That perhaps would have been drunk earlier in normal households but which we at Castle Homolky habitually offer toward the end of the meal."

His glance rested affectionately on his mother, then to his daughter, and passed on to his wife. Everyone was rising. Homolky raised his glass to a dim portrait that hung in a place of honour beneath that portion of the gallery in which the musicians sat. They were silent, but after the Count had given his toast they broke into a solemn tune during which everyone remained standing.

"The Emperor!" the Count said.

All those at table raised their glasses and drank, and there was an awkward silence for a few moments after the last strains of the anthem had died away. Then the company resumed its seats, and there came the scrambling noise of chairs being shifted on the parquet and the jumble of conversation resumed.

The leader of the small group of musicians, after a reassuring glance from the Count, nodded, and the thin, syrupy strains of a popular waltz began. Coleridge sat back, his darker thoughts now obscured and overlaid by the cheerful surroundings and the excellence of the lunch.

He cast a glance at one of the tall windows near the end of the gallery. The sky was overcast, but it did not appear to be snowing. Somehow he did not relish setting forth from the comfort of the Castle into such bleak surroundings for the second time that day. It was probably a reaction after his uncomfortable journey. Only yesterday, and yet already it seemed years removed.

He bent his head to hear what his hostess was saying. To his surprise she was asking about Raglan. His attentions to her daughter had obviously not passed unnoticed, and again he felt awkward and embarrassed. He gave his colleague mild praise; a neutral report, in fact. It was not his place to assess Raglan's qualities or qualifications as a companion for the Count's daughter.

Countess Sylva must have sensed this, for she hesitated and her delicately diplomatic questions ceased. Coleridge hoped he had not given her offence. He felt himself to be somehow poised on the pinnacle of an edifice which was slowly crumbling beneath him. He was too sensitive, really; there was no reason to feel that, but their gathering at Lugos, rather than being an interval of pleasurable scholarship, was starting to generate a tension which was far from what the professor had intended when he had organised it.

He would feel more at ease once he had received Menlow's report. There must be some plausible explanation for Nadia Homolky's experience of the previous night, though Coleridge could not for the moment assign some convincing reason.

To his relief he saw Menlow rise from his seat and, passing along the room, stoop for a few moments' colloquy with his host. He received smiling assent for his absence from table, and a few moments later his tall, gaunt form had passed through the far door. It was the prelude to the general breakup of the lunch-party, and everyone drifted into a smaller and less grand side-room scattered with comfortable velvet-covered divans where coffee and liqueurs were served to the replete guests.

During a lull in the conversation Coleridge found the Count at his elbow. He raised his glass in answer to the Count's salutation, feeling momentarily refreshed, his mind poised on the edge of contentment.

"To the gypsies!" Homolky said mockingly. "You will find the experience interesting, Professor."

In the Gypsy Camp

A KEEN WIND stung Coleridge's face, bringing tears to his eyes, while the smoke and flame from the bonfires warmed his body at the same time. Barbaric music filled his ears, and his sight was dazzled by the light of flares striking back from tarnished mirrors and giltwork on the tawdry stalls set about like a maze on this dark winter afternoon.

The Count had not exaggerated. It was interesting, to say the least, but Coleridge was vaguely aware that the Gypsy Fair represented a dangerous combination. Mingling with the food and drink he had consumed, the brilliance of the lights and the vividness of the music had a dizzy and intoxicating effect on the brain, while the alternation of extreme heat and bitter cold was an invitation to pneumonia.

He would have to be careful. The intoxication came partly from Nadia Homolky, whose arm was twined in his intimately; she nestled into the warmth of his fur coat as she pressed closely to his side, and once again Coleridge was uncomfortably conscious of the dangerously erotic aura emanating from both the younger ladies of the Homolky household.

Now she was brushing against him through their thick clothing as they threaded among the booths, her face alive with mischief and her golden hair caught carelessly in beneath her fur cap.

"Is this what you expected, Professor?"

"I am not quite sure to what you refer," he answered drily, hoping that Raglan or the girl's parents were not in the vicinity. Probably he was reading too much into her attitude; she had been naturally anxious to enlist his services after her terrifying experience, and her carefree manner toward him might well be nothing more than a young girl's trusting nature. At the same time he must be careful not to arouse young Raglan's jealousy through Nadia Homolky's casual coquetry.

They were interrupted by the same roaring noise that Coleridge had heard that morning when descending the narrow path to the waterfall. The girl looked at him excitedly.

"Wild animals, Professor! Don't you find it absolutely absorbing?"

Coleridge shook his head. There was a grim irony in her words of which she was apparently unaware.

"I would have thought you had had enough of wild animals for the moment, Miss Homolky," he said gently.

He bit his lip with vexation at his carelessly uttered words, because the girl drew in her breath and her eyes were again clouded with fear as they had been that morning. Once more the shadows seemed to close in momentarily, and the lights and wild music of the fairground appeared faint and far away.

"Forgive me," he said quickly, before the girl could speak.

She drew closer to him as though his proximity gave her comfort and protection from danger.

"There is nothing to forgive, Professor. I am still a child in some ways, I am afraid. And fairs and such gatherings are an exciting contrast to our somewhat quiet life here in Lugos."

Her eyes were sparkling now.

"They remind me of the days when I was small and Father used to take me to concerts and fairs and outings in Pest."

Her gaze was wide and distant as she spoke, and to Coleridge it seemed as though she saw not the crude booths and the teeming life of the peasants about them, but the gracious salons and ballrooms of the capital.

She laughed then as she caught her companion's glance.

"And the zoo," she said, squeezing his arm. "We have a wonderful zoo in Pest. We must visit it sometime."

Coleridge was again slightly embarrassed by the intimacy of the girl's manner and her assumption that they might together visit the capital on some future occasion. He drew her over to one side where a savage-looking group of Magyars were doing a fire-eating act, breathing great streaks of flame high into the air.

Then the rumbling roar with which he was becoming familiar again sounded, and the girl cast an apprehensive glance over her shoulder.

"It is only the bear," Coleridge said quickly. "I saw it on my way through the village last night."

"Poor beast," the girl murmured sympathetically.

They had come to a sort of clearing in the middle of the booths where a large crowd of people, mostly peasants, but including some of the better-dressed and more prosperous tradespeople, had formed a large circle. Coleridge realised the word must have spread about Lugos very quickly that the Fair was open, since the Count had made his request only an hour or two before. That probably accounted for the makeshift condition of some of the sideshows, because the crude wooden platforms showed signs of hasty erection in some cases and a number of stalls had their canvas awnings pinned up temporarily on wooden battens. Coleridge guessed that the gypsies, above all people, were anxious to earn some money while it was there and that they obviously led a very insecure existence.

The huge brown bear, its eyes dark and unfathomable, was balanced on a large wooden ball which its sharp claws gripped clumsily as it slowly rotated. The animal travelled cautiously over the rough ground, occasionally bowing its head as though acknowledging the smattering of applause which greeted its prowess.

A dull chinking noise came from the heavy metal chain which linked the leather collar round the beast's neck with the wrist of its trainer, a tall, heavily bearded man who appeared, from his richer clothing and proud bearing, to be the chief of the gypsy band, or at least one of its principal leaders.

The bear got down from the ball at last, having traversed the complete circle, and with a squeal of pleasure seized the juicy turnip its master proffered. It squatted on its haunches in the light of the flares, sinking its sharp teeth into the vegetable, which it held between its massive forepaws.

Its keeper, wild eyes flashing and gold earrings jangling, came round the crowd with his fur hat held out to make a collection. Coleridge saw with amusement that many of the crowd were edging away now that the entertainment was over, but the huge gypsy's face darkened with anger and he spat curses at those meaner members of his audience who continued to retreat, this time with alarm and fright.

But Nadia Homolky had darted forward, reaching for her small leather purse. With a disarming smile she counted out some coins into the man's huge palm, and at once his angry manner dissolved into ingratiating cupidity. He bowed low over her hand, breaking into a flood of excited sentences which the girl answered in his own language.

She returned to Coleridge, her features flushed and amused, her eyes dancing in the light of the flares and lamps.

"You have a way with the savage, I see," Coleridge said. "Both of the human and the four-legged variety."

Nadia Homolky laughed, pressing closer to Coleridge's side.

"Come and have your fortune told," she said mockingly. "It will be interesting to see what fate has in store for us."

And she dragged the unwilling savant forward to where a broken-toothed crone beckoned at the entrance to one of the most lurid-looking booths which was decorated with primitively painted signs of the zodiac.

It was getting toward dusk now, and Coleridge's face was buffeted by the wind, chill and bitter after the warmth of the fairground. He pulled away from the girl, seeing Raglan deep in conversation with the Count and his wife a little way behind them. He guessed that the pair were monopolising the young man, either temporarily to separate him from their daughter or to find out a little more about him from his conversation.

Coleridge would have been diverted had he not felt himself in a somewhat anomalous position with regard to Nadia Homolky. She had been vivacious and unconstrained in her manner while they were at the Fair. It had been an interesting experience, but the professor realised, somewhat to his annoyance, that most of it had passed in a blur.

Normally he would have taken careful notes and absorbed all the atmosphere and folkloric implications of these hard, wild, and proud folk who carried on their ancient traditions with an absolute contempt for what passed for modern civilised standards.

It was not only the problems of Lugos and the girl, but also the girl herself with her rich, vibrant personality, that disturbed Coleridge's settled bachelor ideas. Now, he examined her covertly as they walked, their boots crunching in the heaped snow at the side of the road, the icy ruts glittering like steel beneath the faint oil lamps which illuminated the streets of Lugos.

Preserving a deep silence, they walked back across the bridge where his sled had passed Captain Rakosi and his cavalry troop the previous evening. The girl's eyes were on his face, and she again had the troubled look.

"You have not yet heard anything, of course?"

Coleridge knew what she meant without being told.

"It is too early," he said cautiously. "I have asked Dr. Menlow to analyse that material. He is carrying out the tests now. I am hoping he will have some information for me by the time we return to the Castle."

The girl seemed relieved, but still she persisted.

"And then what?"

Coleridge put his hand under the girl's elbow and helped her to jump up onto the narrow pavement inside the bridge parapet as a heavy farm cart approached, the two great horses reeking steam through the nostrils, the creaking of the wheels in the ruts making conversation difficult. The heavily muffled driver, who actually had ice gleaming on his moustache, must have been one of the Count's estate workers, for he gave the girl a respectful salute.

"We must take things as we find them, my dear young lady," Coleridge said, answering her question. "We can do nothing until we have some precise data."

She nodded vigorously, as though the idea were new to her.

"You are right," she said decisively.

There were heavy footsteps on the icy road behind them, sharp above the distant music of the fairground. The couple turned to find a huge bearded figure.

"Forgive the intrusion," said a jovial voice, "but you must not expect to monopolise Miss Homolky during the entire Congress."

Coleridge smiled. It was Dr. Duncan Abercrombie, the Scottish medical man who had gained quite a reputation for his papers on vampirism in the Middle Ages, with special reference to medical aspects of the phenomena.

"You are perfectly correct," said Coleridge.

Inwardly he was pleased at the interruption because he had no wish to draw undue attention to himself and the girl. Already people must be wondering what they had found so much in common, and though Raglan's addresses had been diverted by the girl's parents, Coleridge had no desire to give the young man further cause for jealousy.

Therefore, he was content to drop behind a little, leaving the girl and the burly savant to keep up an animated, bantering conversation in which Abercrombie courteously tried to involve him from time to time. They were almost opposite a part of the village where several side-streets debouched into the main thoroughfare, and Coleridge became aware of the low sound of voices, faint chanting, and the shuffling of many boots.

The two in front had also heard it, and they halted, watching as the pale flare of lanterns and a long file of black-clad people entered the main street from the lane opposite. Coleridge could make out the green onion dome of a large church, faintly visible against the darkening sky. He had not noticed it the previous evening because it had been completely dark when he reached Lugos and he had been facing away from the structure when they had passed on their way to the Fair earlier that afternoon.

People were standing on the heaped snow of the pavements now; half the population of Lugos seemed to have suddenly appeared. A group of black-clad mourners were sobbing brokenly as they followed the draped coffin resting on a farm cart drawn by three black horses. A man standing bare-headed near Coleridge crossed himself and said something in a guttural undertone.

The girl caught the question in Coleridge's eyes.

"The man killed by the wolf," she said in a low voice. "They are taking the body to lie in state in the church. The funeral will be on Monday. Father and all our family will be there, of course."

Coleridge nodded, his mind pervaded by melancholy. He caught a glimpse of Father Balaz now, comforting the bereaved. He must have slipped away from the Castle soon after lunch. Naturally, it would not have been seemly for him to have accompanied the party to the Fair.

"They appear in rather a hurry," he said, sotto voce, to Abercrombie.

The big man had been staring at the peasant who stood the other side of Coleridge, and the latter realised his colleague either spoke the language or at least understood it well enough to make out what the man had been saying.

"They are a very superstitious people hereabouts," Abercrombie said. "The old man there, for instance. He was just remarking to his neighbour that people who die by the bite of the wolf are best underground as quickly as possible."

He smiled wolfishly himself as though at some cruel joke.

"We are in the very heart of folklore here, Professor! I must put that in my notebook."

And he promptly took out a wine-coloured leather-bound volume from a capacious side-pocket and laboriously jotted down something in it under the light of the nearest streetlamp. Coleridge watched the procession tail off toward the distant church until the lanterns were nothing but faint pricks of light in the darkness.

It seemed to him that ever since he had set foot in Lugos, less than twenty-four hours ago, everything had been split into segments of light and shade—the former representing the happier interludes at the inn, at breakfast, and lunch; with darkness represented by the processions centring on the dead man who had just passed him for the second time, the gypsies with their barbaric magnificence, Rakosi and his unsuccessful cavalrymen, the wolf and Colonel Anton, the girl with her weird tale. Even Father Balaz seemed like some bird of ill-omen.

A splendour of epaulettes and befrogged greatcoat grew before his eyes, and here was Rakosi himself, saluting in the lamplight and bowing enthusiastically over the girl's hand. He shook hands with Abercrombie and Coleridge too and then drew the girl over beneath the lamp.

Coleridge was turning away when he became aware that the tall, gaunt figure of Menlow was elbowing its way through the crowd of people which now blocked the street. His face looked worried, and he beckoned Coleridge into the shadowy dusk, out of range of the lamp.

"You have done the test?"

Menlow shook his head.

"That is what I wanted to tell you, Professor. I cannot find my microscope or my case of instruments anywhere."

The Beast Must Die

"THIS BEAST MUST BE KILLED!"

The Count's voice was dangerously mild, but his eyes glittered with anger. Colonel Anton shrugged his big shoulders, his heavy-lidded eyes regarding his host through clouds of Turkish tobacco-smoke.

Captain Rakosi brushed an imaginary speck of lint off the front of his immaculate uniform and put his hands forward to the blazing logs of the fire.

"That is easier said than done, Count."

Coleridge leaned back in his leather easy-chair, keeping his mind blank, his glass of whisky half-drunk. It was completely dark outside now, had been for a long time, but close to the windowpane opposite, where the curtain was not quite drawn, flakes of snow whirled at the glass.

The fall would not be heavy, the Count had said; it was snowing in the wind, as Coleridge would have termed it. It was too cold to snow heavily, but the point was an important one because the Count soon hoped to find time to mount a determined hunt for the wolf.

It was annoying, to say the least, because the lectures were due to begin tomorrow, though Coleridge recognised that the affair was too urgent to Lugos to put off any further. The beast responsible for several deaths and one wounding must be put paid to if local people were to venture abroad safely or sleep easily in their beds.

In some ways, though, the day following—Sunday—would be more convenient. It would be observed by his colleagues as a normal rest day as in their own country, and the debates and lectures were not due to resume until the Monday.

Personally, Coleridge would not mind if it snowed heavily tomorrow, which would be a good excuse to continue with their planned programme and not set off on what might amount to an abortive pursuit of an animal which was dangerous, elusive, and cunning. Assuming that it was one beast they were dealing with, and not several.

But he had promised to accompany the Count and his party, and in all courtesy he could not very well back out. Coleridge ignored the talk of the three men at the fire and let his gaze wander at length over the vast expanse of shelving in the extraordinary library chamber which the Count had designated as their lecture room on the morrow.

It was different from the smaller library in which he had been received the previous night and was situated in another wing of the Castle. Coleridge realised it would not be too difficult to get lost in such a vast and rambling pile. When the opportunity presented itself he would get the girl to draw him a simple diagram, giving the disposition of the principal rooms and corridors. It might be vital if he were to assist her in the bizarre affair in which he was becoming involved.

His mind skirted Menlow's problem; he had asked him to consult the Count on the matter of the missing cases. He hoped against hope that they had simply been mislaid by the servants. If not, it put an entirely different construction on the girl's experience.

Abercrombie, sitting opposite, gave Coleridge a warm smile, puffing out clouds of rich smoke from his cigar, which ascended in slow blue whorls to the beamed ceiling high above. Everyone else had gone to their rooms to prepare for dinner, but the big Scot had expressed a desire to Coleridge and the Count to see the preparations which had been made for their debates. He was a formidable figure, and Coleridge felt an affinity for him, though they had known one another for only a few hours. He would be a useful man in a tight corner; it might be as well to remember that.

The professor shrugged off the thought irritably; he was becoming as highly strung as Nadia Homolky. It had a lot to do with the atmosphere of the Castle, the bitter weather outside, and the long miles of wolf-infested wilderness that lay between Lugos and the city.

He glanced over toward the dais which the Count had had erected by his estate servants at the other end of the library. There were comfortable leather chairs arranged in rows, books and documents set out on tables, the various charts that would be needed for the lectures, rare illustrations culled from choice holdings in the Count's extensive library collection, and a large blackboard with chalks and a pointer.

He had forgotten nothing, even down to the water-carafes ranged at intervals and which would be rewashed and filled with fresh water in the morning; cups, saucers, and coffeepots on a side-table; and an impressive array of wines and spirits on a buffet set against the wall between two of the glass bookcases.

The arrangements were indeed comprehensive, not to say magnificent, and in normal circumstances Coleridge would have been delighted. But now . . . He looked at his silver-cased watch. In another half-hour it would be dinnertime. Despite the lavishness of the lunch, the walk in the snow, the time spent at the Fair, and the long uphill trudge back had restored his appetite.

"What do you think, Professor?"

Coleridge blinked fully awake. He tried to look as though he had been closely following the conversation, knew that he had failed. Anton had a slightly amused expression on his massive features.

"We were just saying," the Count explained patiently, "that in view of the weather it might be better to postpone the hunt until Sunday."

He shrugged.

"Unless you have any objection. And as the first sessions, even of such a small Congress as ours, are all important, it would seem to suit everyone better."

Coleridge nodded, his eyes still on the dancing flames of the fire.

"That is settled, then," said Homolky decisively.

Rakosi went to stand with his heavy leather-clad feet astride, near the fireplace, looking searchingly at each of the four other men in the room.

"I will get my officers to organise a party of villagers. We shall need a good deal of help to flush out this beast. But I shall recognise him again, if we meet, have no doubt of that."

He slapped his braided uniform trouser-leg with a sharp crack that boded ill for the animal, and Coleridge saw a faint smile curve the corners of the Count's mouth. But he got up politely to replenish his guests' glasses.

"You will stay to dinner, of course, gentlemen."

His eyes flickered across to Coleridge.

"And then the professor and I must have a little talk."

He waved his unoccupied hand expansively to encompass the vast, silent library.

"We have much to arrange before the morning."

He was interrupted by a sudden knock at the door, and the gigantic bearded servant entered and exchanged a few quick, harsh words with his master. He went out swiftly, closing the door behind him. The Count rubbed his hands briskly.

"Excellent!"

He handed Coleridge his refilled glass.

"That was a message about your colleague, Dr. Menlow. I am glad to say his instrument cases have been found. They were put in one of the spare bedrooms by mistake."

Coleridge paused by the half-open door of the Weapons Hall. It was, in fact, one of the museumlike rooms in which the Count kept exhibits related to his family history. Coleridge had noted it in an earlier tour of the Castle his host had given him. It had been an excellent dinner, and now he was on his way back up to the library where he and the Count were due to make the final dispositions for tomorrow's Congress.

He had seen Menlow before dinner, and the latter had told him something which had increased his disquiet. It was nothing in itself, but its effect had been to deepen and colour the clouded atmosphere which it seemed to him was spreading within his mind. It was simply that the case containing the supplementary lenses of Menlow's equipment, and on which he depended to make his tests, was missing.

It was not with the rest of the material, and the servants had been unable to find it. Coleridge had had a tactful word with Nadia Homolky, and as a result the Count had made his own laboratory facilities available. Menlow should be carrying out his tests now. The professor would be glad when he had the report. The matter was taking far too long for something so intrinsically simple.

Now he stood irresolute for a moment or two by the Weapons Hall door; the corridor here was lit by the pale flare of oil lamps, and in their flickery light he could see across to the glass cases of weapons, the serried racks of pikes and swords on the walls, and the suits of mediaeval armour on stands, from which the low yellow light struck passing glints.

He went in quickly, his mind made up, and stood, adjusting his eyes to the semigloom. There was no fire in here, and the atmosphere struck chill. His feet roused echoes from the heavy wooden floor as he walked slowly between the cases. He paused again, but there was no sound from the long corridor outside. The walls of the ancient building were so thick in any case that it was almost impossible to hear any noise from an adjoining chamber; only along corridors and up and down stairwells did voices carry.

Coleridge lit a match and, shielding the flame with his cupped hand, proceeded down the great room toward a case he had noted on his earlier tour. It contained more modern weapons, among them some used by the Count. Like all the display cabinets in here, it was not locked, merely secured by a metal catch.

Coleridge's movements seemed furtive and alien to his forthright nature, and he felt almost like a thief as he opened up the lid with his disengaged hand. But he would take the opportunity of telling the Count at some appropriate moment, either tonight or during the following day. He did not want some servant blamed for his purloining the Count's property.

He picked up the big military-type revolver, hefting its walnut butt in his hand. It was a heavy weapon, too heavy for his pocket really, but it was all he could think of. He broke it open quickly.

As he had expected, it was unloaded. He picked up the cardboard box of cartridges that reposed in the case together with all the other hand weapons that nestled there on the velvet base.

Each revolver or pistol had the appropriate carton of ammunition next to it, proving that they were for the Count's personal use. Coleridge just had time to make sure the ammunition was the right calibre for the pistol before his match went out, leaving him in semidarkness.

He closed the case noiselessly and walked cautiously up between the stands, making for the slit of yellow light that spilled in from the door. The butt of the revolver felt cold to the touch, but it gave him confidence. He was halfway between the door and the case when a heavy shadow passed across the lamplight. Coleridge stopped, his heart suddenly thumping.

He had the box of cartridges in his pocket now, but even the empty weapon in his hand was reassuring. He did not know what the shadow might portend, but there was something unspeakably sly and devious about it as it brushed slowly and cautiously between the beam cast by the lamp and the door.

There was a sudden noise as Coleridge's outstretched foot struck the leg of one of the cases. The shadow fled then, quickly and silently down the corridor outside. The swift movement gave Coleridge renewed courage. He reached the door, flung it fully open, conscious of a faint scratching noise which died out along the passageway.

He brought the pistol barrel up, blinking in the yellow light from the oil lamps. Nothing moved in all the wide expanse. Coleridge stood for a moment. He caught a glimpse of himself in a small mirror screwed to the wall opposite. His face looked white and strained, even distorted.

With trembling fingers he took out the box of cartridges and loaded the pistol. He went on down the corridor now without caring how much noise he made. As he had expected there was nothing, and no-one visible in the passages and landings he traversed.

He put the heavy pistol in the left-hand inside breast pocket of his jacket, hoping its outline would not be noticed. He felt sweat trickling down his cheek as he mounted the stairs to keep his appointment with the Count.

Ivan the Bold

COLERIDGE SIPPED his strong black coffee as he shuffled through his papers, his eroded nerves recovering in the mellow atmosphere of the great library. The Count sat opposite, studying the professor's pencilled schedule, while Abercrombie's bearded face caught the light from the overhead lamp as he sat at the table, occasionally consulting his own notes.

"So you think the arrangements are adequate?" the Count asked.

Coleridge nodded, keeping his tones matter-of-fact.

"More than adequate, Count."

His eyes caught the doctor's. He shuffled his papers and cleared his throat.

"Excellent!"

He rubbed his big hands, looking at each man in turn.

"Judging by the programme set out here, our own deliberations will be even more comprehensive than those of the main Congress."

The Count glanced over at the ornate cased clock that stood between two of the massive bookcases.

It was not yet eleven o'clock and the silence was profound;

even had it been daytime, the library was so isolated and high up that little sound would have penetrated from the main body of the Castle or from Lugos itself. The Count had chosen the venue well; it was ideal for such a gathering when one needed to concentrate on lectures, study notes, and debates.

A large brass optical lantern with a metal lamphouse had been set up at the back of the chairs. Hand-coloured slide presentations would add to the interest of the principal lectures. Coleridge wished he had prepared some slides of his own, but Menlow had promised him a set which would illustrate salient points of his later discourses.

He really needed to consult the latter about a number of things before the morning, and he had hoped the doctor would have appeared before now to report the result of his tests. The Count glanced at him as though he had guessed the distinguished visitor's thoughts.

"I am somewhat disappointed at the lack of response to my invitation tonight, Professor," he began hesitantly. "I had envisaged that most of your colleagues would have been here."

Coleridge gave his host a reassuring smile.

"The majority of them are simply tired out with the strenuous day we have enjoyed. I am sure you will find no lack of enthusiasm in the morning."

The Count smiled too. Coleridge realised he had gone to immense trouble in his arrangements, and he wished above all to emphasise that everyone gathered at the Castle had come there simply because of their tremendous interest and application to their specialised subjects. They would hardly have travelled so far and in such bleak conditions had it been otherwise.

The Count may have sensed this, because he became more animated as time went by and he presently rose courteously to pour his guests coffee. He was still over at the side-table when Abercrombie, who had been studying his companion closely, observed quietly, "You look rather pale, Professor."

"It is nothing," Coleridge replied carelessly. "I feel the cold a good deal, and, as I have just observed, it has been a tiring day."

Abercrombie shrugged.

"Even so, Coleridge, I should not overdo it. I understand you drove yourself rather hard at the Congress."

It was true, Coleridge knew, and he was grateful for the big Scot's consideration and concern. He was a medical man, of course, as well as a scholar, and it was obvious that the incident in the Weapons Hall a short while before had shaken Coleridge more than he cared to admit, though there might be a mundane explanation for what he had seen and heard.

The heavy revolver made a strong pressure against his shoulder muscles as he turned in his chair, and he hoped it would not be too obvious to his companions.

He was spared any further conversation on the subject of his health by the Count's return with the coffee cups, and a few moments later there came the clattering of feet on the stairs and the door opened to admit the animated figures of Shaw, Sullivan, and Parker.

"I understand we are to expect something special for the opening ceremony tomorrow, Professor."

It was Shaw, with his silver hair and drooping moustache shining like metal in the lamplight, who had propounded the question. He sat, coffee cup on the table in front of him, blinking in scholarly anticipation.

"Things will hardly be that formal," said Coleridge modestly.

He noticed his fingers were trembling slightly as he put his cup back in the saucer. He had not told his host or anyone else of the shadow at the Weapons Hall door or, even more unnerving, the faint clicking scratch as something went down the corridor.

It was too reminiscent of what Nadia Homolky fancied she had heard outside her room. He wondered what could be keeping Menlow. Something that had started out as a comparatively trivial inquiry was beginning to nag at his nerves.

He became aware that Sullivan, the middle-aged savant with the greying beard, was also looking at him critically. He still wore the suit of dark brown plus-fours he had affected at breakfast the previous day and which made him look as if he were bound for a Scottish grouse-moor.

"Your opening lecture will be on lycanthropy, of course?" the latter said.

Coleridge forced a smile.

"It is my specialised subject. And we all begin in those areas, do we not."

There was a chuckle of agreement from George Parker, the big black-bearded expert on witchcraft, among other things.

"I shall certainly stick to my own brief in my initial talk," he told the company. "I am giving fair notice of that now."

The Count joined in the subdued amusement that ran round the table.

"I do not think anyone here is likely to usurp another's special preserve," Coleridge went on.

He turned to the Count, aware that there was more than normal interest in their deliberations of the morrow. Unlike the highly publicised and extremely crowded Congress they had recently completed in Pest, this private gathering, in addition to being more informal, was also more interesting in some respects.

It was an occasion—there had been others in America, England, and France during the past ten years—where more controversial topics were aired; sometimes, even outrageous hobby-horses ridden.

It was a programme where daring ideas, outré theories, and bizarre conjectures could be expanded upon without ridicule and, usually, without prejudiced reaction from one's colleagues.

The Count, as Coleridge well knew, had done an enormous amount over the years in an amateur capacity to advance these highly specialised interests, and everyone gathered at the Castle for this specific purpose was in his debt.

That reminded Coleridge of a promise made that morning and which now appeared so far distant. So much seemed to have happened to him since his arrival a bare twenty-four hours before, the days felt at least twice as long as they did anywhere else. It was something to do with their strange venue, more with the fresh impressions, new faces, and crowded itinerary; each experience pressed upon the last.

The girl had a good deal to do with it, Coleridge thought, and not only because of her fears and suppositions: the fresh beauty of her face came between the professor and the pages of his books. His scholarship seemed to have lost something of its savour since he had met her.

There was a deep silence in the room now as each man considered what he might be saying at their first session of the morning. Coleridge cleared his throat, aware that the eyes of everyone in the lecture room were turned upon him.

"I asked you about the history of the Castle this morning, Count. You promised to tell me something of it."

He raked his glance about the room. Homolky came over from the fireplace and looked at Coleridge with hooded eyes.

"So I did," he said softly.

Coleridge felt a moment of quick discomfiture. He bit his lip.

"I take it you have no objection to speaking in front of my colleagues?"

The Count shook his head. He was smiling now.

"By no means. We are all folklorists here, are we not."

He went to sit in a big carved chair at the head of the table. The room was very quiet apart from the crackling of the fire, and the rest of the Castle seemed to be lapped in a profound sleep.

Homolky shrugged.

"My home is known among the people of Lugos as The House of the Wolf. As some of you may have noticed, a wolf's head is the motif of some of the furnishings, notably the large and elaborate firedogs which embellish a number of the great fireplaces in the main rooms. It is also part of my ancient family coat of arms."

He had his eyes fixed on a fragment of blazing log which had fallen from the firebasket and smouldered smokily on the hearth, away from the main mass of the fire.

"The association relates not only, as might be supposed, to the native Eastern European wolf, our old friend *Canis lupus*. The derivation comes also from a certain savage ancestor of mine, who enlarged the present building and had a somewhat fiendish reputation for cruelty, to put it mildly."

To Coleridge it seemed as though the faintest shiver ran through the Count's tall frame.

"He was an extraordinary man," the Count went on almost dreamily. "A genius in some ways, a degenerate monster in others. A man of great culture and artistic taste, a gifted amateur painter, an inventor of ingenious machinery that was long before his own time. But within the same envelope there resided a creature who could put his enemies to death with all the perverted refinement that only a sadist of the grand class could encompass."

There was a deep silence in the room now, broken only by the faint crackle of the fire. The Count's voice was so low that Coleridge had to strain his ears.

"He developed instruments in the dungeons below this Castle that were so delicately adjusted, so finely balanced, that his enemies took weeks to die."

Once again Coleridge had the vivid image of the mutilated majordomo who had greeted him on arrival at the Castle, and he was hard put to it to repress a tremor.

"I could show you things . . ." the Count went on absently, his eyes fixed as though on far distances.

"Do you mean to say that all this . . . equipment . . . still exists?" put in Abercrombie.

The Count nodded.

"My father showed it to me once. It is a sort of black museum where every horror known to man in the Middle Ages was practised unchecked. No-one knows how many men and women perished there."

He smiled faintly.

"Of course, this is for your ears only. I never discuss the matter with the ladies of my family, though they know the general outlines of the story. My ancestor's portrait hangs somewhere in the Castle. I will not specify where, as the picture still has an unnerving look to someone like me who knows the man's history."

The Count hesitated a moment, then resumed his narrative.

"Of course, I had the dungeon area bricked up when I succeeded to the title. It is below the modern cellars, and no-one has been there for the greater part of my lifetime. It is better so."

There was a faint stir among the guests, as though they had been held in some sort of spell.

"Your ancestor would himself seem suitable for a learned paper," George Parker put in.

He had intended only to be helpful, but Coleridge saw a wince of distaste pass across their host's face. He shook his head sombrely.

"I think not," he said softly. "Normally, I would say everything is a fit subject for research. But this history is too painful for me personally."

He seemed to recollect his wider audience and paused to glance at each face in turn as if he would imprint the details on his memory.

"Anyone at the Congress is welcome to research the Count in my library," he said slowly. "But I would not advise it."

"Has this man a name?" Abercrombie persisted.

The Count nodded.

"Ivan the Bold," he said simply. "He was known as the Wolf of the Mountains. He was a great wolf-hunter, and you may see many of his trophies of the chase which hang on the walls of this Castle. It was he who gave the Castle its name. In fact, my ancestor's exploits malign a noble animal which is a good mate and parent, loyal to its tribe, and normally kills only to eat when it is hungry."

A genuine smile of pleasure passed across Homolky's mobile features. He chuckled quietly. It was a startling sound in the context of his grim story, Coleridge thought.

"There is an ironic and very satisfying ending to Ivan's history," the Count said. "And one I particularly relish."

He swivelled in his chair, cupping his big hands round his right knee, rocking to and fro as he surveyed the company.

"There is a large ravine not five miles from where we are sitting," he continued. "It is a wild and lonely place, with a grim reputation and always shunned by the locals. Appropriately, it is known as The Place of the Skull."

"A spot where Ivan massacred his enemies," put in Coleridge with a flash of intuition.

The Count stared at him with bright eyes.

"Correct, Professor. It has the same reputation in this province as that of Glencoe in Scotland. Though only some thirty or forty people died there. By contrast, my ancestor killed hundreds. He once drove the population of an entire village into the ravine and slaughtered them to the last man, woman, and child because they had fallen behind with their rents."

He smiled again as though he had been personally present at

the massacre and had discovered something humorous beneath the horror.

Then he went on quickly, as though not wishing his listeners to misunderstand.

"Forgive me, gentlemen. This is not an amusing story, I agree, but there is poetic justice in it. Ivan was out hunting one day, with only two retainers. A pack of ravening wolves appeared, some thirty in number, and cornered the Count and his two companions in the gorge. His household found only some shreds of clothing, their weapons, and a few pieces of splintered bone."

He was smiling openly now.

"Some say that relatives of the dead villagers had gathered a band of peasants together and that they had driven the wolf-pack on to Ivan's party."

He rubbed his hands together briskly.

"I like to think so."

The scraping of his boot on the parquet as Parker got to his feet was an intrusion in the thick, glutinous silence.

"Very interesting, Count," he said blandly.

"The very essence of folklore, if I may say so. And now, if you will excuse me, I will seek my bed. It has been a strenuous day, and we have much to do tomorrow."

He went round the table, shaking hands formally as the others rose. The remainder of the company too made their excuses, and the staircase was loud with their departure. Soon only Coleridge and the Count were left. He waited politely at the head of the stair while his host put a guard over the fire and extinguished the lights.

He heard a faint noise in the gloom below him and, with a quickening of nerves, descended a flight. Menlow's white face floated up toward him like some disembodied manifestation in the yellow lamplight. His lips were trembling as he caught Coleridge by the arm.

"You did the tests?"

Menlow nodded.

"Would that I hadn't. The thing is manifestly impossible, Professor, but the hairs were those of a wolf and the particles of skin those of a human being!"

COLERIDGE COULD NOT SLEEP. Menlow's unexpectedly shattering news had momentarily deprived him of those faculties which controlled the mainsprings of action, his ability to think clearly, and the energy to formulate plans and carry them out. He had had time only for a brief conversation with his colleague. He had sworn him to secrecy; there was no point in alarming the household, though it was obvious that at some point the Count would have to be told.

Coleridge had hoped for a while that there was some possibility of error in Menlow's analysis and calculations, but the latter had been vehement on that point. There was a mystery here which hovered at the edge of brooding horror and clouded Coleridge's mind. He did not know what he was to tell the girl in the morning; he had been at pains to reassure her and to formulate a theory that postulated a perfectly normal explanation for what she had experienced the previous night.

Now that possibility lay in ruins, and Coleridge and Menlow were faced with a set of circumstances that led squarely to the conclusion that the thing which the girl heard had a supernatural origin. That there was a supreme irony in all this was not lost on Coleridge: here were professional savants, steeped in the traditions and study of folklore, who were recoiling from real-life evidence that such manifestations might be true.

Coleridge had not forgotten the sinister shadow he had seen at the entrance to the Weapons Hall and the clicking noise resembling that made by the claws of a four-footed animal which had faded down the corridor. It was the same sound that the girl had heard, though Coleridge had been at pains to avoid facing it in his own mind.

The thought of the Weapons Hall brought the comforting reality of the Count's pistol to the forefront. He took it out now, made sure the safety-catch was on, and put it down on his bedside table, within easy reach together with the spare cartridges. He walked over to the stout oak door and made sure it was locked. It was past midnight and the Castle lay in an unbroken silence, as though everyone and everything in it were frozen like the bleak wastes of snow and ice outside.

Coleridge sat down in a big high-backed chair by the bed and poured himself a whisky from the bottle his host had thoughtfully left on the silver tray on the bedside table. He swilled the liquid round thoughtfully in the glass, watching the yellow lamplight strike glints from its dark surface.

Coleridge at first had a flicker of hope that Menlow might have been wrong; that the sample somehow may have become mixed with a fragment of flesh from his own finger, perhaps lodged there when he removed the wood splinter from the girl's door. But Menlow, in their muttered conversation on the darkened staircase, had soon disabused him of that. The thing was an impossibility.

The animal fur had been growing *through* the human skin. Now Coleridge debated the problem further; he could not sleep when matters of such urgency were gnawing at his consciousness. The Count would have to be told, of course, but not necessarily at once. Coleridge needed time to think. He dare not elaborate to himself, even in the locked privacy of his own room, what such a beast as that roaming the corridors of the Castle might portend for its inhabitants.

For if the girl had been right—and there was no reason to

doubt her—the wolf-thing had gained entry to the Castle by opening doors and turning handles, thus implying that it not only walked upright instead of on all fours, but also possessed human as well as bestial faculties. That conclusion led to gibbering madness, and Coleridge thrust the notion hastily from his mind; his lonely room and the lateness of the hour were neither the venue nor the time for such thoughts.

For Coleridge was an authority on the subject: the loup-garou, as the French called it; the werewolf as the English termed it; and the volkodlak as Eastern Europe had it. Lycanthropy was his special study, but there was a world between the scholarly examination of mediaeval legends and medical case-histories of persons who had believed themselves to be werewolves, and the apparent reality of what both the girl and now Menlow were telling him.

The irony was increased by the paper which Coleridge was due to deliver at the opening session of the Count's private Congress tomorrow. Then he glanced at his silver-cased watch on the bedside table and mentally corrected himself: today, or to be absolutely precise, in some nine hours' time.

Still fully dressed and with the whisky glass in his hand, Coleridge quietly paced the floor of his comfortable room. The fire had burned low, leaving the red glow of charred logs from the forests which surrounded the Castle and which still threw out an agreeable heat . . . a fact which was emphasised by the icy wind which whistled round the turrets and battlements of The House of the Wolf and occasionally stirred the thick curtains at the window, as though they had been disturbed by some spectral breath of a person long deceased.

Coleridge thought again of the Count's sombre history of Ivan the Bold and his retributive death among the snapping fangs of the wolf-pack in the ravine known as The Place of the Skull. He was uncomfortably aware that some hundred and fifty feet or so below him, deep in the earth, lay that sealed and unspeakably vile torture chamber of which the Count had spoken, lapped in an unearthly silence which had not been disturbed for more than half a lifetime.

Unnerved, Coleridge stopped his pacing and again went to try the door of his room. It was securely locked, just as he had left it.

This would never do; he found himself bent over, his ears straining for the slightest noise, his eyes fixed on the handle. A damp bead of sweat had formed on his forehead. With a grimace of disgust he turned from the door, drained his tumbler.

He dropped still fully dressed on the bed, pulling the coverlet over him, leaving the light burning. He knew he was in for an uncomfortable night. The last thing he remembered before falling into a fitful sleep was the comforting image of the shining barrel of the Count's pistol on the bedside table.

Suddenly he was awake, all his nerves alert to danger. The fire was out, and there was a chill in the air. It may have been his imagination, but the lamp also seemed to have burned low. A glance at his watch at the base of the lamp showed him that it wanted but a few minutes to three o'clock. He felt untidy, ached in every limb, and was not at all refreshed by his two-hour rest. There was a stale, uncomfortable taste at the back of his throat, only partly overlaid by the cleansing flavour of the whisky.

He knew instinctively that some faint sound at the farthest edge of consciousness had awakened him. He pulled himself upright on the bed, levering his legs with difficulty to the floor. He felt stiff, his limbs sluggish and unwilling to do his bidding. His head ached too, and his heavy-lidded eyes seemed reluctant to stay open now that he was on his feet.

He groped for the revolver, his senses reviving at the chill touch of the walnut butt on his fingers.

At the same time he became aware of a furtive noise in the general direction of the door. He reached out with a none-too-steady hand and turned up the wick of the lamp. The intensity of brightness, which immediately flung the darkest shadows into the far corners of the chamber, seemed to renew his flagging spirits.

He was wide awake now, the revolver firmly held in his right hand. He walked over toward the door, his senses alert, the heavy pumping of his heart seeming inordinately loud, a pulse throbbing in his throat. The sound came again before he was halfway between the bed and the door.

There was something infinitely stealthy in it; he remembered then the girl's vivid description of her own experience, and he realised she had not exaggerated. A slight scratching noise, as though heard at the far edge of silence; it was darker here than it had been in the area of the bed, of course, and he did not at first notice anything.

Then, as his eyes adjusted, he saw the infinitely slow turning of the handle and realised the subtle pressure that was being put upon it. Coleridge did not reckon himself to be a man possessed of exceptional courage, but he was one of those individuals who prefer action rather than indecision.

There was something so furtive and sinister about the stealthy trying of his door in this dead hour of the night that he understood immediately the circumstances would sap his will if he delayed a moment longer.

No sooner had the resolve been formulated within his own mind than he started forward with a wild cry and reached for the handle, intending to unlock the door and throw it open in one movement.

Unfortunately, or fortunately—he could not afterward decide which—he had forgotten the revolver in his right hand. He intended to grasp the door-handle and at the same time with his left to throw over the key, so unlocking it.

Instead, the barrel of the pistol struck the panel of the door with a resounding crash. The noise had a heart-stopping quality in that deathly silence and was immediately answered by a low snarl in the corridor outside. This was something more definite, and, paradoxically, Coleridge's energy revived. He shouted something incoherent and seized the door-handle firmly this time. The key grated in the lock as he turned it with his left hand.

It was a foolhardy, even suicidal, thing to do, as he did not know what it was that stood there, but even as he opened the door he heard the sharp scraping of claws on the corridor parquet. There was the dim lamp burning near the bathroom door farther down, which was the only illumination.

By its light Coleridge saw the elongated shadow of the furry shape which fled down the corridor in front of him. He stepped out, excitement making his hand tremble. Again the horrific snarl which had all the savage quality designed to strike fear into human prey. The corridor light was distorting and exaggerating the size of the thing, Coleridge knew.

He did not pause to think how it might have come there, but he could see clearly now. It was undoubtedly a wolf, moreover one of the biggest he had ever seen. It had greyish hair on its back, and as it ran, its claws making that extraordinary sharp, clicking noise on the wooden floor, it looked back at him over its shoulder. Coleridge was left with the impression of jagged white teeth and the burning redness of its eyes.

He squeezed the trigger, realised too late that he had forgotten, in the agitation of the moment, to throw off the safety-catch. The beast seemed to sense this, for it had at first jinked aside, as it was still some way from the turn in the corridor. Coleridge knew stark fear then, for it was coming back at incredible speed, its head growing quickly in size as it accelerated from the darkness into the light.

But Coleridge had the safety-catch off now. The explosion of the pistol seemed unaccountably loud. Flame split the darkness, and powder-smoke stung his cheek. The wolf seemed flattened and somehow deflated by the explosion, but he saw it had turned with fantastic agility and was going back, very fast, down the corridor. The air was full of smoke, and Coleridge was conscious of sweat running down into his eyes.

The entire encounter had lasted only split-seconds, and now he ran forward, bringing the pistol up. Perhaps he had grazed the beast, for it seemed to limp on its off hindpaw. It was almost at the end of the corridor when Coleridge was struck a paralysing blow; the pistol fell to the floor with a thump and he groped, searing pain suffusing him.

He was aware that in the gloom he had not noticed a wooden buttress protruding from the wall at shoulder height. He had run straight onto it in his pursuit, momentarily paralysing a nerve.

He had fallen to the parquet now, groping for the pistol which lay a foot or two from his nerveless hand. Again came the chilling snarl from the end of the corridor.

Coleridge felt his senses swimming. As he pitched forward into unconsciousness he was left with one final image on his retina: that of naked human feet rounding the end of the passage. The right leg was limping. Then the darkness reached out and enveloped him.

COLERIDGE BECAME AWARE that the Count's face was coming into focus. He looked concerned and moved forward to press his guest back onto the pillow as he tried to struggle upright.

"Rest. You have had a bad shock, my friend."

Coleridge was aware of a throbbing in his arm. He cautiously flexed his muscles, felt the pain receding.

"I am sorry to put you to so much trouble."

The sentence sounded fatuous even as he enunciated it. His eyes were normal now, and he took in the pistol lying on the bedside table. He was back in his own room again.

"I must apologise," he told the Count. "I borrowed your pistol without permission. I took it from the Weapons Hall."

The Count smiled faintly.

"That is perfectly all right, Professor. You must have had a good reason."

Coleridge nodded. He decided to take his host into his confidence. It was the most sensible course. Things had taken too serious a turn for prevarication.

He glanced at his watch face, clear and sharp beneath the lamp. It had just turned half-past three. So he had been unconscious only a short time. Probably the shock and the pain. Recollection flooded back; he remembered the feet he had seen running away.

He got up, felt a little weak. The Count held him firmly by the arm and helped him to sit. His head was clearing. His host had enormous strength; Coleridge could feel that, though the steel-like fingers were amazingly gentle.

A shadow moved in the room. The bearded servant looked at Coleridge impassively. The Count was already pouring him a drink. He put the glass into his hand. Coleridge caught the taste of cognac, raw and strong on his tongue. Strength flooded back in. He rose, flexing his left arm gingerly. The feeling was returning now. He had probably merely bruised his shoulder.

"Would you like a doctor?" the Count said solicitously.

Coleridge shook his head. His host was incredibly patient. He must have a dozen questions as to why his guest had been running about the corridor in the middle of the night, firing a revolver; but he merely waited, nothing but compassion in his eyes. Coleridge knew then that the wolf-thing had disappeared, that he was probably the only person who had seen it. Otherwise the whole Castle would have been aroused.

"My man was passing the stairs," Homolky volunteered as Coleridge sat down on the edge of the bed and again sipped at the cognac. "His wife is sick, and he had been to collect something from the doctor in Lugos. He heard the shot and came to investigate. He found you lying unconscious. He came straight to me without arousing the household."

"He is very discreet," said Coleridge.

The Count smiled again.

"All my servants are discreet," he said.

Coleridge had been listening to his host almost without understanding the purport of his words. Now came their sense. He looked at his host incredulously.

"Do you mean to say your man was the only person who heard?"

The Count shrugged.

"Apparently. It is the middle of the night. My guests would be sound asleep. And these walls are enormously thick. Perhaps it is better so."

His eyes held the guest's until they seemed to grow inordinately large.

"You are a man of great courage and discretion, Professor. A savant and a scholar. If you discharge a pistol in the corridor of my Castle in the dead hours of the night, you must have had a very good reason for doing so."

"Indeed," Coleridge said.

The Count inclined his head.

"You were firing at something dangerous?"

Coleridge nodded.

"Very dangerous. You may be sure I would have come to you immediately had I not foolishly struck against a protruding beam."

He looked uncertainly from the manservant to his master.

"But I would prefer to speak to you in private about it."

The Count made a subtle gesture to the bearded man, who mumbled something in return and seemed to melt back into the shadows. Coleridge heard the faint click of the bedroom door closing to behind him.

The Count drew over a bedside chair and sat down facing Coleridge, pouring himself a liberal measure of cognac. He sipped it appreciatively, raising it in a silent toast to the guest.

"Now, Professor," he said gently. "Had you not better tell me everything?"

"It is absolutely incredible! We have searched but found no trace of the animal."

Homolky stroked his chin with a strong hand, but there was the very faintest tremor in his voice. He poured himself a little more cognac, concentrating on the task with great deliberation as though striving to preserve the normalities. Coleridge's throat felt dry with talking, and he held out his own glass as the Count advanced the bottle to him. The two men sipped silently, each occupied with his own heavy thoughts.

"What you are telling me, then," the Count said eventually, "is that you fired at a wolf in the corridor outside here, in the midst of my sleeping guests."

Coleridge felt suddenly tired.

"I tried to put the matter as unsensationally as possible, Count. A wolf, moreover, which had apparently just tried the door-handle of my room. A beast which can reason like a man and which has apparently disappeared like a puff of smoke."

He held out his hand as the Count started up as though in expostulation.

"I think there is deadly danger here. Your daughter is involved also. That is why we were examining the broken wall of your outer courtyard."

The Count stared at Coleridge for a long moment, his face draining of blood. He held the stem of his fragile cognac glass as though he would crush it in his massive fingers.

"And why did my daughter confide in you instead of her own father?" he said very gently and deliberately.

Coleridge felt the uneasiness and embarrassment return, but this was the time for truth.

"Because she loves you and her mother very much," he said steadily. "She did not wish either of you worried at that stage. Tonight's incident changes things."

Little sparks were glinting in Homolky's eyes beneath the thatch of white hair. But he looked at his guest with approval and nodded once or twice as though he had come to a decision.

"Your words do you credit, Professor. But I find this very alarming."

He paused, fixing Coleridge with burning eyes.

"I shall have to ask you to be absolutely frank and precise in your answers to my questions."

Coleridge got up and took a turn around the room. He was still fully clothed, and his arm and shoulder felt less painful with every minute that passed.

"You will not need to ask questions, Count. I intend to be most comprehensive in my facts as well as my theories."

Coleridge paused again, looking round the ancient chamber in the golden lamplight. He was suddenly conscious of the hundreds of years of history, mostly barbaric history, that Castle Homolky represented.

And somewhere out there in the darkened corridors and shadowy hallways was the answer to a mystery that was assuming baffling proportions. He came back toward the bed quickly, sensing the Count's barely hidden impatience.

"When I arrived at Lugos," he began, "I found a tragic situation in the village, as you well know. Several horrible deaths, the result of depredations by a band of wolves. I myself saw the mangled remains of a peasant brought in; one of the employees on your own estate, who had been a friend of your daughter as a child. There was a further attack yesterday and another villager injured."

The Count's eyes never left Coleridge's face. His guest looked strained and haggard in the lamplight. He gave a heavy sigh at the professor's words, but he did not interrupt the narrative.

"Yesterday morning," Coleridge continued, "your daughter sought my help and advice. The previous night she had been disturbed by someone trying the handle of the door to her room. It was locked, fortunately. She was about to open it when she heard a snarling noise like an animal. She screamed and heard a clicking sound on the corridor floor as though the beast were running away."

The Count shifted uneasily on his chair, holding his half-empty cognac glass in his listless hand, but still he did not interrupt.

"After that she fainted," his guest went on. "The following morning, when she asked my help, I examined the door of her room and the corridor parquet. I found scratches which looked as though they had been made by an animal."

His face now was grim.

"I also found fragments of skin and fur in a splinter on the panel of the door. I asked my colleague, Dr. Menlow, to analyse it for me. First, he found his microscope and other instruments had disappeared. When your servants traced them, the box containing the lenses was not there, making the instruments useless."

The Count's face was grave.

"You think this was deliberate?"

"I do not know," Coleridge said heavily. "I am merely transmitting some relevant facts. Without going into wild theories, I was examining the broken snow in the area of the shattered wall which contains the outer courtyard of the Castle. I found tracks of a beast which could have been a wolf and which led toward the arcade of the inner court."

The Count rose quickly, seeming to tower over Coleridge, his heavy shadow imprinted on the opposite wall.

"This is fantastic, Professor. What animal can open or unlock doors to penetrate to my family and guests' quarters?"

Coleridge shrugged.

"A very strange animal, Count, evidently. I have not yet finished."

The host laid his hand on the other's arm. His voice sounded tired and dispirited.

"I am sorry. This is an upsetting business."

"I will be brief. This morning's incident was almost a repetition of your daughter's experience. It was most alarming, I can assure you. It was because I was concerned, particularly for your daughter's safety, that I took the liberty of purloining that pistol from your Weapons Hall. While I was in there I saw a strange shadow on the corridor wall and heard the clicking of what sounded like an animal's paws along the passage."

The Count drew in his breath with a quick rasping noise, but he still stood immobile, his shadow dark and distorted on the wall.

"When I opened my door an hour or so ago I could not really believe what I saw. There was a great wolf in the corridor. It seemed to understand that the pistol spelt danger, and it made off very rapidly."

Coleridge paused. He suddenly felt very tired, and his arm and shoulder were paining him again.

"Its action reminded me of the beast Colonel Anton fired at without any seeming effect. Unfortunately, I had forgotten to throw off the safety-catch in the excitement of the moment, or it would have been a very different story."

His eyes met the Count's, and a strange, almost hostile, glance passed between the two.

"The beast knew this also, Count, for it came back toward me as fast as it could, ready to tear my throat out. I had the safety free by this time, and the animal made off again. I cannot be certain, but I think I wounded it slightly in the off hindleg."

The Count's eyes were very bright now as he stared at Coleridge.

"I went to follow, but unfortunately I had not noticed that projecting beam in the corridor and I ran headlong onto it. The pain was such that I dropped the revolver and lost consciousness."

The Count could not keep the astonishment from his voice. "What are you telling me, Professor?"

Homolky's pronunciation trembled very slightly despite his iron self-control.

"That we have a bizarre situation here, Count," said Coleridge in a voice so low that the other had to strain to pick out the words.

There was shock in the big man's eyes.

"I must call in Colonel Anton. What does this all mean?"

"I am not certain," Coleridge said. "There is a dark tangle and much danger overhanging your household."

He cleared his throat with a low rasping noise in the silence of the shadowy room.

"There are just two alternatives. A wolf. Or a werewolf. With the available evidence pointing to the latter."

Nadia

COLERIDGE DRAINED his second cup of coffee and sat staring moodily at the icy landscape spread out far below his window. He had had only four hours' sleep, and his arm still throbbed.

He felt incredibly tired, but his mind was clear. He had the opening lecture of the Congress to deliver in less than two hours, and he was determined to do justice to his theme.

The professor smiled grimly to himself. The subject of his lecture was extremely apposite at this moment. The Count had had his breakfast served in his room, and he sat at a table near the roaring fire, well-being gradually seeping back into his body. Following his conversation with his host a few hours earlier he had deliberately blanked off his mind, forcing himself into exhausted sleep.

Now his brain was incredibly busy, but he had gone over all the ground at length; there was no sense in retracing the situation until he had further data to work on.

He wanted to see Menlow before they went in for the opening session. He had sworn him to secrecy, but he needed to make sure that his colleague did not inadvertently spread the story about the Castle. It would do no good and merely alarm the servants. As the Count had indicated, no-one had apparently heard anything untoward the previous night; the bearded attendant could be relied upon for discretion, and he had not spoken to anyone other than the Count regarding the night's events.

Anton would have to go about his inquiries with circumspection. The Count had already been in to see Coleridge at the same time the breakfast was served; he had communicated these facts to his guest when they were once again alone. Coleridge found it incredible that no-one should have heard his pistol shot and his fall, apart from the man descending the stairs. But there it was.

The guest wing was as isolated as that for the Count's own family; the walls of the bedrooms were several feet thick, as Coleridge had already observed, and as Homolky had himself pointed out. If everyone had been fast asleep—and it had been in the middle of the night—then the incident, however shattering for Coleridge, might well have passed unnoticed. It was only one more strange facet of this wild and romantic household.

He replaced the cup in his saucer with a faint clink that seemed to erode the edges of the brooding silence. His immediate problem was what to say to the girl. The Count had promised he would not speak to her before Coleridge had had the opportunity to do so. And he would, of course, be absolutely forthright and tell her exactly what he had told her father.

That was the most urgent necessity. There was deadly danger here, and there was now no point in minimising it, though he would not speak of what he had finally seen before he had passed out. Coleridge's conscience was already nagging him about the problem of his colleagues. They would have to be told at some stage, and it was possible that they also were in some danger while this thing was prowling around. But there was no sense in alarming the inhabitants of the Castle unnecessarily.

And as his host had stressed, he did not want his wife, and particularly his aged mother, worried at the situation. That was something they would have to meet in due course. And there was another problem, too, in the fantastic circumstances of the whole business: Coleridge had no desire to be ridiculed by his scientific colleagues who might merely suspect him of romantically embellishing his own particular subject.

The thing had appeared to Coleridge and the girl; the Count and his personal servant were the only other people privy to the facts. It was best to leave it at that. There was Menlow, of course. He was a strong-minded person and might have ideas of his own about the situation. Coleridge glanced at his silver-cased watch. He still had an hour and a half yet before he was due to deliver his lecture. He walked over toward the bedside table, reloaded the revolver, and replaced the weapon in his pocket.

He came back and poured himself a third cup of coffee, conscious that thin rays of sunlight were staining the window casement. With the combined warmth of the fire and the coffee his spirits were rising as his physical condition was restored.

Coleridge's mind still shied away from the supernatural theory, but his scientific training reinforced the unlikeliness of an ordinary wolf prowling the corridors, apart from the impossibility of such an animal turning door-handles and trying to gain entry. Wolves, moreover, were normally shy and timid creatures, despite their reputation for ferocity, and they tended to move and hunt in packs. What would one be doing within the Castle, leaving aside the problem of its method of entry?

Again, no-one had seen the animal except Coleridge; it had then completely disappeared, and, certainly from the discreet inquiries the Count had been able to make early in the morning, none of the servants or the guests had seen or heard anything untoward. Menlow's microscope tests posited another theory, and Coleridge was finding it grim and unpalatable, however much it favoured his own particular subject and the whole realm of folklore in which he and his colleagues were so immersed. He would not speak of that until a more suitable moment.

There had been no blood in the corridor; Coleridge had looked before anyone was about. He was sure he had at least grazed the creature's leg, and it might have been limping and losing blood. But there was nothing on the parquet or in the corridor adjoining, not even a few cut hairs that would have given Coleridge some comfort in the nonsupernatural direction.

Though he had found the hole his bullet had made; it had

lodged at the foot of a massive beam at the end of the corridor, about six inches from the floor, which strengthened Coleridge's impression that he had wounded the beast's leg.

Even that left out of account the image of those naked feet running from the scene just before he had lost consciousness. That was the most incontrovertible truth and an aspect that he had thrust firmly to the back of his thoughts. But its reality could not be denied, and its ugliness was growing on him as the minutes ticked by on the face of his watch.

There was a faint tapping at the door now, and Coleridge rose with some relief. It was not good to be alone with these gnawing problems.

"Good morning, Professor."

It was Nadia Homolky who stood there, and one glance at Coleridge's face had told her that her worst fears had been realised.

The girl was silent for a long while as Coleridge finished speaking. Her brown eyes regarded him steadily. Her face had become more anxious as his narrative developed, and she moved forward impulsively and put her small hand over the back of his own.

"I am so sorry I got you involved in this."

Coleridge shook his head.

"This morning's incident would have happened in any case."

And then, as she looked at him with a faint air of disbelief, he went on, "I am certain of that."

Nadia Homolky expelled her breath in a long shuddering sigh and stirred restlessly in the big padded fireside chair next to Coleridge. A bar of light coming in from the casement behind them seemed to strike a radiance from her hair. Once again Coleridge was vividly aware of this young woman's physical attraction, but he was no longer discomfited by it. The strange situation in which they found themselves had made them accomplices.

"I am glad you told Father," she said at last, reluctantly removing her fingers from his. "It is better so."

She put up her hand to her hair, her head on one side as she regarded Coleridge.

"He will not tell Mother and Grandmother?"

The professor shook his head.

"He assured me of that."

He leaned forward, looking at her steadily.

"You have not asked me the most important question."

The girl smiled faintly, though there was still concern at the back of her eyes.

"I am waiting for you to tell me what you think. We are not dealing with a real wolf, are we? Like me, you think there is something supernatural behind it."

Coleridge sat back in his chair. Fatigue had fallen away from him and the ache in his left shoulder was disappearing, though there was massive bruising of the skin, as he had already ascertained. He would get Abercrombie to look at it if there were any medical complications.

"You know what lycanthropy is, I suppose?"

The girl smiled again, genuinely this time. The shadows had temporarily cleared from her face.

"There are two strands, are there not? At least, according to Father. One is a sort of disease. The other, the stuff of legend in which men have the power to change themselves into beasts?"

Coleridge nodded.

"Well and succinctly put. I have devoted several volumes to the same basic propositions."

He was silent for a moment or two as though collecting his thoughts. Then he went on with a rush.

"I do not believe this is a time for scholarly dissertations. I will put things as briefly as I can. And then we must simply follow events as they occur."

A sudden flash of alarm passed across Nadia Homolky's face.

"You think something else may happen, then?"

Coleridge's expression was grave.

"There must be a purpose behind these manifestations. No, I do not think this thing has finished. On the contrary, I think it is just beginning."

He went on before she could say anything further.

"There is a significant difference between the two legends relating to lycanthropy and that of vampirism. The former was believed by the ancients to be a disease which might afflict anyone among them, causing them to behave like ravening beasts. They would discard their clothing, fur would grow on their bodies and limbs, and when the moon was full they would roam the night, seeking victims whom they would savage and destroy in the manner of wolves."

The girl shivered, but her eyes were fixed unwaveringly on Coleridge's face.

"I have heard Father speak of such things. But it is physically impossible, is it not, for such a transformation to take place."

Coleridge nodded.

"Scientifically speaking, yes. But there are many instances in ancient records of a medical condition which was akin to such phenomena. The victims were impelled to discard their clothing, howled and behaved like beasts, and ran about uncontrollably in the light of the moon."

Coleridge paused, a heavy sigh escaping him. He smiled wryly.

"But I am beginning to sound like my public persona. I trust I am not boring you."

Nadia Homolky shook her head.

"Far from it, Professor. Father said the difference between the two conditions of the vampire and the werewolf was that the vampire was a natural evil spirit which exulted in roaming the earth and drinking the blood of the living. But the werewolf was merely an unfortunate wretch visited by some weird and little-known disease which compelled him to do things against his nature. He had no wish to do evil and was thus a victim."

Coleridge inclined his head, enthusiasm flashing in his eyes.

"Your father is perfectly correct in those basic tenets, though the pedant might argue with such a simplistic interpretation."

He smiled briefly at the girl's expression.

"There is a good deal more to lycanthropy and the legends which have accreted round it than that, of course. And the whole apparatus which guards against the vampire is useless in the case of the werewolf. The only basic trait they have in common is that both are confined to the night, creatures of the dark hours. And it was widely believed that the silver bullet was the only antidote to the lycanthrope, the wolf-victim, though that is not strictly correct."

He consulted his watch, noting that he still had a little time.

"You should attend my opening lecture, Miss Homolky. You

may not enjoy it, but you would at least learn a good deal more about this thing."

"I would like to, Professor, if my father has no objection."

Coleridge shrugged.

"I do not see why he should. But if you wish, I will speak to him about it before the Congress begins."

The girl had a hesitant expression, and she bit her lip as though reluctant to go on.

"Please understand me, Professor. I was horrified when you told me of your experiences just now . . ."

"But you were relieved that they had not been confined to you alone."

The girl nodded, catching her breath. She seemed to be listening for something that Coleridge could not hear. Something stirring in the long corridor outside? Or was the guest becoming fanciful, and was she really more concerned in case her father came back and found them tête-à-tête by the fire in Coleridge's bedroom?

Once again Coleridge felt an inward embarrassment. Then his resolve strengthened. This business was far too dangerous and important to let ordinary conventions stand in the way. And Raglan must think as he liked.

"I have still not heard your scientific explanation for what happened last night," the girl went on.

"I have none. I hope and trust there will be some quite logical dénouement. But I know what I saw. It was no hallucination. There was a great wolf in the corridor. I fired at it and struck it a slight blow on the off hindpaw."

He looked at Nadia Homolky grimly.

"It was something I shall never forget."

"But what shall we do?" the girl persisted.

Coleridge's voice was firm and decisive.

"Take precautions, my dear young lady. Any other questions must wait."

He got up and walked over toward the door.

"And now, permit me to escort you to the Congress's opening session."

The Limping Man

THEREFORE, TO THE MAN OF SCIENCE there remains one inescapable conclusion. That this wolf is a true werewolf and lives on through the ages in myth and legend."

Coleridge finished to a thin ripple of applause. He bowed, feeling satisfaction that the paper was a good one and that he had delivered it to the best of his ability. He reached forward and sipped at the glass of water on the lectern in front of him.

"And now, gentlemen, if there are any questions I shall be pleased to answer them."

There was no lacking in response. Abercrombie was the first, as the speaker had thought he might be. Beneath his bluff exterior was a fine, shrewd brain. He would be quick to find a chink in the armour of any unprepared speaker, but Coleridge had done his groundwork well; it was not like him to prepare a sloppy paper, and he was convinced that his reasoning was as accurate as it could be in the light of modern knowledge.

The rest of the area was lost in shadowy speculation, and he had been careful not to exceed his given bounds. He need not have been worried. Abercrombie was courteous and polite. He really wanted to know what was the true medical basis for the holocaust of werewolf trials in mediaeval times, and Coleridge was able to amplify his reply until it became a miniature lecture in itself. He was grateful to Abercrombie for opening out the discussion like this, and he intended to do justice to the subject.

He caught the girl's expression and it was approving, though her eyes held him in a way he would have found uncomfortable if he had persisted in looking at her. She was sitting next to Colonel Anton; he was in full uniform, which meant he was there on official business, and the Star of Krasnia threw off golden glints as he shifted in his seat.

Coleridge knew the colonel would want to question him as soon as the lecture was over. He was glad now that he had said nothing to the Count or the girl about the feet he had seen running away immediately after he had struck himself upon the buttress.

It may have been, in any event, a momentary effect of the blow. A sort of hallucination engendered by slight concussion, though he really could not convince himself of this. And it did not help Coleridge in explaining the other events of the night, or the trying of the door. He knew the animal was immediately outside. Therefore, no other human being would have been near. And he had definitely seen the handle turning. The girl had had a similar experience.

It was not mass hysteria or anything of that sort. Both Coleridge's nature and that of Nadia Homolky did not lie in those directions. And Menlow's test had been conclusive.

Coleridge caught Homolky's eye as he glanced about the big room they were using as a lecture hall. His smooth, practised sentences went on in reasoned, coherent periods, his voice resonant and confident as it carried to the farthest corner of the chamber, while his brain continued to revolve imponderables. The Count was chairman, of course; it was a courtesy the host appreciated, and he had the agenda and timetable for every day and notes on each speaker giving information he would need as he introduced them.

Homolky had a satisfied look on his face; things were going well. It had been a good start to the Congress, and it appeared, both to him and to Coleridge himself, as though this smaller gathering would be as successful as the major Congress just concluded in Pest.

Coleridge's gaze passed on, taking in the pale oval faces scattered about, gradually resolving them into detailed features. He had not been surprised to see the old Countess there; she looked like one of those rather austere oil paintings set about the panelled walls of the Castle, but there was no doubt about her interest in the subjects being debated or her knowledge of his work.

Though the presence of Sylva Homolky, sitting next to her mother-in-law, had been a little more unexpected. Coleridge was encouraged by this gracious manifestation of the interest shown by the host family in their deliberations, and the speaker was pleased to see the amusement and appreciation on the younger Countess's face at some of the more esoteric and erudite jokes with which he had sprinkled his text.

But there was a vague doubt nagging at Coleridge's mind; it had been there for some time, but he could not at first give it conscious recognition. He was bringing his comments to a rapid close now, and he again raked the hall. The stage was brilliantly lit with the rest of the room somewhat in shadow, which was normal for such events, of course, and at first he could not see any visible reason for his unease.

Then he had it. Menlow did not appear to be there. He went round the semicircle of faces again. There was Sullivan, still in his archaic suit of plus-fours; George Parker, his black beard abristle and his eyes alight with enthusiasm; Raglan, who was sitting at a discreet distance from Nadia but eyeing her appreciatively from time to time.

Pools of darker space were scattered between the figures, which stood out almost like tableaux in a museum. Shaw was there too, sitting at the edge of the gathering, toward the front. He did not know why he had not noticed Menlow's absence earlier, or why it had not been mentioned before the lecture began. Coleridge hoped there was nothing wrong; judging by the gathering in Pest it was not like him to miss out on such an important event as the opening session. He would ask during the intermission following the questions; perhaps Menlow was ill and confined to his room. Homolky would send someone to inquire.

And then there was the problem of Anton. The Chief of Police would obviously wish to question Coleridge on his experiences of the previous night. That was likely to be a long and tedious business, as Anton knew little English and the Count would have to translate. Coleridge had already decided to keep his own counsel about what he had seen just before consciousness faded, even so far as Anton was concerned. It would add nothing to the situation except an element of fantasy, which was certainly not needed at the present time.

He should have kept a cooler head, but he had been unwell and off balance when he had confided in his host. After all, there was great danger overhanging the family if this thing was prowling the corridors. It had manifested itself on three separate occasions if the shadow seen by Coleridge at the door of the Weapons Hall could be counted.

What the police chief would make of it all he did not know; he and the girl could only speak the truth, after all. The official had impressed him as being a man of great courage and probity, and he would obviously know the folkways of his own country at least as well as a scholar whose knowledge, however assiduously gleaned from long contact with European peasants, could only be superficial by comparison.

Another question was coming up now, this time from Shaw. It was a good one; a clever one with a trick flaw in it, and he saw the admiration and pleasure in Shaw's eyes as the speaker gently twisted it and handed it back to him. There was a further ripple of applause, in which the girl joined.

It was a well-argued piece of sophistry, based on the turning of skins; the judiciary in the Middle Ages had the delightful habit—founded on the premise that the werewolf in daylight wore his skin reversed, the fur on the inside and the human skin on the outer—of skinning the werewolf-victim alive in order to discover if this were so.

The victim invariably died, which, in the manner of Cotton

Mather and the witch-trials, merely proved his guilt; Shaw had disguised the barb of his question with a neat double-entendre, but Coleridge had parried it equally deftly. He felt a certain dry satisfaction as he turned to a question by the Count himself. But as he argued his point with the smoothness engendered of long practice, he was still disturbed by the absence of Menlow.

His vacant place among the leather chairs was like a gap in an otherwise well-ordered row of perfect teeth in a friend's mouth, taken for granted but shockingly self-evident when one was missing. He wondered too what Anton would say about the use of the pistol in the Castle corridor. There was a faint flicker of amusement on Coleridge's face now; he hardly thought it would matter.

It was the Count's pistol; it had been fired on his own private property, and at a moment when a guest had been in danger of his life from a savage beast. He could still see the redness of the creature's eyes as he finished answering Homolky's question. And it was not as though they were in England or America where a firearm permit might be required.

It was to reduce the situation to a simple domestic process hinging on a bureaucratic whim as to whether he had been licensed to fire the shot or not, and he savoured the quiet joke for a moment or two longer. Something moving at the back of the library caught his eye, and he heard the faint squeak of boots on the polished floor.

For a moment he thought it was Menlow, and relief flooded through him; then he saw he was mistaken, for as the figure emerged from the shadowy distance into the light of the lamps he saw that it was Rakosi. The young captain paused apologetically and then slipped into a vacant chair next to Nadia Homolky, giving her a hesitant smile.

Coleridge brought his remarks to a close with a professional flourish and waited; apparently there were no more questions. He moved mechanically over toward the blackboard, erasing his statistics and the carefully drawn graph. It was something they all did; a sign of good manners. Literally leaving a clean slate for the next man to lecture.

He stood to one side of the platform, watching the girl, only half-listening to the Count's words of thanks; he was roused by the strength of the applause. Apparently his modest efforts had met with success. The Count was by his side, shaking his hand. The audience was rising now, moving over to the side-tables where the dumb majordomo and the huge black-bearded servant stood ready to dispense coffee and cognac.

Coleridge was aware of thick snow drifting down past the high-up window against a dreary sky that was almost the colour of soot. The bleakness of the vista reminded him of his promise to the wolf-hunters on the morrow. He hoped they would not have to rise at some unearthly hour.

The Count was smiling, ushering his guest from the platform toward the refreshment-tables. As Coleridge moved over, following the others, he saw Shaw coming from his place in the auditorium. He walked with difficulty, and the professor saw that he was limping heavily on the right foot.

Death Strikes Again

"So!"

Anton's hooded eyes glared blankly at Coleridge. If he had any opinions on the matter he was not divulging them. He, the Count, and Coleridge sat at one end of the shadowy library, apart from the babble of the refreshment-tables, while Nadia Homolky hovered halfway between the two groups, out of earshot but within call if her father needed her.

The examination had been carried out with the Count's acting as interpreter, and despite the apparent cumbersomeness of the method it had worked admirably; the colonel seemed to be a man who got at the pith of a matter with short, sharp questions, and his barked, equally concise replies to Homolky's own queries had advanced the interview in a swift and efficient manner.

Despite the limitations of communication and the language barrier Anton had seemed sympathetic and absorbed, his thick lips drawn into a tight line as he had listened intently to the Count's version of Coleridge's story. He had jotted a great many points in a large black notebook he produced from his uniform pocket, and it was now covered with pages of data.

If he had any theories of his own on Coleridge's experiences and of those of the Count's daughter, he had kept them to himself; Coleridge was becoming more and more impressed as the minutes went by. Anton had told the professor, through his host, that steps would be taken to patrol the Castle perimeter and that Rakosi had also volunteered the use of his men for that purpose.

But it was obvious Anton had a great deal more on his mind than that, and from time to time he paused, looking blankly in the girl's direction, while his thick spatulate fingers drummed softly on the knee of his braided uniform trouser-leg. There was a pause in the interview now, and the Count excused himself and got up to refill their coffee cups.

Coleridge, following his progress down the room, saw him stop for a brief word with his daughter. She joined them a few moments later. She was now wearing a pale green dress with a long skirt, cut vaguely on peasant lines and held in with a belt of soft leather. Her hair fell in waves across her face, and Coleridge noticed, as she crossed her legs, that she wore polished leather boots that came halfway up the calf.

She spoke easily with Anton; it was obvious the two were old friends, and it was clear to Coleridge, from the isolated phrase here and there, that the girl was telling her own story to the police chief.

It was evident that the family relied on his discretion, and Coleridge guessed that the colonel, who had served with distinction in the Imperial Army, as he had learned from the girl, had possibly also held diplomatic rank at one time. His rough exterior overlaid a good deal of polish, and Coleridge suspected that he too probably spoke other languages in addition to his own, though English was not one of his accomplishments.

The Count was back again, and Coleridge was content to drop out of the conversation, sipping his coffee, his eyes searching the room for Menlow. He had still not appeared, and Coleridge was beginning to feel worried; he was not in his room, as a servant had been to look for him. He turned his eyes back to the police chief. He shut his notebook with a snap and replaced it in his uniform pocket, thanking the girl graciously as he bent his head over her hand to kiss her fingertips in an affectionate parody of a subject being dismissed by his queen.

The Count's amused eyes caught Coleridge's own. Coleridge again glimpsed the tall figure of Shaw, coffee cup in hand, as he talked animatedly with the Countess Irina. He had fallen on the stairs earlier that morning, he had told Coleridge; turning his ankle. It appeared to be even more painful now.

Abercrombie had confirmed this in an apparently casual query Coleridge had put to him later, but a question mark still hovered in his mind that he could not dispel, however much he tried. It would be a startling coincidence, and Coleridge's thoughts were still darkened and distorted with the image of the naked feet running from the menace of his pistol.

It would be a case of the subject's literally biting the savant, had a real werewolf descended on their Congress. The idea was absurd, but it continued to dance round the edges of the professor's troubled mind, like one of those little figures that were sold in the more elaborate toy shops. They hung on wires and were apparently animated by some inner secret life of their own but which in reality came from concealed springs.

Coleridge wished that he could suddenly awake and find himself on the floor of the corridor, suffering from concussion, the whole incident a hallucination engendered by the sharp blow he had given himself by running at full speed upon the beam. But reality often had darker tints and more sharp-edged outlines, and so it was here.

Anton was giving him his hand to shake, indicating that the interview was concluded. They could rely on his discretion, the Count added. A little bell was sounding, clear over the babble of conversation. Coleridge turned back to the lecture platform with a heavy heart to introduce the next speaker.

Coleridge came to himself with a jerk, the thin smattering of applause in his ears. Abercrombie was reaching the end of his dissertation on witchcraft, and he was rounding off his paper in masterly style. There was a positive storm of clapping as he finished, and his eyes caught Coleridge's with pleasure as the latter signalled his own approval and enthusiasm.

But as the Count took the chair again and invited questions from the general gathering, Coleridge was only half concentrating on the business that had brought them there. Even two intelligent questions from the girl and one from her grandmother failed entirely to arouse him from his lethargy, though he had the tact later to add a few words of commendation to the ladies, which brought a glance of approbation from the Count.

Both women were, in fact, extremely well-read and -versed in these arcane subjects, and under any other circumstances Coleridge would have been completely absorbed. But he could not forget the festering suspicions in his mind, and Menlow's continued absence, though not commented on openly by his colleagues, was obviously a source of mounting uneasiness to more than one person in the room.

The Count had twice consulted his watch within the last hour, and his wry glance at Coleridge had underlined the fact that he too was puzzled by this apparently unwarrantable breach of good manners.

It was with relief that Homolky brought an end to the session, and the assembly adjourned. In the afternoon there were more major papers to be delivered by experts in their own field, and in the evening, after dinner, a general debate on the subjects of the day, with the Count in the chair. Coleridge took his host aside as everyone started filing out. Two minutes later he was walking up the shadowy staircase toward the guest wing.

He was startled to see the figure of Nadia waiting at the stairhead. Then he guessed she must have come through one of her secret shortcuts. Her face was serious as he joined her at the top. Impulsively, she put her hand on his arm.

"You're worried about Dr. Menlow, aren't you?"

Coleridge nodded.

"It is not like him to be absent from something so important as the opening sessions of this Congress. I am going to see whether he has returned to his room."

The girl fell in alongside him as he rounded the angle of the corridor.

"I am going with you."

Coleridge took one look at her set, determined face, decided not to utter the sentence which had first sprung to his lips.

"Very well. But please do as I say."

"You think there may be danger?"

The eyes were sparkling now. Coleridge felt the heavy pressure of the Count's pistol against his ribs as they turned the corner. It was a reminder of the seriousness of the situation.

"It is possible," he said, as lightly as he could. "Though he may have gone for a walk and become unwell, of course."

But he knew the sentence was not worth consideration as soon as he had uttered it. The Count had given specific instructions to everyone on the dangers of venturing out alone. And Menlow would not have done it. He was too alarmed at the weird result of his tests for that. Coleridge would never forget his face and the trembling delivery as he crouched on the shadowy staircase the previous night.

Coleridge could not put from his mind, either, the savage snarl of the great beast as it bounded toward him down the corridor. That was something else stamped indelibly upon his memory.

He was conscious that his fingers were none too steady as he put his hand on the girl's shoulder, bringing her to a halt. They were quite close to Coleridge's own room now. He knew that some of his fellow guests were farther down and others were in a second corridor that debouched from the stairhead in a different direction.

It was dim in here with the panelled walls, and there were no windows to break the gloom except, at the far end, up a shadowy stair. Once again Coleridge noticed and smelt the exotic blooms which were arranged in bowls and pewter jugs on chests and tables set along the passage. Botany was not his particular subject, and he did not recognise the flowers. He presumed that Nadia's mother or perhaps the old lady was responsible for the arrangements.

He knew that in such a great house there would be a huge flower room attached to the conservatories where servants would prepare the arrangements under the skilled direction of the châtelaine. He knew also from his experiences as guest at some of the most prestigious mansions and châteaux of Europe that each arrangement for every room and corridor, every table even, would have its own special order and placing, and if there was one bowl so much as out of its designed position by a fraction, the Count or a member of his family would want to know the reason why.

He glanced ruefully across at the huge wooden beam into which he had driven his shoulder. His injury still gave him an occasional twinge. He would let Abercrombie have a look at it at a convenient moment. He knew that the bruise had a horrendous colouration by now; he preferred not to think of it. When he had examined it, one glance at the green-and-black mottled aspect of his flesh had been enough.

The girl was very close to him, and they stared down the corridor in silence.

"Is this where it happened?" she said softly.

Coleridge nodded.

"Yes."

Then he added briskly, "Somewhere about here."

He led the way forward again, their footsteps making heavy vibrations across the parquet and setting the beams of the old walls and ceiling creaking. This section of the Castle seemed alive in a way that stone-flagged and solid-walled corridors could never be; there was something about wood and its springiness, even when cut, sawn, and pinned, that made it vibrant, almost breathing, Coleridge felt. But he must not become too fanciful in this atmosphere, though it was easy enough to do so.

The lamp outside the bathroom was still burning, so dark was the passageway, and in fact Coleridge understood it was lit day and night when guests were staying. They went on past Coleridge's chamber.

"Dr. Menlow's room is just at the top of this half flight of stairs," the girl said. "The first door on the left on the landing."

Coleridge nodded. His throat felt dry and constricted as it had when he had seen the shadow cross the Weapons Hall door.

"I think it would be better if you stayed at the top of the stairs while I went in," he said.

The girl turned a puzzled face to him.

"Why? What do you expect to find there?"

Coleridge shook his head.

"I do not know," he said almost helplessly. "Nothing, probably. But I would feel happier if you would remain in the corridor. I will leave the door open so that you can see me, and I you."

The girl smiled faintly.

"That will be something," she said gravely, as though they were old friends who could not bear to lose sight of one another. The thought gave Coleridge comfort in the midst of his bleak imaginings. They went up the short flight quickly, as though it were better to get things over with as swiftly as possible.

The girl paused at the top while the professor went on. His heart was pounding faintly, but the heavy bulk of the pistol gave him a veneer of courage he was far from feeling. The thick oak door was unlocked and opened smoothly to his touch. The room was very similar to his own, though perhaps slightly smaller. Order and precision reigned throughout. It was the atmosphere that always prevailed in establishments where servants were cheap and plentiful.

The counterpane of the bed showed not a ruckle; either the servants had been in and tidied things or Menlow had never slept there. The fire, freshly made-up, burned steadily in the grate. Coleridge saw his face as a faint yellow oval in a long mirror he passed. The panelling was so highly polished it reflected little dancing points from the fire.

Through the lattice windows with their thick edging curtains were the dark sky and the snow falling steadily; little maggots of doubt gnawed inexorably at Coleridge's soul. He shivered suddenly, forcing himself across the room. There was a great old wooden press in the corner that showed as a darker blur against the darkness of the panelling. There was a ruckling of the carpet near the door that Coleridge did not like.

He had the pistol out as his hand was on the door; little ganglions were quivering in his cheeks and throbbing at his throat. He flung the door open, his nerves excoriated by the harsh jangling of the hinges. There was stale air within, something else too: a pale, shapeless thing that came floating through the tangle of clothing that hung in the gloom.

Coleridge jumped to one side, an incoherent shout forcing itself through his lips. The torn corpse-thing that was Menlow hit the floor with a noise that seemed ripe and unwholesome. There was a lot of blood, and Coleridge had to clench his left hand so hard that he saw his own blood trickling down where his nails had scored the skin.

He heard the girl's light footsteps run toward the open door, and sanity returned to him.

"Keep back!" he shouted, his voice strong and firm now.

He went over with studied casualness and closed the door gently but firmly on her puzzled face.

"Fetch your father," he said through the panel.

He turned to the wardrobe as her footsteps died away along the corridor, but he still held the pistol ready. There was no need, really, for there was nothing else in the room, but he felt better nevertheless.

He went close to the bed and stared over at what lay on the parquet. It was then that he saw something protruding from between the stiffened fingers of the right hand.

It was just a fragment of paper, but Coleridge recognised it as the remains of the envelope in which he had put the specimen of hair and skin for Menlow's analysis.

THE COUNT'S EYES were like two glowing coals.

"What you are saying is that one of us is a murderer?"

"Or a werewolf," Coleridge said with a twisted smile.

The two sat in the smaller library room where Coleridge had been received on the first evening of his arrival, with an ashen-faced Nadia between them.

"I am afraid I have kept something from you. You must forgive me, for I did not wish to alarm anyone unnecessarily."

He had expected an angry expostulation from the Count, but it did not come. The secret sorrow still showed in the penetrating eyes beneath the shock of white hair, but his manner was calm, almost gentle, after his lack of control a few moments earlier.

"What might that be, Professor?"

Coleridge stared at the girl's lowered face. They sat in a semicircle in front of the blazing fire; it was early afternoon and snowing thickly outside now. The three of them had taken lunch apart on some pretext the Count had given the rest of the party. No-one outside these walls yet knew of Menlow's death, though the Count had despatched an urgent message to bring Colonel Anton back to the Castle.

Apparently he had discussed with Rakosi details of the wolf-hunt and had disappeared shortly after Coleridge's lecture, saying that he had urgent business. The Count had been considerably put out by this, and Coleridge would have been glad of Anton's iron authority and sound common sense on the spot. He hoped the police chief would soon put in an appearance, as he was finding the responsibility of his secret burden trying.

He felt guilt, too, about the death of Menlow, though no-one could have foreseen the dreadful outcome of his investigations. Coleridge had immediately locked the bedroom door and given the key to the Count. All they could do now was wait for Anton's arrival. The professor was so absorbed in his thoughts he had almost forgotten his host's question, and he had to repeat it before Coleridge responded.

"Menlow found something so strange, so unlooked for, beneath his microscope lens that he could hardly believe it. I felt the same myself, and I would expect the same reaction from you and your daughter."

It was very still in the room except for the thin flicker of the flames from the fire as they weaved intricate patterns on their way up the chimney set in its handsome carved mantel.

"We shall hardly know unless you tell us," Nadia Homolky put in gently.

Coleridge cleared his throat, which had suddenly become husky. He went on in a rush as if anxious to share his secret.

"Though it is a scientific impossibility according to our present state of knowledge, what Menlow's tests showed was that the specimen I gave him consisted of a wolf's fur growing through human skin. In other words, the classic hallmark of the loup-garou."

Homolky narrowed his eyes, though whether with shock or surprise Coleridge could not make out. Nadia gave a little choking cry but was then herself again.

"Incredible, isn't it?" Coleridge went on. "A real werewolf, apparently. And the last thing we expected. As you will recall, I found the sample caught on a splinter of wood in the door-panel of your daughter's room."

The Count's voice was low and controlled.

"And you believe this?"

Coleridge shrugged.

"I give the facts, as fantastic as they may seem."

The Count persisted, his long sensitive hands quivering in his lap.

"You did not see this sample yourself beneath the microscope?"

Coleridge shook his head, avoiding the girl's eye.

"So we have only Menlow's word for it. And now Menlow is dead."

Coleridge felt irritation rising within him.

"You are not questioning Menlow's sanity, I hope? I would have vouched for him. And only the lateness of the hour last night prevented me from making my personal observations."

The Count nodded.

"Quite. And where is this sample now?"

Coleridge watched his host's cigarette smoke going up straight and thin to the ceiling in the still air.

"I found the remains of the envelope in which I had placed it clutched between Menlow's stiffened fingers. It had been removed."

He looked steadily into the Count's eyes until the other's gaze involuntarily dropped.

"Which indicates to me that someone did not want that proof preserved. Whether the creature was animal or human—or half and half—is for Colonel Anton to decide."

The girl shivered suddenly, and the professor withdrew his gaze from her father to give her a sympathetic glance.

"What it does indicate to me is that Menlow spoke the truth, whatever that might mean to some of us."

He got to his feet and took a turn or two about the room, not seeing the slowly falling swathes of snow through the narrow windows.

"I am sorry this had to happen under your hospitable roof, Count. We must cancel the Congress, of course."

The Count rose with a swift movement, astonishment on his face.

"That is the last thing we must do, my dear Professor! This thing must be discounted as much as possible, to avoid alarm both within my family and among my guests and the neighbourhood. And of course it will give Colonel Anton and the police and military authorities much more freedom to track this thing down."

There was iron in the voice now.

"We must give out that Menlow died of a heart attack. My servant did not go near the bed. We shall say that the body was lying at the side of the bed and so was not noticed by my man."

His eyes swept from Coleridge to his daughter and then back again.

"The Congress must go on!" he said firmly. "We all need distraction under these terrible circumstances."

He lowered his voice suddenly, his eyes fixed on the falling flakes of snow outside.

"And there is a very practical side to all this. Whatever killed Menlow is still within the walls of the Castle. Anton would never let anyone leave until the investigations are concluded and the whole matter cleared up."

There was a sudden babble of voices as Coleridge came into the large panelled room where his colleagues were having afterlunch liqueurs. He found Raglan at his side, his face white and drawn. Rakosi's eyes were on him from the far side of the room.

"Dreadful news about Menlow! I thought something had happened to Miss Homolky."

Despite his tension and preoccupations Coleridge felt a wry amusement at the last words. Even amidst the seriousness of the present situation young Raglan could not keep the jealousy from his voice. He shook his head.

"No, there is nothing wrong. Her father needed her to take notes for Colonel Anton. There will have to be an official inquiry, of course. But it is undoubtedly heart failure."

Raglan fell back, his clear-cut features expressing relief.

"The Congress is cancelled, of course," said Shaw, disappointment mingling with regret in his voice. There was pain too, and he was still limping badly. His silver hair gleamed in the lamplight.

Coleridge shook his head, stilling the buzz of conversation as he raised his hand. He caught the piercing eyes of the old Countess on him; she sat in a place of honour near the fireplace, presiding at the silver-plated coffee pot.

"The Count and I have decided—with your approval, of course—that the Congress should continue. I think it is what Dr. Menlow would have wished. All respect will be observed, naturally."

There was relief on their faces now. Tragic as even an ordinary sudden death would have been, Coleridge could well understand their feelings; they had come endless miles in primitive conditions for this gathering. It was only natural that they should wish to continue, and it was perfectly true that Menlow himself would not have desired otherwise. They were enthusiasts to a man, like all those who followed specialised pursuits.

There was a general murmur of consent, and avoiding further questions Coleridge worked his way to Abercrombie's side as soon as he had the opportunity. They had decided to confide in him alone for the time being; there had to be proper medical authority consulted in the case, and from what the professor had heard the big, bearded Scot was one of the best men in his field.

And his qualifications would be undoubtedly higher than those of an obscure Hungarian village practitioner who would not be specially trained in police work. Coleridge had checked on Abercrombie from the Count's records in the extensive library archives, as he had on all those speaking at the Castle gathering, and he was well qualified to find out exactly how Menlow had met his death.

There was nothing but polite assent on his face as he listened to Coleridge's request.

"I shall be delighted to do what I can to assist the authorities, of course," he said crisply. "But I naturally have no surgical instruments with me."

"Anton has brought a medical bag from the local doctor's equipment," Coleridge told him. "I understand you will find everything you require there. And the Count's extensive laboratory facilities are available for any medical analysis you may wish to make."

"Very well," said Abercrombie.

He put down his coffee cup and wiped his lips fastidiously with a silk handkerchief he took from his coat-sleeve. Once outside the door Coleridge drew his colleague into the shadows of a secluded corridor. They walked slowly down while Coleridge wondered how he could broach the subject. He made up his mind quickly.

"This is a highly confidential matter, Doctor. I would like your word that you will keep everything you learn within the next five minutes strictly to yourself."

Abercrombie gave him a piercing glance.

"You have it," he said after a perceptible hesitation.

"This is not a normal death," Coleridge said. "I have the Count's and Colonel Anton's authority in making this request. We have no wish to alarm the neighbourhood. It is also imperative that the Congress continue. If it did not, it would be necessary to detain everyone here, by force of law if necessary."

Abercrombie smiled briefly in his beard.

"You intrigue me, Professor. It is something serious, then?"

The two men were walking down the corridor a little more quickly now, and their footsteps were magnified and reechoed by the flagstones.

Coleridge nodded.

"Very serious indeed, Doctor. Certainly murder. Perhaps something even more atrocious, if that can be imagined."

Abercrombie shot him a glance in which incredulity was overlaid with distaste.

"You will have to be more precise, Professor."

"I intend to be, Doctor," Coleridge said.

The two men had stopped as though by some obscure process of telepathy. The burly, bearded Scot provided an immensely reassuring presence to his companion; as comforting in its way as the heavy metal and walnut of the revolver in his inner pocket. The corridor was dark and chill, the flagstones seeming damp underfoot, though that was obviously imagination; they were high up here and the flags had been laid over heavy timber flooring, no doubt for durability against the constant wear of the feet of marching men-at-arms when the earlier Homolkys had kept their own private armies in ancient days.

Coleridge again thought of the sealed dungeons the Count had described, which added even more sombre tints to his racing imagination. The far door opened then, letting a shaft of light into the velvet shadow, and a servant came out.

Coleridge drew his colleague closer in to the panelled wall as though he feared something from the man's intrusion. It was partly to do with the atmosphere of the Castle; and he could not dismiss from his mind the naked savagery of those wolf-eyes.

"Anton inclines to murder," he went on. "He is not a medically trained man, of course, and neither am I. So I do not know what to make of the wounds on poor Menlow's body except the obvious factor that he died a violent, unnatural death."

Abercrombie nodded, licking fleshy lips beneath the thick beard, his eyes registering shock.

"How had he died?" he said. "It must have been a terrible experience as you found the body. Did you notice?"

Coleridge shivered slightly. The retreating servant's footsteps died out round the angle of the corridor.

"The throat was torn out. I would put that as the cause of death. Coupled with shock and loss of blood, of course."

Abercrombie stood very still, his head on one side as though he were thinking deeply.

"You know a wolf kills in a very noisy and messy manner," he said softly, an almost dreamy expression in his shadowed eyes. "And the idea of a wolf being able to penetrate the living quarters of this Castle is preposterous."

Coleridge stared at him without saying anything. The big man went on after a moment or two as though he were alone and delivering a monologue.

"The idea of a werewolf is equally ridiculous."

Coleridge felt a sudden stab of amusement.

"Is that not rather a strange remark for a folklorist?"

The burly Scot shook his head, little sparks glinting in his eyes.

"I thought we had already discussed this in general terms, Professor. We are folklorists, yes. Gathered at this Castle for the specific purpose of studying, exchanging ideas, and delivering learned papers."

Coleridge moved his feet uneasily on the floor. The flags seemed to exude a chill which was penetrating to the very bone.

"You have not answered my question, Doctor."

Abercrombie cleared his throat with a deep rasping noise. The sound was an ugly one and appeared to rouse vibrating echoes in the dark, dusty corners of the long corridor.

"We are dealing in folklore, Professor. Not folk-fact. You and I both know that most of these legends, as interesting as they are, are merely legends. Stories, if you like, handed down orally over the centuries from mother to daughter, father to son."

"But there is a basis of truth in many of them," Coleridge persisted.

Abercrombie drew himself up to his full height and looked at Coleridge seriously.

"I wonder you do not cast silver bullets for that pistol you are carrying in your pocket."

Coleridge smiled somewhat shamefacedly.

"You noticed it, did you?" he said lamely.

Abercrombie nodded, his eyes hooded.

"I am trained to notice things."

Then his manner softened, and he put a strong hand on the other's arm.

"But I do not blame you after such an experience. Only I should not make its presence too obvious. Some of our companions may be more nervous than I."

"No-one could describe you as nervous," Coleridge said. "But if a wolf did not kill Menlow, nor a werewolf, what are we left with?"

Abercrombie displayed a strange twisted smile.

"Murder, perhaps. The thought had no doubt crossed your own mind."

He started walking toward the far door.

"But let us just try to find out, shall we?"

The Man From Yesterday

IT WAS QUIET on the gallery. Coleridge went down the shelves, his nerves soothed by the mellow ticking of the clock on the floor below. He was on the flying gallery of the smaller library room where he and the Count and Nadia had spoken earlier. Like the others, he was awaiting the result of Abercrombie's examination of Menlow's remains.

It had already been an hour, and there had been no word; the big Scot was nothing if not thorough, Coleridge mused. Colonel Anton sat as though sunk in deep thought at the circular walnut table near the fire below, but the professor could see that he was covering page after page of his notebook with scribbled annotations.

Now and again the door would open as one or other of his officers came and went after making their reports. There were several of them within the Castle now, but their unobtrusive presence among the servants was not unusual where there had been a sudden death, and they all knew that an inquiry was pending.

Coleridge had not quite caught the term, but he had gathered it was equivalent to an inquest in England and a coroner's autopsy in his own country. It would not be for a week, at any rate; then the truth would have to come out.

The Count was due to join them in the library as soon as Abercrombie had concluded his preliminary examinations. Menlow's body had been covered and discreetly removed to an outbuilding. Abercrombie would find it cold work this weather, Coleridge thought, and then realised that an autopsy called for such conditions; his brain was not functioning properly at the moment.

It was probably something to do with the shock to his nervous system of the events of the past few days. The amazing thing was that, remote from himself and Nadia, the normal life of the Castle went on about them, the true state of affairs unsuspected and unobserved by the staff and Coleridge's colleagues.

The Count was worried, of course, and horrified. Anton suspected murder; while to the others Menlow had simply died of heart failure. Of all the people within the walls of Castle Homolky, only Coleridge, Nadia, and Menlow had had a real glimpse of the truth. Homolky and Anton had been told, but they were sceptics: their minds would move within the orbits of accepted experience, their theories encompassed wild beasts or simple murder.

Coleridge did not blame them. Madness might lie any other way, and he felt far from sane today. Abercrombie was another factor; with his vast knowledge of folklore and his undoubted skill as a doctor he might well penetrate to the truth of the matter, which would provide at once a working hypothesis and a plausible theory for Menlow's death. Coleridge did not wish to think anymore. For a moment he was even sorry that the throbbing ache in his shoulder and ribs had stopped.

At least the nagging pain took his mind off the black thoughts that had been crowding in over the past two days. The image of the girl, clear and bright, was the one sane and reassuring thing in the surrounding gloom.

That and the strength and purpose of such people as Homolky, Anton, and Abercrombie, who would surely come up with some solution to this dark affair. And Rakosi, of course. He was at that moment organising another wolf-drive in the area surrounding the Castle, perhaps hoping to flush out the beast responsible for the local deaths in the wooded area immediately adjacent to the village.

He might well kill the wolf. He was competent enough, Coleridge reflected, but even if he did, it would not lift the horror that was beginning to cloud the very air over Castle Homolky. That was a decidedly deeper and far more bizarre business altogether. He went down the bookshelves quietly, his feet making hardly any noise on the parquet, careful not to disturb Colonel Anton. He could not communicate with him in any event.

But the Count had given Coleridge carte blanche to examine anything in his personal library, and the latter, intrigued with the legends of Ivan the Bold and the dungeons beneath the Castle, was glad to turn his thoughts in another direction. Even if the tales and myths were as equally bloody as the present events, at least they were comfortingly remote in time.

He paused in front of a long set of elaborately bound volumes in brown leather with gold titles on the spines. They were in Hungarian, so Coleridge could not make them out, but a brief examination of the contents of one proved them to be on the Count's own subject of folklore, for there were rough woodcuts of vampiric presences, autos-da-fé, witch-trials, and mass hangings.

These were the commonplaces of Coleridge's studies, and he examined the set with particular interest. He saw that they had been printed at Pest in the mid–eighteenth century, judging by the paper, typography, and style. They were extremely rare and would be priceless, though useless for his scholarship purposes unless one knew the language.

He remained absorbed for some minutes, his mind diverted from the cruelties of the present circumstances to bygone cruelties of an even less tolerant age. He felt rather in limbo for the moment; he frowned at the drifting snowflakes which showed up clearly against the leaden sky as they fell past the big windows set high in the opposite wall.

On the gallery here they were on the same level, and he had a magnificent view of the sheer walls of Castle Homolky: sweeping buttresses, spires, turrets and crenellated battlements, with here and there a glassed-in arrow-slit, and the walls themselves falling breathlessly to the moat, for this portion of the Castle faced the entrance road and the huddled mass of Lugos at the foot.

He replaced the big leather volume absently and moved on, his eyes roving restlessly across the shelves. The sheer weight and number of volumes here with hundreds of gold-embossed titles stretching to the far distance had a hypnotic effect, and Coleridge paused in a sort of embrasure between two sets of shelving. There was an ancient desk here, with an embroidered stool in front of it and on the wall faded photographs in silver frames.

Coleridge sank down gratefully, and, after a glance at the absorbed figure of Colonel Anton at his table near the fire, he again idly turned his attention to the desk and the photographs. There were a great many of them, and they seemed to be old family pictures on which the owner put a great deal of value. Coleridge guessed then with almost absolute certainty that this portion of the gallery had been a favourite spot of the old Countess in earlier years.

It commanded a spectacular view of both the library and the Castle and village beyond; it was quiet and secluded, and when the view tired she would have been able to settle down to her letter-writing undistracted. It did not take Coleridge long to reach these conclusions, for the photographs in the silver frames told their own story.

They were of an earlier style and epoch, and the old Countess undoubtedly featured in many of them; as Coleridge had guessed she had been a great beauty. Here she was at the age of eighteen or so dressed in hunting costume, on horseback, with the frowning mass of the Castle in the background. Another, of the same period, showed a summer family picnic with the falls in the valley below as a striking setting.

Coleridge wondered if the golden-haired little boy who appeared in a number of studies was their host in his tender years; it appeared entirely possible, though it was difficult to associate the two images. The pictures evidently covered a wide span of years, for here was a more sedate but still striking Countess driving a dog-cart; and another more formal study, with the family in front and the servants massed in the background, showed an unmistakable Count Homolky as a young man in a fashionable tweed suit and dark homburg, flanked by his mother and father.

Coleridge wondered why Countess Irina still kept all these things here. Surely she would now be too old to mount the steps to the gallery. Then he remembered she had first received him in the library below, and perhaps there was some access to this gallery which did not necessitate using the spiral staircase up which he had just climbed. Normally, Coleridge would not have sat at someone else's desk in this manner, but there were no personal documents or letters on its cool green leather surface; it was the pictures which absorbed him.

Like a jigsaw puzzle only half-completed by its owner, their fading surfaces and brown pigmentation seemed to hold enigmatic secrets waiting to be solved. Coleridge then saw that there were several newer photographs which stood on a small ledge at the back of the desk. It was obvious they were taken more recently because of the styles of clothing, and the matter was clinched by the factor that the Countess looked a good deal older.

There was one which particularly absorbed him. It showed a young man with a smiling face and a luxuriant beard who stood flanked by a young girl at his left hand and the Countess on his right.

They were smiling into the camera lens as though the photographer had just said something that amused them; Coleridge could see the man's shadow sharp-etched on the dusty ground at their feet. It might even have been the Count who had taken the picture. Or were the three of them sharing some secret joke? It was impossible to tell at this distance in time.

Coleridge was still sitting there staring at the photograph when a shadow fell across the glass. He looked up with a start to find the tall figure of the Count on the balcony behind him. He looked like a ghostly metamorphosis of his youthful self until Coleridge had adjusted his eyesight. But Homolky merely sighed quietly.

"Interesting, are they not, Professor Coleridge?"

Coleridge felt a quick flash of the old embarrassment. He got up swiftly.

"Forgive my idle curiosity, Count. I could not help admiring the desk and was passing the time by glancing at the photographs."

The Count smiled. It was a smile of peculiar sadness as well as sweetness, and once again the guest was struck by the sharpness of his teeth.

"It is my mother's desk, as you have probably guessed. She often used to sit here writing letters, particularly on summer evenings, when we would have the big windows open. A striking woman when young, was she not?"

Coleridge nodded. He saw now that his earlier supposition had been right. Homolky had come from another room or corridor at the end of the balcony behind him, for the door giving access still stood half-ajar. That reminded Coleridge he had intended asking the girl to draw him a rough sketch-map of the Castle and its principal rooms.

Its strange layout, with odd corners and unsuspected corridors, resembled a rabbit-warren and might be vitally important in the present circumstances when, as Coleridge suspected, deadly danger appeared to be overhanging the occupants.

"She is still a handsome lady," he concurred.

The Count smiled again, more naturally this time, glancing down at the police chief, who had not stirred; he went on methodically writing in his notebook at the table below.

"And a wilful one."

His glance returned to the desk and the pictures.

"You will forgive me for saying so, but you seemed inordinately interested in that photograph there."

He tapped with his forefinger on the glass of the study depicting his mother and the young couple Coleridge had already noted.

"The young man's face seemed somehow familiar."

Homolky shook his head, a spasm of what might have been pain swiftly passing across his mobile features, to be erased in a fraction as though it had never been.

"I do not think so, Professor," he said gently. "That photograph has a tragic history. I do not really know why my mother let it remain there, unless as a sort of penance."

Coleridge felt his curiosity quicken.

"Penance, Count?"

Homolky put up his strong hand to stroke his jaw as the two men stood immobile at the edge of the balcony, the falling flakes of snow beyond the window making a bleak background to their conversation.

"My mother was very fond of this young couple. The man was an English doctor, who was said to have a brilliant future. He too had an interest in folklore, particularly the dark legends of these mountains. He was engaged to be married to the young English lady in the picture."

A nerve twitched at the corner of the tall man's mouth as he glanced again at the faded image.

"One might almost say that this moment in time, captured by the shutter of my camera, was the end of happiness for the four people involved."

Coleridge felt all sorts of questions starting to his mind, but he discreetly kept silent, waiting for his host to go on.

"There was a terrible accident," the Count continued without prompting. "The very day after the photograph was taken. It was summertime, and my mother was out driving in the dog-cart. She was coming very fast down the hill leading to the village, which was her way. Somehow she lost control, and the horse bolted."

He paused, licking his lips.

"The doctor and his fiancée were out walking at the foot of the hill, on their way back to the Castle. He managed to jump aside. The young lady was killed."

There was a long silence on the balcony. Coleridge averted his eyes from the Count's, looked again at the blank, happy faces in the photograph.

"You can imagine the effect, the remorse of my mother and the whole family. The reaction was even worse in the case of the young doctor. In the agony of his grief he accused my mother of murder. He swore vengeance, then collapsed. He had a nervous breakdown, and my mother paid his medical expenses and his fare back to England. The last we heard he was confined in a lunatic asylum. My mother specifically asked for that photograph when they arrived back from development, then had the frame made for it and insisted on placing it on the desk in front of her."

A faint shudder passed through Coleridge. He again had a quick flash of the Countess's austere, ravaged face.

"A dreadful story," he said quietly. "You have my deepest sympathy. I would not have asked had I known."

The Count shook his head impatiently.

"It was twenty years ago, Professor. Besides, I volunteered the information. I would not have done so had the subject been taboo to me."

He looked grimly down at the police official working by the fire. He seemed as remote and efficient as though he were operating in another country altogether.

"My mother has suffered, Professor Coleridge, make no mistake about it. But she has a tremendous sense of duty. And she feels it only just that she should have suffered so for a momentary act of carelessness which, you might say, destroyed three lives. Therefore, the photograph remains."

Both men were silent for long moments as though each were absorbed in thoughts of such a sombre nature that they could not be uttered aloud. Coleridge turned away from his host and again studied the photograph which was the subject of their conversation. The smiling, happy faces of the hostess and her two guests—one so soon to be dead, the other hopelessly insane—were cruelly ironic under the circumstances.

Coleridge could still not quite see what obscure motives had driven the old Countess to have it framed and placed there where she could study it every day. It could not be remorse only, surely. But the human heart was like a series of interlocking membranes, on each of which was inscribed some dim and cryptic thought or deed, and the more one peeled off layer after layer the less one penetrated to the heart of the mystery.

He had long ago come to that conclusion as a result of his own researches into the human mind through the arcane world of folklore, and it was something which continued to baffle and frustrate even the trained observer.

But he knew now, again transferring his gaze to the Count, something of at least one strand making up the secret sorrow he had sensed in the Count's own refined and brooding features. They were still standing there when a dark-uniformed official on the colonel's staff entered the room below and saluted the latter, who looked up from his task at the table.

The two men held a muffled conversation which the Count followed with increasing satisfaction. He nodded as the man went out the far door.

"Preparations for the wolf-hunt are complete, Professor. Captain Rakosi and all officers and men who can be spared will beat the woods from the north, entering from the road some five or six miles distant, and drive the beasts on to our guns."

He looked at Coleridge hesitantly.

"I hope I can rely on you, Professor. I can promise we will shoot only those brutes which are suspect. We are looking for the big wolf which the colonel tried to shoot."

"You can rely on me," Coleridge said shortly.

The Count wore a satisfied expression.

"Excellent. We shall go tomorrow under any conditions except those of a blizzard. But all the signs point to the fact that the snow will stop before morning."

The two men were descending the staircase to meet Colonel Anton at the foot when the library door opened to admit the grim-faced figure of Abercrombie.

A Face From the Past

"WE MUST SEARCH the Castle from top to bottom!"

The Count's voice was vibrating with surprise and anger. He took his glass of cognac and drained it at a gulp. Colonel Anton stood grave and silent with his back to the fire. He spoke little or no English and waited patiently until the Count should see fit to translate the gist of their remarks.

"You astonish me with your conclusions, Doctor," the Count said.

"This is an astonishing business," Coleridge put in. "You say it was definitely a wolf?"

Abercrombie nodded.

"I am familiar with their habits," he said. "And my folklore researches in my own particular subjects, together with my medical reading on the wounds inflicted on persons killed by wolf-packs, have made me tolerably *au fait* with the methods employed. Menlow was killed when attacked by a wolf, there is no doubt about it."

The Count gave a swift glance at Anton, who momentarily lifted his eyelids but otherwise gave no audible sign of life.

"You incline to murder, then?"

Abercrombie shook his head.

"The attack was that of a wild beast, however improbable that may seem within the walls of the Castle. You were not mistaken in what you say, Professor."

He smiled thinly.

"My examinations today have been nothing if not varied. I have just been called to examine Shaw, which was why I was delayed. He was in some pain, and I have given him something for it. His ankle is swollen like a balloon, but cold compresses should bring it down within the next few days. Though he must keep off his feet as much as possible."

Coleridge seized this unexpected opportunity.

"There was no wound?" he said quickly, instantly regretting it.

"Wound?"

The Count could not keep the surprise from his voice.

"My apologies for being so imprecise," Coleridge told the doctor. "I meant an injury, of course. I heard that he had fallen on the stairs, and I feared blood vessels might have been involved."

Abercrombie shook his head.

"Nothing like that; merely bruising and swelling. I have sent him to bed so his absence from the remainder of today's lectures need not be construed by his colleagues as anything personal."

He was obviously relaxing with a little banter after his grim task in the cold outhouse, and Homolky went immediately to offer him more cognac while Anton moved over to make room for him in front of the fire.

"I thought you said wolves killed in a very noisy and messy manner," Coleridge put in, somewhat tactlessly. He could see the nerve twitching in their host's cheek again. Abercrombie made a little clicking noise deep in his throat, holding down the contents of his glass to the firelight.

"As a rule, yes. But the animal may have been disturbed before it could finish. No portion of the body had been consumed."

The awkward pause was broken by the Count, who explained in a few succinct sentences the import of their conversation to the Chief of Police. He nodded once or twice, muttering to himself under his breath. His puzzlement was evident, but he put his professional face on it and a moment or two later resumed his seat at the table and jotted down additional notes.

"Could someone in the Castle have let the beast in?" Coleridge asked.

"It is possible," the Count said. "But for what purpose? You are not suggesting that Menlow was murdered by a wolf acting in collaboration with a human being?"

Abercrombie smiled grimly, warming his hands at the fire.

"Even so," Coleridge persisted, "Menlow may have been killed for his knowledge. The results of his analysis were torn from his hand. You are not suggesting that the wolf may have eaten them?"

Homolky shook his head, his face set like marble.

"No, I am not suggesting that, Professor. But there is something dreadful here, which seems to be quite beyond the normal range of human knowledge."

Abercrombie looked at him sharply, his eyes gleaming above the beard. His massive presence had a calming influence on the proceedings, Coleridge thought.

"We must not exaggerate, Count," he said gently. "Who knows what is behind this. But we have to avoid a panic, either in your household or in the village. And I am confident that we can leave everything to Colonel Anton . . ."

The Count drew himself up to his full height, his white hair in startling contrast to his face, beneath the lamps.

"You are right, of course. You must forgive me, gentlemen. But you can imagine my feelings. A stain on my household. A guest has been killed beneath my roof."

"It is not your fault, sir," Abercrombie put in. "And no-one would blame you. But, as you say, an immediate search must be made."

Coleridge felt moved to intervene.

"Discreetly," he said. "This afternoon's lectures must be put back until tea-time. I suggest we make a floor-by-floor search. We will go armed and in twos."

Abercrombie nodded, his bearded face grim with determination.

"Whom would you suggest?"

"We four. And perhaps Captain Rakosi and one of his officers. We will keep Miss Homolky informed, of course. And we will need sketch plans of the building, a copy for each couple involved in the search."

"There is no difficulty in that," the Count put in. "I will make all the necessary arrangements."

He had recovered his poise now that the moment for clear-cut action had arrived. Like Coleridge himself, he was better when some definite plan had been decided upon. He went over to Anton, and the two conferred together for several minutes. Coleridge joined his colleague in front of the fireplace.

The Count was back again.

"I have made the necessary arrangements with Anton. And Rakosi is already here, as you know. My wife and daughter will draw the two copies of the plans you will need. We will visit the Weapons Hall on our way down. I take it you can use a revolver, Dr. Abercrombie."

The big Scot bowed stiffly.

"Tolerably well, Count."

He turned to Coleridge.

"Shall we make up one team, Professor?"

Homolky nodded approval.

"Ground floor, cellars, and outhouses, then. Anton and I will take the upper floors. Rakosi and his colleague the middle floors. All will be made clear from the plans, and we will work out the dispositions privately before we begin."

He paused, frowning, waiting politely while Anton closed his notebook and rose from the table. He wore a black uniform this afternoon with his epaulettes of rank, but the Star of Krasnia still glinted as a dull patch of gold on his chest. His eyes beneath the hooded lids were cold and watchful as he apprised each man in the room. It was good to have someone of his calibre at the heart of things, Coleridge felt.

Homolky was frowning as they all walked in a group toward the door.

"You say the animal you saw had a grey patch on its back, Professor?"

Coleridge nodded.

"I could not absolutely swear to it in a court of law, but that was my impression."

The Count bit his lip.

"This affair becomes more strange with every hour. The big brute which has been causing such depredations in the countryside has fur which is almost entirely black."

"You are sure you are not too tired?"

Abercrombie's eyes were solicitous as the two walked along the gloomy panelled corridor, keeping abreast. Both were armed, and though Coleridge felt slightly ridiculous over their quest in this civilised and highly frequented part of Castle Homolky, it was obvious they might have to rely on the weapons if they were confronted with the prowling beast in the more remote parts of the Castle or in one of the cavernous outhouses which flanked the courtyards.

Coleridge had told the doctor he had had only four hours' sleep the previous night, and now it was beginning to have its effect. He had been sustained by the wine and the conversation during lunch, but that euphoria was wearing off. He had decided to be open with his companion; after all, if he were less than vigilant this afternoon, their lives might depend upon his degree of alertness.

"I shall be all right," he assured his colleague. "If I feel fatigued I will let you know."

Abercrombie grunted, looking about him with a grim expression in the semitwilight. There were oil lamps burning at intervals here, but there were no windows except for those at either end of the long corridor, and strange shadows were cast across the panelling.

They had already carried out most of the Count's plan, and it seemed as though they had been walking for miles. Abercrombie paused beneath the nearest lamp and studied the inked sketch of the ground floor in Nadia Homolky's neat ruling. Coleridge had seen her only for a moment, in the company of the others, before they had set off, and they had no time for confidences; now, her solicitous look and her whispered injunction, "Take care!" were still with him, cutting through the layers of tiredness in which he was becoming enwrapped.

"This appears to be a somewhat fatuous exercise," said Abercrombie.

"Perhaps," said Coleridge cautiously. "I agree so far as the ground floor is concerned. But the cellars and outhouses are a different matter."

Abercrombie shot him a quizzical glance.

"True," he agreed. "But I suppose we have to do it, if only to satisfy the Count."

"And Colonel Anton," his companion reminded him. "He now has a murder investigation on his hands. What are your theories?"

Abercrombie looked at his companion from beneath thick, tufted eyebrows. They were at the end of the corridor now, almost opposite the great barred window. It was lighter here, and Coleridge could see that it had stopped snowing. It might clear up in time for the wolf-hunt tomorrow, after all.

The Castle was becoming a little claustrophobic; it would be good to get in the open air again. The ground floor alone must cover several acres, and he would be glad when he and the doctor had followed Colonel Anton's injunctions. At least they would then have the satisfaction of knowing that they had carried out a thorough search.

They were doing it discreetly, at any rate; the few servants they had met did not appear to think it at all strange that they should wish to inspect the spacious stone-flagged kitchens or poke about in dark closets.

Abercrombie carried his medical bag with him. Coleridge knew that it contained a dark-lantern, at least. He wondered what other surprises the burly Scot might have there. At least they would not have to face the cellars in total darkness. Homolky had indicated on the plan where the oil lanterns were; they were fitted at intervals on the walls, and the two would light them progressively as they went along.

Truth to tell, this was one aspect of their search that Coleridge was not relishing. The Count's grim tale of his ancestor and the sealed dungeons had made a deeper impression than the professor cared to admit. Now he studied the doctor's face, waiting for the answer to his question, which seemed a long time in coming.

"I?" the big man said at last.

He frowned up at the dark sky through the window opposite.

"I have no real theories. At least none that would make much sense or give any comfort to the Count at the moment. I had already given you my tentative opinion before I carried out the postmortem."

Coleridge nodded, looking reflectively at his companion's face. He saw strength and character there. But like the Count, it seemed to carry some secret sorrow. Or was he becoming altogether too fanciful in the strange mediaeval atmosphere of Castle Homolky?

"But after the postmortem," Coleridge went on. "You must at least have modified your views since then."

Abercrombie smiled. His face was completely transformed.

"I see your drift, Professor. You are implying that I did not speak all my thoughts out loud when I was making sceptical remarks earlier. Presumably, in order to save the Count and his family further distress."

Coleridge nodded.

"That was at the back of my mind, yes," he said defensively. "But if you had further thoughts on the matter they would have to come out, would they not? I was thinking of your official report to Colonel Anton."

Abercrombie wrenched his gaze from the bleak scene outside the window and fixed his companion with deep-set eyes.

"Naturally," he said affably. "There are one or two points that occurred to me. But whether this is the right moment to discuss them . . ."

"I would be glad if you would do so," Coleridge said.

The big man shrugged. They were quite alone in the corridor, and he produced the pistol the Count had loaned him from the pocket of his capacious tweed jacket and turned it over in his capable hands as the two men talked.

"Despite our antiquarian interests, Professor, I do not believe in the reality of the werewolf myth. Man into beast, silver bullets, and all that sort of thing. A real wolf, yes, though that seems unlikely. Anton is committed to the theory of murder, is he not?"

"I wish I could believe that it were something so comparatively mundane as murder," Coleridge said.

Abercrombie smiled again. With his reddish weathered face and thick eyebrows he rather resembled one of the more sombre oil paintings that decorated some of the interminable salons and public rooms that he and Coleridge had traversed in their fruitless search this afternoon.

Already dusk was imperceptibly descending outside, making their faces and those of the servants stand out as indeterminate and featureless blobs in the gloom of the corridors, stairways, and courtyards.

"Whether this be natural or supernatural, there is one thing I would commend to you, Professor."

They had quitted the corridor and, opening the large double doors in front, entered a splendid panelled room which neither man could remember having seen before. It was lit at the sides by high, slightly slanting windows that imparted something of the aspect of a cathedral, and the light spilling in from the snow on the roofs round about illuminated the magnificent hammer beams of the ceiling.

Though there was no-one there and would probably not be, perhaps for many days, there was a huge fire burning in the immense stone fireplace, which was surrounded by superb carved panelling.

Large oil paintings marched into obscurity down both walls of the room, which tapered, leading to a gallery at the far end. There were polished refectory-type tables set about down the centre on the softly glowing parquet of the floor, and on them, carelessly piled catalogues and volumes which might relate, Coleridge thought, to the Homolky family's treasures which were scattered about the Castle in equally careless profusion.

"This is certainly more cheerful," Abercrombie observed. "The Count's art gallery, perhaps?"

Coleridge agreed.

"The whole place is an art gallery or museum of one sort or another. You were just about to commend something to me."

The two men paused in the centre of the room, conscious that their footsteps were making unpleasant echoes in the far corners of the vast chamber.

"Motive, Professor," the doctor said enigmatically. "Whether Menlow's death be due to natural or supernatural causes, there must be motive and purpose in it."

Coleridge thought again of the remains of the analysis envelope clutched in Menlow's stiffening fingers. Motive enough there, he would have thought. Abercrombie alone did not yet know of this, or he might not be so sceptical. But there was good sense in what his companion was saying, and he listened carefully.

"Once we establish the motive and purpose," Abercrombie went on, "that may well lead us to the perpetrator of this horrible crime."

Coleridge assented.

"Then you do not think these deaths have anything to do with the great wolf which has been terrorising the village and killing local people? Or the wolf I saw in the Castle corridor?"

Abercrombie shook his head.

"I think we have two things here. Perhaps someone within the Castle let the beast in to confuse matters."

"But you yourself said Menlow's death was due to a wolf," Coleridge persisted.

Abercrombie rubbed the edge of his nose with a great finger.

"So I did, Professor, so I did," he said gently. "But I have not entirely revealed my thoughts on the matter. And it does not invalidate my theory on motive and opportunity. We must watch our companions carefully."

He glanced out the side-windows.

"Judging by the features of the buildings surrounding the courtyard, we have come full circle. It is time to visit the cellars."

His words struck a chill into Coleridge, who watched silently as his companion produced and lit his dark-lantern.

"A fatuous exercise, as I have already observed," Abercrombie went on, trimming the lamp to his satisfaction. "We should certainly have heard something from the servants before now had the beast been prowling these corridors. And if it is supernatural . . ."

He smiled broadly. The two men walked down the long gallery, their feet slapping echoes from the boards. There was none of the Count's electric light in here, only elaborate oil lamps standing on tables and in niches, and the large candle chandelier, though none were lit. Coleridge longed for the brilliant comfort of electric light. The labyrinthine corridors with their shadowy gloom were beginning to oppress his spirits, and more than once he fancied he had seen the pinpoints of animal eyes lurking at the foot of beams or buttresses.

But the yellow rays of Abercrombie's lantern and the doctor's massive presence gave comfort. He paused at the far door, and while he fumbled with the latch the light beams strayed aside, sweeping across a face with tangled hair and wide eyes which seemed so real and vivid that Coleridge almost cried out. He bit his lip and then saw that it was an oil painting, so cunningly recreated from the original by the unknown artist that it seemed to start from its heavy gilt frame.

The lips had a perpetual sneer upon them, and the eyes were so implacable and full of hatred that they appeared to follow the two men all the way down the corridor outside.

"Now for the cellars," Abercrombie repeated.

Coleridge hardly heard him. The eyes and that vicious mouth could belong to only one person in the Count's long ancestry. As Abercrombie struggled at a massive iron-studded door in a bleak stone corridor, Coleridge knew that he had beheld the face of Ivan the Bold.

The Cellars

BE CAREFUL THERE! These steps are loose."

Abercrombie's admonition came too late. Coleridge felt his heel grate on the crumbling block, which moved away, almost sending him headlong. His fingertips scraped frantically across the curving wall, drawing blood.

Then the big Scot had him firmly by the collar with his left hand, the beam of the dark-lantern dancing across the steep descent that looked as though it might lead to hell itself, so black and forbidding did it seem to Coleridge's somewhat fevered imagination. Then he had recovered himself, slightly out of breath.

"Thank you," he said gratefully, his legs trembling slightly.

But there was firm stone beneath him, and as his companion held the lantern downward across the next half-dozen treads, their surface worn into runnels by the passing feet of centuries, he could now see that the way ahead was clear.

"It was fortunate I saw you in time," Abercrombie said drily.

His face, heavily shadowed, appeared vague and insubstantial in the dim light; the black beard powdered with grey at the edges looking as though it were carved in metal. He held the lantern high with a courteous gesture as the two men walked more slowly abreast, keeping their eyes down at their feet.

Soon, a few steps farther, they came upon a lantern standing on a heavy oak bracket set into the wall. The doctor stopped to light it, and by the stronger illumination they could see down to the next curve where a similar lamp was set. Beyond that was velvet darkness.

They descended deliberately, taking their time, each man absorbed in his own thoughts. Their feet made sharp, almost furtive scrapings on the stone blocks, and now and again small particles of grit or crumbling stonework produced little pattering noises which trickled from step to step in front of them, as though something invisible were scampering ahead. The simile was an unpleasant one, and Coleridge quickly dismissed it from his mind.

There was a mouldering smell in here as of the crypt; it was compounded equally of the spicy odour which ancient stone appeared to emanate and of dust, earth, and cobwebs. He wondered idly whether cobwebs did, in fact, give off any smell; but the atmosphere in here certainly brought them to mind.

They had long ago lost to sight the mighty wooden door they had left open at the top of the flight, and now, as they went farther and farther down, the round stair, following gentle curves, seemed to lead them imperceptibly on and the great stone blocks of the curving wall at their left were as massive and as high as a prison.

Oddly enough, the wall at their right was straight, which seemed to infer that they were beneath the main body of the Castle and not under one of the towers.

"Curious, is it not?" Abercrombie observed heavily, stopping to light a second lamp.

It appeared as though he had read Coleridge's mind accurately, and for a moment the savant was startled. He waited while Abercrombie replaced the lighted vessel on the bracket, reassured by the springing back of the shadows but still conscious of the subterranean depths to which they must still descend.

"Don Juan in Hell?" the Scot continued jovially, glancing at his companion.

Coleridge smiled.

"I do not quite follow . . ." he began.

Abercrombie shrugged.

"It merely seemed a long way to go to bring up a bottle of wine for the Count's dinner. Unless he has a more convenient pantry upstairs."

He was making conversation, and Coleridge guessed that he too was beginning to find the atmosphere oppressive. They went on then and traversed three more curving flights, each bend being served by a solitary lamp on a bracket, and each of which was carefully lit in turn by Abercrombie.

Coleridge was conscious that he had a damp patch of perspiration on his forehead. He guessed it originated in the shock he had received on his narrow escape from falling. It also denoted how warm it was down here relative to the rest of the Castle. There must be thirty or forty degrees of temperature difference in comparison with the open air outside.

They had paused now while the doctor lit the last of the lamps and found themselves on what looked like a vast slab of stone; a sort of platform bounded by a metal railing which had evidently been added in modern times, for the metal was painted a shiny black which gave off gleams in the lamplight as though it were wet.

For some moments Coleridge had been aware of another noise which he could not quite place. The air smelt mouldy, almost damp here, and it had a sickening charnel smell which reminded the professor of a badly tended graveyard he had once encountered in a remote part of Italy during the winter months.

Then he heard it again: the slow drip of water, like a thin thread, giving off a monotonous liquid beat in the velvet darkness. His expression must have been strained or startled because Abercrombie gave a short, harsh laugh which sent the echoes flying.

"Water, Professor! You forget we are beneath the moat here. I do not know how deep it is, but we are obviously under the outer wall and a long way below the ice which binds the surface."

Coleridge did not say anything for a moment. Somehow, the fact that they were below water level made the place seem even more dank and ominous. How deep—and how secret, then!—

must be that dreadful dungeon of Ivan the Bold which Homolky had had bricked up all those years ago, as it must lie at some fearful depth in the eternal darkness and silence still so far below them.

He shook off such thoughts with an effort and followed Abercrombie, who was already clattering down a small straight stair made of heavy wood, clutching the handrail firmly with his disengaged hand while he shone the beam of the lantern curiously about with the other.

By its feeble light Coleridge could see massive wooden casks and timber racks of an ancient pattern that stretched out before them, creating aisles that ran forward until they were lost in the far distance of this dark, arched vault. Away to the left there were huge buttresses of smooth-fitting hewn stone blocks, and these Romanesque architectural features ran up in liquid curves to support the arched stone roof far above their heads.

The worn flooring was dry and dusty, and there were the marks of many feet in the dust, no doubt made by the Count's servants as they went to and from the bins and casks to draw whatever was needed for the huge household above. At any other time Coleridge would have been deeply interested in these social minutiae, but his racing thoughts had a distracting effect and he had time for only cursory glances as he cautiously followed the burly back of Abercrombie.

This was a sinister place for such a search as that on which the couple were engaged, and he wondered for a moment why the Count had insisted on the pair of them coming here. It was an unworthy thought, but it indicated to Coleridge how far his experiences within the Castle walls had corrupted his sensibilities and made him suspicious of almost everyone and everything in the circumstances in which he found himself.

There were no brackets or oil lamps within the main cellar area so far as he could see, and it seemed to go on for a vast extent, judging by the faint pattering echoes of their progress which reverberated beneath the arches for an interminably long time before dying out.

It would obviously be disastrous for the two men to separate in here, apart from its impracticability, for one would be without light, and Coleridge instinctively moved closer to his companion. He had drawn his pistol now, a movement which was not lost on Abercrombie because he gave the professor a wry glance.

"A bad place, eh?"

Coleridge nodded.

"I have not seen worse under the given circumstances. It is the perfect area for an animal to hide. Providing it was well fed, it could survive down here for a long time."

Abercrombie held the dark-lantern high, sweeping its beam across a great rack of barrels that barred their path.

"You are right. A wolf can go many days without food and suffer no ill effects. And it could drink from there."

He moved across, into a sort of aisle that ran at right-angles between the line of great pillars and the racks of casks and barrels ahead. The dripping noise was louder now, and as they advanced closer to the side of the vault they could see the lamplight gleam on green slime and a pool of stagnant water that had formed in a runnel where the rough stone floor at the side met the curve of the wall.

Abercrombie moved the lantern beam, tracing the damp area upward to where small beads of water glistened in a crack overhead.

The doctor grunted.

"There has obviously been subsidence at some time, and the pressure on the vault arch has made that crack, allowing a certain amount of seepage from the moat."

He grunted again, sweeping the beam about in a wider arc.

"I should not think it is of any importance, or the Count would have had buttressing put in hand."

He shrugged.

"But we are forgetting our purpose here."

He turned back, and the two men were then confronted by another steep stone stair that led below and which was bordered by a rickety-looking wooden guardrail.

"It is a pity we have no twine or chalk," Abercrombie muttered. "We could then be sure we had searched everywhere."

"Why not keep to this side-wall and work our way up and down the aisles until we have covered the entire area," Coleridge suggested.

Abercrombie nodded in agreement. He was already descending the stair, the lantern beam stabbing nervously in all directions. Coleridge prepared to follow. He saw that the wall at their right was now pierced by worm-eaten wooden doorways that hung askew on great iron hinges of an antique pattern.

His nerves were scalded by a sudden splintering noise. He was just in time to see the wooden handrail give way beneath Abercrombie's massive hand. The big Scot emitted a strangled cry, and then he had fallen toward the wall. He struck the nearest wooden door with a tremendous impact and all his considerable weight.

Coleridge moved forward quickly to see the door splinter inward amid a cloud of dust and his companion disappear. The lantern, falling from his hand, clattered several times on the floor, and the cellar was then plunged into the darkness of the tomb.

With beating heart Coleridge moved cautiously down the staircase on his knees, one tread at a time. An unearthly blackness seemed to press on the eyelids with a physical force. The deathly quiet, broken only by the occasional drip of water, seared the nerve-ends. He had not heard one sound or cry from Abercrombie after the door had given way beneath him; nothing except the faintest slithering as though his unfortunate companion had been hurried to bottomless depths.

He could feel perspiration trickling down into his eyes. He moved slowly but precisely; he had had one split-second vision of the dark-lantern before it had been extinguished in the fall. If he could not find it, he feared for his sanity under these conditions so far beneath the Castle and remote from help. He had a box of matches in his pocket and hoped to relight the lantern and make a search for Abercrombie.

He might be lying injured now not so very far from him, and it was certain that Coleridge was the only man able to help. As he moved gingerly down, searching with his right hand for the splintered end of the wooden railing where it had broken away beneath his colleague's weight, he fumbled awkwardly with his left to remove the Count's pistol from his inside jacket pocket.

It was then that he detected the faint scratching noise, like the sound of claws on flagstones. He had heard it before, and fear coursed through his veins. In that drear place and in the pitch darkness its connotations were enough to unseat the mind, and he fought for control, the trembling fingers of his left hand at length throwing off the safety-catch of the pistol.

The crisp click gave him courage, and he quickly scrabbled to the bottom of the steps. The lantern had been lying at the foot of one of the great wooden casks, and he moved his fingers across the floor in a hesitant arc, almost as though he feared to find fur beneath his hand. The noise he had made had overlaid any further sounds from the vault, and he went swiftly on with his search, deliberately making as much commotion as possible, with black fear gibbering at his elbow.

Relief flooded through him as he felt the warm metal of the lantern at last; it seemed to be unbroken. He put the pistol down quickly, searched frantically in his jacket pocket for the matches. The scratch of the match-head sounded like an explosion, and the resultant yellow flare almost blinded him. He lit the wick with shaking fingers, sweat pouring into his eyes. The yellow light threw the barrels and overhead vaulting into sharp relief, and the shadows jumped backward.

A low snarling noise greeted the light, but Coleridge's nerves were equal to it now. He had the pistol up ready, his hand none too steady. Two pinpoints like eyes at an angle almost opposite made his heart jump in his chest until he saw that it was the beam of the lantern shining on the necks of two bottles. He trimmed the wick until he had the maximum light and then replaced the metal-and-glass shutter, shining the beam in a wide arc as he got shakily to his feet.

Then he called Abercrombie's name several times over, ignoring the thunderous echo of his own voice beneath the arches, straining his ears to catch any response in the dead silence which followed.

He still held the box of matches awkwardly in the same hand as that in which he had the lantern, with the pistol in his left. It was the work of a moment to transfer the pistol to his right. He put the lantern down for a second on one of the transverse beams of the rack holding the casks. He stared at the matchbox unseeingly, the echoes of his shouts still reverberating in his ears.

The box reminded him that he had not smoked a cigar for several days, not since the girl had come to him with her terrifying news, in fact.

It was one of those curious, rather ridiculous pieces of information which jumped to one's mind at difficult moments; perhaps the human psyche blanking off disastrous events with trivia, probably in order to protect the brain. He put the box back into his pocket, moving across to where he had last seen Abercrombie. The place where the door had been now gaped as a black hole in the side-wall.

He froze in midstep as another of those savage snarls echoed and reechoed beneath the vaulted ceiling. It came from the area of blackest shadow that stretched in front of him, between two dusty racks of casks.

He lifted the lantern from the beam with his left hand, bringing up the pistol with his right. His fingers were still trembling slightly so that the yellow beam seemed to shudder and slither over the shadowy ceiling groynes without really picking out detail. But Coleridge's nerves jumped again as he saw, or thought he saw, two tiny red spots near ground-level at the end of the aisle. He heard the faint scratching and clicking noise on the stone floor that he had experienced before; a furtive, secretive sound that seemed to lacerate the nerves.

This would not do. Coleridge decided against following the beast farther into the vault; whatever it was, it would have to come to him. He was comparatively safe here if his nerve did not crack, and he had the revolver. He did not think it would come too far into the light, but it was cunning, incredibly cunning, as he had already sensed.

And there was another fear added to the smell of danger; the fear that Abercrombie might already be dead. He seemed to have fallen into vast, unknowable depths when he crashed through the rotted timbers of the door, and there had been no sound of life from him since.

Coleridge held the lantern carefully and moved over sideways into the next aisle. Something moved with him at the far end; there were two red eyes now, glaring at him balefully from the darkness. It was not imagination, but as soon as he brought the pistol barrel up, they disappeared. The beast was moving with him across the width of the cellar, almost as if it had divined his intention and was keeping pace with him. The professor again felt the sweat of fear descending into his eyes, momentarily blurring his vision.

The light given off by the dark-lantern seemed pitifully small compared to the area he had to cover, and he wished they had had the benefit of large oil lamps in here, such as those that illuminated the staircase above. He cast a quick glance back over his shoulder, toward the steps, and saw another vast shadow pass rapidly across the wall, before disappearing.

He moved over desperately to the side of the cellar. Surely there could not be two beasts. His situation would be desperate indeed if that were so. But at least here he would have his back to the wall. He cast a quick glance to the right, saw something slink between the casks at the far limit of the lamp's range. He fired quickly, the muzzle flash of the pistol seeming to burn a huge hole in the darkness.

He heard the bullet spang off one of the stone buttresses while the long shape flattened itself to the floor before flickering behind a pillar. The entire vault seemed filled with powder-smoke which stung Coleridge's eyes, while the echo went on for a long time.

He glanced swiftly to his left, saw that the shadow near the staircase had disappeared. Instead there came another light scuffle from that direction. He moved back up toward the stairs.

While he was thus occupied, something launched itself from the top of one of the casks. Coleridge fired instinctively, the two shots seeming to split the top of his head. The beast's jaws snapped shut, and it was so close he could smell the stink of its feral breath. He cowered back instinctively, losing his footing, and in a moment of blind panic fell over, upsetting the lamp but not extinguishing it.

The great body passed him, disappearing behind the barrels with a dreadful worrying noise. Coleridge stumbled to his feet.

He still held the pistol, but he was dusty and very frightened. His limbs felt like water. Another charge like this and he would be finished. He picked up the lamp and put it down on top of a barrel, where it gave a good light.

The black hole left by the shattered door was at his left now, and Coleridge got across the intervening space quickly, the comforting solidity of the wall at his back. He heard footsteps then, running down the passage leading to the small flight of stairs above him.

Then the girl's voice, calling his name. Relief flooded through Coleridge, erased in an instant by the hollow, murmuring groan that echoed in his ears, disarming his spirit and reverberating round the vault like some supernatural symbol of doom.

KEEP BACK!"

Coleridge's voice came out in a strangled croak, but he had command of his faculties now. The girl ignored him. She came flying down the steps, her hair in a tangled mane about her, holding a cutlass in her right hand and the glimmering oil lamp in the other. It would have been an absurd, wildly piratical sight under any other circumstances, but to Coleridge her presence spelt salvation.

Her eyes raked his face as she came within the shelter of his arms. He was left with the brief vision of the grey patch on the huge wolf's back; it had disappeared now, and with its absence a semblance of normality seeped back into the cellar.

"You might have been killed," Coleridge said somewhat incoherently.

Nadia Homolky gave him a strained smile.

"So might you," she said. "That seemed equally important to me."

Coleridge had no time to discuss the matter, and the implication of her words did not soak into his consciousness until much later.

"Where did you get that weapon? And why did you follow us?"

"From a rack on the wall on my way through. It seemed as though it might be an effective wolf deterrent. As to the second question, I thought you might need help."

Coleridge gave her a grim smile.

"Even so you were lucky, Nadia. The beast was only a few yards away as you came down the stairs."

He let go of her, conscious of the faint perfume that emanated from her hair. It was the same elusive fragrance that he had noted on the night of his arrival at the Castle. He was already over at the dark space which gaped in the wall. By the light of the smaller lantern he saw that the rough stone sloped downward, the fragments of the broken door partly blocking it. Beyond was something dark and crumpled.

"Bring your lantern, quickly!"

The girl came over, curiosity in her eyes. By the stronger light the two made out the huddled form of Abercrombie; he was lying with his hands on a jagged projection in the rock, a thin trickle of blood on his forehead. The scene resembled the entrance to an oubliette, and once again Coleridge remembered the tale of the Count's ancestral dungeon.

"Is he dead?" Nadia Homolky whispered, casting worried glances about her.

Coleridge was mindful of the need for vigilance; at any moment the wolf might come back for another attack, but their overriding duty was to Abercrombie, to get him from that dreadful place and to see what aid could be given him.

He shook his head.

"I do not know. But even if he is still alive he may be in terrible danger. We do not know where this tunnel leads. And it may get steeper farther down."

The girl set her lips in a stubborn line.

"Let me go. I am lighter than you. And I saw some rope at the top of the steps."

Before he could stop her she had run back up with a brittle clacking of heels on the stone slabs, mindless of the wild beast which might be watching them a short distance away. She returned with a thick coil of new rope, flinging the hair back from her eyes as she smiled at her companion. Her presence gave Coleridge renewed vigour. He was at the opening now, fancied he saw a faint flicker of movement from the recumbent figure below. Then the groan he had already heard. His heart leapt. Abercrombie was still alive.

All thoughts of the wolf were erased. He realised that the second shadow he had seen at the top of the steps was that of the girl moving cautiously down the passage, waiting until she was certain of the situation before rushing to assist him.

A great wave of affection for her passed across him. She was already elbowing him aside, handing him one end of the rope. He secured it round his right wrist, leaning close to the opening. The girl was sliding cautiously inward, and he had her hand with his left. As soon as she had gone some little way down she reached for the fragments of the broken door and handed them up to him, piece by piece.

"This must be one of the old entrances to the dungeons Father had bricked up," she said. "How did the accident happen?"

"The wooden handrail gave way," Coleridge whispered.

He had the absurd notion that they were speaking in low voices to avoid waking Abercrombie. But in reality it was to prevent rousing the wolf which could be lurking at the top of the barrel racks in the shadowy gloom behind.

It would be an appalling moment of danger if the beast attacked now, and Coleridge quickly put the pistol down on the stone sill of the embrasure, close to hand. He threw the last of the broken board to the floor, relishing the sound it made. The vulnerable feeling in the small of his back and neck muscles had passed.

He guessed then that the beast had fled up the staircase after the failure of its attack. It could have made its way through the open courtyards and into the shelter of the forest by now. He reached for the girl's lamp with his disengaged hand, shone the light down into the dark tunnel before him. A musty, foetid smell came from it, and once again he admired Nadia's courage. She was already securing the end of the thick coil round Abercrombie's massive chest, knotting and reknotting it. Deep stertorous breathing was audible from him now.

Coleridge's hopes rose. Perhaps his colleague was only stunned. The girl was crawling back up. He had her firmly by the hand, could feel her trembling by the pressure on his fingertips.

"I think he will be all right," she whispered, her lips close to Coleridge's face. "We must have these dangerous embrasures bricked up. I will tell Father about it."

She lowered herself to the floor, reaching for the lamp. Coleridge was already taking up the strain on the rope and then pulling with all his strength at Abercrombie's recumbent figure. The man's dead weight was enormous, and he could again feel pain in his left arm. The girl came to help him, and they pulled silently together, the breath sobbing in their throats.

Abercrombie's unconscious body made a low slithering noise that echoed and reechoed in the dark tunnel, and little fragments of stone and dust fell clicking and clattering to what seemed like vast depths below the doctor. He had had a narrow escape indeed. As he and Nadia Homolky toiled in close intimacy, the girl's warm breath on his cheek, Coleridge had a vivid impression of the jeering face of Ivan the Bold.

The wolf's presence in the vault could have almost been the malignant return of his degraded spirit from the vault below. The fancy was absurd, yet Coleridge could not shake it from his clouded mind. That was the impression the sinister events at the Castle had upon him, and he was beginning to find it harder and harder to wrench himself free from them.

"One more pull!" Nadia gasped, and then, just when the strain was becoming intolerable, Abercrombie's bearded head appeared in the opening like some battered and bloodied image of a Norse god following an epic battle. He groaned again and opened his eyes slightly, hooding them against the light from the lantern.

"You are safe now," Coleridge said. "Lie still while we try to work your shoulders free."

It was ten minutes more before the two of them had the semiconscious form of the doctor on the cellar floor. Coleridge had tied the rope tautly to the nearest barrel rack, as he was afraid his colleague might yet slip back into the yawning darkness of the oubliette. When he was safe he quickly ran his hands over the collapsed figure. He did not appear to have any broken bones. He was probably suffering from slight concussion and shock.

Nadia had found the doctor's pistol, which had fallen to the floor, and she held it ready in case the wolf returned, but all was silent now in the yellow light of the two lamps.

"I will stay here and guard him," Coleridge whispered. "We shall need help to get him up."

In the event there was no need, for a few moments later there came the welcome clatter of feet on the stairs and then the Count and his servants to see what had happened to his missing guests.

"I owe you my life, Professor!"

Duncan Abercrombie, his head bandaged and his voice weak, nevertheless stretched out his fingers from his bed-sheets and grasped Coleridge warmly by the hand. The latter smiled, despite the gravity of the situation, because there was still a good deal of strength there.

As he had suspected, Abercrombie was an extremely durable individual, and his layman's diagnosis of momentary concussion and shock had been correct.

The Count's own physician, Dr. Istvan, had just left with an admonition to Abercrombie to rest a few days, but the big Scot had expressed his intention of getting up for the wolf-hunt in the morning, though Coleridge and the Count had voiced their doubts at this.

"I have a personal score to settle with that brute," said Abercrombie wryly. "If the beast had disabled you or prevented you from coming to my rescue, I might have slid to my death in that oubliette."

"You must not forget Miss Homolky's part in all this," the professor reminded him. "She rescued both of us, in effect."

Abercrombie nodded, looking at his companion shrewdly.

"She is a girl of spirit, Professor," he said quickly. "And she is obviously greatly attracted to you."

He laughed weakly.

"And you are an eligible bachelor, are you not?"

In spite of himself Coleridge felt a flush rising to his cheek. He had not seen things in that light, but it was obvious Abercrombie had sensed a great deal that he, in his more obtuse fashion, had not noticed.

The two men now were alone. After the alarm and excitement in the Castle and all the resultant confusion, Abercrombie had been conveyed to his own room where he had recovered full consciousness a short while afterward. A large fire burned on the hearth, and the black-bearded servant was stationed just outside the door, in earshot of the bell on the doctor's bedside table, in case he should need anything.

A discreet search had been made of the Castle, and despite the short while remaining before darkness, Rakosi and a few men from his troop had carried out a brief reconnoitre of the area surrounding the Castle. It might have been thought traces of the wolf's passage would have been visible in the fresh snowfall, but they had reported nothing, though it was extremely difficult to make out such tracks in the falling dusk.

Homolky, Nadia, and the doctor's colleagues had all visited the invalid to express their regrets, but Coleridge had lingered for some indefinable reason; a strong bond had been forming during the past hours between the professor and the massive Scot, and both seemed to gain confidence and energy from the other.

Coleridge looked at his silver-cased watch; there were still two more lectures due to be delivered this evening. The Congress went on, in spite of everything. Abercrombie had wished to be there but had finally seen that it would be ridiculous for him to make the effort in his present physical condition. Coleridge had promised to bring him a précis of the proceedings afterward, if he were not asleep.

Now he rose to take his leave, hovering solicitously.

"Is there anything you need? A magazine, copies of the proceedings?"

A spark of amusement flickered in the doctor's eyes.

"No, thanks. I have everything I need here. Including whisky." He waved his hand feebly to encompass the bedside table.

"Goodnight, then."

"Goodnight. And thank you again."

Coleridge closed the heavy oak door behind him, nodding to

the servant who sat on a carved chair just to the right of the entry. He walked down the short stair, deep in thought, subconsciously noting the subtle perfume of the flowers in the bowls placed on the tables at intervals. He met Nadia at the stairhead. She had obviously been waiting for him.

Her eyes searched his face.

"How is the patient?"

"Much better. Thanks to you."

She shrugged.

"I only did what anyone would have done."

Coleridge shook his head.

"You risked your life. And you went down into that dreadful place, not knowing if the doctor were alive or dead. I would say your conduct was exceptional. Your father must be proud of you."

It was dark in the corridor, despite the lamps, but Coleridge noticed the rise in colour of the girl's cheeks.

Aware of her confusion, he went on quickly.

"But you wished to see me, obviously."

Nadia Homolky nodded, her eyes very bright and not at all troubled now.

"Yes. We all seem to be in the same situation, which is rather reassuring somehow."

Coleridge knew what she meant, and he did not reply but fell into step with her as they walked down the corridor in the direction of his own room; content to be *en rapport* with this remarkable young woman. A shadow moved away at the end of the passage, and for a moment his heart missed a beat until he remembered that it was probably nothing more than one of the servants who had been deputed by the Count to watch over the safety of the guests following this latest alarm.

Coleridge was aware then of the double pressure against his ribs. He had forgotten to give back Abercrombie the revolver the Count had loaned him. He drew it out and proffered it to the girl, but first making sure the safety-catch was on.

"I would feel better if you would keep this by your bed. I presume you know how to use it? I will get another from your father for Dr. Abercrombie."

The girl took the pistol with the faintest smile hovering at the corners of her mouth.

"I know how to use it, John. Ask Father. We have a private shooting range here. The countryside round about is far from safe, especially in winter."

It was the first time the girl had used Coleridge's Christian name, and its effect on her lips struck him forcibly. He was thrown off balance for a moment or two. Though she was not looking directly at him, Nadia was obviously studying his reaction, as if she had dared too much and was not certain of his response.

Coleridge passed quickly on to firmer ground by ignoring the situation. They continued walking back down the corridor.

"We must talk," he said quickly.

She nodded, looking at him directly.

"You are going on the wolf-hunt tomorrow?"

"I have given my promise."

"I would like to come too, but Father has forbidden it."

"He is a very sensible man," Coleridge told her. "And you have had enough excitement for one weekend."

He glanced at his watch.

"I have to attend another lecture in half an hour. We shall just have time."

The girl put her hand familiarly in his, just as she had at the Fair.

"Father's private library," she said decisively. "We shall be alone in there."

They had reached the end of the corridor, and the professor fancied he saw the shadow again, slipping away from the stair-head. As it disappeared from view he had a brief glimpse of its owner. Again the uneasiness returned, for he could have sworn it was Raglan lurking suspiciously there.

"BUT WHAT WERE you doing in the cellars?"

It was Dr. Sullivan with his greying beard and crumpled suit of brown plus-fours who asked the question.

He had delivered an excellent paper on demonology earlier in the evening, followed by Raglan with an equally well argued lecture on certain aspects of witchcraft. Despite the alarms and disruptions, the Congress was proving a surprisingly vital and worthwhile event; even if appalling things were taking place beneath its placid surface, Coleridge thought.

It was the quiet hour before dinner now and the company were still in the library lecture-hall, sprawled out comfortably in the leather seats, waiting for their summons below. It had been impossible to keep Abercrombie's accident secret, though no-one outside a small circle had an inkling of the true facts. This was the moment Coleridge had been dreading, and he pondered his answer carefully while drawing at his fragrant cigar, aware of the Count's worried features in the row above him.

All the family were there, including the old Countess, whose clear-minted, brooding face inevitably conveyed to the savant her tragic history. He avoided Nadia's eyes, though he was conscious —perhaps too conscious—that Sylva Homolky was intensely interested in the growing relationship between him and her daughter. In fact he was anxious to talk to her; not on that subject, certainly, but on the matter that vitally concerned them all.

He sensed that she was a decisive and complex woman, and it would be good to get her opinion on the baffling and terrible events that seemed to threaten the people of the Castle. It was obviously impossible at the moment because the Count had not told her or his mother about the true situation. Until he saw fit to do so, no-one else would dare to, not even Nadia. Certainly not Coleridge; it was not his place to break his word to his host, and he sympathised with the man's appalling dilemma.

Now, as he drew steadily on his cigar while pondering his answer, he raked his eyes slowly about the great conference chamber, taking in the details of each of his colleagues in turn. It was difficult to believe that any one of them could be a murderer; let alone anything so fantastic as a werewolf. Yet his training and experience as a collector of folklore and curious facts from all the wild corners of the earth had taught him to discount nothing.

His difficulty was that he possessed so few personal details about his companions. He had looked them up in the official yearbooks, of course, but he knew none of them intimately, and one or two he had never even met before the Congress in Pest. He turned his eyes back to Sullivan. It was this man, if he remembered correctly, who had expressed ironic delight in his colleagues' scepticism when he had first mentioned the wolf-death at breakfast.

And it was certain that to many of the village people the werewolf was a stark reality. He had gathered that much from the Count and Rakosi. The girl, too, had spoken more than once of the strange legends peculiar to that remote corner of Hungary.

Coleridge opened his mouth to mutter some banal excuse that was hovering at the back of his mind, but in the event he was saved by Homolky, who broke in with a disarming smile.

"It is entirely my fault, gentlemen. I asked Professor Coleridge and Dr. Abercrombie to bring up some rare bottles of Tokay for our dinner this evening. And they had some archaeological interest in the ancient foundations of such a Castle as this."

He shrugged deprecatingly.

"I should have known better, and the accident following so closely upon the tragic death of Dr. Menlow fills me with sadness."

Coleridge shook his head.

"It was not the Count's fault. If anyone, it is mine. I had specifically asked to see the cellars. The vast antiquity of the Castle intrigued me, and the Count's stories of his ancestors and the dungeons below had given me the idea for a monograph . . ."

He had said the right thing evidently, for there was an interested babble of question and counterquestion from his colleagues and the Count gave him a grateful nod from his seat in the back row, mopping his forehead with a scarlet silk handkerchief. Rakosi turned his gaze from Nadia and offered the professor an enigmatic glance.

For the first time Coleridge realised how like Raglan he was. Both young men, given the slightly different characteristics imposed by nationality and profession, were astonishingly similar in manner and physical appearance, even down to the trim, clipped moustaches they wore.

The only real difference, it now appeared to him, was the fact that Rakosi wore his elaborate befrogged uniform with an appropriate martial dash and Raglan had on a dark green day suit with a smartly cut waistcoat of the same material. Was it that Nadia preferred young men of this type and character or that they simply gravitated to her?

"It was unfortunate," Raglan agreed. "But certainly no-one would blame you, Professor, least of all Abercrombie. The accident happened to him. And in the event you—and Miss Homolky here—certainly saved his life."

"It is indeed a memorable Congress," said George Parker sombrely, his deep-set eyes looking reflectively round the assembly. "And a sad one, of course. But poor Menlow might have collapsed delivering a paper in Pest, and Duncan Abercrombie could just as easily have fallen downstairs in his hotel."

"It is good of you all to look at it like that," the Count put in.

"That is the only way to look at it," said Parker.

With his strong face, black beard, and athletic physique he reminded Coleridge of someone, but he could not quite place the connection. It was a factor which had been hovering around the edges of his mind for some time now. He dismissed it temporarily. It would no doubt come to him in due course.

General conversation resumed, and he had time to study his companions. Raglan and Rakosi were engaging the girl in some amusing light banter, judging by the smiles which were being exchanged. The Count was deep in talk with his mother, and although Countess Sylva occasionally threw in a sentence or two it was obvious her mind was preoccupied, and more than once Coleridge caught her eyes on him.

Professor Shaw was sitting quite near to Coleridge; he had not known him before the Congress, and he regarded him with more than usual interest. He had the reputation of being a witty and erudite speaker, and great things were expected of him at the opening session on Monday when the Congress would resume after the wolf-hunt. That reminded Coleridge he was due to choose a rifle at the Weapons Hall after dinner.

Following their conversation the Count had had the Hall placed under lock and key, though the professor felt that would not deter anyone of a murderous disposition. He resumed his covert examination of Shaw. Despite his thin, emaciated look, he was a distinguished figure in his well-cut pearl-grey suit, and once again Coleridge was aware of the curious effect the light had on his silver hair and drooping moustache of an iron-grey colour.

At one moment it looked a faded brown, at another like burnished metal. It was a strange transformation, and for one absurd second Coleridge wondered whether he could be wearing some form of disguise. Certainly his even white teeth, slightly canine beneath the moustache, seemed to belong to a much younger man.

The supposition was ridiculous, of course, but was a measure of the effect the atmosphere of Castle Homolky was having upon Coleridge. He gave it up, dropped out of the conversation, and smoked his cigar in a blissfully neutral state while waiting for the sacred hour of dinner.

* * *

Coleridge carried the polished leather rifle-case to his room almost reverently. The Count had chosen him a splendid weapon, and under any other circumstances he would have looked forward to firing it. Perhaps on the private range the girl had mentioned; but not at living creatures, however savage they might be. He had exchanged only a few words with her at dinner.

The news from Abercrombie's sickbed was good, and he had so far recovered it was almost certain he would be with the party the following morning. The Count was strongly against it but had been unable to dissuade him, though the news had lightened the atmosphere at dinner with the consequence that the meal had been relaxed and genial. Even the old Countess had sparkled, though the girl and her mother had continually eyed him throughout the meal in a way that made him feel slightly uncomfortable.

His own gaze had ranged round the table, lingering over his colleagues of the Congress. It was unthinkable that one of them could be responsible for the death of Menlow, let alone those in the village, with or without the aid of the black arts. It was preposterous even to contemplate, and Coleridge soon abandoned such idle speculation and was glad to be taken wherever the lively conversation tended.

And after the meal and the half-hour spent on coffee and liqueurs he had avoided both Nadia and Countess Sylva and allowed the Count to hurry him off to the Weapons Hall. They had put aside the dark questions which occupied both their minds and had stuck to the technicalities of the weapons displayed in the cases and on the walls. So far as Coleridge could make out, all of his colleagues had volunteered to take part in the wolf-hunt, though not all were expert shots.

But the Count had made his dispositions well, and those not familiar with the niceties of the hunt would be under the strict supervision of expert marksmen from his own household or those experienced shots among the guests. Coleridge himself had expressed a preference to be paired with Abercrombie, should the big Scot not be persuaded to stay behind.

Despite the conversation before dinner he did feel some personal responsibility for his colleague's accident, and in the heat and excitement of the wolf-hunt he wanted to make sure the doctor would be safe and protected in his slightly weakened state. The Count had professed himself satisfied, and as the rest of the party were due to select their own weapons a short while later, Coleridge had taken the rifle and ammunition to his own room.

He had been there only a few minutes and was examining the weapon, cradling the butt to his shoulder near the fire, when there came a faint tapping at the door. The rifle was unloaded, of course, but Coleridge first lowered it and replaced it in the case before hastening to unlock the door.

To his surprise it was the Countess Sylva who stood there, still wearing her elegant dinner gown. She looked about the corridor quickly, as though afraid they might be discovered, and held her fingers up to enjoin caution.

"I must speak to you privately, Professor Coleridge. I have vainly been seeking an opportunity all day, or I would not have disturbed you at this late hour."

Coleridge stood aside to let her enter.

"The Castle clock has only just struck ten, Countess," he said in an attempt to appear light and bantering.

It was obvious she had not taken in his words, for she looked dully at the rifle-case leaning against the side-wall and went to sit in one of the big fireside wing-chairs, nervously twisting her elegant hands. Once again Coleridge was struck by her mature beauty. At the same time he hoped the Count would not come here to seek her. It was an ambiguous situation at the best of times, and Coleridge did not want any misunderstandings, particularly where Nadia was concerned.

He went to sit somewhat nervously in the companion chair opposite, with the small table between. It was almost a repetition of the breakfast scene with the daughter herself, and he was momentarily struck with the analogy.

The Countess also evidently felt her guest might put some odd interpretation on her visit, for she roused herself quickly, looking about the dimly lit chamber almost fiercely. Then she turned her extraordinary cobalt eyes full on her companion.

"You will think this a strange request, Professor Coleridge. But it is something I must ask you."

Coleridge was uneasily aware that he might be obliged to

break a confidence, and he put up his hand as though to indicate what an impossibility that would be. But the Countess stopped him with a fierce gesture of her hand.

"Please hear me out, Professor," she said deliberately.

She was breathing heavily now, as though keeping her feelings under control with some difficulty.

"There is something very peculiar going on in the Castle, Professor. I think you know what it is. Or at least a good deal about it."

There was a long silence between them, punctuated at intervals by the soft crackling of the wood on the fire. Coleridge felt for the Countess in her difficulties, and he had no intention of lying to her.

"Had you not better ask the Count?" he said gently.

The tall woman straightened in the chair.

"I am asking you, Professor."

Coleridge shook his head. Already he felt out of his depth with this imperious and passionate-natured woman.

"I wish I could help you, madame. But it is surely your husband's place . . ."

Too late he realised the trap into which his guileless nature had led him.

The Countess gave him a triumphant look.

"Ah, then the Count does know what is involved here. I demand that you take me into your confidence, Professor Coleridge."

Coleridge shrugged helplessly.

"I am afraid, Countess, it is something I cannot do."

The striking-looking woman gave him a bitter smile.

"Or will not do."

Coleridge looked at her steadily.

"You must think as you wish, madame. I would like to say, however, in my own defence, that I am doing my best to assist your husband in a very difficult and dangerous situation. He is a man for whom I have an enormous respect. I could not nor would not forfeit that respect by breaking my promises to him."

The Countess Sylva's eyes flashed for a moment, and she drew herself up again. But he had evidently said the right thing. She was smiling now, and all the bitterness was gone from her expression.

"You are a man I also respect, Professor. I should not have asked you to break such a confidence."

She bit her lip.

"It is just that I have been under considerable strain these last days. I am a person who prefers action to inactivity."

Coleridge nodded.

"I understand perfectly. I wish I could help, with all my heart. But I am sure the Count will confide in you at the earliest opportunity. It was just that he had no wish to alarm his immediate family, particularly his mother."

The Countess nodded, as though the matter was at an end. She got up quickly and came forward. Coleridge had risen also, and she put both her hands in his. They remained so for a few moments, looking into each other's eyes. Then the Countess released her fingers and drew back.

"I sense great danger, Professor," she said quietly. "Stay near my husband if you can. I know you are an expert shot. I am uneasy about this wolf-hunt in the morning. But he will not let me come along."

"He is very wise, madame," Coleridge said slowly. "But be reassured in your mind. The Count will be surrounded by friends. And I will do my best."

The Countess crossed to the door. She stood there a long moment, the firelight flickering on her handsome but saddened features.

"I know you will, Professor."

Then she was gone, the door closing quietly behind her. Coleridge bolted it and undressed quickly, aware of the glacial wind that was howling outside the Castle and slightly agitating the casement curtains. His mind was full of a thousand conflicting thoughts and emotions as he dropped into sleep.

The Place of the Skull

"ARE YOU SURE you are all right?" Coleridge queried anxiously.

"I am fine," Abercrombie grunted.

With his great flapped fur cap and his thick clothing he somewhat resembled a bear as he trudged slowly down the icy slope next to the professor. A few yards away the Count, heading a long line of black figures, prepared to start the wolf-hunt.

It was bitterly cold, but the snow had stopped, and though it was past ten in the morning it was still almost dark, the sky pressing heavily on the bare branches of the trees, the wind whistling keenly about them.

Their feet crunched harshly on the fresh surface of the frozen snow, and the heart pounded with the effort of moving over this difficult terrain. They stopped again as they came abreast of the Count's party. To left and right the long line of guns stretched, supplemented by a few men Rakosi could spare. The remainder were trusted shots from among the village men.

A larger party of people from Lugos, together with the main body of Rakosi's troop, were somewhere beyond the wooded horizon, acting as beaters to drive the wolves on to the guns which now stretched for more than a mile across the icy undulating terrain. With Rakosi's party was a pack of wolf-hounds, belonging to the Count, which were noted for their excellence in the savage sport. Coleridge hoped for a clean shot if he spotted the wolf with the grey back, but he had his doubts.

Menlow's analysis and the superhuman cunning of the beast which had twice menaced him seemed to paralyse the will, and he was convinced in his heart that there was a supernatural basis for the activities of the animal which was swiftly transforming the peaceful interior of Castle Homolky into a place of terror.

What was remarkable was the utter obliviousness of most of the Congress party to what was taking place, literally before their eyes. It was better so, though the Count had a fearful responsibility in the matter. In his natural desire to avoid distress and something like a panic in Lugos and within his own household, he was risking the lives of his guests; though it was true that they knew of the wolf menace and were on their guard against natural dangers.

He turned slightly, his eyes stinging from the wind, waiting for Abercrombie to come up. The doctor seemed to have lost none of his vigour, though the long gash on his forehead testified to his ordeal of the day before. He had a personal score to settle; Coleridge could not deny that. For if the wolf had disabled or killed Coleridge, the big Scot would most certainly have died too in the darkness of the oubliette.

But he would keep close by him; he had promised the Count. He reached into his pocket for the silver flask of cognac his host had insisted they carry. Abercrombie put it to his lips with a grunt of satisfaction, handing it back to his companion. Coleridge wiped the rim of the flask and drank in his turn. The biting cold was erased as the flood of warmth invaded his extremities. He screwed on the cap of the flask and replaced it in his pocket, smiling at Abercrombie's expression.

The Count was beckoning now, and the two men detached themselves from the line to their left and crunched their way over toward him. Coleridge's rifle-case seemed inordinately heavy, and he again felt the faintest twinge from his injured shoulder. The Count smiled encouragingly at Abercrombie.

"If there is the slightest doubt of your fitness, one of my men will escort you back to the Castle."

Abercrombie shook his bearded head.

"I have just assured the professor I am all right."

Homolky bowed slightly.

"As you wish."

He turned to Coleridge.

"I would like you to take charge of the left flank, Professor. I myself will take the right. Between us we should ensure the success of the hunt."

Coleridge felt disappointment. He had promised the Countess he would stay close to her husband. But he could not fulfil that promise unless he first told the Count his reason. He felt resentment growing within him at the impossible position in which he was being placed. But one look at his colleagues, almost indistinguishable in their heavy fur clothing, brought reassurance.

For he had heard Sullivan was an excellent shot. And he noticed that the big bearded servant who always seemed to hover at the Count's elbow was there also, with a fearsome looking long-barrelled rifle which he had already removed from its case. The Count would be safe enough.

But would his own nerve hold sufficiently to protect himself and Abercrombie from any possible harm? In the difficult terrain over which they would be operating, they might become separated. There was always that possibility.

The Count extended a friendly nod and drew back into the line. Coleridge had just time to see Anton give him a formal military salute before the two wings disengaged, each man remaining about ten yards apart. Coleridge stood firm at the wing and waved Abercrombie back. His own section spread out until the farthest men had disappeared.

The guns stretched for over a mile across the ground. All they had to do now was to walk slowly forward and keep their eyes open. The Count had earlier told them that no-one in the line was to shoot until he himself had first fired. And they were not to kill the animals indiscriminately but only those large males which resembled the black wolf they were hunting.

Rakosi's party were beating some five miles back. As soon as the beasts were being driven forward on to the guns, Rakosi would alert them with a pattern of three shots.

In front, the ground descended into a sort of ravine from which a thick stubble of bare undergrowth and tree-boles protruded, then it rose again with woodland until the blue, hard line of the mountains began beyond. It was a difficult landscape, and Coleridge intended to keep close to his companions.

Apart from the natural dangers from the animals they were hunting, it would be easy to turn one's ankle in among the boulders, and anyone foolish enough to be disabled and out of earshot of companions could face a miserable death from frostbite and starvation; particularly as there were so few hours of daylight in these latitudes.

Coleridge turned back as the line stood steady, from horizon to horizon, waiting for the signal. Behind them the black mass of Lugos huddled round the base of its hill, with small scribbles of smoke rising from its chimneys into the sullen sky. Far above, on the heights, Castle Homolky glistened in its frosty overcoat, resembling some grotesque iced cake more than ever, Coleridge thought.

He turned back, breaking out the rifle from the case and loading it quickly, keeping his gloves on. He had just time to secure the safety-catch, noting that Abercrombie at his left was doing the same.

Then the Count had raised his hand and was striding out across the rough surface of the frozen snow. The rest of the line followed suit. Breath smoking from his mouth, his heart pumping steadily in his chest, Coleridge walked forward, his eyes half-closed against the wind. The darkness of the ravine with its icy tree-boles marched up to meet them.

The three shots, when they came, seemed to split the darkened sky, reverberating and echoing across the mountainside until it appeared as though Rakosi's troop had fired a fusillade. Coleridge could hear the hounds now, their shrill voices carried strongly by the wind, then fading to silence as it quickly changed direction.

The line went steadily forward. The signal obviously meant that some beasts had been started toward the guns. But they could still be a long way off, and though wolves could run at tremendous speeds for twenty miles or more, they were familiar with such hunting procedures as the Count was employing today and they would proceed with caution, especially as they were still within the woods.

Coleridge knew it was the Count's intention to drive the animals on and catch them in the open, but it was obvious something had gone wrong with the timetable, as often happened on such occasions.

It would be extremely dangerous if they came upon the wolves within the woodland, for in that situation it might well be that the hunters would become the hunted, and it would be difficult if not impossible to use the rifles among the trees.

For that reason each man was equipped with a pistol and plentiful ammunition. Coleridge turned back and looked for Abercrombie. He was still a little concerned for him, but he was keeping up well, though they had been going for more than an hour. He was only a few yards behind the line, which was extremely ragged now. As always, individual guns, carried away by the excitement, forged ahead, while the less cautious or athletic tended to straggle behind.

Although Coleridge was nominally in charge of the left flank, it was almost impossible to control a party of men strung out over a wide section of countryside, and he hoped for nothing more than reasonable coherence under the circumstances. He waited now for Abercrombie to come up and again offered him the flask. The big man took it gratefully and moistened his lips with the fiery liquid.

"Thank you. Most welcome," he said drily, his eyes reddened and inflamed with the wind.

Coleridge looked beyond him. To his relief he saw that the whole line had paused with him. Over on the right Homolky, a small black figure against the dazzle of the snow, waved also. They would rest for a minute or two and listen for the progress of the hunt.

"You have not changed your opinion of this wolf?" Coleridge asked.

It was a question he could not resist.

Abercrombie smiled, wiping his beard with the fur back of his glove.

"My scientific mind is open to any well-argued propositions," he said cautiously. "You are talking of the beast in the cellar?"

Coleridge nodded.

"Of course."

Abercrombie shrugged, putting down the butt of his rifle on the frozen ground, holding the barrel delicately in one gloved hand. He was so massive the weapon looked almost toylike by comparison.

"I did not see it, of course. But the weather has been very severe. That beast could have taken refuge there in the natural course of things."

"It is possible," Coleridge agreed reluctantly. "But it had the grey patch on its back. It was the same animal which attacked me in the Castle corridor."

Abercrombie smiled again.

"The one which tries door-handles?" he said mockingly.

Coleridge felt irritation rising within him, fought it down.

"You have not seen it, Doctor. I have twice been in danger of my life from the brute. In theory it should have been killed yesterday, for I aimed at its head."

A silence fell between them, broken only by the faint barking of the dogs from over the bare shoulders of the hills.

"There is another thing also," Coleridge went on. "As you may imagine, I have been thinking much about this matter recently. The wolf with the grey patch has been seen only by myself and Nadia. The black wolf we are hunting today had killed long before we came to the Castle. The other, which I am convinced killed poor Menlow, has manifested itself only since the beginning of the Congress."

Abercrombie looked at him blankly.

"What are you suggesting? That one of our colleagues is a werewolf? The idea is preposterous."

Coleridge looked his companion deep in the eyes.

"I did not say so. I am just stating a few facts."

He had a sudden recollection of the photograph in the silver frame on the old Countess's desk. He drew in his breath. It was foolish of him not to have seen the possibility before. But this was not the time to discuss it. This evening perhaps, after they had returned to the Castle.

He turned back to the line. The Count was moving forward again. Coleridge followed suit, conscious that his legs were beginning to ache. There was no doubt that the life of the scholar was not conducive to such strenuous activities. Again the girl's image came before him and the bleak landscape. He dismissed it and peered carefully about him, half-closing his eyes against the piercing wind.

They were descending into broken ground once more, and beyond it was something that looked like the mouth of a ravine; instinctively Coleridge increased his pace. He did not want to be caught in here. Abercrombie was going well, keeping abreast of him. As they descended and the light began to fade from the sky and the tree-branches to close above their heads, Coleridge realised with dismay that the area was more extensive and precipitous than he had imagined.

More importantly, the rest of the line seemed to have spread out to skirt the wooded area, because he could not see anyone else in sight. He pointed this out to Abercrombie. The giant hesitated and then grunted belligerently.

"We two are any match for the odd wolf which might find its way in here. And we should be through this in about twenty minutes or so. If we go back up and follow the others, we shall be a mile behind and unable to catch up."

Coleridge nodded. Abercrombie's words made good sense. The two plunged on, balancing precariously on the icy ridges, sinking lower and lower into a twilight world where the gnarled boles of trees were frosted thick with ice and where great boulders hung awry across a winding path which twisted across the face of the hillside.

They could still hear shouting, presumably from the line of guns, and once the sharp high notes of a horn which could only have emanated from the beaters' party beyond the hills.

Then the sounds ceased, except for the sharp crunch of their boots in the impacted snow, and they were crossing what was obviously a streambed where boulders, splintered boughs, and the dull gleam of ice made a nightmare tangle. Coleridge kept close to Abercrombie, but the rugged Scot seemed in excellent spirits and impervious to fatigue.

"I am well," was all he would say, and Coleridge decided to save his breath.

They had left the frozen streambed now and were going uphill, tracing a zigzag course on the snow. Great belts of trees stretched to left and right and they found them useful, pulling themselves up by the boles of the saplings when the going underfoot got too rough. Once they paused for five minutes to catch their breath and then went on again, refreshed and conserving their energy.

There was no sound from their companions; the only imposition upon the silence was a harsh metallic screeching from the far wood that might have been carrion-crow quarrelling. Coleridge looked at his watch anxiously during one of their halts, but Abercrombie dispelled his anxiety.

"We have several hours of daylight yet. We shall be through this soon and able to sight the others."

Surely enough, a few minutes later they had climbed a bare ridge of thick snow which raised itself from the tree-line; they were in a sort of valley which led steeply to the right. In front of them the skirt of the mountain led upward, almost vertically, with thick bands of pine and fir.

At the left-hand side was a thick sheet of ice which was almost a cliff-face, surmounted by more heavy forest at the summit. There was obviously only one way to go, and Coleridge led to the right, moving steadily downhill all the time between two big stands of trees. They were off the line of the hunt, but that could not be helped.

Tumbled boulders were flung about in this bleak place, and the wind funnelled down from the far summit, making their ears numb and stinging the eyes. Coleridge could hear a faint howling in the distance, but whether it emanated from the hounds or from the prey they were seeking he could not make out. Abercrombie caught his eye and increased his pace a little.

They were still going steeply downhill, the great rolling landscape leading them inexorably onward. To either side windswept slopes reared, crowned by thick clumps of dark trees. It was a drear sight, and gradually the light seemed to be leaching from the sky until they were in a condition of twilight. The howling was louder, and Coleridge's companion looked anxiously about him.

"Perhaps Rakosi has run them to ground," he said. "We would not have known down here."

"Which means they may be driving the wolves in our direction," said Coleridge grimly.

They paused halfway down the slope, conscious of the dark gorge that gaped before them. It was full of blue-black twilight with the mouths of caves halfway up the rocky slopes. The hill on which they stood ran directly into this vast cleft, with cliffs at either side ascending vertically for about two hundred feet. A few yards more and they saw that the far end was barred by more frowning crags, impassable and coated with ice.

The place was an enormous cul-de-sac from which there was no escape. As they stood undecided there came another mournful howling that was taken up from the thick forest that surrounded the entrance to the gorge and spread in a wide horseshoe to encompass all three sides of the valley.

Abercrombie stared bleakly at the great shattered cleft before them.

"The Place of the Skull," he said.

The Bear

THEY PICKED THEIR WAY down the slope, the freezing wind plucking at the skirts of their heavy clothing. Coleridge's breath was reeking from his mouth, and his extremities felt numb despite the heavy flapped fur cap he wore. He rubbed his nose to make sure of his circulation; he did not want frostbite under any circumstances.

They were in among the tangled mass of boulders now. It was shadowy here and a place with sinister connotations, but, as Abercrombie had pointed out, they had little choice. They were trapped and defenceless on the open slope, even with the rifles, if wolves should appear.

But if they could climb up the side of the gorge they could at least hold off any marauding pack until help arrived. It was sound advice, and Coleridge hoped that they would have time to find a suitable refuge before the first of the beasts approached.

That they would do so within minutes was obvious, as the whole object of the beat was to drive all the wolves in the vicinity on to the guns of the Count's party.

The dry rustling of branches in the wind seemed like the padding paws of the pack to the savant's overheated imagination, and he was again grateful for the doctor's presence. It was a fluke of circumstance, and ironic, as Coleridge was supposed to be taking care of Abercrombie in his semi-invalid condition.

The two men walked quickly and in silence, occupied with brooding thoughts. They were through the boulders and came out on a fairly flat space before jumbled scree heralded a steep slope that led up to a series of caves under the lip of the gorge. The caves were at the end of the cul-de-sac and so commanded the whole view of the valley they were traversing. Abercrombie was leading now, and he gave a brief exclamation as they came out into the open.

Coleridge hurried to his side and soon saw what had attracted his attention: heavy footprints, despite the thickness of the ice, which led to a dark huddled figure on the snow. The two men hurried forward after giving worried glances around the horizon. Nothing moved for the moment, but there would not be much time.

The man was obviously dead; his neck was dislocated, judging by the bizarre angle at which it was inclined, and his clothes were torn and bloody. Handing his rifle to Coleridge, Abercrombie nevertheless knelt down and made a thorough examination. As the distorted face came into view, Coleridge was astonished to see it was that of the gypsy at the Fair to whom Nadia had given money.

Abercrombie shook his head grimly and let the big man fall back to the snow.

"Dead."

"But what is he doing here?"

"Simple," Abercrombie shrugged. "Acting as a paid retainer for the Count's party. A number of the gypsies were pressed into service. Perhaps he started off early hoping for an extra bounty if he shot the wolf we were seeking."

He pointed to the gypsy's rifle which lay, barrel twisted and stock splintered, some yards from the body.

"What wolf would do that?" Coleridge asked.

Abercrombie laughed harshly back in his throat, getting to his feet. He took his own rifle from his companion and again scanned the horizon.

The shadows were longer on the ground now, and the chill

wind blew with an intensity that seemed to freeze the heart. Coleridge thought that he had never known so sinister a place; every hope seemed blighted here. All his instincts were against going into the depths of the gorge, perhaps, like the Count's ancestor, to their deaths at the jaws of wolves. But he also knew that was the only way to safety, as Abercrombie had already pointed out.

The latter shook his head, answering his companion's question.

"No wolf did. That was the bear. See the big tracks there. The gypsy thought to profit by the poor brute even under these circumstances. The bear would lead him to the wolves. And be added protection if they were attacked. Wolves usually give bears a wide berth, even in packs."

Coleridge stared silently at the remains of the rifle.

"The bear seized his chance of revenge. He had a cruel master and preferred the freedom of the woods. This gorge seems remarkably fortuitous for the oppressed, does it not."

Abercrombie smiled cynically, as though he relished the situation. Following his eyes Coleridge saw that the bear's chain and halter were lying some yards from the body. The links had been torn apart as though they had been made of paper.

"I do not blame the poor beast," Abercrombie went on. "It has probably gone off into the woods to find some snug cave and rest out the winter. I will not harm it. I rather approve of its moral attitude."

"Supposing it has taken shelter in the caves we are going to," said Coleridge.

Abercrombie shook his head. He pointed out the heavy tracks in the snow that went up the more shallow slope, back toward the valley they had left.

"He has gone that way. He will be miles off by now. Good luck to him."

As he spoke there came a faint howling sound which sent alarm coursing through Coleridge. Abercrombie had heard it too, because he turned on his heel.

"The wolves! We have but a few minutes left. Quickly! Run for the cave."

The Fight in the Gorge

THE FIRST GROUP of wolves came pouring over the ridge, sniffing suspiciously, their heads held back. From the shelter of the cave to which they had hastily scrambled, Coleridge could see the white sharpness of the canines. They were running mute now, and as the first of the beasts gained the entrance to the gorge more followed, some standing sentinel on the slope above.

The professor's throat was dry, and he could feel his fingers trembling slightly on the stock of the rifle. Abercrombie looked at him sympathetically.

"This is my fault, Professor. I am sorry. If I had been more agile, we could have caught up with the others."

Coleridge shook his head.

"It is no-one's fault except my own. I was in charge of the left wing of the guns. It is a mistake which is likely to cost us dear."

He shot a grim look at his companion.

"You have not forgotten the Count's story. This is the place where Ivan the Bold massacred the villagers. And where he and his two companions were themselves eaten by such a pack as that below us."

He looked down to where the first of the wolves had drawn together near the mass of scree at the foot of the steep slope leading to the cave, bonded now with ice and snow. Their eyes glittered yellow and alien as they stared up at the two men.

Abercrombie slapped the butt of his rifle with a great crack that went echoing round the gorge.

"That was centuries ago, Professor. They had only knives. And we have high-powered rifles. Besides, the others will be here soon."

"They will be if they know," Coleridge replied. "I have been greatly remiss."

He quickly raised the rifle, held the heavy weapon out at arm's length, and rested the stock on the heap of boulders that rimmed the cave while letting off four shots in quick succession. The wolves scattered, howling, at the foot of the slope, and the whole cave seemed full of smoke. The detonation went echoing and re-echoing like thunder across the miles of countryside.

Abercrombie kept his eye on the wolves huddled in the gorge below, leaning easily on his rifle barrel. Something like admiration passed over his face.

"You are certainly a cool companion in a tight corner, Professor."

Coleridge shook his head.

"I fear not," he said. "If you did but know I am pure jelly within."

Abercrombie chuckled, his teeth gleaming in his beard.

"Well, that is honest enough. But you surely do not think I feel any different? This is a serious situation right enough, and there is no minimising it."

He looked down morosely to the bottom of the gorge. A huge wolf, evidently the pack-leader which had mottled fur and heavy teeth-marks in its right shoulder, was already picking its way over the bonded scree, testing out a likely route to the cave. The forerunners of the pack were spread out in a semicircle now, staring up at the trapped men. Their eyes were like sinister brilliants which kept an unwavering glance upon them. Coleridge remembered then that few men were able to outstare the wolf.

He could see still more of the brutes crowding over the ridge.

There must have been at least twenty or thirty of them, an exceptionally large pack if he remembered his research on the animal.

"Far enough, I think," Abercrombie said calmly.

He had torn off a small rock from the icy parapet in front of them and threw it at the pack-leader. It landed a foot or two from the brute's nose, splintering some rock and ice particles about it. The wolf awkwardly jumped sideways, to avoid the missile, and gave a howl. Then it was slithering and sliding helplessly down to the bottom again. As the doctor raised the rifle, it squirmed behind a rock with astonishing swiftness.

"There is your werewolf, Professor," Abercrombie said thoughtfully.

Coleridge disagreed.

"I think not. The beast I saw was very distinctive. Darkish, certainly, but with a long grey patch on its back. This is not the one."

"Well, it will have to do for the time being," Abercrombie said drily. "And I fancy this is the signal for attack."

He had no sooner spoken than the great wolf stepped from behind the boulder and gave a long drawn-out howl. As if the pack-leader's silence had been the only thing restraining them, the wolves started milling over the ridge, racing down the slope with a scattering of loose ice to join their companions.

The big leader was back in the shelter of the boulder, but the others came on in a semicircle, running mute. Then there broke out a concentrated howling that made Coleridge sick to hear. He glanced desperately round the great horseshoe slope opposite, but there was nothing now except for the trampled snow, the dark sky with the darker forest, and far off, a mere smudge against the horizon, the silhouettes of two great black birds that winged their way eastward.

Abercrombie's rifle cracked then, and the brutes, howling, ears flat back and eyes gleaming viciously, were slipping and scrabbling up the slope toward them.

Coleridge's ears were deafened by the rifle explosions in the close confines of the cave; his cheeks were stung by powder-smoke, and sweat ran down into his eyes. Still the wave of great grey brutes came on. Mingled with Coleridge's admiration for their courage was his surprise at the slight impression he and Abercrombie seemed to be making on their ranks.

The body of one animal remained motionless where it had slithered to the bottom of the ravine; three others had limped away licking their wounds while the rest still advanced. The two men were working too close to use the rifles effectively; the cave entrance was small and they tended to get in each other's way and, most vital of all, they had little time to reload.

Once, the leading wave of three wolves had got dangerously near to the cave entrance when Abercrombie had reversed his rifle and laid about him, sending them howling from top to bottom of the gorge. At that moment the Scottish doctor had appeared to his companion like some heroic figure out of Norse legend, and it was an image that was to remain with him for a long time.

There was a lull now while the wolves snarled and glowered at the bottom of the slope. The remainder of the pack still stood in a semicircle, looking upward, but there was no sign of the leader.

Coleridge wondered why they had attacked at all; it was alarmingly reminiscent of Homolky's story of Ivan and his companions. Almost as though some malignant force had swept the pack over this ridge and on to the two men trapped within the frowning walls of the gorge. Wolves were highly intelligent animals, and they must surely know that a great mass of men was beating the woods to drive them on to the guns.

Yet here they were concerned only in pulling down and killing two lone men who were nevertheless heavily armed, while they might have made good their escape through the gap formed by this difficult terrain. They were not even hungry so far as Coleridge could ascertain; he was not an expert, but all the animals seemed well nourished and not at all suffering from mange or starvation.

There was another strange thing too, which underlined the respect felt between man and beast. Both Coleridge and Abercrombie could easily have picked off the wolves as they sat at the foot of the slope, yet something within themselves prevented them from doing this; they preferred to wait until the animals were closer and their lives were in danger before firing.

The pack itself seemed to know this, for they were quite content to remain below; but as soon as a rifle was levelled in the direction of any one individual, the threatened beast would flatten itself to the ground and wriggle aside.

Abercrombie broke the silence as if he could read the professor's thoughts.

"Have you noticed how they sense danger when we point the barrels at them?" He laughed harshly.

"We must be mad, Coleridge. We do not even shoot them while we may, without danger to ourselves."

Coleridge smiled grimly, seating himself on the parapet of boulders and keeping a sharp eye on the wolves.

"You have remarkable intuition, Doctor. I was just thinking the selfsame thing. I have an inhibition about killing any living creature. You as a practising doctor have no such scruples, I should imagine."

He joined in the doctor's laughter, which broke the tension.

"I did not mean to imply any lack of professional standards on your part, as must be apparent. But I am sure you know what I mean."

Abercrombie nodded, raking his eyes over the massed pack below.

"I understand perfectly, Professor. It is true I have a respect for the wolf, as well as what is sometimes miscalled the British sporting instinct. If we were really on the point of death, I think you would see a more ruthless side to my nature."

He turned his pockets out, setting the cardboard ammunition boxes on the boulders.

"How are your cartridges lasting?"

"I have plenty for the moment," Coleridge said.

He scanned the slowly darkening horizon.

"I cannot understand why the others have not yet arrived. Our shots must have carried for miles."

Abercrombie shrugged.

"Perhaps they have their own problems to contend with."

Coleridge's ears were still ringing with the concussion of the shots within the narrow confines of the cave, but he now distinctly heard the faint, far distant echo his companion had already caught. They were rifle shots.

"So they may not get here in time," he said.

Abercrombie made a wry expression with his mouth.

"The moment for chivalry is past."

He lifted the rifle, but at the same instant a tremendous howling broke out. The entire pack launched itself forward, scrabbling and sliding with a ferocity Coleridge had never seen before. He was aware only of white jaws, yellow eyes, red tongues and mouths, as he fired into the thick of the press with a sort of madness on him.

He was vaguely conscious of Abercrombie at his side; half-blinded with the flashes, deafened by the concussion, and blackened with powder-smoke, he found himself out of ammunition and no time to reload.

He used the rifle as a club, prodding the barrel into hairy chests and mouths, then listened to the snarls of pain and anger as he reached for the pistol at his side.

He was firing all six chambers into the grey mass when he felt a slacking of the press. The pack broke, drew back a little; then there came a faint pattering like a stick being drawn across a fence. The hot breath of the nearest brute had been almost fanning Coleridge's cheek. Now the animal stood rigid and then fell, stiffly, all four paws out. It was dead before it reached the bottom of the slope.

Abercrombie rose to his full height as the attack wavered and clubbed the nearest brute with the butt of his rifle; he seemed half-wolf himself at that moment. Another animal fell, then another. They had turned and were fleeing to the bottom of the slope, falling over one another in their anxiety to escape.

Now Coleridge could hear the hounds. He saw the source of the timely interruption: the upper slope below the tree-line was black with figures. On the ridge to their left above the cave he made out Raglan, firing at close-range into the pack on the floor of the gorge. Behind him was the tall, lean figure of the Count. And on the far slope, Rakosi, on horseback, spurring on his troop.

The wolves were dispersing individually, fleeing precipitously between the trees, making difficult targets for the rifles of the Castle party, pursued by the dogs. Behind, on the slopes and at the bottom of the gorge, were the scattered bodies of the slaughtered wolves. Coleridge was astonished to see there were only some half dozen or so.

He was conscious of falling; all the strength seemed to have gone from his legs. Abercrombie was at his elbow; he caught the rifle with one hand before it went down the slope. His left was under the professor's arm. He half pulled, half dragged him to sit on the jumbled boulders, forced the flask of cognac between his teeth.

Coleridge spluttered as the fiery liquid coursed its way down. Abercrombie took the flask away and put it to his own mouth. He was barely recognisable; his face blackened and streaked with smoke in which perspiration had ingrained long rivulets. Coleridge realised he must look little better.

Abercrombie replaced the cap on the neck of the flask with a flourish.

"I think we are safe now, Professor," he said.

"IT WAS CERTAINLY STRANGE," Count Homolky remarked slowly. "I have never known such a thing happen before."

"It was my fault," Coleridge said. "If I had not got out of the line it would never have happened. We should have retraced our steps."

The Count shook his head.

"I did not mean that, Professor. I meant the behaviour of those wolves. It is totally contrary to the normal."

He shivered suddenly as though some subtle, chilling wind had passed through the chamber.

"It seemed almost as though that old legend of Ivan the Bold was about to be reenacted."

"The thought had crossed my mind," Coleridge said. "Did you get the wolf you were after?"

The Count turned down the corners of his mouth.

"We glimpsed it once or twice, but always it was too cunning and agile for us. We picked off three or four of the biggest and most savage beasts which looked as though they might be potential pack-leaders."

"You found the gypsy?" Coleridge asked.

"My men conveyed him back to the village. I fear it will not prove a great loss. He was much hated by his own people, and he was certainly cruel to the bear. We will not harm it nor hunt it. And if I know bears it should survive the winter all right."

He smiled thinly.

"Poetic justice, you might say. Like Ivan the Bold. Certainly the Gypsy Fair will be a more amiable function without him. The other gypsies are burning his caravan and possessions this evening. It is their ancient custom."

The two men sat in the great chamber in which they normally took breakfast; it wanted half an hour to dinner, and as they faced one another over a table which held a half-empty whisky bottle, Coleridge felt his courage and tenacity revive.

He had bathed and rested since his return, and so far as he could make out he had received only one small scratch on his right hand, presumably from the claws of one of the wolves trying to get over the top of the boulders into the cave. That was how close they had come.

He had not seen Nadia since his return, but the news of their adventure had been conveyed to her by her father, who had persuaded her to let him rest; they would meet again at dinner. The image of her face was again agreeably before his eyes as he sat on talking to the Count. The two men seemed to be skirting the real hub of the problems involved; Coleridge was content that it should be so for the time being.

Homolky eventually turned his gaze from the heart of the fire.

"Abercrombie did well. He is a remarkable man."

"That is almost an understatement," Coleridge assented. "I should not have survived except for him."

The Count tapped with strong fingers on the arms of his chair.

"It has been a disastrous Congress," he said heavily. "I should never have invited you all here."

Coleridge put a sympathetic hand on his host's arm.

"It is wrong to think that, Count. Who knows, something like this may have happened if the Congress had not taken place. And our presence may have prevented greater harm so far."

A strange change had occurred in the Count's face.

"I am not quite sure I understand you, Professor. Do I take it you know or suspect something which you have not yet imparted to anyone, even my daughter?"

Coleridge shook his head. In truth he had been somewhat startled at his host's reaction.

"It is at the moment only the faintest idea at the back of my mind. If and when it crystallises I will let you know, you may be sure of that."

Before Homolky could reply, the room door opened and Captain Rakosi came in. He wore an undress uniform of some grey-green material, and Coleridge, who had not seen him since his timely appearance at the gorge, guessed that he had come back directly to the Castle instead of first going to the barracks.

He rose and shook hands gratefully with the young man. He had gathered from the Count that Rakosi had been the first to hear the firing, had perceived that it came from the gorge, and had ordered his troops there. On the way they had come across the Count's party and had taken him and Raglan up, riding double, until they had reached The Place of the Skull.

"Most pleased. Most pleased," Rakosi repeated over and over in answer to Coleridge's thanks.

Homolky smilingly waved him down to a seat at his side and poured him a glass of whisky. The three men sat drinking in silence for a few moments. Then Homolky excused himself, and the two men spoke for a while in Hungarian. The Count repeated briefly in English that they were making preparations for a further hunt the following week.

After a few minutes more Coleridge departed and went to his own room to prepare for dinner. He felt drained and exhausted but realised he owed it to his host and the family to put up a casual outward appearance.

He met Nadia Homolky at the door of his room, and it was obvious that she had been waiting anxiously for some time.

* * *

The girl stood very close to him, her breath coming fast as though she had been running.

"I heard what happened," she said. "What a dreadful experience . . ."

Coleridge shook his head gently, putting his hand on her arm. She wore the same evening dress she had favoured on the night of his arrival at the Castle. It now seemed a very long time ago.

"It has probably been rather exaggerated in the telling," he said. "Abercrombie had given a good account of himself, and things were not that desperate."

The girl flushed deeply.

"That is not what I heard, John."

A shadow moved at the end of the corridor. Again Coleridge thought of Raglan and wondered what he represented to the girl and she to him. As though she could read his mind, Nadia beckoned him forward to the room-door.

"We must talk privately. I have been less than honest with you."

Coleridge smiled.

"I find that hard to believe, Nadia."

The girl brushed the hair back from her eyes in a familiar gesture as he opened the door for her to precede him into the room. He closed and locked it behind them, and then they sat down by the fire. As always, the servants had been in to put the room straight and everything was in immaculate order, the logs burning evenly in the great hearth.

The girl came to the point immediately.

"What do you know about Dr. Raglan?"

Coleridge shrugged.

"Very little, actually. Apart from his medical and scholarly attainments, of course. They are on record."

He paused, choosing his words with care.

"Except that he seems very attentive to you."

The girl's eyes were wide.

"I do not quite understand what you mean."

But there was amusement dancing there.

"Surely you are not jealous? Raglan means nothing to me, you must know that."

Coleridge found himself stammering with embarrassment. The situation was novel for him, and he realised he had given himself away with his clumsiness.

"I am sure I did not mean . . ." he began.

The girl interrupted him, her eyes bright.

"I know what you meant, John. But Dr. Raglan is the person I wanted to talk to you about."

She clasped her hands about her knee with a boyish gesture and leaned forward to him.

"A short while after the main Congress party arrived here, Dr. Raglan sought me out. He requested my help on a certain confidential matter. I thought it strange at the time, but I gave him my promise. It did not seem so then, but it may be vitally important in this black business which surrounds us."

Coleridge stared at her in silence for a moment.

Then, recollecting himself, he said, "This may be very important indeed."

"He asked me, in effect, to keep an eye on various members of the Congress and to let him know of any untoward incidents there might be."

"Did he give any explanation for this rather extraordinary request?"

"He convinced me the matter was serious," the girl said. "Otherwise I would not have complied with his wishes."

"What sort of incidents?" was the professor's next question.

"Nothing that I could not have told him without a clear conscience. People's movements and that sort of thing. Who conferred with whom. Anything that came within my own purview."

The girl flushed again.

"I was not in any way acting as a spy, you understand. I would not have stood for that."

Coleridge was silent for a long moment.

"You were convinced his motives were good, then?"

Nadia Homolky nodded.

"He was particularly concerned with my own safety and that of my family. Just as you were, in fact. I could not see any harm in his request."

Coleridge found the silence profound, save for the very faint crackling of the fire.

"What does your father say to this?"

The young woman shook her head.

"He does not know. You are the only other person who does."

"And you think this might be to do with the creature which seems to be haunting this castle. If we are to speak bluntly."

Nadia Homolky picked an imaginary thread from her long skirt and frowned at her companion across the table.

"We are to speak bluntly. It is too late for us to dissemble with one another now."

Coleridge put the implications of this aside and ploughed on.

"You think I ought to have a talk with Raglan? And ask him his true purpose here? Apart from the Congress, I mean?"

The girl bit her lip.

"Perhaps. You are convinced of his bona fides?"

"Certainly. He knows his subjects in every aspect."

Coleridge turned and stared into the heart of the fire.

"I do not think he means any harm. He certainly distinguished himself when Abercrombie and I were trapped in the cave. But we cannot take anyone at face value. There is a darkness and a horror here, and we have no margin for error. I only wish you could have confided in me sooner."

The girl gave a helpless little gesture that reminded Coleridge of the first morning they had spoken.

"It is difficult. I had given my word. And I never break my word if it is humanly possible."

Coleridge accepted the implied rebuke in silence.

"I am sure that is so," he replied eventually. "And it is certainly not my place to criticise your personal conduct."

The girl got up quickly, giving Coleridge a shy little smile.

"I shall go to tell Dr. Raglan of our talk now, so that there can be no misconceptions. After that you two gentlemen must make your own accommodations."

Coleridge joined in her smile as they shook hands formally.

"Thank you for telling me," he said.

The girl left her hand in his a fraction longer than necessary.

"Until dinner, then."

Coleridge nodded.

"Until dinner."

He stood frowning into the fire until he heard the door softly close behind her. As her footsteps moved away he went over and relocked it. He returned to his seat, his mind revolving further possibilities. The problems at Castle Homolky were apparently endless, and Raglan's involvement made little sense either.

He must have sat there a long while because when he again looked at his watch it was almost time to go down. He changed rapidly and made hasty preparations, using the basin in his room.

It was only when he went over to the door that he saw a small square envelope had been pushed beneath it. He picked it up cautiously, as though he feared its contents. He read it twice before its import sank in. It was inscribed in stylish, flowing writing that was unfamiliar to him.

It said simply: "Professor— Have most urgent information to impart. Please come to my room after dinner, at eleven o'clock. Raglan."

The Hanged Man

COLERIDGE EASED THE PISTOL from his jacket pocket and threw off the safety-catch. It was dark and dim in the corridor here. He had had no time to tell the girl of the meeting at dinner, and it would certainly have been unwise to have spoken to Raglan publicly. If the man was genuine and had knowledge to impart to Coleridge, then his life could be in danger as well as the professor's.

It wanted but a few minutes to eleven as Coleridge gained the stairhead, and the Castle clock chimed the hour as he paused outside Raglan's room. He remembered its exact location from the plan Nadia Homolky had prepared for their search of the Castle, and he still had it with him. He had met no servants on the way.

Raglan had excused himself from the coffee room some while before, and Coleridge had slipped out after a discreet interval. He was himself again now. His experiences with Abercrombie had strengthened him, if anything, and he was determined to see the business through until the end. He wondered what his American students would think if they knew he was engaged in a hunt for such a mythical creature as a werewolf in this dark and remote corner of Europe.

Superstition was something that was woven into the very thread of people's lives here; the reverse side of the religious coin, if one liked. Father Balaz had been at dinner, and one look at his mediaeval saint's face, which appeared as though it had a century of suffering carved into it, would have been enough to convince the most confirmed sceptic.

Through the great staircase window Coleridge had been startled to see scarlet-and-yellow flame coming from the village below; then he had remembered that the dead gypsy chief's caravan and all his personal belongings were being burnt according to ancient ritual that evening. He had lingered by the casement for some time, watching a scene of barbaric splendour as the gypsies stood rank on rank on the field of the Winter Fair, their wild chanting rising up toward the Castle on the night wind.

He wondered cynically if the great bear was watching from the warmth and security of some remote cave high above the village. He wished it well, at any event. Then, as the flames flickered and died, and the scarlet splashes, looking like blood against the crusted snow of the housetops of Lugos, faded from sight, he mounted the stairs to his meeting with Raglan, still feeling a great oppression upon his heart.

His mind had been much drawn to Homolky's tale of the tragic accident involving his mother all those years ago; Raglan would be too young, of course. He was only some thirty years old, and the doctor concerned would be in his forties now, at least. But supposing he had escaped from his asylum in England and had come back for revenge? As fantastic as such a proposition sounded, it was no more bizarre than the idea that a genuine lycanthrope might be roaming the Castle corridors.

Coleridge followed his weird train of thought a stage further as he lingered, still outside Raglan's door. There was no way of checking, of course; it had all been so long ago and the man might well be dead by now. Even if he lived, there was no method of discovering in which asylum he was now incarcerated.

But such a possibility would solve Coleridge's greatest problem. Two strands, perhaps? A real wolf killing the people in the village, long before the Congress party arrived; and an insane murderer inside the Castle walls again, returned after twenty years and bent on revenge. Either way, the prospect seemed hardly less dismal. But at least a human being, once identified, could be stopped.

It was a horrifying thought that one of his own colleagues was responsible for Menlow's death. Several of them were the right age and might fit the young doctor's physical characteristics. That still did not explain the wolf's presence in the corridors, but there were many other things also that were unexplainable; if one problem were solved, then more might follow.

Coleridge thrust all such useless speculation from him, took a deep breath, and rapped firmly at Raglan's door. The sounds made a dull, echoing reverberation in the dim corridor that set the blood racing. A very long silence followed. It was so deep that Coleridge could clearly hear the remorseless ticking of the watch in his pocket.

He knocked again with the same result. Then he tried the door. To his surprise it was unlocked. He pushed it slowly open, whispering Raglan's name. There was still no response. He put the barrel of the pistol up as he stepped quietly and cautiously into the faintly lit bedroom.

Coleridge sensed danger, yet he could not assign a precise reason for it. The room looked empty and perfectly normal. It was very much like Coleridge's own; very much, in fact, like all those assigned to the guests. The only differences were that, being a corner room, it had a sort of turret window set into the far angle of the chamber, which must have commanded a magnificent view of Lugos in the daylight. For the rest there was a curious little balcony, reached by a spiral staircase to one side of the handsome carved fireplace.

It was a charming conceit, and for a moment or two Coleridge stood admiring the apartment in the light from the two shaded lamps set on small round tables until he was recalled to the present and his mysterious summons there.

It had evidently been a woman's room at one time—he was reminded of the old Countess's predilection for her writing desk on the balcony—and at the other side of the fireplace there was a superb polished spinet cased in rosewood, which was evidently a lady's instrument, judging by its delicate proportions and floral embellishment in different coloured woods let into the main body of the casing.

Coleridge did not really know why he was taking in all this detail, or why he was concerning his mind with it. Except that it provided a form of distraction under the circumstances of stress in which he found himself. He was becoming resentful, in fact, of the strain; it seemed that he alone had been picked out from all his colleagues to bear this burden while most of them—Abercrombie a notable exception—went their way heedless of the appalling drama that was being played out behind their backs.

It was unfair to think so, Coleridge knew, but it was a measure of the wear his nerves had been subjected to over the past few days. Now he paused, still holding the pistol, feeling rather absurdly self-conscious but at the same time aware of some danger it was difficult to encompass.

Then he had visual evidence of what his nerves had already told him. At the far side of the bed there were some signs of a struggle: a thick bearskin rug had been ruckled and pushed out of position, and the bedspread itself bore marks as though hands had scrabbled at it before relinquishing their hold.

Coleridge felt a cold draught then; he had not noticed it previously because he had been standing near the fire. At first he could not quite place the direction from which it was blowing. He had left the room-door ajar, and now he crept back quietly toward it. Nothing moved in all the dim privacy of the long corridor, in either direction. It was chill there, certainly, but that would not account for this particular draught.

He closed the door behind him and went back into the middle of the room. He was only a few minutes after the time appointed in the note; perhaps Raglan was downstairs and would shortly reappear. As soon as he had formulated the notion Coleridge knew that this could not be so. The urgency of the summons denoted its importance; Raglan would have been here.

Besides, the slight disarrangement of the room had a somewhat sinister import under the circumstances, not only of the present situation but in the entire context of the menacing atmosphere in the Castle.

Still the draught persisted. Coleridge went over and stared at the large stone fireplace. There was some draught from that direction, certainly, but not enough to account for the strong current of air he felt even at the moment. It was icy cold. There might be a window open somewhere, but the notion seemed ridiculous. Or could a pane somehow have been broken?

There were three sets of curtains in the room, covering the heavy leaded casements. Coleridge went round them slowly. The first was to the left of the fireplace, in the far wall. There was nothing amiss there. He replaced the heavy dark red portières and went across to the embrasure near the bed-head. It too was secure. That left only the turret window at the far side of the bed.

Coleridge walked over, still holding the pistol, his throat dry and constricted. He pulled the curtaining back. The draught was certainly coming from here, but at first he could not see anything wrong.

It was dark in this corner of the chamber, and he had to stoop before he saw that the right-hand wing of the lower casement was open. Unlike most of them, it opened outward, and he was slow to see the reason for its gaping darkness. He twice tried to close it to cut off the draught but found on each occasion that something gently resisted the pressure.

Bending lower still he found a rope had been tied at floor level to one of the heavy uprights of the four-poster bed. It was lying parallel with the dark boards, which was why he had not noticed it before. He could feel with his fingertips that it was under heavy pressure. The far end went out the window and down the wall.

Coleridge opened the segment and pushed his head out, oblivious of the cold wind which leapt at him. The whole of Lugos was below, bathed in unearthly beauty in its coating of snow and ice, for the moon was out, riding high and clear of the jagged clouds. By its misty light he could see the body of Raglan hanging halfway down the turret, his legs dangling above the awful abyss. His eyes seemed to look imploringly at Coleridge.

His blackened tongue started from the rictus of the mouth like some monstrous sac, and the rope was about his neck. One hand was trapped beneath it as though he had tried to grasp it to haul himself back up to salvation.

Into the Abyss

COLERIDGE FOUND ABERCROMBIE drinking whisky and soda in the small side-room they had used for taking coffee after dinner. The professor walked like an automaton, his legs stiff and seeming to carry him of their own volition. His brain felt anaesthetised and remote from his bodily functions. But he must have appeared fairly normal because his colleague looked up, merely smiled, and waved him to a leather armchair at his side.

As he sank down and the doctor poured him a whisky from the decanter on the table, Coleridge felt the pressure of the revolver in his inner jacket pocket. He was glad that he had remembered to put it away; he would have looked absurd coming through the Castle corridors holding it in the firing position, though there had been few people about.

He took the crystal tumbler Abercrombie passed him and drank. He felt better immediately. He looked at the big man opposite, noting the scar that creased his forehead. He was immersed in a bundle of newspapers, apparently seeing nothing amiss on his companion's face.

"Would you care to see *The Times*? These came in for me this afternoon. They are a fortnight old, but it does help to keep one in touch with civilisation."

Coleridge took the proffered paper politely, left it unfolded at his side as he sipped his whisky. He had shut Raglan's room-door. He had no wish to alarm the Castle. But he could not confront the scene again without the presence of someone like Abercrombie. And there was the problem of the Count and his family. . .

This was the end of the Congress, of course; it was the end of many things, come to that. Coleridge shut his mind to the mass of bewildering complications that this new death had opened up before him. His mind felt frozen; he would think later. Tomorrow, perhaps. He wondered if Anton was staying in the Castle tonight. He would be glad to leave everything in that officer's capable hands.

He stared at the calm face of Abercrombie. It was incredible that he should be so unruffled, particularly in view of the fact that he also had been through two horrifying experiences since his arrival. The big man looked up, smiling pleasantly.

"Hungary is not the only place in which bizarre things happen."

"What do you mean?" the professor forced out.

"There is a fascinating criminal report here," Abercrombie went on. "A young man called Clyde Beatty, a private detective, discovered a cemetery near Woking in which bullion robbers from London had hidden vast amounts of stolen gold bars. Imagine!"

He tapped the newspaper, his face alight with surprise and interest.

"The stolen articles hidden in the coffins of the dead and transported by rail from Waterloo-road to Brookwood Cemetery direct and under the unsuspecting noses of the police. There is enough material here for a Gothic novel in itself!"

"Indeed," said Coleridge politely.

He had hardly taken in what his companion was saying, did not really know where to begin in relating his own bad news. He hoped for an opportunity, but a sort of paralysis of the soul had seized him. He appeared isolated in his chair, mechanically sipping the whisky and soda Abercrombie had poured for him, his gaze fixed blankly upon his companion but not hearing his conversation or receiving the import of his words.

He wondered vaguely if he were ill. Certainly his experiences since arriving at the Castle were enough to unhinge any man; that and the knowledge which he carried within him. For he alone seemed to have received all the facts, as though he were a cornucopia in reverse, into which all the evil thoughts and impressions of this ancient house were poured, soaking and staining their way into his very soul.

His inmost thoughts now seemed opaque, filtered through muslin. The room in which he sat was somehow all squeezed up, the angle of the fireplace in tight perspective that seemed to bend and distort before compressing itself into an impossibly small area of space. As Coleridge watched it actually came to a point.

He heard a noise then. That too seemed to come from the far distance. He sat watching stupidly as his shattered glass and the remains of its contents dispersed across the floor. Abercrombie looked at him sharply. His face appeared immense as he bent concernedly toward his companion.

"Are you ill? Is there anything I can do?"

Coleridge meant to shake his head, but his neck muscles felt paralysed. His words were enunciated as a strangled croak.

"Raglan. He is dead."

It seemed to take him an immense amount of time to get out the simple sentence. Abercrombie rose to his feet, his face alarmed.

"Are you sure?"

He patted the other's hand solicitously, as though he were speaking to a child.

"Don't worry yourself. Stay there. I will go and look."

He went away, leaving Coleridge to stare at the distorted room before him.

Then the old Countess appeared. She leaned over him, her eyes narrowed to slits.

"There are wolves—and wolves, Professor," she said mournfully.

She sighed. Presently she went away in turn, and he was alone once more.

He was conscious of no sound except the faint murmur of his own breathing and the thump of his heart. Perspiration cascaded down into his eyes. Abercrombie was away for more than a year.

When he reappeared his expression was puzzled, noncommittal. He bent until his mouth was close to Coleridge's ear.

"I have been to Raglan's room. Everything is in order. There was no-one there."

Coleridge gave a gurgling gasp. Abercrombie's alarmed face disappeared as he pitched forward in a dead faint.

The Wolf Strikes Again

COLERIDGE SAW THE GIRL'S FACE first, slowly composing itself from the darkness. Her expression was concerned, anxious. Next to her the Count, equally grave. It was the second time Coleridge had fainted in a few days, and he felt ridiculous and somehow diminished. His throat ached, and there was a vile taste in his mouth. He supposed that Abercrombie had given him something to bring him round, though he was not there.

As recollection flooded back in, he half lifted himself on the pillow, found the girl holding his hand.

"You are all right," the Count said very deliberately. "Just a faint, the doctor thought. I have taken the liberty of having you brought to your own room by my servants."

He glanced at his watch.

"You have been unconscious only half an hour."

The girl cast a defiant look at her father, then remarked bluntly.

"What is this about Dr. Raglan? Abercrombie said you told him he was dead."

"That is perfectly true."

Coleridge sipped gratefully at the tumbler of cold water the girl held out to him. Nothing had ever tasted better. His brain was clear now.

"He was hanging out the window by a rope attached to the leg of his bed. I saw him as distinctly as I see you."

The Count and Nadia exchanged glances; their import was not lost on the man in the bed.

"There was nothing there when Dr. Abercrombie looked," the Count said. "I looked myself. But Dr. Raglan is certainly missing."

He gave a helpless shrug.

"We will do what we can, of course, but things are hopeless tonight. There is a snowstorm raging outside. From my experience it may last for days."

"Raglan was hanging outside the room, with the rope through the window," Coleridge persisted. "Someone must have removed the body."

The Count bit his lip, his eyes turned full upon Coleridge.

"You may well be right, Professor. The Congress must be called off, of course. And in the morning, when you feel better, you must tell everyone why. There is a murderer amongst us. He must be caught."

He drummed with strong fingers on the edge of the counterpane, avoiding his daughter's eye.

"You will tell your wife and mother, then?" Coleridge said.

Homolky nodded.

"I must. Things are too serious for anything but absolute truth. I will leave it to you, so far as your colleagues are concerned. Both Rakosi and Anton have accepted my hospitality for the night, in view of the weather."

He paused.

"Whatever the weather I must be present at the church tomorrow afternoon. It is my duty."

Coleridge had forgotten the funeral service for the dead villager. They would be holding a mass memorial for the werewolf victims in the Castle chapel soon if things went on in this way, Coleridge reflected cynically.

Two of his colleagues were already dead. He felt in his bones that there would be more; the thing was reaching insane proportions. He could not make head nor tail of it, but there was a terrible logic behind the tragedies.

"I was thinking about that sad story you told me," Coleridge said.

He was talking to the Count but looking at Nadia. She kept tight hold of his hand, her lips compressed into a stubborn line.

"Oh?"

There was nothing but polite interest in the host's voice now. The sadness of the ascetic face beneath the shock of white hair was markedly pronounced. At that moment he almost resembled the saintlike features of Father Balaz, Coleridge thought.

"About your mother's accident. And that young doctor . . ."

The Count nodded stiffly.

"I had not thought about him for years until we spoke. Dr. Sanders. The unfortunate confined in the asylum."

"You do not think he may have come back? For revenge? The insane are said to be possessed of immense strength . . ."

The Count's jaw dropped, and there was something like fear in his eyes as he stared at the man in the bed. The girl looked helplessly from Coleridge to her father.

"He swore vengeance, you said," Coleridge continued. "Supposing he has broken out and come here to destroy your family? Human or demon, he has supernatural cunning. I know nothing of the wolf which has been ravaging the village. But I have twice seen a wolf within the Castle. And two people have been murdered; one of them for the knowledge he possessed. The second wished to see me, and he also may have intended to pass on some information. He did not commit suicide, despite the indications. He was murdered before he could tell me his secret."

The Count's face was ashen and he spoke in a hollow voice, like a mechanical doll Coleridge had once seen in an arcade.

"Then we are all in the most appalling danger."

Coleridge looked at the Count's pistol which someone had placed on his bedside table.

"As you value your life, see that the doors of both guests and family are locked tonight," he said slowly. "In the morning we will take counsel."

The Count nodded as though he were slowly awakening from a trance.

"I will leave my men on guard outside the door, Professor. They will remain there all night. You have only to ring if you need assistance."

Coleridge nodded. He felt weak and drained. The last thing he remembered was Nadia bending over him with a reassuring smile.

He struggled awake, aware of pressure on his shoulder. A hideous, distorted face was pressed up close to his own. He reached out desperately for the pistol, felt his wrist gripped in a clutch of steel. As the fog of sleep cleared from his mind he saw that it was the dumb majordomo, who had come to shake him awake. The mutilated red stump of his tongue rolled round his mouth in the lamplight.

He had thrown on his braided uniform over his night-clothes, and Coleridge could now see that it was concern and fear that were agitating him, not malice. The other gripped him lightly by the arm and indicated that he was to follow. Coleridge rolled out of bed quickly, throwing on his trousers and jacket over his night-things; he put on his socks and shoes as the other made imploring noises deep in his throat.

He left his shoes unlaced, hoping that he would not trip on the steep stairs of the Castle. He saw by his watch that it was three A.M. as he went over to the lamp to get the pistol. It was fully loaded, and he still had some cartridges in his jacket pocket. He felt well now but parched with thirst, and he paused just long enough to pour a glass of water from the bedside carafe.

Then he was outside in the dim corridor, stepping over the outstretched legs of the sleeping servants and trying to keep up with the headlong rush of the majordomo as he headed for the upper floors.

Coleridge was wide awake, painfully aware that he was having difficulty in breathing as he ran clumsily up the worn stone steps that ascended in a steep spiral to the next storey. He had never been here before; this must be another private stair to the family's own apartments. The majordomo could not speak to him, of course, but he must have been sent by the Count to rouse Coleridge.

At three in the morning it was obviously urgent, perhaps terrible indeed, to disturb one who was currently regarded as a semi-invalid. He held out the pistol in his left hand, as the stairway was dim and he hoped to be warned in this way of any obstruction; he did not want a repetition of his earlier experience. Once he caught his right shoe on the outstretched lace of the other foot and almost fell headlong.

But his heart was doing its work properly and he felt fit and alert, if a little blown, when they came at length to the end of the spiral and were in a well-lit corridor with parquet underfoot. The majordomo went straight on, not looking back, holding a lamp in his left hand that he had just picked up from a small occasional table standing by the wall.

The horror of Raglan's death burst into Coleridge's brain like a bombshell. Perhaps he had been found, and that was why the majordomo had been sent to summon him to the Count's presence. Coleridge did not know the way here, but the dumb man led him unerringly onward, up two more short flights of stairs, where an atmosphere of brooding oppression seemed to obtain.

Coleridge could not have said why; it seemed, as they came along these dim corridors, as though some sort of blight or pollution had settled upon his soul. The tall man with grey hair grunted again and beckoned him forward to where an open door gaped blackly.

Lamps burned from within, casting a pale, unearthly sheen on everything. Coleridge went to cross toward the entry, but before he could do so he heard a terrible snarling noise. In contrast to his earlier experiences he was ice-cold now, throwing off the safety-catch of the pistol.

A monstrous shadow passed across the lamps, and then some vile thing was in the doorway, jaws slavering, foetid breath foul and stinking in Coleridge's nostrils. He fired as it sprang, was put off his aim. The majordomo gave a strangled cry and was hurled to the floor; the beast went by so close it appeared to knock him down.

Coleridge turned, got off another shot which tore splinters from the wall panelling; he could not see whether he had hit the wolf. It moved so quickly it was merely a fleeting shadow on the far wall. A faint groan from the room beyond sent pencils of fear crawling along Coleridge's nerves.

He helped the majordomo up, the barrel of the revolver trembling. The man appeared uninjured. The whites of his eyes showed as he stared at his companion with blanched features. Coleridge was within the room now, took in the tangled and disarranged sheets of the bed. His nerves jumped again as a white hand sought his own.

The Countess Sylva materialised from the darkness. Blood dripped from the torn shoulder of her silk dressing-gown, her hair hung over her eyes, and the dark blue pupils stared from chalk-white features. She collapsed into Coleridge's arms as he half carried her into the corridor and sat her down on a chair.

"You are safe now," he said.

The majordomo, with great presence of mind, had darted into the bedroom; he came back with a bottle of some spirit and a crystal goblet. The Countess's white teeth danced on the rim of the glass as she drank.

Coleridge was already examining the torn flesh of her shoulder; she appeared to have had a remarkable escape. So far as he could see, the damage was limited to fairly superficial injuries, as though the beast's claws had raked across her once or twice.

He waited until the liquor had done its work. She clung to him convulsively as he sent the majordomo back into the bedroom to find a clean towel. He made a compress and fixed it securely over the wound, the padded shoulder of the dressing-gown holding it in position.

The Countess was calmer, and she made an effort to speak.

"What has happened?" was Coleridge's first question.

Countess Sylva turned dazed eyes from the majordomo's face to his own. The former was drinking now to steady his own nerves, at Coleridge's suggestion.

"There was a knocking at the door earlier. My husband thought it was one of the servants. He found no-one there."

Her breathing was becoming agitated again, and her eyes glanced wildly about the dim corridor like a hunted animal. Coleridge gave the servant the pistol and sent him to stand in the middle of the corridor, in case the animal came back. But he knew in his heart that they had seen the last of it tonight.

"He felt there was something wrong," the Countess continued. "He went out with his revolver, telling me to lock the door. A few minutes ago I heard three taps and opened, thinking it to be my husband."

Her lips were a pure white colour as she stared at Coleridge.

"The wolf came in," she said simply.

A scalding fear came over Coleridge then; he guessed it was delayed shock, and he sought the bottle on the corridor table. His nerve steadied, his arm still round the dark-haired woman's shoulder, he tried to make sense of this new development.

"You have not seen your husband since?"

Countess Sylva shook her cloudy black hair round her face.

"The Castle is vast, as you understand. I do not know where he is, except that he was lured away."

"You were fortunate, madame. How did you managc to avoid serious injury?"

The voice was so low the professor had to bend forward to hear what his hostess was saying.

"I fell behind a big armchair, which took the full force of the beast's attack. I hung on to it and dragged it to a corner of the room, staying behind it. The animal's claws were able to reach my shoulder only. Then you arrived . . ."

Her eyes clouded over.

"For God's sake, what is this curse on our house, Professor?"

Coleridge felt inadequate and impotent in the face of something so black and monstrous that it seemed to inhibit the will. He stood up quickly, throwing indecision from him.

"Your mother-in-law's room. Where is it?"

The Countess pointed dumbly down the misty corridor. Coleridge wished he did not have to go, but there was no-one else and his Boston upbringing had instilled in him a strong sense of duty. Hc took thc pistol from the manservant, reaching down a sabre from the panelled wall.

"Look after madame."

He gently ran his fingers along the frightened woman's jawline.

"Be brave, Countess. Your husband will soon be here."

He moved away from the brightness of the lamplight into an inky pool of darkness, feeling his courage ebb with the fading of the light. His feet made hardly any noise on the parquet, he was moving so slowly, but his fingers were firm on the butt of the pistol. He did not think there would be anything there; the beast had done whatever it set out to do.

He no longer thought of it as a fact of natural history. Either it was of supernatural origin, able to open doors and turn handles as well as knock on wood, or there was, as some in the Castle had surmised, a human agent behind this using an animal as its nemesis, which was almost as fantastic a possibility.

But beyond Coleridge's present fear and his presence in this darkened corridor was the image of a young, strong face in the silver-framed photograph on the Countess's desk on the upstairs gallery.

Had that young Dr. Sanders indeed returned from his asylum, as a man in his forties or early fifties, burning with vengeance? Or had a werewolf brushed paths with man, as the legends and stories in Coleridge's ancient books opined? Was there, in fact, any sense at all in this holocaust of death and suffering in which Coleridge was embroiled?

He was in complete darkness now but, turning, could see the small, tragic tableau made up by the huddled figure of the dishevelled Countess in the lamplight with the white-haired majordomo nearby; his shadow and that of the upraised sabre making a fine, dramatic silhouette on the panelled wall beyond, thrown there by the yellow glow.

There was a window at his back, and through it, dimly seen, the calm relentless descent of driving snow. But more light was growing ahead, and a few yards to his left Coleridge could see where the open door of an adjoining room gaped blackly. He went forward with unsteady steps, holding the pistol with its four unexpended shots, reluctant to cross the threshold but knowing that he must.

There were two lamps burning here, and by their light Coleridge made out, as though in thickly carved detail, a scene of unparalleled horror.

Death Comes to the Countess

THERE WAS A DEEP SILENCE in the room, and over it, the smell of death. To Coleridge it was unmistakable. He lingered in the doorway, his legs turning to water before he had a grip on his eroded nerves. He lowered the pistol then. There would be little use for it.

The room was a large and comfortable one, as befitted the titular head of the Homolky family. The walls were panelled, and the eye was led naturally to two points: the great four-poster bed with its wealth of Gothic carving which seemed to take up most of the far wall and the huge, elaborately carved fireplace in which a vast fire was leaping. A spiral staircase, similar to that in Raglan's room, stood in the far corner and led to a long gallery below the ceiling, where the lamplight gleamed on the massed gilt spines of thousands of books.

Coleridge took all this in in a fraction of time. He stared at the tangled mass of bedding that had been dragged from the four-poster into the centre of the room. Its strange and anarchic shape was composed of whorls of white drapery, reminiscent of the pattern of seashells, against which the gouts and stains of blood stood out in sinister contrast.

For a moment Coleridge could make out little else, as it took a short period for his eyes to become adjusted to the gloom. That the room belonged to the old Countess was not in doubt; there were silver-mounted photographs of her on a bureau which stood near the door and which Coleridge had passed on his way in. There were flowers in bowls too, and these touches of tropical elegance added undertones of grotesque mockery to the charnel scene.

Coleridge moved a little farther forward, his shoes making an ugly scraping noise on the parquet. The action naturally brought him closer to the bed and at a slightly different angle. It was obvious the bedding had been dragged toward the fireplace. Coleridge knew what he would find in the huddled mass on the other side, and he was not anxious to advance the moment.

He had control of his nerves now, and he put the pistol back into his pocket. He moved again, infinitely slowly, as though dragged reluctantly by some force outside himself. He had often noticed the same thing in spectators at a street accident, for example; their horror and repugnance overcome by human curiosity that impelled them to come forward for a closer look.

A clock ticked somewhere in the heavy silence; Coleridge had not been aware of it before. Now, it seemed a grating intrusion on what had become a funereal place. He stopped again, his stomach turning over. A beam of yellow lamplight shone on the whitened, neatly severed arm that lay apart from the bedding like some obscene waxwork exhibit. It undoubtedly belonged to the Countess; he recognised the rings.

The extensive system of blue veins, so typical of the very old, and the thinness of the wrist would have identified the pitiful fragment even without the decoration; a bright corona of blood ringed the upper arm where it had been bitten clean from a point near the shoulder. Coleridge was trembling uncontrollably now but he forced himself on, avoiding the thing on the floor, remembering to look carefully before placing his feet.

He had not far to go. Another yard took him to the object of his search. The Countess lay half in the light, half in the shadow. Her eyes were open, but the face was extraordinarily placid, as though she had had no time for alarm before death was on her. The professor guessed that she had probably died of shock before the extensive wounds were inflicted.

She had made no attempt to defend herself. The wolf-creature had probably dragged her from the bed by the arm before severing it; Coleridge hoped the old lady had been already dead by then. It had next returned to savage her throat. Despite the wounds, any one of which would have been sufficient to cause death by itself, there was surprisingly little blood.

But then a person of that age might have little, and a sluggish circulation could account for it. Moved by some obscure shaft of compassion, Coleridge turned slowly back to a big leather wing-chair that stood in the window embrasure. He took from it the voluminous silk dressing-gown that was draped across it and gently covered the Countess's remains, hiding the shocking countenance from sight.

Then he went back and carefully eased a section of the sheeting over the fragment on the floor. He moved a few yards toward the door, his head bowed as though in silent prayer. The lamps shone on, yellow and indifferent, as though the scene had been an ordinary domestic one, typical of the thousands that must have been enacted in this elegant room.

Coleridge was still standing there, wishing himself vast distances from such pain and problems, when he heard hurried footsteps in the corridor outside and a flood of hysterical conversation in Hungarian. He quickly pulled himself together and walked toward the doorway. He was just in time to meet the dishevelled figure of the Count, tall and gaunt in his dark grey dressing-gown, his eyes wild beneath the shock of white hair.

"Don't come in!" Coleridge warned.

The big man stared unseeingly at the disordered room over Coleridge's shoulder. Then he seemed to crumple. Coleridge put his arm round his shoulder as his host sagged toward the floor.

Theories & Counter Theories

COLONEL ANTON'S FACE was grim. He confronted the members of the Congress and the family who were sitting on the leather chairs of the conference room, with the police chief on the dais. Professor Shaw and the Count had been translating question and answer, and the process had necessarily been a long one. The only member of the Count's family not present was the Countess Sylva, who was under guard and recovering in a private sitting-room on the ground floor.

She would not return to her bedroom, and Coleridge could not say he blamed her. He himself had had a private interview with Anton and Rakosi before dawn when, through the Count, he had explained in great detail, aided by the dumb servant's written deposition, the events of the night.

Now he half listened to the discussion that went on about him, knowing that it would do little good. The Count had not mentioned the professor's own theory of Sanders: it would all have seemed too fantastic and bizarre for the police officer.

The snow was still coming down thickly this morning. There would be difficult conditions for the Count's sombre expedition to the village church. In addition to the peasant's funeral there would be a melancholy procession from the Castle when the hastily constructed coffins of the Count's own mother and Menlow would be taken to lie in state.

Coleridge felt he should go with the others, but the events of the night had taken their toll and he had slept for less than three hours in toto. The Count had insisted that he should remain to assist Anton and Rakosi. All the conference members had volunteered to attend the service as a mark of respect for Countess Irina but had also been asked to remain by the Count personally; it was obviously more important to discover the perpetrator of these devilish crimes at a Congress which now appeared to be cursed.

The girl was staying too; not only to comfort her mother but also to be near Coleridge. She had not said so, but he could feel it as he watched her downcast head in the front row of leather chairs.

Rakosi sat next to Anton on the platform, his face sad and stern, as he followed the police chief's discourse; the Count, apparently fully recovered from the ravages of the night, occasionally translating.

Raglan was still missing. Extensive searches had been made, but he seemed to have disappeared as completely as though he had never existed, while heavily armed parties had made a minute search of the Castle, including the cellars. Already there had been whispers among Coleridge's colleagues; most of them had been at first sceptical at the werewolf theory, but now it appeared that Raglan himself was suspected of the outrages.

Coleridge wondered how long it would be before their resentment turned upon him. After all, he had suspected, if not known, the situation for some time but had not confided his thoughts to the general company. He turned uneasily in his chair, taking in the melancholy features of the dumb majordomo who stood, tall and erect, in his semimilitary uniform at the side of the hall, ready to do the Count's slightest bidding.

His eyes rested with approval on Coleridge and passed to the next in line. Anton's monotonous question and answer went on;

where had everyone been during the night. In bed and fast asleep, of course. No-one had seen or heard anything, even when Coleridge had fired the shots. The Count had been making his investigations in far corners of the Castle; he thought he had heard something and had pursued it with his pistol and the lamp. He had seen nothing and had later come to realise he had been lured away, leaving his family at the mercy of whatever was prowling the corridors. No-one had mentioned the question of how the wolf could have gained access to the old lady's room.

The only person who had seen anything, other than the Countess Sylva and Coleridge, was the majordomo; he had written down, for the Count and for Anton's official file, his own account. Though Coleridge had not seen it on this occasion, the tall man had had time to notice the telltale grey patch on the wolf's back.

It was over at last, and everyone drifted across to the side-tables where Nadia Homolky presided at the coffee urn, the majordomo dispensing strong liqueurs for those who needed them. The melancholy, ravaged face of Father Balaz appeared in the room, snow still glistening on his black robes. He sat at one end of the chamber, coffee cup on lap, talking earnestly to the Count and his daughter, no doubt offering support and comfort.

All those in the hall seemed in a state of suspended shock. Coleridge found himself studying them intently. He had no doubt now that one of them must be the murderous presence who haunted the Castle corridors.

"But why did you not tell us of this before?"

Shaw had difficulty in keeping the irritation from his voice. His attitude summed up that of the others, Coleridge thought. Not that he blamed them. Both he and the Count had been playing a dangerous game by remaining silent. But Coleridge had bowed to his host's wishes in the matter.

And it was true it would have done no good even if he had warned his colleagues. They were frankly sceptical of the werewolf theory, even now, and inclined to lay suspicion on Raglan, whose disappearance had only crystallised their feelings in the matter.

Menlow had been on his guard, but even he had been taken unawares. Coleridge himself had had lucky escapes; and if what the girl had told him pointed in the direction of the professor's suppositions, even Raglan had been carrying out his own investigations into the matter. So he had been on guard too, but that had not prevented him from being hanged from his own bedroom window like a helpless fowl.

Coleridge still inclined to the murder theory; why should Raglan have killed himself? Unless the whole thing had been an elaborate charade, staged for his benefit. He could not rule that out, of course. Such things had happened before, leaving murderers a free hand to prowl the night and prey on further victims. Or someone could have removed the body in Coleridge's absence.

It would have needed immense strength. All of the members of the Congress fitted that bill, including the Count himself; though some were in middle age, they were of imposing stature and in excellent health. Coleridge blinked. Shaw was repeating his question. He answered to the best of his ability, making things sound as plausible as possible while at the same time avoiding laying the blame on the Count.

As Coleridge finished, Shaw seemed mollified and the discussion became general.

"And now we must remain here at the mercy of this thing," said Dr. Sullivan aggrievedly. "While this policeman carries out his fruitless investigations."

He still affected the suit of dark brown plus-fours which made him look as if he had just come from a Scottish grouse-moor, and with his greying beard appeared a typical savant. But he was deceptively muscular, and his age would have fitted Coleridge's theory.

The professor's thoughts were still centred on his somewhat wild ideas about Dr. Sanders and a possible escape from an asylum somewhere. It seemed the only explanation which made sense. That was leaving aside the wolf-attacks in the village. If one presupposed them to be the natural result of preying bands of wolves driven down from the high mountains by hunger, that broke the attacks into two sections.

Those that were entirely natural, presumably perpetrated by a band led by a large black wolf; and attacks within the Castle area by a large animal with a grey patch on its back. With the creature's incredible cunning, lethal ferocity, and magical habit of appearing and disappearing without first being seen, Coleridge was inclining more and more to the supernatural. Could there be such a thing as a real-life werewolf? One, moreover, which had been incarcerated in an asylum for a large part of its life?

If that were so—and one had to assume a natural time-scale—that limited his possible suspects to men at least in their mid-forties, certainly no later than fifty. Sullivan was in his late forties, he would have said. His eyes wandered over his companions, quietly drinking their coffee, until his brain felt exhausted with the seemingly patent absurdities of his quest.

His new theory also presupposed that the werewolf had first killed some member of the Congress and had taken his place; it seemed even more unlikely, until Coleridge remembered that Sanders had been a fully qualified medical practitioner who was also an expert on folklore.

Shaw was holding forth again now. Today he wore a thick grey tweed suit with a matching waistcoat, and his green wool tie was knotted in tightly beneath his high celluloid collar. He had something of the look of a Spanish hidalgo with his silver hair and drooping moustache of the same colour; though tall and emaciated-looking, he was possessed of immense strength.

This had been demonstrated to Coleridge when he had been helping to rearrange the platform for the Congress meetings a day or two earlier. He too was about fifty, the professor would have said.

He caught Abercrombie's eyes fixed upon him with a sympathetic expression. The scar on his forehead where he had gashed it falling down the oubliette now showed as a slightly less livid mark. His big, capable hands held his coffee cup steady as he stirred it, making a faint chinking noise over the murmured conversation of the girl, the Count, and Anton at the far end of the room.

Coleridge owed Abercrombie a great deal. He turned his gaze from the Scots doctor's reddish face with its great black beard to

Captain Rakosi, who was today wearing another of his seemingly inexhaustible supply of smart uniforms. He did not waste time on him, as he was far too young to be the man he was seeking. And if he had been, that disposed of Coleridge's ideas of the English doctor.

The trouble was that none of the people in the room could be fitted easily to a faded photograph of a smiling young man dating from a period some twenty years earlier. People changed so much and it was almost impossible to relate thickened features, coarser physical characteristics, beards, and an increasing weight with slim young folk whose faces life had not yet moulded into lines of character.

He turned his gaze back to George Parker. He had very strong, almost striking features, made even more memorable by his jet-black beard. His teeth were square and sharp, his hair very thick. Coleridge had already thought that of Shaw, but his hirsute appearance seemed almost like the result of makeup. He put Parker's age at about forty-five to fifty, which placed him squarely within the age-range that fitted his most plausible theory.

Coleridge had not dismissed the Count. He had been conveniently absent at the time; he was powerfully built and immensely strong. Of course such a supposition was mad and entirely demolished his earlier ideas, but supposing the old Countess was immensely rich and the Count somehow in financial difficulties? Such things did happen.

Coleridge brushed aside these weird suppositions out of hand; it was yet one more indication of how his entire balance had been upset since coming to Castle Homolky. As well suspect the bearded servant; the dumb majordomo; Eles, the proprietor of the inn in the village; Father Balaz; Colonel Anton; or Nadia herself!

He turned thankfully, aware that the stalwart Chief of Police had come over to him, extending his hand. He still wore the Star of Krasnia winking on the front of his uniform. Shaw was at his side too.

"He is thanking you for all you have done here," Shaw said, stroking his silver-grey hidalgo's moustache.

Coleridge took Anton's strong hand, again feeling slight embarrassment. He was aware of Nadia Homolky's eyes on him.

"Please tell him I only did what anyone else would have done," Coleridge said.

Shaw translated, and the police chief's eyes opened wide. He smiled, baring his strong teeth, shaking his head. The grip on Coleridge's hand became even more fervent.

"He will speak to you after the funeral," said Shaw, finishing the translation.

The gathering was breaking up. Coleridge went over to catch Abercrombie's attention unobtrusively. He urgently needed the big man's advice.

Missing

THIS IS AS WEIRD a business as I have ever heard of," Abercrombie said.

He put down his coffee cup. The two men were almost alone now in the great conference room.

"But you have come out of it with notable esteem, Professor. If it had not been for you, Countess Sylva would have been dead too."

He smiled faintly, his expression plainly composed for the sole purpose of cheering Coleridge up.

"You will be able to dine out on it for the rest of your life."

Coleridge's face remained bleak. The business was too tragic and serious for speaking of lightly, even though he knew the big Scot was intent only on boosting his morale. The other put a heavy hand on his shoulder with bluff concern.

"What does this village doctor think?"

"Dr. Istvan?" Coleridge said. "He is the family doctor, I understand. He also doubles as police-surgeon, so you will have a deal to talk about when he has carried out his preliminary examinations."

"So long as he doesn't think that I have spoiled his instruments the last time," Abercrombie said sardonically. "I meticulously cleaned and polished them before returning them to their cases."

Coleridge shivered slightly. The conversation was assuming a charnel flavour that he was not anxious to sustain.

"I have something important to ask you," he went on quietly.

Abercrombie spread his hands wide.

"I am at your service, Professor, as always."

"I will wait until the room has cleared," Coleridge continued. "I do not wish anyone to see us."

He held up his hand to enjoin caution as the Count's shadow fell across them.

"I am deeply grateful to you, Professor. I hope to make my gratitude more tangible at some future date."

Coleridge got up.

"It was nothing, Count."

The other grasped his hand, looking deep into his eyes.

"On the contrary, it was a great deal. Things are bad enough, but I could not survive without my wife. You must forgive my emotion, Professor Coleridge, and you, Doctor; but these events of the past few days have hit me hard."

"We are all deeply concerned," Coleridge rejoined quickly. "Please say no more."

He stepped back and the other passed on quickly, followed by Rakosi and the girl, who had time only for a brief smile at Coleridge. The room was empty now, and the two men followed, loitering behind deliberately, until they could hear the sounds of the dumb majordomo clearing up the room behind them.

The man must have a lonely and unrewarding life, Coleridge thought; though no doubt the Count looked after him well. There were compensations living in such a great house, insulated from the troubles of the wider world. Though the evils of that world now seemed to have polluted that privacy.

"You were saying?" Abercrombie continued, now that there was no-one within earshot.

"I want you to look at something," Coleridge went on. "And then give me your honest opinion."

He shot an apologetic glance at his companion as they went down the staircase; he remembered Menlow's trembling and frightened features, which strengthened his resolve. This was no time to weaken; the menace which overhung the vast house had to be rooted out.

"My opinions are always honest," said Abercrombie affably, though his eyes expressed a cautious interest.

"I have a theory which is so fantastic," Coleridge went on, "that no-one but you would probably believe it."

The big doctor gave his short, harsh laugh.

"Everything about Castle Homolky is bizarre," he said. "And certainly, nothing you could suggest would be as weird or horrible as the events you have already witnessed."

"That is true," Coleridge agreed.

They were in a busier part of the Castle now, where female servants brushed by with averted eyes, and the two men lowered their voices to an almost inaudible whisper.

Eventually, after climbing several more flights of stairs in the other wing, they had reached the entrance to the Count's private library, which was Coleridge's destination.

"What do you think about Raglan's disappearance?" Coleridge ventured.

Abercrombie shook his massive head.

"I do not know. It is all of a part with the blackness that surrounds us."

The two had paused on an airy landing that was surrounded on three sides by windows. The thickly whirling snow made a suitably bleak background for their conversation. The blizzard was now so concentrated that it obscured everything but the immediate architectural features of the curving walls of the Castle, some buttresses, and occasionally a glimpse of Lugos far below, seen as though by lightning, between driving curtains of white flakes.

"You cannot really think that Raglan is responsible for these murderous attacks?"

Abercrombie stroked his heavy chin beneath the beard. Today

he wore a dark suit with a blue bow-tie; his sombre garb seemed to merge into the shadowy panelling that surrounded him, so that only his face floated clear, rather like one of the mediaeval portraits of the Count's ancestors in the heavy frames that hung in the gallery at ground-level.

"Again, I have no real thoughts on the matter. The entire business is pure insanity when considered from a logical scientific standpoint."

"You are sure Raglan's body could not have been concealed in the room when you went to ascertain my story?"

Again the emphatic shake of the head.

"The window was firmly closed. There was no sign of a rope. And certainly no corpse tied to the leg of the bed, if that is what you mean."

The thoughtful eyes were fixed on Coleridge's now.

"There was, however, a distinct chill in the air, despite the fire."

Coleridge was quick to seize the point.

"You see! The window had been open. The murderer may have returned to remove the body."

Abercrombie shrugged disarmingly, as though to humour his companion.

"You may well be right, Professor. I am not arguing with you. I am merely reporting what I myself saw and experienced. Which was very little in comparison to your story."

That reminded Coleridge of something else.

"You did not think I was overwrought? My collapse came shortly after."

Abercrombie's eyes were solicitous.

"Not at all. Such a collapse is often the result of pent-up emotion being released. You had been under severe strain during the previous few days. The death of Menlow. Your experiences in the Castle corridor. Your rescue of me from the oubliette. And finally our horrific experiences in The Place of the Skull. Think no more of it. I pride myself on my own strength of character, but I was close to collapse after the fight in the gorge."

He reached out a massive hand and patted Coleridge's shoulder clumsily.

"What was it you wished to show me?"

Coleridge recollected his mission here. He quickly led the way forward. As he had hoped, the library was empty, though a cheerful fire gleamed and there stood the chair, still in the same position, which Anton had occupied while he was making his notes at the circular table. Coleridge realised for the first time just how taciturn the Chief of Police was; he had not yet committed himself to any theory regarding the violent deaths within the Castle walls. Or outside it, come to that.

The small library was one of those rooms in the Castle devoted to the luxury of electric light, and the professor threw the two big brass switches fitted just inside the door. Yellow lamplight pricked the gloom, both from overhead chandeliers and from graceful iron wall-fittings. Coleridge ushered his companion up the staircase on to the balcony toward the Countess's desk.

Abercrombie stood silently by his side at the balcony edge, his eyes slowly sweeping across the silver-framed photographs that decorated the walls and rested upon the upper shelf of the desk. Again Coleridge felt oppressed by the silence and the weight of centuries which seemed to hang tangibly in the air here.

"Do you see anything familiar?" he asked.

The big doctor with the fading scar on his forehead made a helpless gesture of his arms.

"Should I?"

Coleridge felt momentary exasperation. He was not being exactly helpful. What should his companion make of such a large collection of faded pictures, when he himself had taken such a long time to arrive at his cloudy theory?

He started to explain, having difficulty in progressing beyond his halting introduction. Then, as he continued to expound his ideas, Abercrombie's expression became one of concentration. He moved forward, sitting down to examine the pictures more closely. He still said nothing, and Coleridge, gaining confidence from his silence, went on at a faster rate.

Before he could finish they were interrupted by the opening of the door below. It was the Count who stood there; behind him were the reassuring figures of Colonel Anton and Captain Rakosi.

The Count looked up toward the balcony curiously but was obviously too well-bred to ask what they were doing there.

"Forgive me," he said quietly. "The colonel has left some important papers here."

To Coleridge it sounded as though he were the host and the Count apologising for intruding on his privacy; another wave of unease came over him.

"I beg your pardon," he said hastily. "I had taken the liberty of showing the doctor some of your rarer books."

"By all means," replied the Count courteously. "I have already indicated that you may use the house as your own."

He bowed slightly, including both men in the gesture. Anton had darted forward to retrieve a heavy black leather briefcase from the foot of the table-leg. He smiled affably, and then the three men had withdrawn, the door closing softly behind them.

"What is your point?" Abercrombie remarked after what seemed like a long silence.

Again Coleridge plunged clumsily into his narrative, but the words flowed more easily now. Abercrombie gave a heavy sigh when he had finished. He bent forward to examine one of the photographs more closely.

Then he straightened up, making a slight clicking of the teeth. His eyes were alive and questing now, as he turned to Coleridge.

"What do you think?"

"There may be something in your theory, Professor."

"But does the photograph remind you of anyone?"

Abercrombie shrugged, his face seeming enormous in the mellow light of the electric chandelier suspended far above their heads. Behind him, through the high windows, the snow still fell, though not quite so thickly now.

"It does, now you come to think of it."

With a heavy finger he tapped the face of the young doctor in the photograph Coleridge had indicated.

"Do you not think there is a marked resemblance to one of our colleagues? Making allowance for the passing of the years, of course."

Coleridge's eyes were fixed unwinkingly on his companion. He did not dare break the silence. A shadow seemed to pass across the floor below, and a door creaked. Abercrombie's expression remained unchanged, and he seemed not to have noticed. He tapped the photograph lightly once more.

"George Parker, is it not? Examine it more carefully, and you will see what I mean."

Coleridge's heart was suddenly thumping in his chest. He leaned forward and studied the picture until his eyes watered. He now saw what Abercrombie meant. There was a definite likeness, making allowances for age and increasing corpulence. He wondered why he had not noticed it before.

They were bent in reverent examination of the picture still when there was a furtive pressure on the floorboards below. Abercrombie looked down sharply. This time a shadow hovered before the rapidly closing door. Coleridge went down the steps quickly, trying to move as quietly as possible.

The stair outside was a big one and was built at right-angles, affording an unimpeded view. A heavy figure was on the first landing, going down fast, its progress muffled on the thick carpeting.

But Coleridge had a clear view in the light from the casements. The heavy beard and massive features of George Parker were unmistakable.

Coleridge stood looking down from the large circular window, the reflected light from the snow making a blanched image of his features in the glass. Beneath this superimposition was spread the distorted Castle walls going away at a mad angle and, below, the huddled mass of Lugos. The snow had briefly stopped now, and the dark procession stood out with the insignificance of a file of ants.

The height was too great and the scene too indistinct to make out enough detail, but one of the figures at the very front must have been Father Balaz, then there was a gap and a few more figures, followed by two dark oblongs in a cleared space. Coleridge guessed these would have been the coffins of the old Countess and that of his late colleague, Dr. Menlow.

He felt he should have been there, but it was not as though these were the actual funerals; the coffins would rest in the church for several days, and he would have time to pay his respects later.

The cortège moved with infinite slowness. It resembled the progress of ants even more vividly from this height; just so had Coleridge, on many occasions, seen a body of ants move heavy weights in like manner until they had achieved their objective.

He could not make out the Count, but the three figures walking a little apart behind the second coffin might have been him, Colonel Anton, and Captain Rakosi.

Perhaps the Countess Sylva was watching with her daughter from some other window, Coleridge reflected, as he felt a profound melancholy pass across him. It was not merely the atmosphere of the Castle and the dark mystery that surrounded all of them; it was as though some enormous force of evil, supernatural and infinitely cunning, had invaded his soul, and he needed all his strength of will to throw it off.

The procession had passed beyond the first courtyard now and had again penetrated within the Castle buildings. Coleridge waited to see it emerge into the main courtyard fronting the moat and so into wheeled vehicles for the journey to the village below. It would be dusk soon, and lights were already pricking the huddle of mediaeval houses. The glare in the sky beyond would be from the Gypsy Fair, while an area of mellow incandescence from the large square could only emanate from the houses round about and from the grandiose hostelry, The Golden Crown.

No doubt Herr Eles and selected members of his staff were even now waiting at the head of the steps to join the procession and pay their own respects. The cortège had reemerged from the front entrance of the Castle; there was a short delay while the coffins were loaded amid long lines of bareheaded Castle employees. Then, the pawing horses showing their impatience with the cold, the Count and his parties swiftly entered two covered vehicles, and the cavalcade set off with a loud cracking of whips and creaking of wheels over the hard-packed ice.

Coleridge was about to turn away when he was aware that

another image had joined his own in the wide quadrant of the window. He found the girl beside him; she looked pale and diminished by the tragedy in the family. Her eyes were turned incuriously to the far vista where the dark procession wound its way down the precipitous road; the same along which the old Countess had once so imperiously driven her dog-cart with such tragic results.

Coleridge felt cool fingers shyly touching his palm, and he quickly closed his own over Nadia Homolky's as they stood there, quiet and rigid, as though in some predetermined compact, until the melancholy file of humans, vehicles, and animals had turned the bend in the road.

For a long time, though they could not see it, they could hear the progress of the cortège, echoed, reechoed, and magnified by the narrow confines of the houses and by the height at which they were receiving the sounds. Instinctively Nadia moved closer to Coleridge, and the two stood in unspoken sympathy for what seemed like a long while.

In the circular window Coleridge could see something gleaming in a corner of the girl's eye that resembled a reflection of the frozen icicle on the cornice outside. They were held by an intangible bond there, in the gathering dusk, and did not return to full consciousness of their surroundings until darkness had descended.

Coleridge parted from her outside her mother's sitting-room; the two still had not spoken of their various thoughts and fears, but neither now needed speech. They seemed to sense all the nuances of emotion of which they were individually composed. As he left the girl and mounted rapidly through the dusky corridors to the upper house, Coleridge's feelings were an amalgam of hope and despair; he dare not give visible expression to the former, but the latter was gathering like some unseen force, permeating every fibre of consciousness.

He gained the library at last; the staircases, landings, and corridors were empty of everything except small everyday comforting sounds. The soft tread of well-trained manservants on the lower floors, the clink of tongs as a maid replenished coals on one of the ever-rapacious fires, a faint snatch of concerned gossip in a foreign tongue at the intersection of a passage, the sound of glasses being washed from some distant pantry, and, once, the clatter of cutlery laid on bare boards, possibly for some servants' hall meal.

They were comforting in their way, being universal in application, and the professor lingered a moment, his hand on the door. Then he proceeded directly inside. He did not switch on the electric light; there was enough shimmer from the snowy rooftops spilling in through the high windows and from the fire for him to see by. He went up the small staircase, cautiously and catlike; once on the balcony he moved quietly along, adjusting his eyes to the gloom.

He was at the old Countess's desk now, anxiously searching the faces in the framed photographs. He felt a tense quickening of excitement, as a man fronts a situation not entirely unexpected.

For the photograph which depicted the young doctor, his fiancée, and Countess Irina had vanished.

COLERIDGE CHECKED THE PISTOL and replaced it in his pocket. It had been a trying day, perhaps the worst since he had come to Castle Homolky. The Count had excused himself from company after returning from the funeral service and had disappeared to his own quarters, presumably to comfort his wife.

The tea-hour had been a melancholy affair, taken this afternoon in the great chamber used as a breakfast-room, the guests served by soft-footed servants whose strained faces and frightened demeanour bespoke their secret fears.

Nadia had not put in an appearance since he had left her at the sitting-room entrance, and Father Balaz had presently retired to his refectory following the service. Coleridge had said nothing to Abercrombie of the missing photograph, but he had kept a discreet watch on Parker and the remainder of his colleagues, uneasily aware that he too was the object of their own scrutiny.

Colonel Anton had returned to the Castle with Rakosi, and both men had taken refreshment apart with the Count's family in their private quarters, no doubt to discuss the general situation and to compare notes. Coleridge knew that Anton intended to question him and his colleagues again after dinner, and he wondered idly, as he prepared for the meal, what the phlegmatic Chief of Police made of it all. No doubt he was treating it merely as a murder investigation.

Coleridge smiled wryly at his use of the word "merely"; one could not imagine more horrific circumstances than those prevailing at Castle Homolky, but the truth as suspected by Coleridge himself was almost too fantastic to be borne.

He turned as there came a tap at the door. It was the Countess's voice which came to him through the thick panel. He eased the pistol back into his pocket, going quickly across to open the door. Countess Sylva had her injured arm and shoulder in a sling and looked pale, but she was otherwise composed and calm.

She was dressed in black, which made her pale complexion stand out like an oil painting in the subdued yellow light from the lamps in the room. She held out her hand, a sad smile curving her lips. Once again Coleridge was taken with the astonishingly deep blue of her eyes and the perfect teeth, just failing to achieve perfection through their sharpness. Her fingers were cool and soft to the touch.

"I just came to thank you for my life, Professor."

Coleridge gave her an awkward little bow.

"I only did what anyone would have done, madame."

Despite himself, he was inwardly touched at her gesture and the vehement shake of her head at his disclaimer. She seated herself in front of the fire with a gracious movement, at his extended invitation, and he was reminded of their earlier interview under such dissimilar circumstances.

"I was sorry I could not take you into my confidence," he went on quickly. "But I presume you understand everything now."

She nodded, keeping her eyes down toward the fire.

"My husband has told me. We shall be eternally grateful to you."

She raised her head and looked the professor frankly in the eyes.

"What do you make of Dr. Raglan's disappearance? You do not imagine he can be responsible for these awful murders?"

Coleridge shook his head.

"I think he has been murdered too. Like Dr. Menlow, for the knowledge he possessed."

"Exactly," the Countess said calmly.

"And Colonel Anton?" Coleridge ventured. "He does not seem very forthcoming."

Countess Sylva laughed softly, but there was little humour in the sound.

"Colonel Anton is a remarkable man, Professor. Do not underestimate him. His imagination does not run to lycanthropy and werewolves in the night. But he understands murder and the criminal mind. I think he has his own theories, but he will say nothing until he is certain."

Her slim fingers tightened on the arm of her chair.

"And he will strike when the time is ripe, you can be sure of that."

Coleridge looked at her for a long moment.

"He has a difficult task," he said at length. "Ought he not to have mounted a search for Raglan outside? I know the weather is severe . . ."

The Countess shook her head.

"He and Captain Rakosi have done everything necessary. They are certain he is still within the Castle. The weather will simplify things."

Coleridge was puzzled.

"The weather? I do not understand."

The Countess gave a thin smile.

"The blizzard, Professor. It may last a week, and we shall be isolated here just as though we were in some peasant cottage a mile or so within that mountain range opposite. It suits the colonel, of course, because he could not let anyone leave until he has cleared the matter up."

She shrugged.

"We are all suspect, are we not?"

Coleridge gave her grudging assent.

"It is not a very pleasant prospect. Cooped up with a murderer. And with Colonel Anton suspecting everyone."

The Countess again smiled bleakly.

"You are right, Professor. It has its ironies, does it not, for the murderer cannot escape, either. My husband has a score to settle for poor Mother. And if it should be this man Sanders . . ."

Her eyes were burning and very hard now.

"Unless he be truly supernatural. And I do not think he has finished with us yet."

Dinner was only a slightly less sombre affair than the hour of tea. There had been another alarm in the course of the afternoon, this time from the village. A message had summoned Colonel Anton from them under the most appalling weather conditions. He had taken over an hour on foot to reach Lugos, where a young girl, venturing only a few yards to bring fuel from the family woodshed, had been seized and half-eaten by an enormous wolf.

Later it had been seen by several people, watching nervously from their windows, and had actually been fired at by some courageous villager, apparently without effect. Anton was convinced that the beast was the large black one which had led the pack and was not connected with events at the Castle. The tracks were already covered with drifting snow, and he had given up the impossible task of tracing the beast and had returned, half-frozen, to the Castle.

He now sat at the Count's right hand at the head of the table and regaled those nearest with his clipped account of this latest tragedy. But as horrific as the incident was, he was still more concerned with the heart of the mystery at the Castle.

Coleridge recalled something which had been told him; or had he imagined it? Something almost as disquieting as the other matters which concerned his disturbed mind. That the Count himself benefited enormously from his mother's death. The thought was too base to contemplate, Coleridge felt; but he had to weigh it in the balance against the other probabilities in this dreadful affair.

The suspicions against Parker were growing inside him. As Abercrombie had pointed out, there was a marked resemblance between the young doctor in the photograph and his middle-aged colleague; as he had already learned, their ages coincided; Parker had certainly been hanging about the library when Coleridge and Abercrombie were discussing the matter; and now the picture, which might have established a connection, had disappeared.

Like Raglan, in fact; as though neither the human being nor the inanimate object had ever existed. Coleridge had still not told the Count about the missing photograph; it would do no good and he already had enough on his mind.

Now the professor listened dully as his colleagues discussed the matter and argued among themselves. Some had ingenious theories regarding Raglan, but none that made any sense. The professor himself remained convinced that the incredibly cunning, not to say diseased, brain which had perpetrated these horrors had been responsible for Raglan's death as well as Menlow's.

Both had been silenced for the information which might have threatened or revealed the identity of the monster, and Raglan's body was probably concealed somewhere about the Castle. There were hundreds of places in such a vast conglomeration of buildings where it could lie for months undisturbed. There were still more important factors involved, however.

The grudge against the Count's family would not end there. The attack might be renewed upon the Countess, who had escaped with her life only because of the servant's presence of mind in fetching Coleridge.

The Count himself was at risk; and, most important of all now to the professor, the girl's life could be in deadly danger. Coleridge guessed that the invisible avenger could be destroying the Count's family one by one and might preserve the Count till last, in order to prolong his agony.

All along Coleridge had known that he himself was a prime target. But he was an expert shot, armed and known to be armed, and two attempts at least by the wolf-creature had been turned aside by his vigilance.

That reminded Coleridge of another complication. He had not noticed Shaw limping lately; he seemed to have made a remarkable recovery. He remembered Abercrombie saying something about the cold compresses having done wonders and that the swelling had gone down overnight.

He knew the doctor's thorough examination of Shaw's leg probably absolved him from suspicion, but he would keep an eye on him, nevertheless. One strange factor from the previous night had returned to him during this dreary and austere day. He could understand something tapping on the younger Countess's door, causing her to open it.

But the old Countess had been attacked in her bed. Surely she could not have slept with the door unlocked during the present circumstances? But that was apparently what she did. The Countess Sylva had told him—and the Count had since confirmed it—that she was absolutely without fear and had refused to lock her bedroom door in her own house, as she termed it.

As Coleridge had suspected, this might well have saved Countess Sylva's life, as the beast had evidently entered the old Countess's unlocked room first and killed her before turning to the daughter-in-law.

Which had given time for Coleridge to arrive on the scene. He sipped absently at his glass of wine, wearying of these endless thoughts which tumbled and revolved in his brain.

Anton was talking now, the Count quickly translating. The Chief of Police would hold a conference later in the evening, in an adjoining room. Neither the girl nor her mother had appeared at dinner, and Anton and Rakosi would question the Count, Coleridge, and his surviving colleagues in an attempt to arrive at some definitive solution to the mystery.

Coleridge caught Abercrombie's eyes on him as he rose from the table. He read them as being as sceptical as his own.

I HAVE A SCHEME which may bring this business to a conclusion," said Abercrombie.

He regarded Coleridge sternly.

"It is one not without some risk and rather resembles what we British, in respect of our Indian Empire, refer to as staking out a goat."

The two men sat in a strange octagonal chamber which the Count had designated as a smoking-room. It was comfortably furnished with leather divans and armchairs, and the richly panelled walls were hung with weapons and trophies of the chase. A tremendous fire roared in the chimney, and from the way it bellowed one minute and then appeared to damp down the next, Coleridge inferred that there was a great gale blowing outside, even though camouflaged by the immensely thick walls of the Castle.

In fact the blizzard was at its height, as the Countess had predicted, and Coleridge did not relish being trapped here for another week or more with someone who seemed intent on taking further lives. He shifted uneasily in his comfortable wing-chair as he stared at his companion, blinking in the light of the electric chandelier overhead which denoted that the room was one of the Count's more important and favoured apartments.

They were alone for the moment; dinner had been early at the Count's special request. It was still only nine o'clock, and they were due to meet for the colonel's conference at ten. The rest of the party had dispersed temporarily to their rooms, but Coleridge guessed that they would soon reassemble, as none of them now liked to be alone. Not that he blamed them. Even the servants were affected by the general atmosphere, though there was no reason to think any of them were at personal risk.

"I am not quite sure I understand," Coleridge said in answer to Abercrombie's remark.

"I was referring to tiger-hunting," Abercrombie went on. "A goat is used, generally tethered at night with the hunter in a tree above, ready to shoot the tiger when he appears to kill the animal."

His eyes seemed to burn with great intensity. He rubbed his thick hands together. Coleridge's cigar-smoke went up straight and even to the richly carved ceiling of the panelled room.

The doctor gazed broodingly into the fire as though he could see the creature they sought somewhere in the flickering flames. Coleridge had noticed there were two of the massive wolf-head firedogs here. They seemed to glare mockingly at the two men as the firelight caught their polished surfaces.

"We are dealing with a wild beast, if your theories are correct," Abercrombie continued after a short silence.

"And cunning as he may be—wolf or werewolf, if you insist on your extravagant thesis—he will not be able to avoid taking the bait."

"Which is?" Coleridge prompted.

Abercrombie crossed his legs, clasping his thick fingers together across his knee.

"The solution to this whole mystery, including the identity of the murderer," he continued calmly. "The announcement of vital evidence which has come into our hands, preferably at the colonel's conference tonight."

Coleridge tapped out the ash from his cigar in a carved onyx tray at his elbow.

"Which is what? We have no such evidence."

Abercrombie chuckled.

"I have been giving the matter some thought. The murderer does not know, cannot be sure, that we have no evidence. I will get to that later. We will manufacture some, if necessary."

Coleridge understood now. His experiences were obviously adversely affecting his thinking processes.

"That is the bait of which you are talking?"

Abercrombie nodded.

"Exactly."

Coleridge was smiling.

"And you want me to be the goat, staked out, as you put it?"

Abercrombie was smiling too.

"If your nerve is up to it. It is not without a certain risk."

Coleridge made a wry mouth.

"I should have to know more. You are proposing a remote location, I take it. And though I do not care for your analogy, I see your point."

Abercrombie rubbed his palms together with a heavy rasping noise.

"I have not mistaken my man. And I see the idea appeals to you. I shall be there, of course, to see that no harm befalls."

"One would hope so," said Coleridge drily. "Suitably hidden, of course."

"Naturally," Abercrombie put in. "I will not tell even you where I shall be concealed, or you might give the situation away."

Coleridge looked at him dubiously.

"Supposing something prevents you from taking up your position?" he queried. "What happens then?"

Abercrombie shook his head, little glints of humour dancing in his eyes.

"You are no worse off, Professor. You have your pistol, have you not."

Coleridge stared at him without answering. Though, as Abercrombie said, there was a strong element of risk, the more he thought about the plan the more he liked it.

"Supposing this creature will not come?"

Abercrombie shrugged heavily.

"Nothing is lost. We will not announce the location, so he will have to keep you under surveillance. But we should make it plain that you will retrieve the evidence from wherever it is hidden and place it in Anton's hands tonight. Before midnight, say."

Again the dubious look passed across the professor's face.

"Ought we not to let Anton and Rakosi know what we purpose?"

Abercrombie shook his head emphatically.

"Nobody must know. Otherwise the scheme will not succeed."

He bit his heavy lip.

"If only we had some evidence, something plausible that he could not resist. For if you have proof of the culprit, then he cannot afford to let you live."

Coleridge felt impelled to frankness.

"There is something," he ventured. "Indisputable proof relating to lycanthropy in this case. Menlow had the scientific test results. They disappeared with his death. They will now reappear according to my story."

He leaned back in his chair, his eyes fixed on the ceiling.

"I have made up my mind, Doctor. I will be your bait. But I trust you will play the part of the hunter with all your considerable energy."

Abercrombie gazed at him with approval.

"You may be sure of that," he said fervently.

"We need not waste time in idle speculation now. You have merely to say you have hidden the evidence for security. You will retrieve it from a distant part of the Castle before midnight. That should be sufficient. The odds are you will be watched from then on."

He leaned forward and fixed his companion with dark eyes.

"But you must make the story plausible. Your life may depend upon it."

Coleridge nodded, stubbing out his cigar.

"I will do my part, so long as you do yours."

"Capital!"

The doctor jumped up, beaming on his companion.

"That I can promise. And now, as it is just about to chime ten o'clock by the timepiece in the corner, I think we should rejoin the good colonel."

Anton had gone back exhaustively through the events of the past few days. None of Coleridge's colleagues had anything to contribute to their previous depositions. The tedious business of question, translation, and answer had gone ahead, and now, at almost half-past ten, Coleridge felt that little had been added to their earlier interrogations.

But he did not underestimate Colonel Anton. The Chief of Police had listened intently to the answers of everyone in turn and had made copious notes. Coleridge knew that he had collated and compared them with depositions made previously, and he also knew that any discrepancy would have been observed at once.

So that he was rather cautious when it came to his turn. Anton had closed his hooded eyes as he listened to the translation of the professor's answers. He still wore a dark uniform, with the holster of his pistol buckled at the waist, and with his heavy black moustache drooping over his thick lips resembled some rough Mexican revolutionary, Coleridge thought. He was smoking a strong black cheroot this evening, and the thin, pungent smoke went up in slow whorls to the ceiling.

They sat in the room in which they had taken dinner, and the relief of everyone at being there was almost audible to the senses. It was obvious that all the guests in the Castle would have preferred even an interrogation from the colonel to the lonely solitude of their own rooms and the melancholy of their thoughts.

During the course of the examination it had become clear that further search had been made for Raglan, but his disappearance still remained inexplicable. Anton did not think he had left the Castle precincts, and Coleridge was inclined to agree with him. It was still snowing thickly, and even at the time of Raglan's disappearance it would have been almost impossible to have quitted the Castle without visible tracks having been left in the fresh snow.

Coleridge thought he had introduced his own part in the proceedings rather cleverly. He had been guided by Abercrombie, who had promised to make him an opening that would seem both logical and inevitable. Coleridge had to concede that he had done it most skilfully. There had been general discussion following the interrogation when Anton, through Rakosi, had asked the members of the Congress for their suggestions.

Some, notably those from Shaw and Sullivan, had been even more bizarre than the truth as Coleridge saw it, and Abercrombie had not been slow to capitalise on this. He had subtly insinuated that the authorities were hampered by lack of evidence. His eyes in the reddish face had flickered to Coleridge at this point, as already arranged, and the latter had broken into the debate as though reluctantly drawn.

His strong card was that he inclined to the supernatural, which lifted the cloud of suspicion from his companions. The atmosphere visibly lightened as he went haltingly on, and he noted Abercrombie's glance of approval. As he talked, Coleridge covertly studied his companions' faces. Shaw's emaciated form, with his silver hair and drooping moustache of the same colour; Abercrombie's bluff expression and bristling black whiskers; Dr. Sullivan's grouse-moor exterior, with his greying hair and middle-aged heaviness; George Parker's stocky athleticism and his veiled expression beneath the luxuriant black beard.

These, the sad survivors of a Congress which had started out so auspiciously; Coleridge felt a stab of self-pity for the specialist interests of an outstanding event which had been destroyed at the whim of a madman, but he immediately suppressed it. He was choosing his words with care now, and as he went on he could see that Abercrombie, though his attitude was nonchalant and his eyes cast down upon the table in front of him, was following his discourse with complete absorption and approval.

Coleridge was past the worst now. He hinted at possible evidence which had just come to him; he covered himself by saying that the shock of his recent experiences had driven it from his mind. There was a slight stir around the table, but the professor could see no disbelief in the faces raised to his own. He had remembered something which Menlow had entrusted to him; he had not realised its significance at the time and, on the doctor's instructions, had hidden it carefully. This did not really square with what he had told the Count, but the latter made no comment.

With the violent death of his colleague and the subsequent events which had crowded in, it had slipped his memory, Coleridge went on. Anton's thick fingers had been drumming on the table to cover his mounting interest as the Count's translation continued. Now his hooded eyes were sharp and clear, focused almost brutally on Coleridge.

"Where is this material?" Homolky translated.

"Well hidden," Coleridge replied. "I will search for it when this meeting breaks up and bring it to the colonel's room before midnight."

Coleridge could see mild puzzlement spreading on the police chief's heavy features as the Count translated. This was the vital moment, and he hastened on as though to cover over the cracks in the thin façade of lies he had constructed.

"Why not tell the colonel where it is?" Homolky transmitted.

The professor shook his head.

"I am not quite sure. The events of the past few days have confused my mind. I have no desire to waste police time. I would prefer to search by myself in case I have made an error."

He paused, looking round the room, while the Count passed on the message.

"I have no wish to look foolish, particularly if I have forgotten where I hid the material."

Anton smiled thinly, nodding his head. Evidently Coleridge had said the right thing. The tiny detail of looking foolish, the natural desire of every man to avoid being made ridiculous in front of others, had swung the balance.

Coleridge felt a slight bead of sweat banding his forehead. He avoided Abercrombie's eyes, though he could sense the big man's approval of his performance.

Anton nodded in the end and rapped out two brisk sentences to Homolky, shutting his notebook with a snap. Rakosi pursed his lips, putting his hand on the butt of his pistol, which was buttoned into his gleaming holster.

"Very well," said Homolky, after what seemed like a very long time to the professor. "Colonel Anton understands your position and your desire to help the judiciary. He will be in his room, available to you until midnight and beyond."

Coleridge was aware of the general glances of approbation that were being cast upon him by his colleagues. He avoided looking at George Parker and instead concentrated on the colonel and the Count. He had no further ideas of his own, and Abercrombie's suggestion was the only one which might cause the beast to rise to the bait.

The meeting was breaking up now. Colonel Anton paused opposite Coleridge and gave him another fierce stare. Then he nodded, as if in approval, and held out a hard hand for the professor to shake.

"At midnight," Homolky translated.

Coleridge nodded.

"I shall be there," he said.

Silver Bullets

COLERIDGE EASED HIS WAY along the dimly lit corridor with a racing heart. He was not sure whether his unknown adversary had taken the bait, but he had been conscious for some little while of certain furtive noises that seemed to echo faintly in his rear. He was proceeding toward the highest part of the Castle where the Count had his laboratory and floral houses. Abercrombie and some of his colleagues had already been there, but so far the professor had never visited that remote portion of the house.

Abercrombie had indicated to him where he must make his pretence of searching and had described it to him accurately; he had also undertaken to make sure the laboratory and the other apartments involved in his plan were unlocked. He had left the conference as soon as it had concluded, so Coleridge guessed he would take up his position for surveillance immediately, which gave him some comfort under the present circumstances.

The large revolver made a tight pressure against his chest

muscles as he walked slowly along, orientating himself by the faint light which spilled in at the far end of the corridor. The Castle clock had just struck a quarter past eleven, which gave him plenty of time.

Abercrombie would have arrived some while before this, as they had broken up shortly before eleven. He would have to be early in order to be fully prepared to deal with the thing which Coleridge believed to be carefully dogging his footsteps now.

He needed all his reserves of strength and energy not to flee headlong down the passage at the faint scraping noises in his wake, and he forced his strained nerves under control while he edged slowly along in the deepening gloom. He had studied the plan the girl had made before setting out from his room tonight, and he thought he knew the way well enough, but it was difficult under these circumstances of darkness and silence and he hoped that he had not mistaken a turn on the narrow spiral staircase up which he had just advanced.

He had followed Abercrombie's advice and had first gone to his room, as though to make preparations. This would give anyone time to gain the guests' quarters, to keep him under surveillance, and then to follow if he believed the story Coleridge had told. Abercrombie was right; if there were evidence to give a name to the lycanthropic presence which had already taken so many lives, then the thing could not afford to let him deliver it to Colonel Anton.

Coleridge realised he was taking his life in his hands yet again; but in the meantime he had the comfort of the pistol and for the long-term the solid, dependable presence of Abercrombie, presumably concealed somewhere among the plants of the hothouses far above.

The professor understood pipes from the furnaces which heated certain parts of the house were channelled upward to the glassed-in conservatories, perched among the roofs of the Castle, where they would be sheltered from the wind, yet would catch the maximum amount of sunlight.

He was at the end of the corridor now and paused again, waiting for his eyes to become adjusted to the light. There was another narrow stair in front of him, obviously mediaeval in construction and made of some sort of close-bonded granite, smooth and polished by the feet of centuries.

Nothing had changed here except for such concessions to the nineteenth century as the curving metal handrail which followed the stair at his right and the narrow glass windows with heavy wooden frames which covered the occasional arrow-slits at the outer wall. By the ghostly light coming in Coleridge could see that the outside ledges were covered inches deep with snow, and frost filmed the glass so thickly that he could catch only a glimpse of whirling flakes.

A sort of sick dread seemed to coat his soul here in this lonely, silent place where he was remote from all help, bound on such a grim and incredible mission, and where the only sound was his muffled footfalls scraping on the bleak stone. Coleridge had covered two turns of the stair, and light was growing about him. This gave him confidence, and the coming of the light had renewed his courage.

He went quickly up the last two flights, conscious that there were more echoes in his wake than there should have been. He stopped at the top, hearing another step far below that had halted at almost the precise moment, but not quite. Fear was growing within him; if he waited too long, he would not have the tenacity and willpower to complete his purpose.

The long polished corridor in which he stood was lit by oil lamps at intervals, and he crossed to the nearest, first making sure that the place was empty. He consulted Nadia's inked plan of the top floors—or was it her mother's? Not that it mattered.

He soon located his position and saw that he must now move to the left to cross the centre of the vast tower in which he stood; if the sketch was accurate this should bring him to a sort of balcony which led to a huge timbered hall stretching between two of the towers. These would obviously be later structures, perhaps built by the Count's father sixty or seventy years ago. Coleridge had heard that there were even indoor tennis courts at Castle Homolky, as well as a swimming bath and the shooting range of which the girl had spoken.

The whole estate denoted vast wealth and feudal privileges in which cost was the least consideration. It was equally obvious that to such a family as the Homolkys, isolated in a very primitive community as they would have been all those years ago, it was necessary to invent their own amusements; what better place to indulge such comforts and refinements than under the vastness of their own roof?

All these thoughts had passed through Coleridge's mind in fleeting seconds as he refolded the plan and put it back into his pocket. It made an ugly crackling noise which seemed to flutter beneath the low ceiling of the passage, and Coleridge gave a quick glance to left and right before going on. Nothing moved in the corridor, but still the faint, furtive noise sounded a long way down the stair he had just quitted.

Abercrombie had done his work well. As Coleridge mounted higher, so the light grew, and with it, warmth, which seemed to exude from the polished marble floors of the corridors at this dizzy height. He found the balcony, which had lamps lit along its whole length, and ran across its slatted solid timbers, careless now of the heavy rumble it made behind him.

Beneath him was a dark, warm void, and he could hear water dripping somewhere; perhaps below him were the cisterns which supplied the hothouses and the laboratories. The balcony, which was glassed in at the top, led to a sort of foyer floored in paved coloured tiles which bore Roman motifs. Coleridge had the pistol out now, and he was alert to every shadow, every nuance, of his echoed progress.

The light still grew before him. He opened a glass door and was in what was obviously the Count's laboratory: there were retorts and racks, test-tubes, bottles of chemicals, shelf after shelf of specimens in jars, aisles of mahogany filing cabinets doubtless containing documents relating to the Count's researches, gleaming microscopes on the desks and benches.

There was electric light in here, coming from fittings suspended from long cords in the glass ceiling. There was also an enormous weight of snow upon the heavy iron trusses, Coleridge could see, but judging from the clear patches in the glass roof it was obviously melting from time to time because of the warmth within.

And it was warm after Coleridge's long climb up among the draughty stone staircases. He walked down the gleaming aisle of filing cabinets, making sure the place was empty. There was almost no sound up here apart from an occasional creaking noise which he took to be either the weight of snow upon the iron girders supporting the roof or perhaps the wind buffeting the great mass of ice.

Beyond him was a green jungle where writhing vegetation rioted among the white metal staircases and balconies, giving the Homolky hothouses the appearance of some fantastic spa; perhaps Baden-Baden or Vichy, seen as though in a distorting mirror or in some troubled dream. Coleridge was no botanist, and he could not identify many of the colourful blooms that trailed gaudy blossom like blood or brilliant orange across the vista. It was an incredible tropical contrast to the bleakness outside.

Then he remembered his role, thinking he might well be watched from among the heavy banks of blossom. He quickly put the pistol back into his pocket, hoping that Abercrombie was securely placed to come to his aid quickly if danger threatened. He opened the big glass door in front of him and stepped into a heavy, cloying atmosphere that seemed as oppressive as the Matto Grosso.

The white balcony appeared to sway and give rather too much for Coleridge's sense of security, and he instinctively clutched the railing at his right elbow. It was very hot indeed, and he hoped this would not take too long. Perspiration was already making his shirt stick to his back.

He paused, looking down into the vast arena spread below him where pools of water bearing great tropical lily pads gave back the electric light a thousandfold.

He and Abercrombie had worked out exactly what he was to do, but Coleridge, consulting his watch, deliberately slowed the routine. He was convinced he had been followed here, and he had to allow time for the creature to discover him at his task.

He went along the balcony and onto a sort of ornamental teak bridge in the Chinese style, red-painted and frail-looking, that spanned an awesome drop and led to the opposing balcony. It was a huge place, and Coleridge could glimpse other greenhouses beyond, faintly seen through the vast sheets of glass, but the lights were switched off in those and he knew that whatever drama had been planned for tonight would be played out here.

He walked quickly across the teak bridge, anxious to get off it, and did not breathe more easily until he had gained the other side. He first wanted to make sure he had an escape route near before committing himself fully to the scheme he had agreed with Abercrombie. He could now see that the balconies ran round all four sides of the enormous conservatory; that they were connected by catwalks and staircases to each other and to other gangways and staircases that led to the ground floor.

He had his foot on the first step of one of these, in the act of going down, when the half-hour struck from the Castle clock, enormously magnified up here at the very top of the vast edifice and brought clearly in the bitterly cold air outside by the strength of the wind that was driving the snow.

There was now no sense in delaying; Abercrombie was obviously in position, and whatever creature had been following him on the staircases of the lower Castle had had time to reach the conservatories. This was the worst moment so far as Coleridge was concerned, and he felt his limbs beginning to tremble as he set off down the series of stairs that led to the ground floor of the glasshouse.

He felt exposed and insignificant down here, under the light of the overhead lamps, and his eyes flickered from one set of white-painted balconies to another, but nothing moved in the artificial yellow glare.

The green foliage, broken by the crude colours of the exotic flowers, rose thickly about him the farther down he went, and he again caught the heavy, cloying stench that appeared to have something unhealthy and decadent about it. The greenery was more dense than he had supposed, rising in a wall high above his head and full of shadows. The large fleshy leaves looked artificial and rubbery; others like wax flowers of foliage, shining and still in the stagelike atmosphere.

The dark water of the lily ponds reflected the lights in

crescents, spirals, and stars as he walked quickly along, his feet rattling on the pierced metal flooring that was designed for quick and easy drainage. There was a sort of aisle in the centre, between two of the largest semicircular ponds, that acted as a focus of attention; in the very middle of the aisle, Abercrombie had told him, was an ornamental palm let into heavy trunking. It was in the earth at its foot that he proposed to dig.

The foliage was so high now that Coleridge could see only dripping green shadow on all sides of him. It was a bad place, but at least there was the outlet of the staircases and he could see all the broad blankness of the airy white balconies from here. He walked over swiftly, the revolver heavy against his chest muscles, and selected a small trowel from a rack of implements that was screwed to a metal railing here.

He took one more look round the high arcading of this gigantic horticultural cathedral before kneeling to dig at the foot of the palm. As he did so an enormous shadow passed across the lighting, and the ferns at his back stirred.

Before he could regain his feet there was a snarling sound that raised the hairs on his neck, and the gigantic wolf with the grey patch on its back broke cover and stood for one horrifying second glaring at him.

Then, as he shouted and cowered away, it launched itself at his throat.

Coleridge had fallen clumsily and rolled over, which saved his life. The beast's charge carried it so close, some of the rough hairs of its flank rasped across his cheek and he could feel the warmth of its reeking, foetid breath. He shouted again, and this seemed to alarm the creature because it swerved in midflight and cannoned into a large iron upright, seeming to make the whole conservatory shake.

Desperation now had given Coleridge a clear head. He had the pistol out, tugging it free of his pocket, throwing back the safety-catch. Its click was enormously magnified by the acres of glass around them. The animal seemed to understand the sound because it went straight on without stopping.

The explosion appeared tremendous in that vast space; the wolf trembled as it went up the opposite staircase, and Coleridge saw with triumph that he had slightly wounded it in the off forepaw, because it was limping and trailing blood. It was vulnerable then. Before he heard the crack of breaking glass in the background, he loosed off another shot which whined viciously off a metal stanchion.

Fear flooded through Coleridge as the wolf disappeared into thick foliage at the top of the staircase. There was still no sign of Abercrombie. Everything was silent again, except for the distant drip of water somewhere. This was even worse than what had happened in the previous seconds, and Coleridge then knew real fear.

He was drenched with perspiration which ran down into his eyes, and he rubbed with the back of his unoccupied hand to clear his vision. Nothing moved in all the wide expanse of glass but the very faintest agitation of fronds, which seemed to herald the passing of the lurking menace. Coleridge was on his feet again and, crouching, made his way to the foot of the nearest staircase; it was almost opposite the one up which the wolf had disappeared, and he dare not follow that closely.

Then followed perhaps the worst five minutes of his life. He was to all intents and purposes alone in the pitiless glare of the electric light; the tropical softness of the enormous conservatories about him; the only sound the faint liquid beat as water dripped onto the dark surface of a pool; the stealthy whisper of slowly moving fronds eating away at his nerves; every shadow in this clouded jungle a potential danger.

He held the revolver ready as he eased up the metal staircase, every tread seeming to squeak and protest in an exaggerated way. The man-beast had supernatural cunning; Coleridge had no doubt of that. There had not been a sound since its disappearance into the dense green undergrowth, but the professor knew that fierce yellow eyes watched and noted his every movement from the shadow.

He was near to breaking point when he heard the footsteps, reverberating and magnified on the metal treads of the balcony. Relief flooded through him; that would be Abercrombie. Surely enough, there was the bearded head, white teeth gleaming as he stared from the foliage high overhead.

"There you are, Professor."

A pistol flared as Coleridge, bewildered, sagged against the balcony. He saw the heavy figure of Abercrombie break cover from the greenery. He clutched his stomach and tottered at the edge of the railing. Coleridge could hear distant shouts now, and the sound of running feet.

He turned as the pistol flashed again, could not believe what he saw. For Abercrombie was perched high among the forest of metal struts and columns that supported the roof, his face alight with triumph.

"There is your werewolf, Professor!" he cried, smoke ascending to the high ceiling from the barrel of his pistol.

The bearded figure on the balcony was going down now, taking a great section of the metal railing with him. He bounced once or twice on the lower balconies, making the gigantic structure of the conservatory vibrate and echo as though at any moment the whole thing must collapse. The man and the heavy mass of metal plunged into one of the lily ponds in a high plume of spray, and then the body reemerged, rocking slightly, arms and legs star-shaped as though crucified. Red stains spread out across the dark water.

Coleridge felt sick and turned away. He was aware now of the white shock of the Count's hair on the high balcony. The military figure of Colonel Anton, pistol drawn, strode to the edge of the railing and stared down grimly. Coleridge could see Rakosi clattering briskly down one of the far staircases. The whole high dome was full of the distant echo and murmur of voices as others hurried to the scene.

Coleridge was aware that Abercrombie was at his side, his clothes smothered with dust, pain distorting his features. He looked long at the body in the pool.

"I am sorry I had to expose you to that, Professor. I could not shoot when the wolf jumped because you were between me and the target. I had to make sure."

Coleridge nodded. He felt too shocked and shattered to fully comprehend what had happened. He let the other take his arm and guide him down the stair and across the main floor of the conservatory to where the obscene thing in the pool floated gently. There seemed to be much blood now.

Colonel Anton's harsh orders were spitting out. Coleridge saw the Count run back; whether to get more help or to keep the servants away he did not know. He could see the pale ovals of horrified faces at the edges of the high balconies. Rakosi ran past him with a rake he had found somewhere. He waded into the pool and prodded at the figure, drawing it slowly toward the edge. Coleridge stared uncomprehendingly as the captain bent to turn it over.

Abercrombie went to help him, and with much grunting and straining the two levered the corpse onto the floor of the conservatory. Coleridge found himself looking at the blanched features of George Parker.

Abercrombie glanced at him sympathetically.

"As we suspected, Professor. And a true werewolf."

He shrugged massively, his eyes on the immaculate figure of Colonel Anton, who was stiffly descending the white staircase with his drawn pistol still in his hand.

"I have come round to your way of thinking," Abercrombie went on. He looked again at the dead face of the man-beast.

"I used the Count's laboratory up there. With his permission, of course. For a special purpose."

He tapped his pistol significantly.

"I used silver bullets, to make sure this time."

Wolf or Werewolf?

I THOUGHT YOU did not believe in werewolves," the Count said.

The Countess shrugged. She looked white and her arm was still bandaged, but something of her old immaculate beauty had come back to her.

"I do now," she said grimly.

The blizzard had blown itself out within the week, as predicted, and most of the guests had already left. There was just Coleridge and Abercrombie; the former was saying goodbye to Nadia on the floor below while the doctor finished his packing.

The Count stirred his tea with a faint tinkle of the spoon in the silence of the small drawing-room, which faced the front of the Castle and had a fine view over Lugos and the rolling hills beyond. Dusk was starting to fall, and lights were burning small holes in the wide expanse of snow.

"Dr. Istvan's report was a surprise," the Countess said, almost dreamily, as her cobalt eyes gazed unseeingly out the window.

"But a great relief," the Count rejoined. "Mother would never have locked her door, so her end under those circumstances would have been agony."

He smiled at his wife sadly.

"She was already dead when the wolf savaged her. That would have appealed to Mother."

"She was very old," Countess Sylva said softly. "And I had noticed a slight failing in recent months. It was her heart, Istvan said. She could have died at any time."

"If Sanders, or whatever this creature called himself, had not stopped to attack Mother, you would be dead now," said the Count.

His wife's hand sought his across the tabletop. They sat there in silence for some while, almost awkwardly, as their love was so deep and intimate it was almost too difficult for them to give it audible expression.

"Poor Raglan," she said.

The Count's eyes were smouldering now.

"Poor Raglan," he repeated. "Coleridge was right. He had been hanged from the window bars. And the professor did see him there. But the thing came back and cut the rope. He plunged straight down through the wooden roof of one of the courtyard outhouses."

"And the snow covered everything over," the Countess added.

Her eyes went to the small black notebook which lay by the Count's right hand.

"If it had not been for this diary, which Bela brought to me an hour or two ago, so much would have remained vague and unclear," her husband said.

"I am still uncertain . . ." the Countess began. "I hope you are going to tell me."

The Count gave her a thin smile, emphasising his sharpened teeth which were characteristic of the Homolky family.

"I always tell you everything, my dear. Raglan hid this diary under the mattress of his bed. It was his insurance in case anything happened to him."

"I hope he was what he appeared to be," the Countess murmured. "There has been so much deception . . ."

The Count nodded.

"The diary makes it clear that Raglan was the folklorist and writer whom we knew by repute. He was an official delegate to the Congress in Pest. But what we did not know was that he had recently been appointed to the staff of a lunatic asylum near Manchester, in England."

There was surprise in the Countess's eyes now.

"The one in which Sanders had been incarcerated?"

"Exactly. He had escaped some months before, so Raglan did not know him personally or what he looked like. All he had to go on was an ancient photograph. But he found in Sanders's room an old copy of *The Times*. There was an article in it about the forthcoming Congress in Pest later in the year. It had been heavily ringed round in ink by the patient."

"Together with some material about our own miniature Congress at Castle Homolky," the Countess put in softly.

"Exactly. Raglan had to come here in any event. He also hoped to track down the asylum's escaped patient. From what he says in his diary it was a long chance, but one he felt he had to follow up. For he knew from the case-notes of the tragic background to the man's history, of course."

"So he enlisted Nadia's help and also hoped to warn Coleridge," said the Countess.

She abruptly changed the subject.

"What do you think of the professor as a prospective son-in-law? Is he not a little old for her?"

The Count chuckled.

"I see no objections. He is only about forty-three. Nadia will be nineteen in a week's time. Coleridge is a handsome and distinguished man. Wealthy as well, which also helps."

His wife smiled archly.

"You are becoming cynical in your more mature years."

The Count held up his hand.

"Practical, my dear. I think they will make a very good match. And in any case Nadia is as headstrong as you. We could never stand against the two of them. And the young always get their own way, do they not?"

They were interrupted by a tapping at the door. Coleridge was there with the girl.

The two men clasped hands warmly. It was almost dark now, and from the drawing-room windows Lugos with its lights and the crisply spreading snow looked like a fairy-tale village. But everyone in the room knew what lay beneath and were not deceived.

"The black wolf was shot this morning," the Countess offered.

Coleridge nodded, his eyes fixed on the golden beauty of Nadia.

"Colonel Anton told me. It relied on the laws of chance once too often, it seems."

He turned apologetically to the Countess.

"Nadia and I are meeting in Paris in six weeks' time. With your permission, of course. There is much to arrange. And I have some business there before returning to London to take up a new post."

"You promised to learn Hungarian," Homolky reminded him. "You will then be able to take advantage of my private library."

Coleridge smiled.

"I had not forgotten, sir."

He looked round slowly, as though wishing to imprint the room on his memory.

"I must go now. Abercrombie is waiting for me below. And you have, I believe, kindly arranged for the night-sleeper to Pest to stop for us."

The Count nodded.

"That is so. You must not be late. But you have plenty of time to catch the train. We will come down with you."

The Countess was the last to leave the room. In front of the table which held the silverware and the empty tea-cups, the tall windows glowed like a stage-set. Lugos was spread out below, ghostly, mysterious, and unreal, as though it were composed of pasteboard, paint, and theatrical lighting.

On the horizon the sky was stained angrily with the fires of sunset. The dusk came on inexorably.

Raglan's Diary

MOONLIGHT BLANCHED the window-frames and fell in bars of silver across the sharply angled roofs of Lugos. The Count and Countess were still at the table, this time with brandy-glasses between them. Far across the distant hillside Coleridge's sledge, driven by the same man who had brought him there, stood out as a large black speck against the bleak landscape.

"You promised to tell me what else was in Raglan's diary," the Countess reminded him.

The Count's tall figure remained standing at the window. Then he sat down abruptly.

"So I did, my dear. So I did," he said absently.

He reached over for the bottle and poured a second offering into each of their big balloon glasses. They silently toasted each other in the moonlight spilling through the casement. The only other light in the room came from two red candles in a silver candelabrum that stood upon the table.

"Raglan's diary is a remarkable document," the Count went on eventually. "I shall preserve it among my archives. Either he is a madman, or my own sanity is in question."

He smiled quietly to himself.

"Perhaps a little of both."

He turned to face his wife.

"Have we had a mad werewolf under our roof? Or have we all been the victims of hallucination?"

The Countess paled slightly, plucking at the sling which held her injured arm.

"That animal was no hallucination. Many people saw it. And it appeared and disappeared as though by magic."

Homolky nodded grimly.

"Just so. But a mad werewolf, bent on revenge! It passes belief."

He pondered deeply.

"I wonder whether Mother had recognised him?"

"Had you not better tell me what you have learned from Raglan's diary?" the Countess went on. "The creature Sanders—or perhaps I should say that man, Parker . . ."

The Count shook his head, abruptly interrupting her.

"Who said anything about Parker? If Raglan is not mad, then Abercrombie is the man. Or the were-creature, if you prefer."

The Countess got up, blank amazement on her face. Her voice was agitated as she replied.

"But the man Parker . . ."

"Just another innocent victim, if Raglan's diary is to be believed."

There was a long silence between them. The Countess sat down again, breathing heavily.

"But ought he not to be arrested?" she said. "You let him leave our roof . . ."

There was a strange tenderness in the Count's eyes as he gazed at his wife.

"My dear girl, on what proof? That of a weird diary of a man who apparently hanged himself, and who may have even taken his own life in an insane fit?"

The Countess leaned forward.

"You know he did not."

There was a grim expression in the Count's eyes.

"Yes, we know. And with the aid of Raglan's little black book we can piece together some of the apparently inexplicable events here."

He tapped the small volume in front of him.

"Raglan's attention was first drawn to Abercrombie when he saw him drop some sort of capsule into Menlow's wine one evening. The doctor did not know he was observed, and Raglan resolved to keep him under observation."

"That was why he enlisted Nadia's help?"

The Count nodded.

"Without drawing our daughter's attention to any one man. Raglan felt it might be too dangerous."

"And not without cause."

The Count got up and took a quick turn about the room. He came to a halt and stared at the diminishing speck of the sledge upon the horizon.

"He pieced together a remarkable chain of events. Abercrombie was always there to guard Coleridge, was he not? He turned up time and again, ostensibly to save his life."

"After having first risked it?" put in the Countess shrewdly.

"According to Raglan," said the Count, "Abercrombie took him to the cellars to destroy him. He first had to disappear before metamorphosing himself. He did this by the effective trick of dropping through a half-rotted door leading to the oubliette."

The Count smiled sardonically.

"He had no doubt already inspected it. Not only that, he was in no danger. It was blocked by masonry a few feet below where Coleridge found him."

"Once in the dark he reappeared in his wolf-guise," the Countess breathed. "But Nadia interrupted his scheme."

"In the confusion he regained the oubliette," the Count went on. "Raglan thought Coleridge had wounded the wolf. He recognised the cut on Abercrombie's forehead as a graze from Coleridge's bullet and not an abrasion caused by his fall into the dungeon."

"This becomes more and more fantastic," said the Countess.

"Does it not?" her husband replied. "But it is the only sequence of facts that fits. Raglan went further. He says Abercrombie brought on that pack of wolves in The Place of the Skull to destroy Coleridge, the only man in the Castle, apparently, who had an inkling of the truth. The irony was that the one man who held the key was not even suspected by Abercrombie at that time.

The Countess took another sip of brandy. Some of the colour now was coming back to her cheeks.

"Raglan's theory was that Abercrombie fired to miss the wolves," said Homolky, "his accomplices in the matter. There were only some five or six bodies in the gorge, all shot by Coleridge, according to Raglan. Abercrombie only began to fight in earnest when Raglan and Anton's party arrived at the gorge and when the beasts were almost upon them. Coleridge was interfering with his revenge, you see, and had first to be removed."

"So that we could all be destroyed," said the Countess with a shudder.

She drew closer to her husband as they sat staring at the blanched moonlight on the window.

"Menlow was given a drug to weaken his resistance when the man-beast attacked him," the Count went on. "But again Coleridge interfered when Abercrombie destroyed Raglan. Abercrombie suspected Raglan had left some records about him; perhaps he knew he was on the staff of the Manchester asylum. Abercrombie needed time; it is my own theory that he administered some drug to Coleridge to incapacitate him. He then went to Raglan's room, cut the rope suspending the body, closed the window, and removed the cut end."

The heavy silence was broken this time by the Countess.

"Why was George Parker in the conservatory at all at the crucial time? Another innocent man."

"They were all innocent men," said the Count heavily. "That was when Anton intervened. He could not let Coleridge face that danger alone. He and Rakosi followed. He was the first to search Parker's body. He found a note in disguised handwriting arranging a rendezvous with Coleridge at the conservatory. No doubt Abercrombie had hoped to remove it himself, but the authorities were too quick for him. He has given up now and left with his revenge unaccomplished. For the time being, at least."

"How can you be sure of all this?" the Countess persisted.

Her husband shook his head, a grim smile still lurking round his lips.

"I cannot. The whole thing is fantastic. And one wonders what has happened to the real Abercrombie."

Now there was an alarmed note in the Countess Sylva's voice.

"You have not told Coleridge this? That his close friend and protector is responsible for these horrible murders. Ought we not to warn him?"

The Count shook his head again.

"It would do no good. There is no way on earth we can prove all this. And any city police-force would laugh at such primitive superstition. For the same reason I have not told Anton of this diary. I have no doubt he has reached his own conclusions."

The Countess looked long and deep into her husband's eyes.

"And you really believe all this? Wolves and werewolves? That the entire lycanthropic legend of mediaeval times has been enacted beneath this roof?"

The Count's eyes were solemn.

"I do believe it, Sylva. You remember that Professor Coleridge wounded the wolf in the conservatory. The wound was on the right forepaw, according to his deposition to Colonel Anton."

He sighed heavily, turning his head to the window.

"As I said goodbye to Abercrombie, he winced slightly when we shook hands. I noticed that he had a bandage round his right wrist, which he tried to keep concealed as much as possible."

The Countess got to her feet, alarm on her face.

"What are you thinking of? Word must be got to the professor. It is a long journey to Pest. Coleridge will be quite unprotected if this creature strikes again."

She looked at the passive figure of her husband with exasperation.

"Do you hear what I am saying? We must think of Nadia."

The Count shook his head, laughing low in his throat.

"Do not distress yourself, my dear. Coleridge is safe enough. I have seen to that."

He drew the Countess to him, and the two stood staring down at the tiny dot that was now dwindling to insignificance in the vastness of that plain of ice and snow.

THE BREATH REEKED from Coleridge's mouth like smoke as the sledge breasted the rise, the runners creaking in the icy ruts of the unmade country road. Beside him, swathed in furs, the burly figure of Abercrombie was silent. The driver was silent too, despite the beauty of the moonlight, as though the terrible happenings at Castle Homolky had laid a blight upon the entire neighbourhood for miles around.

It was the same driver who had brought Coleridge to the Castle, seemingly at some vast distance in time. Where he had been voluble and forthcoming on the outward journey, now he seemed taciturn, almost frightened. Coleridge realised he had never learned the man's name. He must remember to ask him and give him a good tip when they arrived at the station.

He opened his heavy fur coat quickly and glanced at his silver-cased watch. They still had more than forty minutes before the night express was due and only a few more to their destination. He turned in his seat to look back. Far away, beyond the lifeless glare of the frozen river, lay the dark huddled mass of Lugos and, high above it, on its moated rock, the great decorated ice-cake that was the Castle.

There was a flare of red light coming to the right of the village, and Coleridge remembered the Gypsy Fair. He wondered whether Nadia was looking from her window, like some mediaeval princess, to catch the last glimpse of their conveyance.

Abercrombie broke the dismal silence at last.

"All's well, eh, Professor?"

His white teeth glittered in the black beard as he stared sympathetically at his companion.

"But at what a cost," said Coleridge sombrely.

Abercrombie's eyes dropped.

"You silence me there, Professor. But you have your life, at least. These things are inexplicable."

He shrugged and huddled deeper into the furs of the sledge. The two horses were working hard now as they went uphill, and there, several hundred yards ahead, were the dim lights of the station. It was a lonely place, and Abercrombie placed a big hand on Coleridge's fleshy shoulder.

"Civilisation, Professor! You will think this a mere dream when the lights of Pest are about you."

Coleridge shook his head.

"Say a nightmare, rather."

All the episodes in which he had taken part were beginning to come back now, with the cloudy vision of an opium addict's dream. The only sane things that emerged from the misty images that beset his brain were the calm beauty of Nadia Homolky's face and the strong, controlled presence of her parents in the background.

He shook the mood from him with difficulty, conscious of the icy cold, like the touch of steel upon his face. He groped about his feet for his briefcase and his valise. The briefcase with its useless documents for a Congress which death had interrupted in the most violent and horrific form and which would now never be resumed. He was tempted to hurl it into a wayside snowdrift but suppressed the urge.

His companion was made of stronger stuff and would not understand. Besides, he had saved Coleridge's life on more than one occasion and the professor had no wish to make another exhibition of himself; the giant Scot had already seen him ill and suffering from the effects of nerves. He did not want to further diminish himself in the doctor's sight.

They drew up at the remote country station where the dim oil lamps swung in the wind, casting huge gusty shadows on the platforms. There was no sound but the creaking of the weather-beaten signs, which made a melancholy noise on their rusted chains. As before, Coleridge could not make out the unpronounceable name.

Abercrombie had his own baggage down and was already paying the driver. Coleridge came over to shake hands and add his own tip. The driver thanked them both in his excellent English and bade them a good journey. And then he was turning the horses and in a few moments was a diminishing speck in the tumbled mass of ice and snow.

Abercrombie led the way across the planked platform. At the station-master's office that worthy, in his best braided cap and uniform, greeted them excitedly in Hungarian before studying their tickets at great length. He then led them to a freshly dusted waiting-room, where a wood fire burned in the stove, and left them. His figure was rapidly lost to sight beneath the thick ice that rimed the windows.

Coleridge went to stand by the pane, clearing a space at a corner so that he could see the train's arrival. They still had half an hour. Abercrombie stood quite close to him. His eyes had a yellow fire in them, almost like an animal's. He looked reflectively at the professor's throat.

The two men turned as the door to an inner office behind them opened. Abercrombie unobtrusively drew away. Colonel Anton's beaming face appeared in the opening. He wore his shabby cap with the rubbed braiding, and his hooded eyes twinkled above the heavy moustache. The red tabs on his uniform overcoat made vivid bloodlike splashes beneath the overhead lamps, and the Star of Krasnia twinkled at his breast.

Behind him came the dapper figure of Captain Rakosi, in full dress uniform. Both men wore swords as well as pistols. Anton glanced from one to the other and drew himself up in a salute.

Abercrombie stared regretfully at his companion; he pulled his right sleeve even more tightly over his glove.

Colonel Anton beamed benevolently on the two men as he moved forward with the captain.

"We have urgent business in Pest! We go together, yes?" he said in passable English, to Coleridge's considerable astonishment.

The thin whistle of a distant train interrupted the small tableau. Coleridge glanced up at the clock on the waiting-room wall, surprised to find it was some twenty minutes early.

Anton slapped his pistol holster, his teeth strong and gleaming in his smile.

"In case we meet werewolf again! Silver bullets! Effective, yes!"

He roared with laughter and led the way out to the platform where the faint lights of the train were already showing.

The blanched moonlight shone down on the wild and desolate scene as the four men stood waiting, Rakosi and Anton taking up position on either side of the professor. The station-master hovered pompously with a lantern. Abercrombie, a huge, massive figure, stood apart from the others, his shadow thrown long and heavy on the boards.

His eyes glowed with pale fire, and he held his head tilted to one side in the unearthly beauty of the moonlight.

Faintly, very faintly, so that the others were not even aware of it, his hypersensitive ears caught the howling of the wolves, his brothers, in the wind.